a year of being SINGLE

a year of being SINGLE

FIONA COLLINS

ONE PLACE. MANY STORIES

HQ
An imprint of HarperCollins*Publishers*
1 London Bridge Street
London SE1 9GF
This paperback edition 2016
1

First published in Great Britain by
HQ an imprint of HarperCollins*Publishers* 2016
Copyright © Fiona Collins 2016
Fiona Collins asserts the moral right to
be identified as the author of this work
A catalogue record for this book is
available from the British Library

ISBN: 978-0-00-821146-2

Set by CPI - Group(UK) Limited,
Printed and bound in Great Britain

FIONA COLLINS

lives in the Essex countryside with her husband and three children, but also finds time for a loving relationship with a Kindle. She likes to write feisty, funny novels about slightly (ahem) more mature heroines. Fiona studied Film & Literature at Warwick University and has had many former careers including TV presenting in Hong Kong; talking about roadworks on the M25 on the radio; and being a film and television extra. She has kissed Gerard Butler and once had her hand delightfully close to George Clooney's bum. When not writing, Fiona enjoys watching old movies and embarrassing her children. You can follow Fiona on Twitter: @FionaJaneBooks

PROLOGUE

They had a charter. An unofficial one. It wasn't written on parchment scroll in swirly feather quill or drawn up on foolscap by a portly, provincial solicitor or even scrawled in biro on the back of a magazine. It wasn't written down anywhere. But it was a charter, nonetheless, and it went something like this:

They were independent women – self-sufficient, autonomous. They could change their own light bulbs and the batteries in their smoke alarms, refill their own windscreen wash bottles in their cars, put out their own bins, carry their own suitcases, take their own cars through the carwash and unscrew the lids on their own jars. If they didn't know how to do something they would ask each other, as one of them probably would. Or they would ask Google and work it out.

They would provide each other with emotional support and babysit each other's children. If one needed another, they would come over.

They had freedom, they had power; they could please themselves and would make sure they did.

None of them had a man. None of them wanted a man. None of them needed a man.

And they would be single for one year to prove it.

CHAPTER ONE:
IMOGEN

If Imogen had screamed out loud, no one would have heard her. If she'd screamed, it would have been swallowed by the unconcerned Paris traffic roaring below. If she'd screamed, nobody would have given a monkey's. Least of all, the giant male ape inside her sumptuous hotel room.

She was standing on the tiny balcony of a massive hotel room, on the top floor of an enormous hotel. A room that she was paying for. The Ape's contribution was zilch. He thought it enough to enjoy the room and the balcony and the whole posh Paris hotel experience as fully and as enthusiastically as possible. Especially the bar, the breakfast buffet, the three gorgeous restaurants and the extensive room-service menu. He'd enjoyed the whole trip. He'd larked about photo-bombing people at the bottom of the Eiffel Tower, stuffed his face with madeleines at Blé Sucré – whilst attempting a French accent that made him sound like a crumb-spitting Pepé le Pew – and danced up the escalator to the Louvre with a silly grin on his face… Oh, he'd had a great time.

He was enjoying himself at this very moment. As Imogen grabbed the balcony's railing and flung her head up to the heavens and the grey Paris sky – to ask, Why? Why another bloody loser? – he was stuffed into a Chesterfield armchair and tucking into another sodding triple-deck club sandwich, irritatingly picking up each triangular section by the cocktail stick that held it together, and nibbling round the stick like an appreciative beaver. It was his fifth that weekend.

When he was done, he'd probably sniff, scratch his balls, burp and top it all off with a long and loud fart. This man couldn't possibly be The One! He shouldn't even have been a vague *someone* in her life.

He was a waste of space; he was lazy, greedy and quite repulsive. She'd been really stupid with this one. She wanted to get away from him as soon as possible. Their train home couldn't come quick enough.

Imogen's perfect nails dug into the palms of her Shea Butter-moisturised hands, and she silent-screamed again.

Thirty minutes before, she had arranged her legs into an attractive position on the bed. She had adjusted the long tulle skirt of her dress. Fanned her hair out on the pillow. The pillowcase alone probably cost two hundred euros. The suite was how much? Eight hundred and ninety-five euros, for one night. Imogen had thought it would be worth it. To stay in the same suite as Carrie Bradshaw in the last episode of *Sex and the City*. She had thought it would be romantic. It had turned out to be anything but.

Like Carrie, Imogen had been waiting, but not for Aleksandr Petrovsky, fiddling with a trendy light installation in a gallery somewhere across the city, but for Dave Holgate, who had been locked in the bathroom for absolutely ages and was showing no signs of coming out.

What the hell is he doing in there? she'd thought, picking a down feather off the bed and tucking it under the coverlet. *He's been at it for over twenty minutes*!

She'd sat up and sighed. She was bored and uncomfortable, and beginning to feel ridiculous with her hair fanned out like that. She wasn't bloody Rapunzel. She wasn't even some young, hopeful ingénue – she was a forty-year-old woman who had been there, done that and got several disappointment-stained T-shirts. She should be well beyond hair-fanning. She should be well beyond pinning any kind of hopes on any kind of pathetic man.

At last Imogen had heard the toilet flush and Dave had come out of the bathroom, in his boxers. He'd looked dishearteningly tubby. He'd put on a fair bit of timber since she'd met him, three months ago. As he stood by the window to the balcony and scratched his large bottom, Imogen sighed again. Oh dear. It appeared *she* had turned him into this chubby monstrosity. It was all those meals out they'd had, wasn't it? All those dates. Dates she'd embarked on with a hope that gradually went the way of Dave's greedily guzzled food: down the pan.

Their first month of dating – very successful and full of laughs, actually – they went to mid-range restaurants in London. His choice. The second, they started going to restaurants in hotels. Her choice. They did the rounds of all of them: the Marriott, the Dorchester, the Landmark, Claridge's. Imogen *loved* restaurants in five-star hotels. She loved the whole thing: concierges in top hats showing you in, the clack of heels across marble lobbies, the uniformly attentive waiting staff and the fact there were hotel rooms above you where all sorts of glamorous things were happening – chocolates on pillows, Hollywood stars ordering room service, lovers loving each other, secret assignations. One day she'd be proposed to in one of these hotel restaurants.

It wouldn't be Dave who would be proposing to her, at least she hoped not. By date six and the restaurant at The Mandarin Oriental, she'd realised he was a lost cause, but unfortunately it was too late. On a high, she'd stupidly booked a trip to Paris after their first, misleadingly brilliant month. A month that had ended with an email landing in her inbox advertising Luxury Hotels of the World, and her reaching happily for the phone with unfounded excitement.

She had had to persevere with him. They had Paris; his name was on the damn tickets. She'd thought if they kept going to all those fab hotel restaurants, even after she knew they were wasted on him (though his stomach would have said the opposite), they might somehow elevate their relationship, elevate *him*.

They didn't.

Equally and idiotically optimistic, Imogen had thought the romantic setting of the Hôtel Plaza Athénée might magically transform him, after three months of dating and dining, to someone she wanted him to be.

It hadn't.

'I'd give that ten minutes if I were you,' Dave had said, with another giant sniff and a ping of his straining waistband.

Who said romance was dead?

He'd crossed the room and huffed his backside into an armchair, knocking a book that had been sitting on one arm to the floor. He hadn't moved to pick it up. It was Imogen's: *The Unbearable Lightness of Being*. She'd hoped to instil some culture in Dave somehow, by leaving it lying around. Fat chance.

Then he'd crossed his muscly, hairy legs. The foot that was raised pointed towards her, like a joint of meat. One big toe was nonchalantly being aired. It was a *really* big, fat big toe. Hairy, too. She was revolted. And not for the first time.

'I can't wait to get out of here,' he'd sighed happily and inexplicably, all his actions suggesting the contrary. 'I fancy pie and mash tomorrow night. Or we could go up Romford dogs. My treat. Who said I wouldn't treat you like a goddess?' He'd chuckled to himself, enjoying his own joke. Imogen had smiled sarcastically and resisted the temptation to flip him the bird. Instead she'd flapped her tulle skirt in a huff, allowing him a quick glimpse of her redundant Agent Provocateur underwear. He didn't even seem to notice. What a waste. He didn't deserve the underwear, the skirt, the suite. It was all wasted on the fat pig. *She* deserved better.

Dave Holgate had turned out to be huge mistake. She'd plumped for him for a *change*. A change from the steady and long-term succession of upper class twits and rich, Impressive On Paper city boys she had selected and then discarded – for being commitment-phobes, or freaks, or crashing bores, or arrogant sods, or cheats, or already married, or all of the above. She had thought a more down-to-earth man like Dave – a man not quite so Good On Paper – could give her what she wanted. Adoration, a good laugh and, perhaps, commitment; God knows no one else had come up with it.

Dave was cheeky, happy-go-lucky. He spoke estuary English, he talked about blokes not chaps, geezers not guys, unlike her posher consorts. He liked pie and mash and liquor, pints of lager, a night out at the dogs. Okay, he wasn't as rich as the others, but, as she'd found to her cost, money wasn't everything, right? *She* made a decent wage. And Dave had a very decent job halfway up a very ambitious ladder in the world of maritime insurance.

When she'd met him, at a bar in Spitalfields, she had viewed laugh-a-minute Dave as a work in progress. He wasn't her usual impressive, finished article; he was someone who seemed impressed by *her*. He said he was lucky to have met her. Said she was different. Feisty, funny, classy. And she'd liked him, before he'd revealed his irritating true colours on that sixth date. (In hindsight, she wondered, did he have a *rule*? Six dates and it all hangs out?) He'd relaxed, got comfortable, *too* comfortable. He began referring to women as 'birds'. Stroking his stomach as though it were a puppy. Eating with his mouth open. Her heart had sunk as swiftly as his decorum had deserted him.

For Paris's sake, she'd valiantly tried to pretend the true colours weren't shining through. She'd tried to ignore the fact that he was absolutely *terrible* in bed. When he'd laughed her into it that first month, he'd seemed quite good (although she *was* really drunk) but subsequent encounters had proved highly unsatisfying. Imogen had to do all the work, she had to go on top, he'd eaten too much, his 'belly' was hurting, could she shift over to the left a bit…?

The awful truth was that he was as far from her perfect man as you could get. She knew that even if he was the marrying kind, any proposal from him would be highly indecent and wholly unwelcome.

Only her good friends knew it, but Imogen wanted to get married. To everyone else, she put on a pretty good act of thinking it was all a load of rubbish, this marriage lark – she was ballsy, she was career driven, she took no nonsense or prisoners – but she wanted it. She wanted The Day, the years, the life; she wanted to be someone's wife. When it finally happened, she would surprise everyone who didn't know her as well and say she was trying marriage out as a giddy experiment, that if she made it to seven years like Madonna and Guy Ritchie it would be something. That it was a hoot, a mad adventure. But deep down she took it all quite seriously. That's what this succession of no-hopers had all been about. Her end game was for one of these men to turn out to be *amazing*. Amazing enough to be her perfect husband.

One of these days, one of her Good on Papers would come up with all the goods.

Dave, less Good on Paper and pretty dreadful everywhere else, was never going to be that amazing guy. Imogen should have known it. She laughed to herself bitterly that she ever thought he was *remotely* marriage material, that she went to dinner after dinner with him hoping he'd magically become someone else.

If he *had* acted strangely protective over his bags or had anxiously patted his jacket pocket, as though checking something was there, at the start of the many amazing meals they'd had in Paris, she would have had a blue fit. The man was repugnant.

Three hours after she'd silent-screamed on the balcony, Imogen was on the Eurostar, sitting across from a slumbering Dave who was soporific from carbs and several hot chocolates with squirty cream and marshmallows. His eyes were firmly shut, greasy eyelids twitching slightly; hers were fully open. She not only saw the wood for the trees, she saw the entire forest and it was desolate and scrappy.

She'd had it. Men were a waste of time. Useless, hopeless, feckless disappointments, every one of them. She didn't want to get married! What was she thinking? Why be saddled with one of the losers? She had a good life, a good job and good friends. It wasn't like she even believed in love. Or wanted it. Love had happened to her once – just the once – and she had come out of it very, very badly. Love was not for her.

She didn't even want to go *out* with any of these no-hopers any more. She was dumping Dave as soon as they stepped foot back on English soil and he'd put his last fast-food wrapper in the bin. And then she was swearing off men. For good.

CHAPTER TWO:
FRANKIE

Frankie's silent scream was made at the sink, after another unappreciated Sunday roast. Three and a half hours it had taken her. Three and a half hours! Roast beef, roast potatoes, six – six! – different types of veg because the fussy so-and-sos all liked different things, Yorkshire puds, stuffing and gravy. The whole bloody works. For her family to wolf it down in five minutes without a word of praise or thanks; abandon all their plates amongst cutlery scattered like dropped straws; and push back their chairs, leaving them all out from the table like boats in a flotilla.

She was left sitting alone at the kitchen table, as usual, unhappily polishing off all the roast potatoes because she'd damn well cooked them and they were really nice, not that any of those ungrateful sods had the consideration to tell her so. Well, her three-year-old had grinned whilst eating one, before she'd taken it out of her mouth with her hand and gleefully mushed it onto the table. It was a kind of appreciation, Frankie supposed.

From the rest of those ingrates there had not been one expression of thanks, not one murmur or slight hint that anything was remotely delicious, or even just passable. Or even edible. Although they did eat it. Some of them. Some of it. Not enough. Not enough for the slaving she'd done.

Her cheeks were bright red from the oven, her hair had frizzed up from the vapour off the vegetable pans; she had an exclamation mark of gravy on her white, straining T-shirt.

As Frankie scraped four whole *starving children in Africa*'s meals into the stinky pedal bin and clattered the dirty plates into the sink, her silent scream spiralled upwards like steam from a boiling kettle.

Last night Frankie had run away for the night to the local GetAway Lodge. An out-of-the-blue, unprecedented, solo flight away from the house and the husband and the four children. A long-overdue escape.

She'd been dreaming of it for months. Every now and then, in that house, she had imagined what it would be like to just take off to the local budget hotel, on her own, for a night of solitude. For a single night away from it all. She'd had that GetAway room in her mind's eye like a beacon in the dark. She'd craved it. She could see it. She could almost smell it. Clean, sterile. A navy blue headboard and a single, solitary scatter cushion. An inexplicable strip of shiny material running near the bottom of the bed. A dark brown wooden unit housing a television. A black and silver kettle. A small wicker basket containing packets of not-very-nice biscuits and diddy milk cartons and sachets of sugar and sweeteners: these meagre offerings would have to be supplemented with a carrier bag of chocolate and treats from the nearby service station.

There would be a bathroom that smelt of bleach and had three toilet rolls, one on the holder and a tower of two on the floor, on a silver stick thing. A single wardrobe with hangers that couldn't be wrenched from the rail. A rough, thin dark blue carpet.

She would add magazines, a book and silence. Bliss. Peace and quiet. No one to talk to. No one to talk to *her*. No one to bother her. More than just 'me' time. Way more. Time to save herself.

Yesterday, she'd finally gone. She'd fled to The GetAway Lodge on reaching the end of an extremely frayed tether that had been fraying for *years*.

It had been just after three on Saturday afternoon and Frankie had been upstairs considering whether to tidy the children's bedrooms or not. They were all absolute tips and if she tidied they would only be absolute tips again in a couple of days. What was the point? She'd decided not to bother. On her way down she'd noticed an open screwdriver set on the hall floor and was coming to tell her husband, Rob, off about it. She found her family in the sitting room and had stood in the doorway, surveying the scene.

The carpet had been used as a litter bin. All her carefully (long ago, when she thought it had remotely mattered) chosen sofa cushions had been thrown all over the place; one was even balancing on top of the television, which was blaring way too loudly. Children were draped on the sofas and the floor, all eating something they shouldn't. One was meandering around with a piece of French bread in her hand, dropping crumbs on the carpet like an errant Gretel from *Hansel and Gretel*. There was lots of annoying larking about. Noise. Mess. Chaos. Downright disregard.

The meandering child kicked a small yellow football (long since banned) against the radiator. It made a jarring, reverberating thwack and a wedding photo in a silver frame, sitting on a small shelf above, wobbled then fell with a heavy *plonk* face down on the carpet. It was a wonder it hadn't smashed. Nobody moved to pick it up.

The kids carried on screeching and larking about. Rob lay on the sofa watching *Deadly Sixty* and let a second Mars Bar wrapper fall from his outstretched arm onto the carpet.

It was nothing out of the ordinary. It was a scene that was pretty commonplace in that household. But Frankie had suddenly pictured herself standing in exactly the same spot five years from then. Ten years from then. Standing in the doorway, with everyone bigger (including Rob, probably, if he carried on eating all that chocolate) but absolutely nothing changed. Chaos, disorder, disregard. Nothing would *ever* change, would it?

'Would anyone notice or care if I just left you all to it?' she'd said.

There was silence.

'If I just walked out and didn't come back?'

Still silence.

Something crunched within Frankie. A switch that had been threatening to be pressed clunked down with a thump. She'd had enough. She turned and slowly walked back upstairs, like a robot.

It had all ground to a halt. Her enthusiasm for family life. Her energy for any of it. Her cooking mojo had been worn down to a nub. It had disappeared on a wave of non-appreciation and apathy. She didn't want to iron another work shirt. She didn't want to pick up another cowpat of compressed jeans and pants that Rob simply stepped out of before getting into bed. She didn't want to look for another missing item whilst a shouting man stomped round the house. She didn't want to load or unload another dishwasher. Or put anything else in the bin. Or answer any more questions. She loved them all so much – well, Rob, not so much, let's be honest here – but they were driving her mad.

If she ever got time to do a full day of housework and get the house pristine, there were five brilliantly effective saboteurs who could trash all her good work in seconds. There really *was* no point. And she had a few stock laments that she trotted out almost daily to completely deaf ears: 'Why is there cheese all over the floor?', 'Why does no one, *no one*, hang up the bath mat but me!' and, 'For the love of God, can't you, just once, put things *away*!'

No one had explained it properly. No one had spelled it out to her. She'd had this ridiculous, fuzzy vision of marriage and babies when she was younger: a sweet-smelling, talcum-powder-dusted oasis of flowers and baby bubble bath and sunny days and holding hands with her husband while her beautiful children ran fresh-cheeked through a meadow. No one had spelled it out to her that marriage and babies actually meant years and years of drudgery.

And, most devastatingly, giving up any semblance of your life. The life you had before.

She was done.

Except she could never be done. This was not a job she could resign from. She had to stay here for ever. In that house. With that husband. With those children…

She had to get out.

Now.

Or she would go stark, staring insane.

Frankie went into her bedroom, silently packed a small overnight bag, and walked out of the house. She was shaking but determined. She was going.

The GetAway Lodge was five miles away. As she'd driven there, 'Young Hearts Run Free' had come on the radio and tears had clichéd down her cheeks. She was a lost and lonely wife. Well, not lonely. The opposite of lonely. She was surrounded by loads of the buggers. But lost, for sure. Self-preservation. That's what needed to go on today. GetAway Lodge, GetAway Lodge, GetAway Lodge. She was coming. It had been a bright light, an oasis, a little piece of heaven in the distance.

She'd gone, breathless, to reception and asked for a room for the night. The girl there had looked at her in a funny way. Was it because Frankie's surname was Smith? Frankie had almost laughed. Was this young girl – clearly hung-over and looking like she had hastily slapped Saturday's make-up on top of Friday night's – expecting some swarthy fella to suddenly appear from behind the potted plant, in a jaunty necktie? With a lascivious look. And dubious shoes.

'Just you?' the girl had said, her over-drawn eyebrows twitching and vodka breath distilling over in Frankie's direction.

'Yes, it's just me.'

After checking in, Frankie had walked to the neighbouring petrol station and bought four magazines, three bags of Minstrels, a Galaxy, a Boost and a large bag of salt and vinegar Kettle Chips. Then she'd returned to her lovely room, and ate and watched telly until midnight. Unhindered. Uninterrupted. Unbothered. She'd replied, *I'm fine*, to each and every one of several texts from Rob, once she'd told him where she was. He shouldn't have been surprised. She'd threatened it often enough. His texts had started off angry, then worried, then resigned. He obviously thought she was just having an *episode*. She could visualise him, on the sofa at home, trying and failing to work out when she'd had her last period, before returning to his television and snacks.

I'll be back tomorrow, was the final text she'd sent, at about midnight, before she'd turned out the light and snuggled down, alone, under the white cotton sheet and the limited comfort of the dodgy striped comforter. The thought of being *back* had filled her with dread, but for those rapidly passing hours of bliss, she was free.

Frankie had arrived home at ten this morning and it was like she'd never been away. Actually, it was worse than if she'd never been away. She had let herself quietly in the front door. Shoes had littered the hall. A child's padded jacket had been flung on the second stair up. A congealing, pink plastic cup of milk had been randomly placed on a windowsill.

She'd walked into the kitchen. There had been remains of a Saturday night takeaway strewn all over the table, an empty styrofoam burger box open on the floor like a Muppet's mouth, an almost-empty bottle of lemonade on its side on the worktop, a sticky dribble coming from it and dripping down the under-counter fridge. Cupboard doors and drawers were gaping; there was a sink full of dishes and empty tins filled with water, and an overflowing bin. For God's sake!

'Rob!'

Silence. There had just been the slight rustle of the white plastic bag the takeaway had come in, left redundant on the table and flicking in the chilly January breeze coming through the wide open back door.

'*Rob!*'

'In the garden!'

They had all been out there. Rob, in his bright red fleece and Timberlands and, despite the weather, those bloody shorts she detested, the ones with the tar stains on the knees. Harry and Josh, duelling with cricket bats. They duelled with anything these days: light sabres, plastic pirate swords, and if it came to it, rolling pins and tubes of tin foil and cling film. At least they were doing it in the garden; they usually fenced at the top of the stairs when she was trying to come down with a massive basket of laundry. Tilly was doing cartwheels on the wet grass in double denim, and three-year-old Alice was plomped on her bottom on the overgrown lawn (where was the waterproof-backed picnic blanket?) and noshing on a very unseasonal choc ice. Half of it appeared to have exploded over her face, and all the children looked overexcited and under-dressed.

'Mummy!' Tilly had hollered, mid-wheel, and Alice had run over to Frankie and wiped her chocolatey cheeks on her mother's leg. Frankie hugged Alice, waved 'hello' at the other children then retreated back to the kitchen, where she'd started tidying up. Within ten minutes, Harry had come into the kitchen for something and ended up telling her she was ruining everything, as always (she had dared ask him if he had finished his science project for school tomorrow) and Rob had stormed into the kitchen demanding to know where his phone was.

'How the hell should I know?' said Frankie, swiping at a ketchup splodge on the table with a sodden yellow sponge.

'It's been moved,' growled Rob, ominously and incorrectly, and he marched off upstairs, huffing about 'turning this place upside down until I find it.'

'Oh, bog off!' Frankie had mumbled, under her breath, then felt her spirit die a little as she remembered she'd promised them a big Sunday roast this weekend.

She'd only just got back, but she wanted out again.

Frankie gave a deep sigh as she peeled a Brussels sprout off the floor with one hand and scraped a strand of frizzy hair off her face with the other. The blissful night at the GetAway Lodge was becoming a distant memory. As soon as she'd stepped through the door and seen those littered shoes and the congealing cup of milk, the wife and motherhood juggernaut had started its engine and it was now rumbling again at full, reluctant pelt as she cleared up the aftermath of the roast dinner. She scraped more dishes in the bin, wiped the table, put the table mats away, swept the kitchen floor, etcetera, etcetera, etcetera. She still wanted out. She wanted her P45. She'd had enough.

She shook her head and tried to rally, which was quite difficult as she'd just stood on a squished, half-chewed potato and nearly slipped over. She'd *chosen* this life! She'd wanted this husband, these children. She'd not said 'no' to any of them, when she had the chance. They were hers and she was theirs. She just had to get on with it. *Embrace* them. Continue to smother them all in love and roast potatoes…

It was no use. She felt worse than before she'd escaped. Crisis point had been reached and there was only one solution. A solution that would give her time on her own, like those blissful hours at the GetAway Lodge, at least every other weekend.

It was radical. It was major. It would cause a hell of a lot of upheaval. But it could be done. She knew a school mum who had this very set-up. Free, blissful time on her own every other weekend. Every other Friday she'd have a chilled night with her girlfriends. Every other Saturday she'd go out and get wrecked. Alternate Sundays she'd lie on the sofa until 5p.m., her shoes from the night before still toppled together on her (Frankie imagined) white, fluffy rug. She wanted some of that and there was only one way she could get it.

Frankie chucked the flattened roast potato into the bin and kicked the dishwasher door shut.

She could leave Rob.

CHAPTER THREE:
GRACE

Grace's silent scream was at the side of a Sunday morning football pitch whilst having a bit of mindless small talk with Charlie's mum.

'Oh bless, look at my Charlie, one of his socks has fallen down.'

'Oh yeah. Yeah, look at him. Oh bless.' Grace smiled and put her hands in the back pockets of her skinny jeans. She didn't really know where to put them. She barely knew where to put herself.

That bastard! How could he do this to me?

'At least they've got good weather for it. It was chucking it down yesterday.'

'Yeah, that's right. It's cold, but it's nice to see the sun.' Another smile, another platitude. Grace didn't really know what she was saying.

Cheat! Liar! I'm never going to let him come back. Ever.

'Goal! Yes! Go on, Charlie!'

'Yay! Brilliant. Well done, Charlie.'

No man is going to hurt me like that again.

Grace grinned in what she hoped looked like happiness, or at least something that didn't look like her soul had been wrenched from her body, and she and Charlie's mum walked towards the brick changing rooms.

Anyone glancing at her would think she was a normal, contented football mum enjoying the bright, crisp January day, the white clouds scudding across a chilly marine sky and her son's hat-trick. That the worst part of her day would be cleaning muddy football boots and scouring the freezer for what to cook for tea. To a casual onlooker, Grace knew she would look *perfectly* at ease.

Blimey, she was good at this, she acknowledged. She should maybe have been an actress, instead of someone who worked in a hat boutique. No acting required there. Well, maybe a bit. She sometimes had to tell old battle-axes they looked nice in their pink mother-of-the bride hats or *anyone* they looked good in a fascinator.

Charlie's mum had certainly fallen for her act this morning. She had no clue that Grace's husband of twelve years had admitted to her before football this morning that he was cheating on her.

Grace had kicked him out. Kicked him to the kerb. He'd talked to the hand 'cause the face wasn't listening. They used to watch programmes like that together. *Jerry Springer*. At the weekends. They loved trash TV. They'd laugh smugly at all those pathetic people airing all their hilarious, dirty laundry in public. The affairs, the drama, the grubby awfulness. Awful Jerry. The terrible people with mullets and missing teeth. Those appalling beefed-up bouncers hamming it up and marching around. It was the sort of programme you could really enjoy for an hour or two, before it started making you feel ill.

She now felt *really* ill: sicker than she'd ever felt. A terrible, grubby drama had played out in her own kitchen and James's dirty laundry had flapped everywhere like filthy pigeons' wings, whacking her in the face and making her fight for breath.

He'd talked to the back of her head as he'd packed his bag. Each time he'd tried to wheedle his way out of things, she'd turned her body. Every time he tried to say it wouldn't happen again, she'd edged further away. Eventually, she'd found herself in a corner of the kitchen, by the bin, facing the tiles and thinking they needed a good scrub.

She'd heard the front door close. She'd turned round to find James gone and Daniel standing by the fridge, with his football bag. Grace had to find a way to tell him.

That his father had done the dirty on her and wouldn't be coming back.

Grace smiled again at Charlie's mum and nodded at a story about the funny thing Charlie had said at dinner last night. Her silent scream was nowhere near loud or long enough.

The Wednesday before, at about half past seven in the evening, she had grabbed James's phone to check the weather for Daniel's district cross-country rally the next day. She needed to know exactly what to bring: fleeces or raincoats or both. (James wasn't coming of course; too busy.) She wanted to get the bag of water and energy-boosting snacks packed and ready for the morning. She wanted to be organised.

Grace kept a pristine, and ridiculously tidy and organised home. Everything had its place. If things didn't work or weren't needed, they were gone. If there was a mess anywhere, it was eradicated immediately. Her friends always teased her and said that you needed to hold on to your handbag in that house; if you put it down on a table for longer than five seconds, Grace would chuck it out.

Her phone was upstairs. James's was on the hall table. As she'd picked it up, she saw there was a thumbnail photo on the screen. It looked like a breast. A naked breast! She quickly clicked on the photo and made it full-size. Yes, a breast. A big one. Bigger than hers, certainly. With a really dark, erect nipple. It was just the one. Not a pair. Sender: *work*. The breast looked like it was lying on a bed, on its side.

Grace had been so startled. What the hell was this and who'd sent it? *Work*? That was a bit vague. She swallowed and threw the phone back down on the table. Oh God. Was James cheating?

'What the hell's this?' she'd said, furious and unnerved, as James came out of the downstairs loo, fiddling with his tie. He'd looked at the phone and laughed.

'It's nothing,' he'd said. He said a friend had sent it to him, that it was just a photo doing the rounds: one of those photos blokes pass around 'for a laugh'. Hilarious, she'd thought. He did always think it all a laugh, that sort of thing – looking at girls on the street, gawping at *Baywatch*-type beauties on the telly. She'd catch him at it and he'd say, 'What?', all laughing innocence.

She accepted his explanation, but still, she wondered about it, after he'd slid his phone into his briefcase, kissed her fleetingly on the lips and left the house. He had a very important meeting that day: he was high up in oil. They'd met when he'd been further down in oil and Grace had worked in the millinery department at John Lewis in Oxford Street.

The photo wasn't especially porn-y. The breast wasn't edged in black lace or peeping out of red PVC. It didn't look sensational enough to be something shared over and over, however pervy and childish the men were. It looked like a real woman's breast, on a real woman's bed; it looked *personal*. But, she'd really wanted to believe him. She liked a quiet life. Her, James and Daniel. The three of them. She was desperate to believe him and for life to carry on as normal.

So it had. For four days she'd bought it.

Until this morning. Way before her alarm was supposed to go off so she could wake Daniel for football, Grace had been woken by a random truck clattering down the road. She couldn't get back to sleep so lay there for a while. James was sound-o. Over his sleeping body she could see his phone on his bedside table. He'd been a bit funny with that phone since the breast episode – protective. He'd even started taking it into the bathroom with him.

She'd got up and, careful to avoid all the annoying creaks in their new-build floorboards, had tiptoed round to his side of the bed and picked it up. She knew his password, tapped it in and swiped. There was a message on the screen.

Bleach!

Bleach? How strange. What did that mean? And who would send that? His mother? Why? James didn't *clean* – and neither did his mother, actually. Was it a random message sent by mistake?

Then she saw it was from '*Work*'.

Her heart pounding, she clicked open the message thread. From the top of the screen, in their jaunty speech bubbles, the messages went like this:

Great night on Thursday!

Mmm. Great, great night! Thank u ☺

Did you get that gravy off your blouse?

Blouse? When was I wearing a blouse? ;-)

At dinner, sexy!

Oh yes I remember! Briefly. Yes, I managed to get it off.

With a lot of scrubbing? Friction?

Funny. Ha.

Then in the same grey reply bubbles:

No.

Bleach!

James stirred in his sleep, made one of his little noises. Grace carefully placed his phone back on the bedside table, walked into the en-suite bathroom and quietly threw up.

When she'd staggered back into the bedroom, her face red, her eyes bloodshot, her hands shaking and an awful taste in her mouth, she'd paced, left to right, right to left. No, no, no, no, no, no, no. No, no, no, no, no, no, no. This couldn't be happening. This *couldn't* be happening.

This was happening.

She'd sat on the bed, on James's feet.

'Ow!'

'Wake up.'

He harrumphed, turned over and pulled the duvet over his head.

'Wake *up*!'

'*What?!*'

'Wake up, NOW!' She was hissing; she didn't want to wake Daniel.

Reluctantly, James sat up. Grace shoved the phone and the messages in his face.

'You're having an affair.'

He actually snorted! It turned into a cough. He ran the back of his hand across his mouth.

'What! You've *well* got the wrong end of the stick! That's just a client I went out for dinner with. Just a random client.'

'A random client you call *sexy*?'

'For God's sake. That's just a turn of phrase! Business speak.'

'*Sexy* is not a turn of phrase!' she snarled, in a terrified whisper. 'Come on, James! I'm not a bloody idiot! I suppose rubbing and friction is some business jargon, too! Was it *an all-hands meeting*? Did you have an *ideas shower*? She said her blouse was off! You're shagging her!'

His head was lowered. He wouldn't look at her.

'That was *her* breast,' she said quietly.

'What breast?'

'You're unbelievable, James. The *breast* on your phone.'

'Oh, that.'

'Yes, that!'

He shrugged. 'A tit's a tit,' he said. His hair was all sticking up and he had a five o'clock shadow. She used to find it endearing. Now she just hated him.

It was typical of the sort of thing he always said, with that cheeky, handsome smile of his. *Tits are just tits; there's no harm in looking; more than a handful is a waste* (although considering the size of *Work*'s, he didn't stand by this sentiment). She was appalled to realise that she actually used to find it funny when he spoke about women like that. Everyone did. He was a *good bloke* was James, a laugh. If he said things like that, people just shrugged and smiled. He could get away with it. He was a top man. The best.

Grace had had a lot of boyfriends; she was one of those girls who always had a boy waiting in the wings. They were all okay, nothing special. Not quite good enough for her. Then James had come along. He *was* special. Tall and dark blond and ridiculously handsome. Funny and brilliant and surrounded by adoring people – his mum, his brothers and sisters, his work colleagues. Everyone she met when she was with him told her what a great guy he was: she was surprised he didn't receive applause just for walking down the street. She had thought, yes, *at last*. James was special. James *deserved* her; at last there was somebody who did.

That was all gone now.

'A tit – God I hate that word – is *not* just a tit! I want you to admit it, James.' James was ruffling his sticky-up hair like Stan Laurel, but he still looked unruffled, unaffected. 'So I can kick you out. Have you been sleeping with someone: yes or no?'

'What?' He turned his baby blues directly towards hers. Those eyes with the eyelashes that were longer than hers. Those eyes she had stared into on their wedding day and seen *everything* in.

'Yes or no? Tell the truth. I'll respect you more.'

Another hair ruffle. Was he about to do the Stan Laurel whimper? Unlikely. He wasn't the whimpering kind. He tried to turn on his age-old charm. He smiled his slow, sexy smile and narrowed his eyes. 'If I tell you the truth would there be a chance I don't have to go?'

'Yes.'

He paused, then said, 'Okay, then it's true. I'm bang to rights. Sorry, Grace.' And his winning smile became a pleading smirk, one that always made her stomach flip and made her forgive him anything. Not now. She felt like she'd been punched in the gut. She would have collapsed onto the bed next to him if she could bear to be that close. She would never put her body that close to his again.

'I lied,' she said. 'You have to go. Now.'

She knew he would have loved to slam the back door as he left, but he chose not to let the entire neighbourhood know he was highly displeased. He was all about appearances, our James. And Grace had to keep up hers.

She'd had to swallow down the tears she wanted to cry her heart out with and take Daniel to Sunday football.

That evening, after the football kit had been washed and tumble-dried and Daniel had gone to bed with his iPad, Grace put love in the bin. Large cream, wooden letters that spelt L.O.V.E. to be exact. They used to sit on the mantelpiece in the living room, when love had meant something. Along with them she dumped a wooden plaque that said LIVE, LAUGH, LOVE and a slate heart that had hung in the kitchen on the wall by the fridge that said MR and MRS. It left a lighter, heart-shaped space on the paintwork. She frowned; she'd have to touch that up.

The lid of her posh, soft-close bin settled back into place and she opened the fridge and took out a bottle of wine. She wasn't much of a drinker, but tonight she needed wine. She'd stopped off at the Co-op on the way home from football to get some while Daniel had waited in the car. A glimpse of herself in the reflection of the shop's chiller door had horrified her. It was a catastrophic hair day. Really bad. The wind on the football pitch had whipped her thick, blonde curls into an unruly bush. A cowlick bounced on her forehead. James liked her hair; he always said it was cute. Bastard. Maybe she'd straighten it now; maybe she'd iron out everything James had ever liked about it.

She stood by the fridge and poured some of the bottle into the glass ready and waiting on the worktop, and her eye caught her calendar. It had three columns, one for James, one for her, one for Daniel. She used three different coloured pens for each of them, perfect and precise.

She quite liked it when her friends called her 'Princess Grace'. They didn't mean it nastily; she wasn't *princess-y*: she didn't have pouting hissy fits and expect people to bring her cucumber sandwiches with the crusts cut off, on velvet cushions or anything, nor was she a J-Lo style demanding diva. But she did like kitten heels and pale pink nail varnish, cashmere cardis and pretty ballerina flats. She never overdid her make-up or wore tarty clothes. She liked small, delicate stud earrings. She would be horrified at anything remotely Pat Butcher. She was a princess but not *princess-y*: if she had the perfect life she had worked hard to get it.

She believed in morals. She believed people got what they deserved. Her favourite book, as a child, was *Charlie and the Chocolate Factory* and she knew *exactly* what Roald Dahl was saying. Good children were given chocolate factories; awful children got what was coming to them. Follow the path; toe the line.

She took a pair of scissors from the kitchen drawer, carefully cut off James's column from the calendar and threw it in the bin. The calendar was now lopsided so she took some Blu-Tack and glued the drooping corner to the back of the kitchen door. Then she took the green pen from her neat pen pot and threw that into the bin as well.

She was done. With James. With men. If James, the very best man of all, had turned out to be a traitor, a hurter, a destroyer, then there would be no more men for her. H.O.M.E as declared in big letters on the wall of her living room was now just about her and Daniel.

Men were a mistake. A big mistake.

And no man would ever hurt her again.

CHAPTER FOUR:
IMOGEN

Imogen fastened the buckles of her favourite, perilously high ankle boots and admired her legs in the mirror. She had dressed carefully for tonight. Okay, she was only having Frankie and Grace over for drinks and nibbles, but she liked to make an effort at all times. She liked skirt-ready legs, shiny hair and foxy make-up; it was just the way she'd always been. She smoothed down her black pencil skirt, flicked a silver cuff high up on her toned, bare arm and made her way downstairs.

She'd been looking forward to this night for *days*. Ever since the Dave Holgate incident. And especially now her friends were manless, too. She'd been really surprised, when she'd phoned up Frankie to tell her about Paris, with lots of exaggeration thrown in she knew would make her laugh, to learn that Frankie's Rob had just moved out.

'Really?' Imogen had said. 'I know he's a lazy git, but I didn't think you'd ever do anything about it.'

'Yep,' Frankie had replied. 'He's gone. I kicked him out on Tuesday night. And I feel *amazing*.' Indeed, Imogen noted, there was a lightness to Frankie's voice she had not heard for a long time.

Frankie was one of Imogen's oldest friends. They'd grown up together just a few streets from where they both lived now, Chelmsford in Essex, a surprisingly pretty place to live and not too stereotypically Essex… People didn't go round in orange tans and inflated lips shouting 'ream!' and 'I ain't done nuffin!' at each other. They'd gone to the same town-centre primary school and remained friends despite going to different secondary schools – Frankie to a St Philomena's, an all girls' school that sounded like St Trinian's and which she travelled to on a riotous bus, in a rolled-up skirt; Imogen to the dull and grey local comprehensive, which she walked to in sensible buckled shoes. Frankie had run amok and not got a lot done. Imogen had been a right little swot and excelled. But throughout it all, they remained thick as thieves.

They reminisced all the time about their teenage years. The things Frankie got up to at school. The way Imogen would refuse to open the door to her when she was revising. The summer nights they spent in a tent in Frankie's garden, scoffing still-warm cakes dripping with melted butter icing that they'd baked super quietly at midnight.

After school Imogen had gone off to London to fly high in an exciting career and Frankie had packed away her hitched-up skirt to muddle along as a secretary at the local technical college, before marrying local guy Rob, who'd been in the sixth form at Imogen's school.

Imogen had reluctantly moved back to Chelmsford two years ago, when her mum got ill. There was a new build for sale a few doors from Frankie's 1930s semi and walking distance from her mum, who had never moved. Encouraged by Frankie, Imogen bought it. She was momentarily worried when she found out Frankie already had a really good friend in the street, Grace, who dared to be younger than them, but thankfully Grace turned out to be absolutely lovely and really great company.

They became the three of them, and they talked about *everything*. So when Frankie told Imogen on the phone that Grace was also now single, having kicked her husband out for being unfaithful, Imogen had called a summit meeting – in other words, a *huge* gossip, with loads of wine.

'I'd love that,' Grace had said, in a wobbly voice, when Imogen had knocked on her door before work one morning to invite her. 'It's ages since we've had a night together.'

'Far too long,' Imogen had replied. 'Bring a bottle. I'm going to get *loads* of snacks in. Let's see if we can't cheer you up.'

Female company was all Imogen craved at the moment. She'd avoided men, as an entire species, since she'd dropped Dave off at the Gatwick Express and sent him on his way without so much as a peck on the cheek. She'd have booted him up the backside, if she could. What an absolute loser he was. She was literally glad to see the back of him, as he trundled his stupid suitcase up the pavement away from her to the taxi rank, in his stupid slightly too-short jeans and his stupid try-hard navy blazer, with his stupid thinning hair flapping in the breeze. He'd even been so thick-skinned as to say, 'Call you later, babes,' before he'd ambled off, despite her telling him it was over and she didn't want to see him again. Honestly, some men were so thick!

Indeed, he'd called her, at work the next day, as though nothing had happened.

'Oh, Dave,' she'd said. 'I'm going to have to be blunt. It was fun – well, some of it – but frankly, you're a bit of a tosser. Don't phone me again. Goodbye.'

And that was the last man she'd spoken to all week. She usually chatted to men at work – there weren't many, admittedly; she was currently temping for a small TV production company and most of the people in the office in West London were women – but any she came into contact with, she now avoided. If someone approached her at the water dispenser, say, Tom the IT guy, or Robin, the new runner, she smiled politely and walked away. Did not engage in conversation. Did not compute. Her flirt button, usually highly active, was switched off. She stopped browsing LinkedIn for eligible bachelors who worked in the city. And she became aloof and full of disdain towards the builders on the street outside her office.

She usually loved the attention; she was forty, she lapped up wolf whistles where she could get them. Now she crossed the street and kept her head down. They could all sod off. She'd had enough of all of them. She was done with men; down with men, the works.

'Heels?' Frankie was at the door, looking bemused. She was wearing skinny jeans, knee-high boots and a longish floaty, cream top under her coat that Imogen recognised as All Saints. Frankie had had it for years, though it hadn't had an outing for several. 'We're not going out anywhere, are we?'

'Nope,' said Imogen. 'I just wanted to wear them. You know I get depressed if I'm not in heels.'

'I know.' Frankie smiled. 'Well, can I come in? I've got the password.' She held up a bottle of White Zinfandel.

They'd loved the Secret Seven as kids. They particularly loved the whole secret password thing. They'd always had them, especially for getting in the tent. Silly ones like 'bottoms' and 'Andrew Grant', an annoying boy at school, were hilariously employed as one of them 'knocked' and the other had control of the zip. Now, the passwords were in the form of wine or chocolate.

'Of course! Seeing as it's you. Come on, Grace!' yelled Imogen, suddenly. Grace was coming out of the modern house opposite and walking down her drive. Imogen had seen her there earlier, saying goodbye to Daniel when

James had come to collect him for the weekend. She had looked inconsolable.

'I've got gin,' said Grace, brandishing a bottle as she approached. Imogen knew she was trying her best to sound cheery.

'Good girl!' said Imogen. 'I've got the ice and a slice.'

Grace joined Frankie on the doorstep. Style-wise, she looked great. Perfect. Pretty. White skinny jeans, a fluffy, faux-fur jacket, and jewelled ballet flats. Her face told a different story. Her eyes were dull and hollow-looking and her expression was haunted.

In contrast, Frankie's face looked open; her eyes bright, her complexion clear. Rob had all four children tonight and for the first time ever he had them for the *whole* weekend, Frankie had told Imogen with excited delight, when she'd invited her over. She had laughed merrily and trilled, 'I'm free! Free as a bloody bird!'

Imogen was glad. Frankie had been so damn angry recently, but now the frown line '11' at the top of her nose had gone. Imogen hugged both her friends fiercely.

'Okay, my love?' she said to Frankie, after releasing herself from Frankie's enthusiastic embrace. 'Missing the children?'

'Not yet!' Frankie replied, breezily. 'Let's get this party started!' she sang, in an American accent, and she headed into Imogen's hall, holding the wine aloft like a bayonet.

'And are *you* okay?' Imogen asked Grace, who was still hovering uncertainly on the doorstep.

'I'm getting there, sweetie,' said Grace, with a brave smile. Imogen linked her arm through hers.

'Nothing a shedload of booze and a stack of snacks won't cure,' she said, and she led her friend inside and closed the door, before sighing with contentment. The gang was all here. A man-free girl zone. Alcohol. Crisps and nuts. Mini poppadums and dips. Chocolate eclairs. Posh chocolate chip cookies. Heaven.

'New sofas?' said Frankie, disappearing into the living room. 'Very trendy.'

Imogen's house was a three-bedroom brand new house with a drive and a small square of garden at the front, a bigger square garden at the back and a brown fence separating her from next door. Exactly the same as Grace's. The inside, she'd tried to jazz up a bit. She missed her trendy London flat in Putney, where she used to live, and if she couldn't replace its character she could at least try to give her new house some of its style. She'd put up huge black and white canvases and framed cinema posters everywhere. She'd had real solid oak floors installed and the walls painted white throughout. On a good day, it looked like a hip art gallery.

'Yeah,' Imogen replied. 'I got them from the King's Road. Cool, aren't they?'

Once they were all settled on the two new white leather sofas flanking Imogen's designer glass coffee table – laden with everything they needed and plenty they didn't, but would scoff anyway – Imogen raised her glass of rosé.

'To us! Oh, Grace, honey, don't cry.'

'I'm not going to cry!' protested Grace, but her bottom lip was wobbling, her eyes were filling and her voice had gone all weird. 'I will *not* cry over that man!'

Frankie reached across the table and squeezed Grace's hand; Imogen put down her glass and grabbed the other one; and Grace clung on to both hands and managed a weak smile.

'It looks like we're doing a bloody séance,' observed Frankie. 'With crisps.' Grace's face broke into a grin.

'That's more like it!' said Imogen, as they let their entwined hands drop. 'Princess Gracie, we'll get you

through this. You're so much better off without that bastard.
We all are. Chin up and bottoms up! Let's have a big old
drink and put the world to rights.'

Two hours later they were all very, very drunk. Imogen's
boots were off and under the coffee table. She lounged on
the cream rug with her head propped up on one hand and
the other lovingly stroking the soft pile. She adored her
gorgeous, very expensive, Pure New Wool rug; it was the
first thing she'd bought when she'd moved into this house,
and it was perfect.

Frankie was slumped – but still managing to hold her
glass upright – over the end of one white sofa, her head
wedged on one arm and her legs curled up under her. Her
boots were off too, as well as her socks, and her toenails
were painted a very surprising and dazzling bright red.

Petite Grace was sitting crossed-legged on the floor, her
customary shell-pink toes grazing the rug. The nibbles had
all but gone, the rosé bottle was empty and they'd moved
onto Grace's gin, which was disappearing at an alarming
rate.

For the past half an hour, Grace had been telling them
about her awful discovery of James's terrible affair and
Frankie and Imogen had been shaking their heads and
providing the verbal equivalent to soothing foot rubs. They
had exclaimed and consoled and agreed and reassured and
gasped in all the right places. She'd just come to the end
of the story – she had kicked James out; she was a single
mother.

Grace unfurled her legs and turned to Frankie.

'Do you think you're being a bit harsh, Franks?' she
said. 'With Rob, I mean. He didn't cheat or anything, did
he? Yet you've chucked him out.' Grace's wide blue eyes
had gone bloodshot. Her pretty doll mouth looked a bit

dry. She grabbed her ever-present tin of vanilla lip balm from her pretty embroidered bag and quickly applied some to her lips.

'No, he didn't,' slurred Frankie. 'And yes, I am. Probably. But I need to be harsh for my own bloody sanity.'

Imogen could sort of see where Grace was coming from, asking that. Grace had kicked James out for being an utter cheating bastard. Rob had just been Rob. His intrinsic *Robness* was his only crime. But, the man *was* a lazy, inconsiderate slob and Frankie's situation was nightmarishly chaotic – all those kids, all that mess. Something had to give, and she could hardly kick one of the kids out, could she? Not yet, anyway. Didn't they have to be at least sixteen?

'He's not a *bastard*, though, is he?' continued Grace. Her head was beginning to loll. 'Not like James. I'm glad we're all in the same boat now – without men. But I feel a bit sorry for him.'

'Oh, come on,' said Imogen, raising her head. 'He's a nice guy, is Rob – he used to run the tuck shop at school, for God's sake, and sometimes sneak me a free packet of Opal Fruits – but he *is* a right selfish sod.'

'*Thank you*, Imogen!' said Frankie with all the impassioned enthusiasm of a drunk. 'Thank you! *Exactly*. And when you have four kids the last thing you want is a selfish slob of a husband, hindering not helping. I need a break! I just need a break. A protracted one. Possibly permanent.'

'Do you miss him?' asked Grace.

Christ, Grace was pretty, thought Imogen. Just such a pretty girl. Still young, too. Thirty-four! That was nothing. Grace could get anyone. She really shouldn't be wasting another second on that horrible husband of hers. She was so proud of her friend for kicking him out.

'God, no!' said Frankie, sitting up and rummaging in an empty packet of nuts. She unearthed one, right in one corner, and triumphantly popped it in her mouth. 'The house is tidier, it smells nicer, no one is going on at me. And I only have to cook one dinner. It's heaven! Think of all the *great* things about not having a man in the house. There's loads of them! Actually, I've got a question,' she said, coming to a perch at the edge of the sofa.

'Go for it!' mumbled Imogen, chomping on a mini poppadum.

'Okay,' said Frankie. 'If your other half is the sole breadwinner and goes out to work and your role is stay-at-home mum, does that mean the partner is required to do absolutely *nothing* at home?'

'Give me an example.' Imogen was examining her nails.

Frankie sighed. 'You're so lucky you don't have to worry about all this!'

'Too right, and now I'm taking myself out of the game I'll never have to.'

Frankie stuck her tongue out at her. 'Right okay then. Example. When he makes himself a snack, is it perfectly acceptable to leave all his crockery and stuff on the counter above the dishwasher and not actually in the dishwasher?'

'God, no!' said Grace.

'*Hell*, no!' shouted Imogen.

Frankie was warming to her theme. She rose further from the sofa. 'When he gets home from work, is it acceptable to take off his shirt and underwear and suit and dump them all on the floor in the corner of the bedroom even though the laundry basket is *just there*, a foot away?'

'No!' Imogen and Grace yelled.

Frankie was standing up now. 'When he gets back from an IT conference in bloody Milton Keynes, is it okay for him not to unpack his own case, because he believes *I'm going to do it*, and when I don't do it, out of protest, is it okay to leave the thing there unpacked for *three whole weeks*?'

'You do realise you're shouting, love?' said Imogen, ignoring the fact they'd all been yelling their heads off.

'Of course I'm shouting! I'm furious! So, is it acceptable?'

'Of course it's not!' Grace had been shouting and laughing along, although they all knew she'd done everything at home and wouldn't let James help even if he'd tried to.

'But you're free of him now, honey,' said Imogen. 'All that nonsense is gone.'

'Free, free, free,' Frankie sung, in the manner of the Nelson Mandela song, then slumped back down on the sofa.

'Are you missing *it*?' said Grace in a quieter voice.

'It? What?'

'Sex.'

'God, no!' exclaimed Frankie. 'I'm well over all that! It just takes so bloody loooong. I can now get some sleep.' She stretched her bare feet out luxuriously in front of her and sighed contentedly as she admired her nails. 'You, Grace?'

'Sometimes. I suppose he hasn't been gone long, anyway. But it's fine, I can manage without it.'

'I've got a banana,' offered Imogen, sitting up and pointing one out. She'd left her pale blue fruit bowl on the table in the pretence any of them would be remotely healthy tonight. The banana was nestled between a couple of apples and the whole ensemble looked like a fruity part of the male anatomy. They all giggled. Frankie did a guffaw and a snort and nearly fell off the sofa.

Grace grinned. 'Ha, no I'm fine, thanks,' she said. Then her face dropped. 'I hate him,' she said, sadly. 'I *miss* him. But he's a bastard who doesn't deserve me. I won't have him in my life any more. I'm never letting him come back.'

'Good!' shouted Imogen. 'Good! We don't need them! If I never see a pair of men's underpants again it'll be too soon. I don't care even if they're David Bloody Beckham's! Good riddance to the lot of them!' She grabbed the banana from the bowl and attempted to use it as a gavel, on the table. The end broke. Frankie snorted again.

Grace picked up the abused banana and took it to the kitchen. She'd been tidying up all evening; whenever they'd finished a wrapper of something, she'd get up and take it to the bin.

'For God's sake, leave it!' Imogen had shouted good-naturedly, at one point. 'The world's not going to blow up if you leave an empty packet of Minstrels on the table! Sit down!' Grace had laughed and taken it well. She'd sat back down and smoothed out the empty packet in the middle of the table, as though it was a centrepiece at a wedding.

Grace would be okay, thought Imogen. She was a good girl. A bit too tidy and sensible, but highly fabulous. She reckoned she'd flourish without a man. Come into her own. They all would. They'd all be absolutely *brilliant* without men. It was almost a revelation. Why had it taken them all so long?

'We should have a charter!' she screeched, suddenly. She lurched up off the floor and started jumping up and down in front of her white marble fireplace.

'A charter?' said Grace and Frankie, in unison.

'A charter! You know, a mission statement. What we believe in.' She tapped out points with her finger on the palm of her hand. 'No men, at *all*. No dating, no husbands, no nothing. We're independent. We're self-sufficient. We help each other. We look after each other. We fix our own stuff.' Her voice rose to a near shout, a clarion call. 'We don't need 'em, we don't want 'em!' She felt impassioned, fired up, *drunk*. 'We have sworn off men. We should form a club!'

'Not the Secret Seven, again?' groaned Frankie. 'I don't want to drink ginger beer and go snooping round the neighbourhood in my pyjamas!'

'No,' said Imogen. 'Not a club, then. But we should make a declaration. That we're going to be single. Let's see if we can do it!'

'For ever?' asked Grace.

'Maybe not *for ever*…but let's see if we can do it for a *year*!' enthused Imogen. 'Yes! A year of being single. The three of us. A strong, powerful, kiss-ass trio. We'll be like Charlie's Angels but without the Charlie.'

'Or the Bosley,' added Frankie, helpfully.

'I'm not sure,' said Grace, doubtfully. 'It all sounds very Sisters are Doing it for Themselves. Very Germaine Greer. Do we have to wear hemp sandals and not shave our legs?' She picked up a couple of crumbs off the carpet with her fingernail and deposited them on a plate. 'And I'm not sure I *have* sworn off men,' she pouted. 'Just James, and anyone else who wants to hurt me.'

'That's all of them, then!' exclaimed Imogen. 'We're not going to put up with them any more! We're going to have a year of being single. Are you *in*?'

'I'm in!' whooped Frankie.

'Grace?'

'Okay,' said Grace reluctantly. 'I guess so.'

'And no,' declared Imogen. 'We don't have to wear hemp sandals. I wouldn't be seen dead in them.'

For the next three hours, the three of them laughed, chatted, sang along to an old Whitney Houston album, managed to fend off Frankie who wanted them to all stand up and sing 'I Will Survive' into remote controls, demolished a whole loaf of toast and Marmite and finished off four bottles of cheap bubbly they ordered from their local Indian takeaway. They were slightly disgruntled they were charged £2.99 each for them, when they usually came free with a curry.

At 2a.m. Imogen awoke to find herself sprawled face down on the carpet. Grace was next to her, curled in the foetal position. Some of her blonde curly hair was trailing onto Imogen's left arm. And Frankie hadn't moved from the sofa; she was now flat on her back with one leg dangling down to the floor and her mouth wide open. Imogen raised herself up, slowly; her head hurt.

'Hey, sleepy heads! Drunkards!' Frankie opened one eye. Grace opened both, with a start. 'Do you want to stay over? I can just throw a couple of blankets over everyone.'

Grace rose. Her Kim Basinger in *9 and a Half Weeks* hair was sticking up everywhere and a stray piece of toast dangled from one frizzy ringlet. She had a smear of Marmite at the corner of her mouth.

'No, thank you,' she slurred, 'I should get home. Daniel's got football in the morning.'

'Daniel's with James, honey. Remember?'

'Oh, yeah. I forgot.' She looked devastated. 'I want to go home, though,' she said, like a small child.

Frankie reared up like a lovelier Frankenstein's monster. 'Me, too. I'm going home to my lovely empty bed. Thank you, though, darling.'

They hauled themselves up, with Imogen's help and some exaggerated heaving, and staggered out the front door. Frankie had forgotten so much stuff – phone, shoes, cardi, all littered around the living room – and Grace scooted round and picked it all up for her, before shoving it in the carrier bag the bubbly had come in. Frankie could barely hold on to it.

'I'm not kissing either of you,' said Imogen, on the doorstep. 'We all stink of booze and Marmite.'

'I love you,' slurred Frankie, going in for a hug anyway.

'Love you too,' said Imogen, turning Frankie like a spindle and pushing her up the drive.

'Love you both,' said Grace. She was veering on tiptoes up the drive. 'I don't know what I'd do without you.'

'Ditto,' said Imogen, 'you drunken idiot. Now get to bed, the pair of you. Text me in the morning.'

She watched them weave up the drive. God, they'd all feel terrible tomorrow. But they'd feel better, too. As she closed the door on her two best friends, Imogen smiled to herself. She loved those girls. They were the best.

They may not have men now, but they had each other and that was a lot.

CHAPTER FIVE: FRANKIE

Today was the first Sunday Frankie had spent on her own for *years*. It had been bliss, so far, despite the hangover. God, she'd enjoyed it last night, at Imogen's: fun, laughter, a good old drink and lots of lovely food, and at the end of it, Frankie had staggered back to calm and order. No children. No Rob. For once her house didn't feel like the polar opposite to Imogen's trendy one or Grace's ridiculously clean, ordered one. She'd got into bed alone and sighed with contentment. It had been fabulous and she'd *loved* Imogen's plan for the three of them to be single for a year. That would work for her. Easily.

This morning, she'd indulged a slight headache without being leapt all over, or being begged to put bacon on, and 'where are my socks?' – all the usual chaos. She'd stayed under the covers reading until ten o'clock. The day stretched wonderfully before her.

On Friday evening, Rob had picked the children up at five o'clock for his first weekend with them. He was staying at his mum's, but she was off to Tunbridge Wells for the weekend. They had all gone off with him quite happily, even Alice. There was no clinging, or hanging on to legs, or wailing. They'd waved cheerily; she'd waved cheerily back. She knew she should be feeling sad about her children leaving her for the weekend. Guilty, even. But she couldn't quite conjure it up. Not at that moment. Shamefully, she'd just felt relieved.

This was really going to work. She was going to be a much better mum now she wasn't with them all the time. And an even better one now that Rob was out of the house. She didn't *want* to be the mum who wandered round the house flinging pants angrily into laundry baskets and crashing bowls into dishwashers. The children were going to really appreciate the new, less stressed her.

As soon as they'd gone, she'd cleaned the house from top to bottom. It was perfect, and she was going to enjoy the peace and quiet for the whole blissful weekend. No kids, and no Rob. She was ecstatic he no longer lived there.

It had not been pretty, the night Rob had gone. The night she'd told him she couldn't do it any more. It had been three whole days after Escape to GetAway Lodge.

She had been in the shower, having just got Alice to sleep. That shower was the first chance she'd had since six o'clock that morning to have some peaceful time on her own, but it was hardly an advert-quality experience. First, Tilly then Josh had banged on the door, yelling about various things and she'd yelled 'I'm in the shower!' until they'd gone away. Then Rob hammered on the door loudly, startling her because she didn't know he was home from work yet, asking her where his blue joggers were. She'd shouted back that she had 'no bloody idea'.

When she'd come out, his work shirt, pants and socks were on the floor next to the laundry basket. She disposed of them. He'd also left a coat hanger on the bed along with a pair of smelly, rolled-up black socks, which were dangerously close to her pillow. She'd picked up the socks between finger and thumb and, with a look of disgust, got rid of those too. Same with the coat hanger. She'd smoothed the cover (she *hated* a messy, un-smooth bed) and went downstairs.

In the kitchen, three cupboard doors were wide open, and a drawer had been left so far out it was in danger of crashing to the floor. It was the drawer next to the sink where he put his keys, but his keys weren't in it. They were on top of the fridge. An empty crisp packet was on the kitchen table. A half-empty bottle of water was on the worktop, its lid off.

Typical Rob. It was nothing he need worry about; he knew she'd be along at some point, on her rounds, picking up and clearing up after him. That was her *job*. She had always hated this sorry little argument of his: *she* didn't help *him* with his job, why should he help her with hers?

'Domestic services,' he called it. 'That's your department,' he said, as though it was a department she had ever remotely aspired to. It was certainly a department that never *closed*, she often thought.

Usually she would sigh and go round shutting all the drawers and doors and putting things in the bin and the recycling box. That day, she'd had enough. She'd already thrown Rob's shirt, pants and socks, and a coat hanger, out of the bedroom window.

She'd systematically gone round and opened every single cupboard door in the kitchen, then all the drawers. Then the fridge door, the microwave door and the oven door. Then she'd walked into the sitting room where Rob was on the sofa with the football on, tapping away at his phone with a vacant look on his face. He hadn't even glanced up.

'What's on the menu tonight?' he'd said. Frankie had stood right in front of him.

'I can't do this any more,' she'd said, in a low voice. There was silence. He obviously hadn't heard her. He didn't look up; he didn't stop tapping.

'I can't do this any more,' she'd said. Louder.

'Eh?' Rob had said, glancing up. 'Can't do what? If you're going to get huffy about cooking dinner tonight – again – we could always just have a salad. I'm not that bothered. I had a big lunch out. Steak.'

'That's nice for you,' Frankie had said. And a salad wasn't less work, she'd thought. There was all that chopping.

She'd raised her voice an octave. 'I can't do this – us – any more. The mess. The lack of respect. The whole lot. I'm done. I want us to split up.' The words had just spilled out of her, like rubbish tumbling out of an overflowing bin or dirty pants spilling out the top of a laundry basket.

'Oh, ha, very funny,' Rob had said. 'Sit down. You don't have to make me anything. You can order us a takeaway if you like.'

'I don't want to sit down and I'm not joking,' Frankie had said. 'I need a break. I need a break from you. I want us to split up.' She knew the look on her face was not normal; she knew she probably looked slightly unhinged. Deranged. She was shaking. She felt sick. Her voice sounded weird. She couldn't believe she was finally saying this.

It was awful. He hadn't believed her. When she'd tried again to explain why: the never-ending mess, the lack of help, how bloody overwhelmed she was; he had just not got it. She had resorted to screaming, 'I'm sick of you!' which had resulted in two things: the distant shriek of Alice, upstairs, startled by a post-bedtime argument that involved adult voices and not those of her older siblings, and a shout back from a palpably furious Rob.

'Well, I'm sick of *you*!' he had hollered, causing Alice to cry louder and Josh to exclaim from upstairs, 'By Jove! What's going on down there!' He liked to experiment with different personas. The current one was a posh country gent. In previous incarnations, he'd been a barrow boy from the East End, a whiny American teenager and Julian Clary. 'Moaning all the time, nagging all the time,' Rob continued, his face red with anger. 'It's no picnic for me either, I can tell you!'

It had degenerated from there. And concluded with Rob emptying the contents of his gym bag onto the bedroom floor, refilling them with some clothes and a hastily compiled wash kit, and going to his mum's for the night.

'Where's Dad going?' Harry had said, appearing on the landing.

'Oh, just to Nana's,' said Frankie. She still had the shakes. 'He's going to do a few jobs for her.'

'Really?' said Harry in mocking disbelief.

'Yes,' said Frankie. 'Go and get on with your homework.'

She had watched Rob, through the bedroom window, getting into his car. At first he stepped over the clothes and coat hanger on the drive, then he opened the boot of the car, retraced his steps and shoved them inside.

She didn't feel sad; she only felt relief. Any guilt that threatened was swept away by the thought that he was angry too. Angry rather than distraught. That made it slightly easier for her. She didn't want to *destroy* him. She just wanted him to go away.

Frankie shook the horrible memories of that night from her mind. It was done, he was gone, and she now had the rest of a luxurious Sunday before her. She was going to spend much of it on the sofa with chocolate and a couple of box sets. She was going to wallow in the marvelousness of this new kind of Sunday.

At 2p.m., whilst enjoying *Grey's Anatomy* and a bar of Dairy Milk, she was rudely interrupted by a text.

Rob.

This is hell.

Tell me about it, she texted back. (She had a silly urge to add 'stud', for old time's sake, but decided that was madness.)

Blimey, it's hard work.

Tell me about it, she texted again, then switched her phone off. Single for a year? *Easy peasy lemon squeezy.* Make it a lifetime.

Rob brought them back late by half an hour. Despite having the time off, she was really happy to see their little faces. He said he couldn't find his car keys. He said after much frantic searching they were eventually found inside Alice's shape-sorting pot. How they'd laughed, he said.

Frankie didn't laugh. 'You need to be more responsible now.'

The smile on his face faded and he looked angry. It had obviously been a *long* weekend.

'I shouldn't *have* to be more responsible! *You* should be doing all this! You should be being my wife!'

'Tough – now maybe you'll appreciate what I did for you.'

'What? Ruin my life?'

The children looked slightly stricken. Frankie hugged them all fiercely in turn, then bundled them in and up the stairs to watch a DVD, leaving her and Rob to pull stony faces at each other on the doorstep.

He sighed. 'I'm moving into one of my brother's empty buy-to-let flats next week, for the foreseeable. It's about ten minutes' drive away.'

'How nice.'

'Can I come back the weekends that I don't have the kids, and work on Kit?'

Rob was building a kit car. It was a sort of giant yellow Meccano car, which he kept in the garage and added bits to when he could afford them. When it was done, it was going to be a flash-looking sports car with one of those noisy, throaty engines and one day, presumably, he would just drive off in the bloody thing, *alone* – it only had two seats. Frankie had always been quite resentful about Rob and Kit. *She* didn't have time for a hobby! Imagine if she locked herself in the garage every weekend, only coming out to demand bacon sandwiches and cups of tea.

'No,' Frankie said. 'I just want to be left alone.'

'But you won't see me! You don't see me for hours at a time when I'm in there.'

'Quite. So no, you're not doing it. Sorry.'

'You're being a bit of a bitch, you know, Frankie.'

'Maybe I am. Maybe I've been pushed to it.'

His next sentence was said with a kind of venom. 'I'm actually wondering if you might be slightly mentally ill.'

She laughed, loudly. 'Ha! That would be convenient! Well, don't think about sending me off to some sanatorium, Sue Ellen style.' He looked blank. He hadn't been a *Dallas* fan, as a kid. He didn't watch much telly, in the eighties; he was always out on his bike or doing Airfix in his room. 'Then you'd have to have the children full-time. You'd have to give up your job!' He didn't look suitably chastened, so she decided to get herself on a roll. 'Don't forget, you've only been allowed the luxury of that lovely job all these years *and* have children, because I've been supplying the childcare and the –' she sneered '– *domestic services.*'

'What?' Rob's face was a picture. A picture of a man who'd been told something totally outlandish. 'Don't be ridiculous. My job has allowed *you* to be a nice little housewife and mum and swan round all the time!'

'*Swan round!* I've been bringing up your children and making sure your life runs smoothly. What a bloody cheek!'

Rob looked flabbergasted. 'You chose this life; you *chose* to be a mum and housewife!'

'I didn't choose to be a baby-making slave! We were supposed to be a *team*. But we haven't been, have we? Not at all. I may as well have been a single mum!' An indignant, Ready Brek glow was turning her face all red, but she didn't care. 'So now I'm going to *be* one. And…and how dare you use a word like "housewife"!' She spat it, with scorn, as though it were the worst insult he could throw at her. 'Nice little housewife? That really says everything I need to know.'

'What's wrong with the word "housewife"?' Rob asked, in all innocence, and she could have killed him. 'You really are losing the plot, Frankie! You're a nutter.' He shook his head, as though she were an errant child who needed a nice sit down with a drink and a biscuit. Then his voice softened. Oh, here it comes, she thought. 'Perhaps you just need time,' he said. 'Some headspace. More chill-out time.'

What on earth? This wasn't 1990, the Second Summer of bloody Love! It had been one of his favourite eras. Did he think she just had to put on some Happy Mondays and sit in a field with a load of people waving glow sticks and she'd be fine?

'You used to be such a laugh,' he said. She had been, she knew. They'd *both* been such a laugh. Had such a laugh. He still was, probably. Except now he laughed on his own.

'Maybe I don't find anything funny any more.'

'No.' He grimaced. Yes, it was an actual grimace. He hates me almost as much as I hate him, she thought. 'Maybe you'll let me come home when you come to your senses.'

She shut the door on him. 'Maybe I already have.'

CHAPTER SIX:
GRACE

'Happy Valentine's Day!'

'Happy Valentine's Day!'

The women clinked their glasses together.

'Pretty good way to spend it,' said Imogen. 'Better than being knee to knee with fifty other couples at a restaurant, all paying over the odds for beef in a pink sauce and heart-shaped cheesecake!'

'Oh absolutely!' declared Frankie. 'Or sitting at home staring at your joke Valentine's card, which depicts you as a cartoon harridan in curlers, and wondering where it all went wrong.'

Grace smiled and nodded but she didn't share their sentiments. She was not relieved to be single on Valentine's Day. She was not happy to be out with the girls instead of at home in the warm with James, a huge bouquet of flowers in the silver crackle vase on the sideboard, a card professing his undying and everlasting love on the mantelpiece and a Marks and Spencer's Meal Deal for two on the coffee table in front of them. He would have run her a bath with candles and Jo Malone; she would be in a perfect dress and heels and ready for a kiss. It was always perfect. She would have done anything to be stuffed in a restaurant with loads of other couples, even if most weren't speaking to each other. She would have done anything to just have her nice husband back – the one who hadn't yet cheated – but he was now doing lovely Valentine's stuff with another woman.

She'd had to be dragged out. Imogen had popped round the other night and told her that as Valentine's Day was on a Friday this year, they should have a girls' night on the town. Stuff all the happy couples and all the saccharine rubbish, she'd said, they should celebrate being single and fabulous. Grace had muttered something non-committal about it sounding lovely, but hadn't planned on actually going. She didn't want to celebrate being single; she hated it. She missed having a man and missed being in a relationship. But Frankie and Imogen had her sussed and had turned up at six o'clock tonight, in their going-out finery and a bottle of plonk, and had practically pushed her out the door.

Now here she was, in a bar festooned with red balloons, while a DJ played a souped-up version of 'Love is in the Air' and a load of singles who had no one to go to dinner with pretended they were about to enjoy themselves.

'Well done, girls,' said Imogen. 'One month single! And it's been a walk in the park, hasn't it? I've absolutely loved it,' she sighed happily.

'Hear hear,' said a grinning Frankie. 'It's been *bliss.*'

Grace grinned too but she wasn't feeling it. All she could think about was James in a nice shirt, feeding her a mouthful of M & S scallops over a flickering vanilla flame and some Norah Jones. She couldn't bear it.

'Right,' said Imogen, taking a large sip of her bubbly. 'Remember what I said. We're implementing a Don't Talk to Men rule. The first rule is, if a man approaches and tries to talk to you, you do not respond. You turn your back if you have to. Got it?'

'Got it!' said Frankie.

'Grace?'

'Yep,' said Grace miserably.

'The second rule is, we all help each other to enforce the rule. The third rule is, if a *group* of men approach, we deflect them en masse and send them on their way. If we're going to be single for a year, we have to be serious about this. Clear?'

'Clear!' shouted Frankie, as though she were doing CPR in an episode of *ER*.

'Yay,' said Grace, weakly.

'Come on, Grace,' entreated Imogen. 'Get with the programme! We don't *want* men, remember? We're going to be single for a year and *love* it!'

'Okay, yeah!' said Grace and punched the air in a salute. She knew Imogen would only keep going on if she didn't swear her allegiance to the cause. Frankie grabbed her raised fist and shook it triumphantly.

'Good girl!'

'Yes, that's my girl!' said Imogen. She made them chink their glasses again and down their drinks in one.

It was quite funny at first, when the men were bald and ugly idiots with not an ounce of charm between them. It was easy to send them packing. A man would approach. He'd be ignored or told to go away and he'd *go* away. It was no loss to anyone. Certainly not to Grace. Then a really gorgeous man started looking at her from across the bar.

Tall. Dark blond hair. Lovely eyes. Nice white shirt. She looked back; he looked back. He looked over; she looked over. Eventually, he walked across to them. He stood directly behind Grace and tapped her lightly on the shoulder. Imogen, like a hawk, spotted his hand and slapped it down.

He scowled at Imogen but was undeterred. He tapped Grace on the shoulder again and said, 'All right?'

'Hello,' Grace said, smiling at him.

'We're not talking to men,' said Imogen, cutting in and planting her face in front of his. 'I'm afraid you'll have to bog off.' This man was obviously not used to such treatment. He cocked his head to one side in amusement and apparent disbelief then pulled at Grace's arm, trying to get her out of the circle. Imogen had to step it up.

'She's not interested. Crawl back to your hole, there's a love.'

His face was a picture. It was not a picture Grace liked.

'Lesbians!' he said, shaking his head at Grace as if to say, 'Your loss', then he walked back to his mates, in a bowling gait he hadn't employed on the way over. She saw him laughing with his friends and immediately scouring the bar for fresh prey; he wouldn't be wasting any more time.

Grace plastered a bright smile on her face.

'Thanks, Imogen,' she said, but internally she sighed a deep, highly disappointed sigh. She was gutted. Okay, he was a bit of a wally saying that about lesbians, but he was *gorgeous*. And just her type. Tall, dirty blond hair, a naughty grin. How unfair!

She tried to tell herself Imogen was right to dismiss him so smartly. That he was a man and it could only end in disaster. What would be the ultimate best that could happen? He would be wonderful, they would date, fall in love, he would ask her to marry him, then, eventually, he would cheat on her... Still, she wished Imogen hadn't.

No other man dared approach. After plenty of vodkas had been consumed and they hit the dance floor, they were a ring of steel. Many a man tried to infiltrate and many a man was repelled; Imogen had somehow acquired the dual superhero powers of elbows of titanium and a threatening stiletto heel. Frankie once laughingly tried to have a little boogie with an eager young pup in a suede jacket but he was shot down in flames.

'It's only a laugh!' shouted Frankie.

'Never give in! Never surrender,' Imogen yelled back, over Calvin Harris. And she was almost unbearable when Beyoncé's 'Single Ladies' came on – wagging her finger, wiggling her backside, giving it all that. Grace just went along with it. Imogen *was* right, though, she thought, looking round the packed dance floor. These men *were* all no-hopers: men who hadn't got a valentine either, who were out on the prowl, on the pull, to see who they could get. She still *hated* being single, though.

'Can I get you a drink?' a man suddenly said, from her right. He was young. White T-shirt. Floppy hair. Killer smile.

'No, thank you.'

'Why not, gorgeous?'

'I'm not interested.'

He laughed. 'I'm not used to women saying "no" to me.'

'Well one is now.'

He shook his head, still laughing. 'I suppose a shag's out of the question then?'

'Please go away.'

And he was gone, with that killer smile and a shrug, moving on to try someone else.

Her hangover wasn't too bad. Daniel was at James's this weekend so she didn't have the full-on Saturday packed with activities she now did to make up for the weekends she missed with him. She'd spend the day watching trash TV and nibbling on things.

It was 8p.m. Grace poured herself a glass of wine – a little hair of a small dog would help no end – and got down the laptop from the bookshelf. She popped some Adele on the music system, stretched her legs out in front of her and placed the laptop on top of them. Time for some mindless surfing.

She flicked through this and that. Fashion blogs. ASOS. Facebook. Ugh. Why had she opened Facebook? She hated it. It was a mocking reminder of the life she thought she had.

Before James had gone, she'd been one of those smug, show-offy Facebook mums, constantly sharing photos and happy news with her one hundred and four friends, mostly other mums from Daniel's posh school. She'd post photos of the three of them on days out, on holiday or at home in the garden, on idyllic weekends. She'd share photos of meals they'd had in restaurants or ones that James had cooked. He was quite an accomplished husband, when he was one; there had been lots of pictures of him smiling proudly over a plate of tuna steaks and chunky chips, piled in a Jenga grid, like they'd seen on the telly.

Daniel's achievements had also featured prominently in her Facebook photos. Daniel in his Taekwondo outfit, doing a high kick or whatever it was called; Daniel with a fish he'd caught at Hanningfield Reservoir; Daniel at sports day. She'd even posted nauseating photos of her and James with corny captions such as 'My best friend, my soulmate, my everything,' while she grinned cheesily and he smiled that lazy, sexy smile of his. Sometimes, to her now extreme horror, she'd even said she felt 'blessed'.

In the post-James days, she posted nothing on Facebook. Nothing at all. She just scrolled through other people's stuff, getting angry.

Family life was gone. It was no longer to be celebrated. And, despite opportunities to temporarily drown her sorrows with her friends, the weekends without Daniel were awful. James was making sure of it.

He was purposely unreliable with pick-ups and drop-offs. The very first weekend he'd had Daniel, he'd been two hours late picking him up on the Saturday. Then on the Sunday he'd, without notice, brought Daniel back three hours early, which hadn't given her enough time to get rid of the hangover from that girls' night in at Imogen's. She'd hated greeting them both at the door with a still-puffy face and unwashed, dandelion-clock hair.

She remembered that, despite his premature arrival and the fact she may have still smelled a little bit boozy, she'd fallen on Daniel in relief. Her boy – she'd missed him. Daniel had looked mildly horrified, shrugged her off and bounded upstairs to his Xbox, leaving James on the doorstep, attempting to give his famous grin as an apology. She'd ignored it. She'd quite enjoyed throwing him a curt 'goodbye' and shutting the door in his face.

Later, she'd asked Daniel how it had gone.

'Fine,' he'd said, giving all the usual detail boys of ten like to give.

'What did you do?' asked Grace.

'Not a lot. FIFA 15 and we got a takeaway.' Informative. She didn't dare ask if Daniel had met 'that woman'. She'd made James promise that when he had their son he wouldn't see her, but who knows? He could have bribed Daniel not to say anything. She'd rifled through Daniel's rucksack for new Match Attax cards but found nothing.

Her ex's timekeeping had remained purposefully awry since. Just to wind her up. Grace sighed, re-adjusted the laptop to a more comfortable position and sipped her wine. She'd probably get the same tomorrow, when

James was due to bring Daniel back. Oh, so much to look forward to.

Work had been a nightmare as well. Gideon had been *horrible*.

When she'd heard, just before her job interview, that the owner of Hats! hat shop was gay, she wasn't expecting a camp, gossipy and 'fabulous daaarhling' cross between Gok Wan and Jack from *Will and Grace*, but she hoped, if she got the job of course, they'd get on well and have a laugh together – she'd always wanted a gay best friend. Grace got the job, but unfortunately, Gideon disappointed: he was sour, dour and grumpy and totally lacking in charm. Grace often thought he was in the wrong trade: he would tell a woman she looked downright awful in a hat and he swore too much in front of the customers and not in a manner that was remotely hilarious... She still remembered the faces of three rather genteel-looking women when Gideon had emerged from the stock room one time, a cardboard box in his arms, and had announced in an over-loud voice, 'Oh, pissing hell, isn't life all such a fucking *drain*.'

Still, his bluntness was, in a strange way, very good for business. Women left his shop in exactly the right hat, often a complete departure from the one they came in for. If something suited them, he made sure they had it. And the hats were gorgeous, so that helped.

This week she'd finally told Gideon about James, expecting him to pull something from the bag in terms of empathy and sympathy (deep, *deep* from the bag), but all she got was a terse, 'Them's the fucking breaks' and, 'I hope you've got a packet of tissues on you; I don't want you snivelling all over the ladies.' She should have known better. She'd been right not to tell him. But once she had, she found the week very hard as she had to put on a horrid brave front that she couldn't let slip. She wouldn't have needed the tissues – she had not and *would* not cry over James – but she'd stupidly hoped Gideon might rustle up some support if she was feeling a bit down.

It was all hard to get used to. Being alone. Being without James. When you'd hero-worshipped someone for so long, what did you do when your hero has gone?

He *had* to go though. He had betrayed her, and he *knew* that would be the end of them. When they used to hold each other at night and say how much they loved each other, she told him if he cheated, that would be it. He'd be out. 'Absolutely, sweetheart,' he'd whisper. 'Absolutely. But that's not going to happen.' Now she knew he didn't mean he wouldn't cheat, but that he intended never to be found out.

She would not be hurt again. She had to compartmentalise James somehow, put him away in a mental box and lock it tight. And any future man would have to give her a cast-iron guarantee he wouldn't cheat on her. She would make him write her a contract, in blood.

She flicked up the blind and looked out of the living room window. The street was really quiet when Frankie's kids were not around at the weekends. Three of them at least would usually be out on bikes, or squealing from the trampoline in their back garden until quite late, all weathers, all seasons. She knew she wouldn't see Frankie tonight, either. She'd been going on about a date with *Mad Men* and a bottle of Shloer. And Imogen was with her mum.

Grace was on her own.

She took a slug from her red wine. Adele was warbling about finding 'Someone Like You'. She was feeling slightly tiddly already. She wasn't a big drinker. She didn't subscribe to Facebook slogan drinking: 'Wine o'clock',

'Mother's little helper', 'For instant happy woman just add wine' etc, etc. There were people who responded to anything at all with 'wine!' She'd never been one of them, and she would *never* refer to having a 'cheeky' glass of *anything*. Yet, since James had left, she had been reaching for the wine. Her wine o'clock appeared to be the moment that bastard left her.

Feeling like a criminal, she quickly opened a new tab on Google Chrome. Hook, Line and Sinker. An online dating site. She'd heard it mentioned by a couple of mums from school, usually accompanied by a lot of shrieking – one was still dating a man she'd met on it. Grace quickly clicked onto her preferred age range: thirty to forty. Most of the men she scrolled through made her scream aloud they looked so grisly or pathetic or downright *predatory*. A few looked like serial killers. But, surprisingly, some of them looked okay.

She didn't dare tell Frankie and Imogen, but she needed a date for something. She had a 'do' coming up and there was no way she could go on her own.

Nana McKensie, James's grandmother, was soon to be celebrating her one hundredth birthday and had arranged a huge family trip to the theatre. Grace was determined to go. She was extremely fond of James's grandmother. Spry and as mentally agile as they came, you'd never have believed she was approaching her centenary. She still lived in her own home, still pottered round her garden, and still went out for fish and chips with 'the girls' every Friday lunchtime. She could text and use the internet and even had a Twitter account. Grace thought she was fabulous, and had gratefully received an email from Nana McKensie after she and James had split, to say she 'must' still come, and she *must* bring a plus one. Sadly, it couldn't be Daniel, who of course had been invited – he would be away that weekend on a school trip to Paris.

Grace needed a plus one who would *show* James. She took another gulp of wine and entered her details on Hook, Line and Sinker's registration page before she could change her mind. She felt like she was doing something very furtive and very naughty. Well, she was! Imogen and Frankie would be *horrified*. Without thinking about it too much, she 'friended' a couple of different men from the local area. One looked quite sporty, another looked like he was on a night out with mates, a pint in his hand. He looked jolly. Friendly.

Almost immediately she got back some dodgy *booty call* type messages, one asking to see her without her top on. Oh God. She browsed further down the rows and columns of men. One guy looked nice. His hair was a little bit longer, he had an open, kind-looking face and a T-shirt with a puppy on it. She messaged him. Five minutes later, as she was appalled reading about a man who enjoyed sniffing people's feet, a message popped into her 'Hook' box.

'Hey babe. Are you up for sex? I could cum over.'

Yuk, yuk, yuk. What a sleaze. That puppy had been very misleading. Is that what *all* the men on here were like? Hook, Line and *Stinker* was more accurate. She closed down the browser in disgust and slammed shut the lid of the laptop.

Surely there were classier, more sophisticated dating sites? Tinder? No! God, no, not that. Not a sugar daddy thing either, though – she'd heard all about *that* site. She took another large glug of wine, opened the laptop up again, and googled 'classy dating agency, Essex'. The first result that appeared was The Executive Club – yes, that sounded more like it, but when she clicked onto the website, all the men in the sidebar were ridiculously good-looking. Almost *revoltingly* good-looking. Oh, she should have known. This was an *escort agency*. It said so. *Gorgeous men at your service*, it proclaimed, at the top of the screen.

Curiosity got the better of her. The wine was swilling pleasantly around her system. Adele was now 'Rolling in the Deep'. She read the text in the middle of the page: *male chaperones to make you feel special... the perfect man for a dinner date... kind, courteous and handsome and know how to treat a lady... gorgeous straight men who love the company of women.* She quickly scanned down the photos. Most of the men looked smarmy, had goatees, were in dinner suits, or suits and ties; a lot were channelling Mr Grey or The Bachelor, from that American TV series. One looked like Gary Barlow and was straddling a ridiculously tiny bike saddle, dressed in pink and grey Lycra.

She stopped at the next photo. 'Text Greg,' it said, underneath. He looked nice. Late thirties? Navy blue short-sleeved polo top. Dark blond hair. Handsome grin. Most of the other men had closed-lipped knowing smiles, or one eyebrow raised, like ridiculous Roger Moores; Greg had his face half turned to the camera and was smiling like a normal person. It was a very informal photo. It was as though he'd quickly put up a casual photo with plans to put the real one up later...when he got round to posing in a dinner jacket and hauling up his left eyebrow.

She studied him. He didn't look like an escort. He looked like an older boy next door – if the boy next door was a cross between Brad Pitt and Liam Hemsworth, that was, not the low-rent Ron Weasley lookalike who always wore a grey tank top, as was actually the case.

Text. Okay. She could just text him, if she wanted to. She could hire him, *if she wanted to*, to go to the theatre with her for Nana McKensie's one hundredth. She could afford it. James was paying her maintenance for Daniel, she had her earnings from *Hats!* and her gran had left her some money, a few months ago. She'd never told James; she didn't know why. This money was just *hers*, to be put by for a rainy day. And if this wasn't a rainy day, she didn't know what was.

A male escort. It was almost hilarious. Once, years ago, in the large circle of her and James's London friends, a rather hapless bloke called Ed had turned up for dinner at Wagamama's one night with a really stunning woman. Everyone had been really surprised – Ed hadn't had a woman with him for months and he was definitely punching above his weight with this one. They all stared at her for most of the night, and tried to get him on his own so he could be quizzed.

After loads of booze, and when Stunning Surprise Girlfriend had gone to the loo, Ed was drunk enough to 'fess up, after unconvincingly trying to make out he'd met her in a Tesco Metro. She was an escort. Once, just once, he said, he wanted to turn up with a stunning girl on his arm and have everyone wondering.

They never saw her again. Ed must have spent too much money on cocktails, or perhaps he didn't want any 'extras', as at the end of the night he saw her off into a taxi with a chaste kiss on the cheek and they all went to get a kebab.

Grace remembered it was a cold night and how happy she'd felt when James had put his arm round her to pull her in close. When James had kissed her in the street after purposely making them drop back from the others. God, he was handsome. She was his and she loved it. She'd been spectacularly happy… Oh God.

She put James back in the box in her mind and slammed down the lid. James was gone.

After pouring the remainder of the bottle into her glass and taking a huge swig, she grabbed her phone and quickly sent a text to 'Greg', before she chickened out, or wondered too much if that was his real name.

Hi, just want to make an enquiry? Grace.

As the text sent, she got up and skipped a bit, nervously, around the room. Then sat back down again and stared at her phone. A text appeared.

Hi Grace, hope you're having a great evening. Would you like to know my prices and range of services? ☺

She panicked. *Range* of services! This was actually real, wasn't it? Oh God. She was in danger of completely bottling it.

I'm not sure! Frantic texting fingers.

Do you just want to chat?

Okay.

Oh, relief! Yes, just chat, they could do that.

If that's okay? she texted again.

Yes, that's fine. Tell me about what you like?

Oh God!

Do you mean sexually? she texted. *I'm not sure a lady like myself is ready for such a question!*

No! In general. What do you like doing?

She thought, sucking on the end of a pencil. Sucking on the end of a pencil! She shouldn't be sucking on the end of anything! She threw it down on the coffee table.

Dining out and roller-skating?

Where had that come from? She hadn't roller-skated since she was fifteen. Although she did really use to enjoy it, especially if she went with a boy. There was nothing nicer, she thought, than skating round to songs from the charts, holding hands.

Interesting! Would you like to book me for either of those activities?

He didn't want to chat, did he? It was all just about angling for a booking. She felt a horrible wave of terrified, horrified shame wash over her. An escort! What on earth was she thinking? She drained her glass of wine and wondered if she had another bottle lying around somewhere.

No thank you. Sorry. I'll get back to you.

CHAPTER SEVEN:
IMOGEN

Imogen left her mum's house to walk to the train station. She took in a deep breath of the damp, cold mid-March air, the month still in lion mode not lamb. She'd stayed over last night and it was a relief to be out of there.

If she was honest, she felt trapped at her mum's – the green carpet everywhere, the tired décor, the carriage clock on the mantelpiece loudly ticking the hours away. It was claustrophobic. Last night she'd retreated to her old bedroom at 9p.m. when Mum retired, and had read lying on her stomach on the bed with her feet dangling off the end, like she'd always used to.

Her bedroom was exactly the same as it had always been. Peach, tiny floral print wallpaper. A scratched white desk with flaky bits of exposed wood, long before shabby chic became fashionable. A sink in the corner. She was the only one of her friends who had one and she used to have it edged in Aapri facial scrub, a tiny bar of wrapped soap, Anne French cleansing milk and an Impulse body spray: Temptation. Still there, on the wooden, wall-mounted shelves, were an ancient Pippa doll (hair cut off, of course) an old cassette machine onto which she'd tape the Top 40 (swearing if the DJ dared talk over the beginning of a record), and a 1986 annual, full of tips on how to get a boyfriend.

In that peach room she had dreamed of having a man. A Prince Charming. The person to take her way from all this. (Ha! Well, that hadn't worked! She was right back where she started.) She saw how it affected her mum, being alone, with no man to share her life with. Imogen's father, or the sperm donor, as she liked to put it, had not stuck around. Mum had had a wild and passionate affair with him in her late teens, then he'd moved back to Brazil. That wasn't as glamorous as it sounded: he wasn't Brazilian, he just lived there. He'd made little contact once he realised he had a daughter, only sending the occasional, half-hearted cheque. When Imogen was a teenager she'd dreamed of flying to Rio to build a relationship with him but now she didn't; he'd proved himself not to be worth the effort.

Imogen, the serious schoolgirl with the A grades, was not going to end up alone. She was going to bag herself a great man. The best she could possibly get, and she'd work at it as hard as she studied. She treated having boyfriends at school like a career, trying to climb a rung up the ladder each time. Each boyfriend had to be better than the last.

She reached the end of her mum's road and headed smartly down the next. She felt happier the nearer she got to the train station – there were shops and convenience stores and takeaway places and noise and smells and life. She was more comfortable in an urban environment; suburbia didn't suit her. She'd loved drunks shouting outside her window at 3a.m. in Putney, all the noise and the bustle. And she loved going to London to work, despite the fact she hated her current job. Thank *God* it was Friday.

She had become an actors' agent at twenty-two, after being an assistant agent for three years and an intern for one. She had been one of eight agents in a big company. It was a busy, glamorous job – sending actors for castings, negotiating contracts, dealing with actors' egos, schmoozing casting directors and producers at lunches and dinners. She loved it.

Her glory days, she called those early years. She went to places like the Met Bar and the Titanic. She got drunk and went home to Putney in mini-cabs. She knew a lot of TV blondes and once snogged one of Supergrass's roadies, in the VIP area of a festival. She drank red wine in fancy restaurants until her teeth were black, and she'd grin at herself in posh Philippe Starck-type toilets that had no locks on the door, and think she not only had it all, but she had it all before her. They were the good old days – apart from one small blip. Her days in the sun.

She smiled as she remembered them, as she fed her ticket through the barrier and climbed the steps to Platform One. Her glory days had lasted for a long time. Even after she'd had to move back to Essex, she'd tried to keep them going. She was still out every night, watching plays and productions with up-and-coming actors in, attending networking dinners in trendy restaurants and, before the Man Ban, dating the most eligible and unsatisfactory men in the capital.

The last train back to Chelmsford had been a good way of separating the wheat from the chaff. After ten past midnight bad decisions about men were all too easy to make. The only time she'd missed it and had to get a cab all the way home was after a fantastic night salsa dancing with an investment manager from Deloittes. Their revelry had ended drunkenly at 2a.m., the cab cost her £140 and there had been no return on her investment. Deloittes Man turned out to have a wife, five children and a house in Mayfair that he got a £15 taxi home to.

The last train to Chelmsford had also stopped her from bringing any men back to the boxy new build she was slightly ashamed of. That's what hotels were for.

Imogen got on the train. She frowned, as the only remaining seat was next to a woman eating a very smelly 'breakfast bagel' that looked like it had a full B&B fry-up stuffed into it. She squeezed as close as she could to the window, got out her Kindle and wondered exactly how, last November, she had suddenly got fed up with it all. Being an agent. At the time her thought processes seemed quite clear: she was forty, she fancied a career break, a change. She'd been an agent for twenty-two years. She couldn't climb any higher with it. She'd done it all. It was getting boring.

She thought she'd see what was out there. Sniff around a bit. Maybe get a job in a different field, like television. Television production, maybe. She had a lot of skills. She could temp. She'd met someone who'd told her it was brilliant. You could get a foothold in the door of a new industry but at the same time enjoy a sense of freedom. You could walk out that door whenever you liked. And there was no pressure. Imogen was sold.

She left her agency, Potters, in a triumphant cloud, with a loud and boozy champagne send-off, then, within days of joining a temp agency, got a job at Yes! Productions, covering someone's maternity leave.

She pushed open the door there now. The trendy reception area always met her with a pepper and ginger biscuit-infused room spray that made her sneeze. She'd suffered it all week and had just about had enough of it.

'Morning, Imogen.'

'Ach-oo! Sorry. Morning, Fred.'

She always had to show her pass, everyone did, no matter how long they'd worked there. Fred once refused to let Marge the cleaner in, because she'd forgotten hers, and she'd worked there for ten years. It was an independent production company. They made sitcoms and the occasional gardening programme for the BBC.

As she walked to her desk, a formidable figure was lurking.

'When you're ready, Imogen.'

'Yes, Carolyn.'

Carolyn Boot. Tyrant was way too mild a word for her.

Carolyn disappeared into her office. Imogen would follow, in approximately one minute, once she'd taken her coat off, to have her Daily Diary Meeting with her. It was Friday the 13th, but every day was unlucky for Imogen at this job.

Imogen had had the misfortune of being Carolyn Boot's personal assistant for the past three and a half months, and it was hell. Working for her was not so much like walking on eggshells, but tiptoeing on a tragically thin sheet of ice, where one wrong move could place you into the black, icy water that was Carolyn Boot's disapproval. Nothing was ever good enough; nothing was ever done quickly enough or accurately enough or with enough *expediency*, one of Carolyn Boot's favourite words. And it was so *easy* to get things wrong! Especially with that threat of utter contempt hanging over you.

It was totally mad, really; Imogen had been an *agent*, for goodness' sake! But this woman could reduce *anyone* to a quivering wreck. Employees, especially the younger girls – well, they were all younger than Imogen – quaked when she walked in the office. She could fell a conversation with a pointed glance. She had a way of telling people off that reduced them to tears. And when Carolyn Boot laughed, someone had better laugh along with her.

Imogen picked up her pad and pen and walked into Carolyn's office.

Carolyn Boot took her shoes off in the office and walked around in her stockinged feet. Tan tights, usually. Woe betide if anyone else did, though. Elaine Marks tried it once and got a right telling-off. The old cow also did this really bizarre thing where she would kneel on the carpet by the side of an employee's desk – the high kneeling, where the bottom doesn't touch the legs – stick her head right next to them and mutter earnestly. It was a misguided attempt at 'chumminess', Imogen suspected. Carolyn stank of cigarettes and colleagues were too scared to reel back from the smell. She also had a despised Leslie Judd from *Blue Peter* haircut.

'Take a seat.'

Carolyn was propped on her desk, her legs dangling like splints and her tights bunched round her toes. Imogen sat on a low chair facing her.

'Have you sorted the talent for next week's dinner at Four Bridges?' Talent didn't mean tasty men, or anything like that – not that Imogen would currently care – it was a poncey word for actors, creative people, producers, whatever… You could use it to describe anyone with the merest sniff of the stuff. Carolyn *loved* the word. She used it at least six hundred times every day.

'Yes, Carolyn.'

'And don't forget the electrician's coming next Thursday.'

'All in hand, Carolyn.'

One day a week, Imogen had to go to Carolyn Boot's house in Oxford and sort out all her domestic arrangements. It involved things like waiting three hours for a courier delivery, tending to plants and doing the recycling. It was not really what Imogen had imagined for her new career. Even a temporary part of it. Watering some old dragon's begonias and shuffling her husband's junk mail into a recycling bag one day a week (yes, amazingly Carolyn Boot was married), and working under her cruel regime in the office the other four.

For twenty more minutes, Carolyn gave out orders and Imogen bitterly noted them down. What parallel universe had she made herself wander into?

Finally, she returned to her desk. But soon after, the stench of stale fags and coffee breath alerted Imogen to the fact The Kneeler was by her side.

'I forgot something important,' said Carolyn. 'Could you please make sure you order three sets of duck wraps and four sets of finger rolls – turkey *not* ham – for tomorrow's Acquisitions and Agendas breakfast meeting. Graham Grinch likes a light bite. Those hideous bacon things you organised last time didn't go down at all well.'

'Yes, Carolyn.'

Carolyn stood up and padded back to her office and Imogen swiftly sent an email to Teresa, who worked the other side of the partition.

If that cow kneels at my desk one more time, I'm going to bosh her over the head with my hole punch, she wrote and sent, in a matter of seconds.

Bish, bash, bosh. An email swooped straight back.

Imogen's heart jumped up to the top of her head. It was *her* subject line ('Ughh!') but the email was from Carolyn Boot.

I beg your pardon? Come into my office.

She hastily checked her sent emails. She'd definitely sent it to Teresa. What the hell had gone wrong? She fired off another email to her colleague.

Are your emails being forwarded to Carolyn Boot?

Too late, she realised Carolyn may get that one, too.

Teresa popped her head over the partition and hissed, 'Yes! For today. I'm being monitored – every email I send or receive, after that "sending the wrong letter" incident.' Teresa had recently sent out a letter to some very important Talent, inviting them to a Facilitatory Brainstorm Catch-all, *three years ago*, as she'd used a template letter and hadn't changed the previous date. 'Bloody hell, Imogen!' She'd read the email, then.

'Bollocks,' said Imogen, and she rose from her chair and went to the guillotine.

Carolyn was behind her desk this time. Her face was set hard. Hatchet face, hammer face, sledgehammer face, thought Imogen. A face of an old boot. She felt sick with fear. She felt like a child sent to the headmistress's office. A foot soldier sent to be court-martialled.

Then she remembered who she was, who she had been and who she was *supposed* to be and almost laughed to herself. Why was she frightened of this bloody woman? Why was everyone frightened of her? She didn't need this. She was an *agent*! People were supposed to suck up to *her* – not that she'd ever be so officious, so nasty, or so downright up her own bottom as this awful bloody woman. Plus, she was way too old for this nonsense.

Carolyn opened her mouth to speak.

'Before you say anything,' said Imogen, 'and I'm sure it's going to be just delightful, I've got something to say to you.' She went and stood right in front of the desk and looked over Carolyn. *She* wasn't in her stockinged feet. She was in four-inch heels and she used her height for extra power. She told Carolyn exactly what everyone around her had been longing to say – for years, probably.

'Just because you happen to be Controller of Executive Demonstrative Facilitative Relations, it doesn't make you a better person than everyone else. Smarter, maybe. Luckier, definitely. But not *better*.' Carolyn made to protest but Imogen shut her down. 'Let me finish. Your *job* does not give you the right to lord over, belittle, terrorise and frighten people. It just doesn't.' Carolyn tried to open her mouth again but Imogen ploughed on. 'You're an awful old bag. Everyone thinks so. Even *you* know so. You get business done by striking fear into people. There's just no need for it, Carolyn! It is possible to be successful *and* nice, you know. Lots of other people manage it.' She took a deep breath. 'I'll sum up, if I may. You're an absolutely hideous, horrible old BOOT. And I'm not going to work for you a second longer. Goodbye.'

And she turned on her high heels and walked out of there, leaving a flabbergasted Carolyn sitting at the desk, her mouth hanging open like a trapdoor. Carolyn's *actual* door had been open. If anyone had dared, there would have been *An Officer and a Gentleman*-style applause and loud whooping. As it was, Imogen quietly got her bag, gave Teresa a wink, and walked out of the office. She said goodbye to Fred, emerged from reception and got straight on the phone to her old friend Marcia Lacrosse.

'Marcia!'

'Imogen, darling!'

'Are you still looking for an agent to be your number two?'

'You bet your last shiny penny I am! Come see me?'

'I'm on my way.'

Three Tube stops later and Imogen was at the Marcia Lacrosse Agency in Soho. When they'd met, twenty years ago, Marcia was an agent at a rival company to Imogen's. They'd hit it off immediately at some networking art gallery schmooze-fest, bonding over some limp sushi that smelt a bit off. Marcia was fabulous fun. She was about a decade older than Imogen and had a very loud laugh, a huge, swaying bottom and a selection of very expensive handbags. She was one of those women who believe their handbags said all there was to know about them; she always held a giant one before her, in a differing rainbow of colours depending on the day, like a shield. Then she came into shot. A severe black bob, laughing hazel eyes and plum lipstick.

Together she and Imogen were a delightfully bad influence on each other. They'd had many memorable 'think tank' meetings in trendy London bars back in the day, which often ended with one of them being sent home drunk and disgraceful in a taxi – usually Marcia, who had once been discovered flat out on the floor of the ladies' of the hottest venue of the moment, giggling into her Dictaphone.

Imogen smiled to herself as she pushed open the pale blue door of the ML Agency's tiny Flora Street entrance. That bloody Dictaphone! Marcia had always been *obsessed* with it. At random, and usually in the middle of a conversation with someone, Marcia would lower her chin to it. 'Jerome Cleaver possibility for *The Dark Horse*,' she would whisper urgently. Or she would walk down the street murmuring, 'Casting for *Danger in the Manger*, Tuesday next. Thinking Sam Burrows, Timothy Tampari or that guy with the navy roll-neck.' Or she would give herself instructions. Once, in a bar, she'd been whispering in it, 'Can you lay a finger on that, soon as,' and a passing man had surprised her by saying, 'Don't mind if I do.'

Imogen couldn't wait to see her. It had been at least six months. She'd heard on the grapevine that Marcia had been looking for a co-agent, but hadn't considered it while she blundered into her laughable new 'career'. Now, it was just what she wanted.

Imogen headed up to the office, treading carefully on the narrow, royal-blue carpeted stairs, which still smelled like furniture polish and old curtains. Heating whacked up to oblivion was belting out of Marcia's open door. The enormous sash windows were wide open and papers on Marcia's huge antique desk were ruffling in the stiff March breeze. There was some music playing – 'Tubular Bells'? – and there was Marcia, over by the filing cabinet, wearing some sort of woolly, hot pink sarong wrapped round her body like cling film, with her arms and legs stuck out of it, surprised. A huge pair of sunglasses on top of her head pushed two parts of her wiry black hair into horns.

'Darling!' Marcia stepped forward and embraced Imogen in a giant hug. Over her pink shoulder, Imogen could see a man in the corner of the room, sitting in a brown leather chair. He had the open-mouthed, vacant glare of an American gangster. 'That's Tarquin,' said Marcia, releasing Imogen from the hug. 'I'm marketing him as the UK's Tony Soprano. Hoping to get him into 'Enders. Say hi to Imogen, Tarquin.'

'Hello there, Imogen,' said Tarquin, standing up. 'Pleased to make your acquaintance.' Tarquin had proper Queen's English received pronunciation, with cut-glass vowels. He sounded terribly posh. It didn't match his look at all. Marcia must have sensed Imogen's surprise. She started to chuckle, her encased pink bottom jiggling as though desperate to be set free.

'Oh, he's a terrific actor, aren't you, Tarquin? Give Imogen your best cockney.'

Tarquin cocked his head on one side, ground his eyebrows into a knot and curled his lips into a snarl. 'All right, Ma?'

'Very good,' said Imogen.

'They're looking for a new landlord for the Queen Vic,' said Marcia. 'I reckon Tarqs will have it in the bag.' Marcia suddenly grabbed her Dictaphone from the desk. 'Please call Derango's tomorrow and arrange canapés for three. Capish. Manyana,' she muttered into it. Imogen smiled. 'There'll be plenty more where that came from. Actors, I mean. If you're in?'

'Of course, I'm in!' said Imogen.

'Fabbo. Can you come in Monday? I'll get a desk all set up for you? You happy in the eaves, darling?' she said pointing to a corner of the cramped office that had a desk crammed under a sloping roof.

'More than happy,' said Imogen.

'Got potentials you can poach?'

'Absolutely.'

Marcia walked over to a laptop on a shelf and started tapping frantically away on the keyboard, like Jerry Lee Lewis. 'Well, duckie, see you Monday then,' she said. And that was that: Imogen was an agent again.

Imogen decided to walk into Chinatown and get herself an early bird dim sum dinner to celebrate. This was going to be great. A boutique agency. Working with Marcia, in a team of two, where she would have so much more control… *This* was the change she needed. Not moonlighting in telly with a horrible boss. What had she been thinking, leaving the business?

She was walking along Grafton Street. Before she'd decided to swear off men, she'd have had her radar up, looking to see who was looking at her, sussing out the rich and available from the not so rich and available, enjoying the stares and returning them tenfold. Not any more. These days she let them look but she didn't return the favour.

She was an attractive woman. Not anything close to beautiful, but she made the best of herself. Her hair was as straight and shiny as she could make it. Her skin was kept in tip-top condition. She bought expensive cosmetics. All that made up for her slightly Roman nose. Her slightly square chin. Both from her dad, she suspected, from the grainy black and white photos she'd seen of him, at age twenty, lounging in a deck chair in Hyde Park, with shorts and flip-flops on. She did have dazzling eyes though. She got those from Mum. Emerald green and able to fell a man at thirty paces. She used to utilise them whenever she could. Now she was happy not to bother.

She received a few whistles, an idiot in a high-vis jacket blocked her path and waved a sandwich in front of her face and a good-looking guy in a smart navy suit looked her up and down. She gave him a withering look. Sod off. Who needed men? She certainly didn't. She'd loved her year of being single, so far.

A large black car was half blocking the pavement. A grey-haired man, late fifties, early sixties, was standing in front of a cashpoint machine in a grey suit, getting some money out. There was a half-person width gap between him and the car. Idiot, she thought. She could have gone out into the road and walked around the car, but she couldn't be bothered, on principle. And the road was teeming with people and bikes and traffic.

'Bad form,' said Imogen, as she turned her back to him and squeezed between him and the car. She flattened her bag against her flat stomach. Her bottom brushed his. Ugh. She didn't particularly enjoy bumping bums with strangers. Not even at nights in salsa clubs.

'Apologies,' said a low, distinctly American voice. It didn't come from the man standing at the cashpoint; it came from the half-open, tinted window in front of her.

Imogen stopped and peered in. A whiff of expensive leather upholstery went up her nose. It was the first thing she noticed. She was attuned to luxury; the leather was a very expensive-looking soft honey beige. The second thing she noticed was a man leaning confidentially against the honey leather. Dark suit and royal blue tie. Salt and pepper hair. Large nose. Twinkling blue eyes that over-rode it. Dazzling, *sexy* eyes, in fact. Overall effect: bloody handsome.

At the sight of Imogen's face, he grinned. She restrained a grin at the sight of his, although other parts of her body were simultaneously breaking into smiles.

'Tosser,' she said. And she averted her eyes and strode forward, releasing her body from the unwelcome compress of the older man's bum.

As she reached the boot of the car (it was a quite a long car – very flash), the man's voice came through the window again. Louder this time.

'I'm Richard. Pleased to meet you.'

She stopped, turned and stuck her head back through the window. It had now been wound down almost to the bottom.

'You're a Dick?'

'Ha, *you're* quick. No, I'm Richard.'

'Dick,' said Imogen, choosing to ignore him. 'There's quite a few famous dicks. Dick Turpin… Dick Emery… Dick for Brains,' she said. 'Actually, I couldn't care less what your name is. You shouldn't park here. You're causing an obstruction.'

He grinned again, and shrugged. Nice tie, she thought. He really was very well groomed and smart. His shirt so white, his suit so immaculate. He would have been just her type, before the Man Ban. 'London's rammed today,' he said. 'There's nowhere to park. I just took my chance. I won't be here long.'

'I hope that's true.' She gave him her best withering look. 'Then you can bugger off back to America. I'm sure New York is desperate to have you back.'

'How do you know I'm from New York?'

'I know the type.'

'Oh, really?' He raised his eyebrows and gave a slow smile.

'Yeah, really. Right, well *I'm* buggering off now. See you.' But it was hard to tear her eyes off his. They were amused, mocking, enticing. Above that big old nose. It was a strange but highly sexy juxtaposition. She felt rooted to the spot. She didn't want to go.

'Have dinner with me.'

'Do what?'

'Dinner. I heard there's a joint called Nobu. I'd like to go.'

'Oh, I've already been, thanks. Loads of times.'

'Come again? With me?'

How bloody forward! Typical American. What a cheek. Still. Despite the pact with Frankie and Grace, *despite* the fact she was supposed to be single for a year – and had been enjoying it – she was tempted. She loved the food at Nobu, this man looked hot and sexy and she was celebrating a new job, wasn't she? A few months ago she would have jumped at the chance of this irresistible combination. A few months ago even just *one* of these things would have had her jumping up and down and saying 'yes'.

Resist, resist, she told herself sternly. Just say no. You're off men. They're useless, hopeless wastes of space. The road to nowhere. The road to ruin. Damn. If only they weren't. If only there was still the slightest glimmer of hope that one, just one of them, would be perfect. What if *this* man was *that* man? What if she let him go and he was someone worth hanging on to?

There wouldn't be any *harm* in going for dinner with him, would there? It was just a little dinner. And a girl's got to eat. She'd gone out with men on less of a pretext: because the guy had Gucci shoes; because she'd stalked the bloke on LinkedIn then hung around the pub in the city nearest his work for an hour, until he'd come in; because it was a Tuesday... Okay, no pretexts at all; she'd just wanted to date them. Yet, none of those guys had worked out well at all. They never did. Actually, maybe this man could serve as a *reinforcement* of her new ideology, a final underlining of what she now believed...

Damn him and his sexy big nose and sexy blue eyes!

She didn't have to tell anyone.

'You know there are actually two Nobus?'

'Yes. Park Lane and Mayfair. I'm thinking Park Lane.'

'I was on my way to have dim sum, actually,' she said. Good. Excellent. *Go* for dinner with him, but on your terms. Take control. 'That's what I fancy.' It wasn't the only thing.

'I can do dim sum.'

God, that accent was intoxicating, thought Imogen. She'd had a couple of Americans. A Texan living in London who she'd dated for two weeks – it had all ended when he suggested a three way, with a blow-up doll – and a super arty Californian art dealer, who she'd thought would be super interesting, but had turned out to be super dull. He never ate after 6p.m. and didn't drink alcohol. She'd been taken in by that accent before and it had never worked out. She feared she remained a sucker for it.

'On the other hand,' she pretended to hesitate, 'I could just as easily go home to a ready meal for one and a date with *MasterChef*.'

'I have no idea what either of those things are,' said Richard, laughing. And what a laugh. Sexiest laugh she'd ever heard. 'Look, we'll go for dim sum. I'll get Nigel to phone ahead.' Nigel, the man at the cashpoint, was now back in the driver's seat and twiddling with the radio.

'You don't *book* dim sum,' said Imogen. 'You just turn up.'

'Whatever,' said the most gorgeous man on earth. 'Hop in.'

He swung open the door, took off his seat belt and eased along the back seat to the far side. An action that made her focus on his thighs. Lord, they looked firm under his suit trousers. She could see his shoes, too. Black and just the right kind of shiny. Shoes maketh the man, everyone knew that. She had dumped a man or two for bad taste in shoes. Had once actually fled a bar before approaching her date because his roosted position on a stool had exposed a pair of perforated lemon suede loafers.

This American's shoes were nice. She bet he had very expensive socks, too, and that his feet never smelled. Oh bugger it, *no one needed to know*. And it would be rude not to, really, now he had moved across to make room for her.

She got in before she changed her mind. Nigel was suddenly at the door and shut it for her. The car smelt wonderful. That leather, and an expensive-smelling New York male cologne. Wow. She was like a fly in a very luxurious honey trap.

She had a moment of panic. She was safe, wasn't she? Nigel was here. He looked a bit like her next-door neighbour, Mr Roper, the one who mowed his lawn at ten o'clock at night in the summer. He didn't look like the sort of man who would suddenly and dramatically lock all the doors, wind up all the windows and speed off to some deserted industrial estate somewhere, whilst Richard's face turned black as night and his lips twisted into a maniacal grin as he reached for a knife from the side car door pocket… She was safe; she was sure of it. Somehow.

The doors didn't lock and they moved slowly off into the London afternoon traffic. Nigel sang softly along to Bruce Springsteen, on the radio. Richard smiled at her, his eyes all blue and sultry. She now felt panic of a different kind. What the hell was she doing? She was reverting to type again, wasn't she? This was exactly the type of man she was supposed to be avoiding! Rich, powerful, impossibly groomed, charming, persuasive. The type of man she'd swerved when she'd lowered her sights to Dave Holgate. She was supposed to be avoiding *all* men, and had been, quite successfully, up until all of three minutes ago. What was she thinking, getting into a handsome stranger's car?

She had form for it. Being reckless. There was the life insurance guy who'd come into her office for a meeting with her boss and left with an afternoon rummage; the ridiculously rich guy she'd met by email and slept with on a houseboat after a night at the opera; the blind date she'd jumped on the Orient Express with… The only men she wasn't reckless with were actors. She *never* dated actors. Not after The Blip.

She was always reckless with *this* sort of guy. Get a grip, she thought. This wasn't *Mr Big*! There weren't balloons in the back of the car! She wasn't going to have an on-off relationship with this man for ten years and end up married to him and living in an amazing apartment overlooking Central Park.

As the car was now in stationary traffic, she reached for the handle. She feared not for her life, but for her sanity. She didn't want to be doing this, after all.

'I'm not a serial killer, honest,' said Richard. 'I work for Universal Re.' He reached into the silky inside pocket of his jacket, and handed her a card.

She glanced briefly at it then passed it back to him. '*American Psycho* worked for a swanky bank. You could still be a serial killer.'

'Pierce and Pierce.'

'Sorry?'

'That was the name of Patrick Bateman's company in *American Psycho*. It was fictitious. Made up. And his company was investment; mine is re-insurance.'

'Re-insurance? Isn't insurance boring enough the first time around? And I know what *fictitious* means. We invented the English language, remember.'

Richard nodded, smiling, his eyebrows slightly raised and teasing.

'You seem to know a lot about *American Psycho*,' she said. 'That's suspicious in itself. You know what suspicious means, right?'

'Ha ha, touché!' Richard's eyes crinkled when he laughed. He had very attractive lines. How old was he? Late forties? How annoying it was that lines could look extremely sexy on a man's face but never a woman's. 'I've seen the movie, that's all. Look, I'm not a serial killer. Call one of my colleagues if you want to. I'm here in London for six months. Working at the Gherkin.' He went to pull his card out of his pocket again.

'No, it's okay.'

'Good. It's all fine and dandy then.' He leant back, relaxed. He was a big man. Not fat big. Broad big. She imagined serious pecs and huge 'guns' under that crisp white shirt. She envisaged strong, hairy legs and sexy feet and toes. She pulled her eyes away from him and tried to be interested in what was going on outside the window, which was difficult, as all she could see was a static and traffic-blackened brick wall. The car was still not moving. It would have been much quicker to walk.

'I'm someone who takes chances,' Richard said, behind her head. 'And I like the look of you and hopefully you like the look of me.' She turned back from the window. Locked her eyes onto his. Oh sod it, he was gorgeous, why not just enjoy the fact? 'So we'll go have a little dinner. That's how it works, isn't it? People who like the look of each other go out on dates. I'm sure dating in London is not so different to New York.'

'Do women jump into the back seats of cars with strange men in New York?' she asked. 'Okay, don't answer that! We're a bit more cautious here. Have you been to London before?'

'Nope, first time. But I know all about the well-documented British reserve,' he said. 'The renowned stiff upper lip. Never let your guard down, don't show emotion and when the going gets tough drink a nice *cup of tea.*'

'Stiff upper lips and cups of tea served us well through two world wars, I'll have you know.' *I'll have you know?* Who was she, her dear departed nan? And what was she going on about? Soon she'd be prattling on about Eccles cakes and ration books. 'Which we *won,*' she couldn't help but adding, unnecessarily.

She really didn't want to get onto this. Did they really want to get into a discussion about GIs and Winston Churchill and all that *standing shoulder to shoulder* business? Although she wouldn't mind standing shoulder to shoulder with this man, or indeed putting any part of her body against his.

She sighed. Did he have to mention tea and British reserve? He was so fabulously amazing, she hoped he didn't turn out to be awfully disappointing – one of those Americans who laughed at all the stereotypical things that British people supposedly did, and bought Union Jack tea cosies thinking they were beanie hats and went around saying how quaint everything was. Surely, he wasn't like that?

He was laughing. 'I'm teasing,' he said. 'I know you Brits hate it when we *Yanks* – I'm kidding, we hate that, too – start going on about English clichés and putting on terrible accents that make us sound like Bert from *Mary Poppins*.' He smirked and gave a slight wink. 'I've never seen an upper lip here that was particularly stiff, and all the guys in my office drink coffee. It's the only thing that keeps them awake for all that boring *insurance*.'

Now it was Imogen's turn to laugh, but her laugh quickly faded away when she realised Richard was staring quite intently at her mouth. Was he looking at her lips, her *upper lip*? She had an urge to not be bloody reserved in the slightest and kiss him right there and then, in the back of his car.

She moved her head out of his laser stare and sat back, aware she'd been perched forward since she'd got into the car, like a budgerigar. She had a proper look around her. She was half expecting a drinks cabinet thing to automatically open up from somewhere, James Bond style, or a glass screen to pop up between them and Nigel, trapping her in the back seat and leaving her to the mercy of Richard. She quite liked the idea of that, to be honest, which was ridiculous, as five minutes ago she'd been terrified at the very thought.

'So what do you do?' he asked. Now it was her turn to study his mouth. She noticed his teeth. Super white. Nice. His lips were on the thin side, but curved upwards at the corner, like a fox's. Tasty.

'I'm an agent.' Yes, she was. She was an agent, again. Hoo bloody ray.

'CIA? Federal?'

'Ha, funny. No we don't have silly things like that in this country, as you probably know. We just have the police. Oh, and MI5, though I'm still not exactly sure what they do.'

'Literary?' He gave the word four full syllables. It sounded sexy.

'No, acting. I'm an actors' agent.'

'Movies?'

'Television. Mostly.'

'Cool job.'

'Yup.'

'I bet you're damn good at it.'

'As a matter of fact, I am.'

'English rose,' he said, smoothing his tie. Oh God, don't look at his hands, she thought: if he's got nice hands as well, you'll be powerless. She was a stickler for a man's hands. And if they pleased her, she knew that they would *please* her. Neat clean nails, large, firm-looking hands, just the right slight smattering of hair on the backs – and she was a goner. Richard's hands were perfect. She got tingles in parts of her body she'd rather not mention.

'I beg your pardon?'

'I'm afraid I'm wandering down stereotype alley here, after all, but you're one of those English roses, aren't you? Winslet, Thompson, Pike. Is your name Rosamund or Abigail or Imogen?'

'Actually, it is. It's Imogen. Imogen Henderson.'

'Bingo!' said Richard, looking ridiculously pleased with himself. He looked like a small boy who'd found a nickel on the sidewalk. (Imogen congratulated herself on her American analogy.)

'Very lucky,' said Imogen. 'Aren't English roses supposed to be blonde, though?'

'I think so, officially. But I'd like to expand on that. I'd like to expand that to gorgeous brunettes with sparkling green eyes and a knock-out pair of legs.'

Imogen blushed, conforming to the stereotype after all. An English rose, eh? She'd never been referred to as one of those before. And she wondered if she was too old to strictly qualify for one. No matter, she could go with it.

'You know your British actresses,' she said, trying to deflect the attention elsewhere.

'I've watched a lot of British movies.'

'Yeah, yeah,' she said. 'Let me guess. *Notting Hill*, *Four Weddings and a Funeral*, *Love Actually*?' The usuals.

'Yes, those. But quite a few others, too. I've seen a lot of British films. From all the eras. Ealing comedies, Powell and Pressburger, kitchen sink dramas. *Kes*. Even the odd *Carry On. Ooh matron*,' he said, in cod Kenneth Williams. Imogen laughed. He actually made Kenneth Williams sound sexy. 'I like British movies. My favourites are *Trainspotting*, *Shallow Grave*, *The Full Monty*. The 90s is my era.'

'Oh me too,' said Imogen. 'Especially for music. Blur, Oasis –'

'– James, Suede, Elastica,' he added. He knew his stuff. 'Sleeper, The Stone Roses, Dodgy…'

'*Dodgy*! There's a blast from the past! Fabulous.'

They grinned at each other. Wow. He liked British films and knew his Britpop. Impressive.

'What's your favourite Blur song?' she asked.

'"The Universal".'

'Mine too,' she said. Now she was more than impressed.

They both paused. Looked at each other. The pause was kind of electrifying. She needed to break it as it was almost unbearable.

'I like a lot of American movies, from the 90s,' she said. '*Goodfellas*. That's my favourite movie of all time. The long shot, going into the Copacabana club, just genius.'

Richard nodded. 'Yes, I know it. Ray Liotta and Lorraine Bracco.' Now *he* looked impressed. She started to show off.

'I met Paul Sorvino, once,' she said, 'in the 90s. He was Paulie, in *Goodfellas*. I met him at a party.'

'Cool. Cool guy. I'm in awe of you already, Imogen.'

'Are you, Richard?' She was flirting now and she knew it. The conversation had got...exciting. Movies, music... they were on the same wavelength. She wondered what other areas they might be in tune on.

'Yes, ma'am.' Oh God, it was corny, and she knew he was saying it slightly tongue in cheek, but the way he said *ma'am* made her feel weak at the knees. Oh goodness. They were doing so well, keeping away from all the clichés. She really shouldn't be seduced by the cliché of a charming American. Good Lord! This wasn't *Yanks* (although she loved that film! Richard Gere? Hello! Who didn't?)

She felt her face colouring, so she turned to the window again. The expensive car would have purred had it been going faster than nought. Instead, it was stop start and it had started to drizzle.

She was excited about going for dinner with this man. She hadn't been this excited about a man in ages. The last time she'd been really excited was when she'd been convinced a hot-shot guy from the Bank of England, whom she'd dated for five months, was going to propose to her. They were in the restaurant at The Flagship Hotel. He kept looking at his dessert. Trifle. She became convinced there was a ring in the bottom of it. She was wrong. He just really liked raspberries. In hindsight, she didn't really want him. She certainly didn't love him – love was for mugs. She just wanted the perfect proposal and the perfect marriage.

Why was she thinking about marriage? She was sworn off men! She had to remember that! God, it was tough, though. She was really struggling at the moment, to be honest.

She felt a hand rest lightly on her leg. She nearly shot off the seat and up to the plush, quilted ceiling. Richard was looking at her with a quizzical look on his face.

Bloody hell, he really was handsome. She was slipping. The ban was rapidly wearing off. Help!

'So,' he said.

'So?' she said.

'We're just about here.' The door was opening. Nigel was outside. She stepped out. Richard came round from the other side of the car doing that sexy thing where a man reaches round to his back and tucks his shirt in. He was tall. Really tall. She'd been out with a couple of tall men, but they were more of the beanpole variety. He was tall, broad… All man. Oh God, she really shouldn't be swayed by this stuff.

She looked up and down the street before they went in to Sai Kung Palace, which was ridiculous. Frankie and Grace were hardly going to be up in London, and no one else knew about her vow to be single for a year, or the fact she was not supposed to be anywhere *near* a man as gorgeous as this.

CHAPTER EIGHT:
FRANKIE

Friday the 13th of March. Unlucky for some, dead boring for others. It was only Friday night but Frankie was bored already. She had absolutely nothing to do this weekend, and the novelty of the children being with Rob was beginning to wear off. She was fed up with having literally no one to play with.

She missed the children. The last couple of weekends they'd gone to Rob and his buy-to-let she'd stuck on a happy face but had had a little cry after the car had pulled away. She *missed* them. It was so *quiet* once they'd left the house. She was beginning to hate the weekends they weren't with her.

They'd been gone about fifteen minutes; Rob had a day off and had picked them up at four. He was pretty chipper these days, she thought. There'd been no snarling recently, no barbed comments; he just picked the children up on a Friday and returned them on a Sunday, usually with a smile on his face. She didn't get any complaining texts from him now, either.

She texted Imogen at work but got no reply. It was Friday. Frankie bet she was going out after work... There'd be a play, or a drink somewhere with those young girls in her office. Imogen still liked her nights out even though she wasn't dating. Grace was also out tonight, at a Taekwondo class of all things! She'd told Frankie now she was single she wanted to take up some new hobbies and as Daniel already did it, Taekwondo was the poison of choice. It takes all sorts, thought Frankie. ('Poison of choice' were her words, not Grace's.) It wasn't something *she* fancied.

Bored, bored, bored. She felt at an utter loss. The weekend loomed before her dull and empty.

She lay on her bed and looked out the window at the sky. That cloud over there looked like a sausage dog. The one just above the telegraph pole resembled Boris Johnson's hair. She heard a car pull up outside. She hoped it was someone exciting. She hoped it was Rob bringing the children back and saying he couldn't have them after all this weekend.

Oh no, she thought as she clambered to the window and looked down at the street. A black Fiat Panda was parked at the kerb and her parents were climbing out. She'd been avoiding them since she and Rob had split. She knew it was awful, but she couldn't bear to tell them. She'd kept contact to a few truncated telephone calls and prayed they wouldn't pop round.

Frankie's mum and dad were Old School with a capital O and a capital S. Pam had been wearing print floral dresses on her self-confessed ample frame since the age of thirty, hadn't worked since the Dark Ages (last known employment: the broken biscuit counter at Woolies) and firmly believed that a woman's place was in the kitchen, or sometimes, the garden, butchering laburnum bushes, or sometimes, the living room, where she enjoyed looming over Ted and his nightly tea on a wicker tray, making sure he had enough salt and pepper or mustard or brown sauce, and was the gravy hot enough, or should she throw the whole thing back in the microwave for another five minutes? Pam was a terrible cook, a lover of shop-bought Battenburg and she liked things how they used to be; she took no *truck* with new-fangled gadgets or 'women's lib' (interchangeable), and she believed men were to be served.

Ted enjoyed being served, despite the terrible food. He was a very quiet man. Well, he had to be. There couldn't be two overpowering, hysteria-prone people in that relationship; they would detonate each other and explode in an almighty mushroom cloud over Essex. And that would be a worry.

The *blasted modern age*, as Pam put it, gave her cause for lots of worry. She had an abject fear of the internet, for example, and was always cutting snippets out of the paper (i.e. the *Daily Mail*) about its dangers and popping them in the post to Frankie. While she was at it, mobile phones, iPads, iPods, games consoles, the 'Wee', the 'Wee You', Gameboys, DVDs and satnavs were also the work of evil, and if she found any evidence of this in the paper, she would also let Frankie know, via a pair of pinking shears and Royal Mail. Frankie was never sure if all this hysteria was down to genuine, loving concern for her family, or whether Pam just enjoyed sitting astride a very high, old-fashioned horse. And slipping things into envelopes.

As she let them in, Frankie felt slightly sick, and not just because her mother was thrusting yet another sodding pot plant at her she knew she would kill within days. Did she *really* have to tell her mother she and Rob had split up? She just knew what her mother would say.

'Oh, Francesca!'

There it was. Her mum's constant lament. She'd said it all the time when Frankie was young: if she fell over; if she dropped an ice cream on the ground; if, as a teenager, she was upset over a boy, failed an exam or attempted to go out the front door in a too short skirt and a pair of white stilettos…and it appeared Pam couldn't give it up.

'Oh, Francesca!' Pam was perched on the sofa; she never sat back properly. It was as if she always had somewhere she'd rather be, something she really should be getting on with, instead, usually some badly done, martyr-ing domestic task.

Her bag was also perched, on her lap. It was ready for every eventuality that bag, like a cracked yellow leather version of Mary Poppins' carpet bag. Everything was rammed in it: a tape measure; a jumbo box of plasters; scissors – paper and nail; tweezers; anti-bacterial hand wash; two hankies; three carrier bags made into micro size by clever knotting; a ball of string; emergency Murray Mints; a packet of chocolate digestives; a Mills & Boon; spare keys, socks, pants and one of Dad's vests; and a vacuum-packed cagoule and matching rain hat. It was as busy and as crowded as Pam's mind. Frankie thought both needed a good emptying out.

'What on earth have you done that for?' exclaimed Pam. Her chins were rippling above her expansive body. 'Rob's done everything for you!'

'Has he? Like what?'

'He married you and gave you four children!'

'Yes, I see.' Frankie nodded. 'Or, you could argue, I married *him* and gave *him* four children.'

Pam wrinkled up her nose in disgust and incredulity. 'But he's your right-hand man!' she said.

What planet was her mother on? Dad had never been *her* right-hand man! She would never let him. Her parents' life was a ship that Pam captained alone.

'Well, that's it, Mum, really – he's not, is he? He's not a right-hand anything! Or a left-hand anything!' He was the back end of a pantomime horse, more like. 'He was a hindrance, Mum. You really have no idea.'

Right-hand man! She couldn't get over that. Why was her mother talking as though husbands and wives were a team? She and Dad weren't a team. Pam wore the trousers and Dad did as he was told. He ate up all his dinner up like a good boy, took out the bins every Friday and turned all the electrics off at night, including the sockets for the television, the Teasmade (defeating the object, surely), the kitchen appliances and the ancient trouser press he'd used religiously since 1975. You can never be too careful, you know. Mrs Godfrey next door, well, her sister-in-law said there was a woman on her street who once forgot to switch the plug off from behind the toaster when she went to bed and when she woke up the next morning the whole house had burned down...

Pam clasped her handbag to her breast, as though for dear life. 'But at least he was *there*, dear! You need him, don't you? Oh poor man, chucking him out like that! Now you'll be one of those terrible single mothers – I feel quite ashamed!'

'Oh, Mum. Please don't feel ashamed. There's nothing wrong with being a single mother.'

'You'll be the first one in the family!' exclaimed Pam. She was right. Both Frankie's brothers were happily married with no signs of unrest and no one in Pam's generation had ever done anything so mortifying as kicking a husband out. 'How do you think that will *look*?'

'I couldn't really care less.'

Pam looked absolutely horrified. 'Oh, Francesca! And poor, *poor* Rob.'

'I'm sure he'll be okay,' said Frankie, without a smile. Poor Rob was probably enjoying his nice, new flat. He could eat Pot Noodles to his heart's content and never have to put the empty pot, or the lid, in the bin. He could leave a trail of clothes on the floor from here to Timbuktu without anyone nagging him about it. He could even bring women back, if he wanted. *Was* he bringing women back? She wondered. 'He can live in a pit. He's probably loving it. He found a flat really quickly,' she added, hoping it would turn the tide of consternation.

The lady was not for turning. 'I think you've made a dreadful mistake, Francesca. What do you think, Ted?'

Ted said nothing. He'd once been a managerial type, commanding a staff of hundreds in a shoe factory, and a very strict parent who took no nonsense. Now, he was just prone to rueful shrugging and the odd conspiratorial wink at Frankie and her brothers, who had both escaped Up North.

'It's just what I have to do,' said Frankie. Despite her bravado, she was cringing. Frankie still didn't like being told off by her parents or, solely these days, by her mother. It made her want to retreat. If she was a turtle and had a big old shell, she'd be in it. She tried valiantly to change the subject.

'How's Mrs Peacock?'

Pam loved nothing more than wobbling her chins, putting her hands on her hips and telling her daughter in great medical detail all about the ailments, diseases and sudden deaths of people Frankie had never met in her life. The tactic worked. Pam rambled on about Mrs Peacock for a good ten minutes, the final two of which Frankie was gradually steering her to the door, handing her her jacket and handbag and saying she'd got things to do and she really must be getting on with them. Ted trailed behind.

Pam managed one more 'Poor Rob,' as she squeezed into the passenger seat of the Panda, and Frankie firmly closed the door. She returned to the sitting room and sat in silence for a bit. She was relieved her parents had gone but now she just felt…flat. Friday evenings when the kids were here were noisy chaos, now there was…nothing. No MTV, no video games, no Mario cart, FIFA 15, iPads, Wiis, Wii Us, television or YouTube videos…all the things that gave her mother the horrors.

She turned the telly on but nothing caught her eye. She checked her phone again. Nothing. She leant over to her magazine rack and pulled a selection of magazines onto her lap. *Heat*, *Marie Claire*, *Chat*. Amongst them was a craft magazine she'd bought in a mad moment. There was a pretty bag on the front that you could make. A bag she'd never be able to produce in a million years.

She flicked idly through the magazine. The bag was beyond her, but maybe there was something she could try and do. Rob had a hobby – his stupid kit car. Imogen had all her plays and stuff, although strictly speaking that was work. And Grace had started some crazy martial arts nonsense. Maybe *she* could have a hobby.

The magazine was a riot of pastels and full of girly, arty farty 'makes' but on closer inspection, not for the faint-hearted or the thick of thumb. Everything looked quite tricky, complicated. Knitting? Not a chance. Crochet? It looked way too intricate and time-consuming; she knew she wouldn't have the patience. Upscaling furniture? – oh Lord, that was far too much of a stretch. She was rubbish at painting; she'd ruin whatever it was and consign it to the tip.

What else? Making sugar flowers for cakes? She'd be hopeless. She wasn't really a baking, cake-y, cake decoration person. She'd tried to make cakes for the kids a couple of times but something always went slightly wrong. There'd be one layer that went all wonky, or she would misread the recipe and not make enough icing, or make icing that tore off half the cake with it when she tried to spread it on. Or she'd make a cake that looked perfect, but when she'd get it out of the tin there'd be a large, uncooked crater in the middle of it.

Often things had to be glued and patched together with the icing that there was never enough of. If there was a missing or burnt bit, she'd put a mark on the plate so if Rob's mother came over Frankie would know which side of the cake to avoid when cutting it.

Ah, here was something. Cutting things out to make a pretty bird mobile. Alice would like that for her room. She read further. Perhaps not. There was a lot of talk in the magazine of 'die-cutting' pieces of paper and it was mentioned again here – whatever it was, it sounded utterly hellish. Sorry, Alice, she thought. God, she missed her. She felt a horrible lump in her throat whenever she dared think about her.

She quickly turned the page. Découpage? What on earth was that? There was a kit that came free with the magazine – fifteen thick printed papers in squares with pretty, shabby chic patterns on them. She detested shabby chic. Rubbing paint off the corners of things to show a grubby bit of something underneath, ditsy, dolly frilly things with polka dots on, floral cabbage print cushions and 'toil of no joy', or whatever it was called. Still, some of these papers were quite pretty. The one with the butterflies was nice.

The instructions suggested gluing the papers onto a wooden box. Did she have one? Her jewellery box. She went upstairs to get it. It was one of those ones where you pull out descending drawers on metal-concertinaed hinges, which could potentially make it quite complicated. Still, how difficult could it be, sticking bits of paper to some wood?

Forty minutes later, Frankie was muttering and shoving tiny bits of cut-up paper in the bin. The jewellery box was also in a bin – the big black one that lived down the passageway next to the garage. She'd shoved it in a Tesco carrier bag and buried it under a bag of rubbish in a tantrum-y rage. There was glue everywhere. And biscuit crumbs. And a lot of it was on the floor.

Sod hobbies. She wouldn't be attempting them again. She ambled to the kitchen to replenish the biscuit tin. The sofa was the only place for her; the television her only pursuit.

She lay there for a while. After the sixth biscuit she felt revolted with herself. She was overweight and underfit. She'd turned into a slob and kicking Rob out had made no difference.

Before she'd had Alice, she'd been doing okay. Her eldest was nine, her youngest was four; the baby days were done and all the children were at school. She had been able to relax a little bit. She still had all the housework, chores, running around and general chaos to cope with, but she also had six free hours to herself every day. Six hours! In time, she'd thought, she would maybe get a job. In the meantime, she'd get a bit of her life back.

She'd sorted out her hair, her nails, her knackered skin; she smartened up, toned up (exercise DVD at home, thank you, Davina) and had time to breathe and regroup. She had begun to feel on top of things again. She'd even started dressing up and going out, dinner with friends, nights out with Rob. Things were settled, great even, and she felt excitement, for the first time in ages, about the future. She wondered what job she might do. Before having kids, she'd been a PA at the technical college, then at a pharmaceutical company. She'd thought she could contact that company again. Or somewhere else. If you were a PA you could PA anywhere.

Then, despite well-intentioned but fairly mediocre once-a-month sex and Rob having had a vasectomy (she *knew* he should have sent his sample to the lab to prove it had worked; he'd said it must have done – his 'nuts' had been on fire for five days), she got pregnant again. With the arrival of Alice – who of course she *adored* – everything had gone belly up, although belly *down* would be a better description, along with everything else that could no longer fight gravity.

She had shifted all her 'baby weight' three times over, fairly easily. (What a stupid expression, she thought. The babies had only weighed eight pounds each – it wasn't their fault she had taken pregnancy as an excuse to eat her body weight in cake for nine months.) This time, she could not. Was it an age thing or had she just lost the will, with four children to look after? (Including Rob, make that five.)

Whatever, after Alice, a fat tummy, wobbly thighs, chubby arms and horrid-looking back fat stubbornly refused to depart. Everything just sat there, mocking her, and she felt powerless to do anything about it. She was fit for nothing except lying on the couch and eating biscuits.

The couch. Wasn't there a new thing? Couch to 5k, or something. She'd read about it on a blog she sometimes read: Beautiful Mummy World. It was a blog she read with acute sarcasm, scoffing – and often scoffing chocolate – at perfect mummy Lucinda Del De'Ath (Frankie liked to shorten her to Lucy Death: the death of all sense), in her wafty linen outfits and her Chihuahua seed suppers and her organic lemongrass colonic cleansing shakes. It gave her a good laugh. Lucinda had mentioned Couch to 5k when talking, as she did extensively, about fitness. Of course Lucy Death didn't do it – it was far too pedestrian and working class; she did yoga in five hundred degree heated rooms wearing five hundred pound designer fitness tights – but it had been mentioned, with a slight sneer, as something the plebs might enjoy. If they couldn't afford to fly to LA for a Soul Cycle class, or have the will to be suspended upside-down from the ceiling in Cirque du Soleil-style purple strips of cloth whilst doing a Downward Dog, they might like to consider it.

Frankie grabbed her phone and googled Couch to 5k. She had run once, a million years ago, before she had kids. She and Rob used to run. She'd had an iPod and some Nike trainers and they'd pounded the streets in the evenings after work. She missed it, she realised, though she hadn't thought about it for years.

Couch to 5k: here it was. Week One, a five-minute walk followed by twenty minutes of alternate running and walking, leading all the way up to Week Nine and a thirty-minute run. It didn't look too bad.

She rooted through her wardrobe. There, at the back, under an old breast pump and a bright orange T-shirt from the 90s, which said 'Stupid Girl', was a very creased pair of pink, Lycra leggings and her battered pair of Nike trainers. It all came flooding back to her: the sound of rubber on tarmac, Nirvana in her ears, her boobs wobbling in her largely ineffective sports bra. She could do it again, couldn't she? She could run. Of course she could! In fact she was such an old pro, she was pretty confident she could skip straight to Week Six.

She stripped off her skinny jeans, revealing a knotted sock secreted up the left leg she'd failed to notice all day, and pulled on the leggings. Boy, they were tight. She'd been a size ten in those days, not the chunky size fourteen she now was. They stretched over her bottom and thighs to the point of see-through, but they were just about okay, she supposed. She had nothing else. She added socks, the trainers and the 90s T-shirt. It was chilly out but she remembered how quickly running warmed her up, and it wouldn't get dark until seven. She was going to do this!

As she shut the front door behind her, she suddenly felt a little silly and utterly self-conscious. There would be people staring at her, small children pointing and laughing. Oh God. She nearly went back in again and slammed the door. Instead, she went through the gate, into the back garden and out to the back alley that ran behind her row of houses. She'd go to the end then head along the river. If she was going to look ridiculous there would be fewer witnesses that way.

She ran. At first her earphones kept coming out, everything was wobbling, the lack of sports bra was a bad idea. The back alley was full of nettles and brambles and she spent a lot of it hopping over doggie do's and broken glass. But, as she headed down the path that snaked next to the river, she found her feet. She had the wind in her hair, the road beneath her steadily plodding trainers, 'Sounds Like Teen Spirit' in her ears...

She'd been going about ten minutes when she had to stop by a tree and catch her breath. She had a stitch. She couldn't remember having one of those since school. Clutching at the tree's gnarly trunk, she staggered against it, gasping.

Moments later she realised she wasn't alone. 'Are you all right?' said a voice.

She looked up, embarrassed. She probably had been making a too-theatrical job of bending over at the hip, clutching her side and grimacing. Well, if you're going to have a stitch, you may as well make sure it's a good one. Life-threatening.

Standing there was a man, also in running gear, but far from looking an utter fool in his. He had on navy shorts, a navy hoodie and white socks and trainers (Rob had those trainers, she noted) and he looked great in them. This man didn't look like he was trying to out-neon an 80s go-go dancer. He was also very good-looking. He had shaggy sort of nineteenth-century hair and blue eyes that looked like they'd had a manly lick of the mascara brush. Incredible eyelashes. He wouldn't have looked out of place up on a Jane Austen horse, in military uniform. He was far too good-looking a man to see her looking like this.

'Oh, I'm fine, thanks,' she puffed. 'Just a stitch. A runner's occupational hazard.' She stood up and did what she hoped was an athletic-looking lunge-type stretch. 'You know what it's like.'

He looked like he didn't. 'First run?'

What? How the hell did he know that? And it wasn't her first *ever* run. She suddenly realised her leggings had gripped themselves up her bum in an enormous wedgie and she had an unbearable urge to prise them out, which of course she couldn't do. She wriggled a bit to try and dislodge the wedgie but it stayed firmly in place.

'No, course not. Is it *yours*?'

'No. I run 4k every day.'

'Oh right. Show-off,' she said and she now had an irresistible urge to stick her tongue out at him, so she did.

He looked surprised, then to her surprise, he burst out laughing. 'I like your spirit,' he said. 'So are you following a programme?'

'Couch to 5k.'

He nodded. 'That's a brilliant programme. I actually run a local Couch to 5k meet-up, if you're interested. We meet in the Tesco car park, Sunday mornings. Ten o'clock.' He pointed over to Chelmsford's main Tesco's, the other side of the river.

'Oh right, thanks,' said Frankie, staring at his bicep. 'I'll think about it.'

'Great. Well, nice meeting you.' There was a beat as he looked at her with his ridiculously long-eyelashed eyes and she enjoyed looking back into them.

'You too.'

Right. Should she set off at a casual, nonchalant jog, or go straight into an authoritative power run? Hang back and let him go off first? She didn't know which way he'd come from and which way he was going. He smiled at her, turned and broke into a run. Phew; she was going in the opposite direction.

As she got into some sort of stride, successfully avoiding the random giant swan that had decided at that moment to amble from the riverside and cross her path, she wondered what his bum looked like in his shorts and turned her head. To her horror he had turned back too and was grinning at her.

Damn. The see-through wedgie. How embarrassing.

CHAPTER NINE:
GRACE

Grace had been secretly dating for a month.

She'd met five different men. All of them (shamefully) had been from Hook, Line and Sinker. She'd decided to give online dating a go, after all. Well, she didn't have much of a choice. Nana McKensie's birthday do was fast approaching and she was running out of time. Over the course of four weeks, from mid-February to mid-March, Grace had bitten the bullet, picked the best of a bad bunch and had been on five dates with five men. There was supposed to have been a sixth, a 'Tim', but he'd cried off from dinner at the last minute, citing scheduling difficulties. She took this to mean he was married with five children. It was no loss – she'd had enough of the dating by then, anyway. It had been very disappointing.

The night she'd joined the dating website and almost been side-tracked by an escort, she'd ended up (red wine speeding her progress) 'friending' and getting in touch with sixteen different men. Six she'd agreed to dates with. She'd met the first four men at lunchtimes, asking them to come to the little Thai restaurant in the street behind the hat shop and having Gideon on reluctant stand-by with an emergency call and a sick grandfather should she text the word 'help'.

Number One had been a nice enough chap – a bit dull, an accountant – but he talked about himself non-stop. If she tried to offer up anything about her life, his eyes glazed over and then he'd say 'anyway...' and carry on. She'd learnt an awful lot about him: he liked jigsaws and watching documentaries about avalanches; he'd been married for fifteen years but his wife had left him for a driving instructor; he had two daughters who were doing really well at school (great!); he'd once shaken hands with Johnny Ball outside the old White City studios whilst queuing for the National Lottery draw. It was all fascinating. She'd left him with a weak handshake and a desire to never see him again.

Two and Three were fairly indistinguishable – both thin of hair, both tall and skinny-ish, both nothing like their photographs or their profiles. One had professed a love for fine wine; he hadn't, he sank five pints of cider over pad thai and green chicken curry. The other had declared himself a rock climber; he looked like he wouldn't be able to climb a post box.

Four was an Aussie who had a laugh like a drunk hyena who'd enjoyed one too many tinnies round the barbecue before he'd set off (she called on the sick grandfather for him), and Five she agreed to meet for dinner because he said he was a foodie. It was excruciating. He'd insisted on going to one of those chef's tables for a ten course 'tasting menu' and all he did was talk about all the food he'd ever eaten and where and keep trying to feed her forkfuls of stuff when she was trying to speak. Just awful.

It had all been terrible. Soul-destroying. Depressing. Even hilarious, if it had only happened to somebody else. And, apart from Gideon, she had nobody to talk to about it. For the whole month she'd not said a word to

Frankie and Imogen. She didn't dare! She was supposed to be single, not massively letting the side down by dating a succession of internet randoms. It was another reason she'd done lunches – she was worried about being seen going out of the house at night. She'd risked it only for the Saturday dinner date with The Taster, when James had had Daniel, and she had driven there and back like a fugitive. If her friends had spotted her coming or going, she would have pulled a long-lost, fictitious auntie out of the hat.

Online dating had been a disastrous experiment. There was no one she could take with her to Nana Marie's one hundredth birthday celebrations and she was getting desperate. Frankie had offered to go as her plus one, which was very sweet of her – Frankie hated musicals – but taking Frankie would not have the desired effect. She wanted to stick one in James's gullet; she had to turn up there with a man.

Desperate times called for desperate measures. She'd remembered Greg, the escort, and two days ago she'd got back to him.

Are you free on Friday please, as I'd like to book you for dinner?

She'd needed a glass of red in order to do it, but she needed *him.* He was a cheated-on ex's only hope. She'd ask him to take her to Nana McKensie's do and pretend to be her boyfriend, but first she'd have a trial date with him to check him out. What if, like men Two and Three, he was nothing like his profile picture? What if he talked like a mouse on helium? She wasn't Debra Messing and this wasn't *The Wedding Date*… He could have advertised as Dermot Mulroney and turn out to be David Brent. She'd have a date with him, suss him out and if he was suitable, she'd take him to Nana's theatre night.

Luckily, he was free.

Grace checked her reflection in a shop window. She was on her way to meet him now.

She didn't want to look like she was 'up for it' in any way, neither did she want to look boring and frumpy. It was silly, really. He was a male escort; he probably didn't care what she looked like, but *she* did. She'd gone for glam but not too glam – black skinny jeans, nice top with a hint of sparkle, a little navy blazer, and some heels that were high but not too high. She didn't want to be wobbling around if she got drunk, not that she was planning to.

She walked down Moulsham Street. She was petrified but very excited and strangely proud of herself. She was going on a date on *her* terms. She was in control. Her heart was under her own protection. It actually felt liberating – she'd booked a man for dinner and there was nothing wrong in it. Nothing at all. It was merely a *business* transaction. One that could save her life.

She prayed he was what he'd said on the tin; it was the 13th of March today (Friday the 13th – lucky for her, she hoped) and the theatre trip was the 1st of April. Nana always said all the best people had their birthday on April Fool's Day. She also liked to say 'time is of the essence'. This had never been truer.

Maggie, James's youngest sister, was babysitting Daniel. She'd turned up at half seven with a huge tote she'd plonked on the kitchen table and started pulling stuff out of. Sweets, chocolate bars, magazines, knitting. Within seconds it was spread all over the table. Grace resisted the urge to grab a wicker basket from a shelf and shovel it all in it. She liked Maggie though. She was fun and Art School – always in a scarf, all year round, always giggly, always really nice. Daniel deemed it very uncool to have a babysitter at his age, but he liked Maggie a lot too. She told great jokes and she liked Star Wars Lego.

Maggie had broken rank from James's adoring siblings by being pretty disgusted with her brother's behaviour, and thought Grace was out on a nice date with a man she'd met at a sandwich shop near work. Frankie and Grace thought she was at Taekwondo – the new, adult class for the fitness-minded over thirties. Her friends would appreciate that: self-defence training. It fitted in well with the silly single for a year ethos. And if she really needed self-defence tonight, she supposed she could always have someone's eye out with her stiletto heel.

'You look great,' Maggie had said, as Grace went out the door. 'I hope the date goes well.'

'Thank you,' said Grace. 'Me too.'

Grace had booked a taxi, which met her at the other end of the road. She'd told Frankie she was getting picked up by someone in a white suit for Taekwondo, and hoped her friend wouldn't see her skittering along the street in her going-out gear, her head down. As she got into the waiting cab and shut the door, she gave a sigh of relief. She'd got away with it, so far.

She tottered into the restaurant. Her feet were hurting already. They may not have been the highest she owned, but her shoes were cripplingly tight. She'd hardly worn this pair; she'd bought them online at House of Fraser a couple of years ago, stupidly anticipating lots of romantic date nights, which had never materialised. At least they were getting an outing tonight, however nefarious.

The restaurant was small, obscure and Italian. Luigi's. She'd never been there before and didn't know anyone who had. There was no way she was booking one of the chains, Prezzo or Café Rouge – far too dangerous. It was better to go somewhere off the beaten track, with questionable reviews. As soon as she went up to the little wooden podium thing, at reception, she could see Greg over the shoulder of the tall girl with the fake, maître d' smile.

He was wearing a pale blue shirt. His hair was close cropped – he'd had a haircut since his photo. He was wearing a pair of glasses and studying the menu. He was, immediately, gorgeous and, apart from the haircut, looked *exactly* like his picture. Her heart started thumping in her chest. She felt light-headed. He was really here. Well, he wouldn't stand her up, would he? She was paying him. But still, she was almost surprised to see him. And she had to walk over to him somehow, in these heels.

'Hello!' said the girl at the podium, faux-brightly.

'Hi, erm…my, er, date is already here. Over there. He's at the table.' She made to point at him then realised that looked appalling and lowered her finger.

'Mr Powers?'

'Er…yes?' Mr Powers? *Greg Powers*? It sounded made up, yet it suited him. He was so handsome he could easily be James Bond, or some dashing spy hero from those TV series in the sixties.

'I'll take you over.'

Grace followed the girl who was like a gazelle with a swingy ponytail. The girl was gliding. Grace was stomping slightly, not sure where her centre of gravity had gone. At one point she had to steady herself on the corner of a passing table.

As they neared him, Greg took off his glasses and smiled. She noticed his eyes were very blue and his teeth were very, very white. Yep, he was gorgeous.

He stood up, walked round to where she was standing, awkwardly, her bag over her shoulder, and leant over and gave her a kiss. He was so tall. Really tall. And God, he smelt good. A pleasant musky scent whooshed up her nose as he kissed her. His lips felt soft. And he was exceedingly good-looking close up, in just the way that Mr Kipling said it.

'Are you okay, Grace?' His voice was deeper than she expected.

She knew she was standing there like an absolute lemon. 'Yes, fine thank you.'

'Shall we sit down?'

'Okay, then,' she said, 'seeing as we're here.' What a stupid thing, to say, she thought. She was a dork. They both sat down.

'What would you like to drink?'

'A white wine please. Large one.'

He smiled. 'Need a bit of Dutch courage?'

'What do you think?'

She quickly placed the folded white napkin in front of her on the lap and grabbed the menu. She gripped it to stop her hands shaking.

'It's really nice to meet you, Grace,' smiled Greg. 'Been to this restaurant before?'

'No,' said Grace. 'Have you?' This was a very good question. Had he already sat at this restaurant with a long succession of women? Was he *known* here? Were all the staff, at this very moment, sniggering at her – the latest on the ever-looping conveyor belt of the sexually desperate? Then she remembered how bad the food was rumoured to be, via TripAdvisor. He hadn't been here before.

'No,' he said. 'Would you like me to order for you?'

'Order for me? Is that all part of the service?' She finally dared to look up at him.

'I don't know. Perhaps it should be.' He looked at her with those blue eyes. The triangle of skin she could see under his shirt collar looked warm and tanned. 'You're nervous,' he told her. His voice really was deep. Not gravelly, just low. Great for pillow talk, she expected.

'Very,' said Grace, with a small smile.

'Me too,' he said.

'You?'

'Yes.'

'How come? Aren't you an old pro at this? If you excuse the pun.'

'No,' said Greg. He leant towards her and lowered his voice. 'I wasn't going to tell you,' he said, 'but you've got the kind of face that makes me want to. I've got a small confession to make.'

'Oh?'

'You're my first,' he said.

'Your *first*?'

'My first client.' He laughed a little. 'Jeez, it sounds weird saying that!'

'Oh!' said Grace. 'Your first client. Really? But your photo must have been up on that website for at least a month.'

'Yes, it has. I've been biding my time. Waiting for the right person to be my first client.'

'Oh.' She was the right person for him. Interesting. Strangely it made her feel even more nervous. 'So you're *new*. What did you do before?'

'I'm in between jobs. I want to start my own marketing business and I need to raise some capital. A mate of mine suggested I do escorting. A female mate, actually. She suggested I had all the right credentials.'

'I bet she did,' said Grace, raising her eyebrows. 'So you're planning to fund a whole new business from women like me. Investment angels.'

'Yes,' said Greg. 'I suppose you could put it like that.' He was unflinching in his gaze. His very blue eyes looked into hers without blinking.

The gazelle returned to the table.

'Can I get you guys some drinks?'

He hadn't been here before and Grace was his first client. They could just be your average couple having a meal out. A real couple. For the first time, Grace smiled at the gazelle and didn't mind her long-limbed perfection quite so much.

Greg ordered drinks, and rattled off their food order, too, in an accomplished manner. He said things in what she assumed was the correct Italian. With the accent and everything. She was sure he had even pronounced *focaccia* properly.

'How about you?' he asked, after the gazelle had glided off. 'What do you do?'

'I work in a hat boutique.'

'Oh, interesting. Married, kids?'

'Well, if I was married I'd hardly be here.'

'You'd be surprised.'

'Oh. My husband and I have separated. I have a son. I'm a single mum.' Ugh, it sounded awful saying that. She hadn't said it before. The 'mum' bit she didn't mind, the 'single' bit she hated with a passion.

'Well, good for you,' said Greg, disappointing her for the first time. What did he know? It wasn't good for her at all.

They sat in silence for a few moments. The gazelle returned with their drinks and Grace fell on her glass of wine like a desert wanderer arriving at an oasis. She took an almighty glug. That was better.

'So,' she said. 'I'm the first person who's hired you. The first person you've gone out for dinner with.'

'Yes.' Greg smiled. 'First victim.'

He hadn't slept with anyone for money yet, she thought. There was yet to be anything seedy about him. He wasn't a seasoned pro who'd already shagged thousands of sad, lonely old spinsters, dripping with gold jewellery and lost baggage and bitterness.

The wine was warming her stomach. She took another gulp. 'Do I get a discount, as you're obviously still in training?'

'Ha. I hope it doesn't show.'

'It doesn't. I wouldn't have guessed, on first seeing you.'

'But you like the fact I'm an amateur.'

'I guess I do. It makes you seem less smarmy.'

'I hope never to be smarmy.' Greg laughed.

Grace laughed too and drank some more of her wine. It was going down very well. She began to relax a bit. This man didn't have loads of well-worn clients he was wearily doing the rounds of. He wasn't putting his bow tie in his trouser pocket night after night as he gambolled down the plush steps of one glamorous apartment building after another. He was as new to this as she was.

'But you are *going* to have sex with people?' she blurted out, a little too loudly. She looked around, but nobody seemed to have heard her. There weren't many people there.

'Probably, later on,' said Greg. 'I will earn more money that way.' She admired his honesty. He was someone who knew what he wanted and how he was going to get it.

'Are you going to train for that?' she asked glibly, looking sideways out into the restaurant, vaguely focusing on the dessert trolley, which was rumbling past their table. Ooh, tiramisu. She might have that later. She couldn't look at him.

'I don't need to,' said Greg. She looked back at him. She couldn't help it. 'I know what I'm doing.'

Grace was no stranger to *frisson*. She'd had lots of *beginnings* to lots of relationships. Loads. But she'd never experienced frisson like this, not even with James. Frisson sizzled up and down her body, an electric cattle prod playing over her skin in a figure of eight. Frisson took her by the hand and led her down the garden path with a rocket in her knickers. *I know what I'm doing.* Good Lord. He was incredibly sexy. He was looking her right in the eye. Please don't wink, or anything corny, she thought, or you'll spoil this very enjoyable moment. Please don't ham it up.

He didn't wink. He didn't ham it up. He just sat with his eyes not moving from hers. She would like to say she was torn between being repulsed and turned on, but that wouldn't be right – she was just turned on. Quick. She had to divert her mind. Where had the bloody dessert trolley gone?

She grabbed the passing gazelle and tapped her somewhere near the knee.

'Could we have another bottle of white, please?'

'Sure.'

'You drink fast, for such a small person,' commented Greg, after the gazelle had gone.

'I know, sorry. Will it be women only that you sleep with?'

'Women only. I like women.' She wished she hadn't asked. He was looking at her intently, again, as though he found her the most attractive woman in the world. Pull yourself together, she willed. Divert your energy from the front of your pants! He's an *escort*! He may have practised that look in the mirror. And it wasn't going to matter *who* he looked at. Any age, any size, any kind of woman. As long as they had money in their purse.

She stared into the bottom of her empty glass as though it held the meaning of life. She briefly thought about getting up and leaving. Then, she realised, this man couldn't hurt her, he didn't have the *power* to hurt her. It was all fine.

The gazelle brought their starters and another bottle of wine. It was *more* fine the more wine she sipped. This man was good-looking and good company. He was exactly as advertised. He'd be perfect to take to Nana's do. And this was *nice*. It was nice to be sitting opposite a nice man in a nice restaurant, not side by side on a silent sofa, with a man's smelly feet up on a footstool, or, more usually, alone on that sofa while that man was out shagging another woman. *No, stop that.* She didn't want to think about James.

They finished their starters and had their mains. Their conversation was easy and flowed as freely as the wine. Greg was charming, attentive and those blue eyes had her captivated. He was spectacularly good-looking. She knew the gazelle fancied him too; as she cleared their plates away she smiled at him for just a little too long.

'Dessert?' he asked.

'Why not?' In for a penny, in for a pound, she thought.

They ordered one tiramisu, to share. She hoped he wasn't going to spoon food into her mouth, like they did in the movies. Wouldn't that be a cheesy, escort-y thing to do? Perhaps he was saving that for further down the line. Perhaps there was a whole list of things he was yet to employ. A wink with every smile, a stroke with a finger down a speckled forearm, an exaggerated look up and down a body as a client arrived. She took a slug of wine and imagined more. A hand placed on a shoulder, another reached across a table to take a variety of women's being held out eagerly – from smooth and pale, to wrinkled and over-tanned, or those women's hands that were chunky, like men's, with loads of rings. Would he help women into their coats at the end of the night like they did at the hairdresser's? Gyrate opposite them in nightclubs, in a horrible Michael-Douglas-in-*Basic-Instinct* V-neck jumper? Would he have a *repertoire*?

At the moment he was still fresh and green. She liked the fact he wasn't yet a practised, jaded, cynical *escort man*. And thank goodness she had suggested this awful restaurant and it wasn't his choice – she didn't like to think of him in weeks and months to come, sitting opposite a succession of random women at the same table. She was his *first*.

She pulled herself up short. She shouldn't be jealous of future women who would be paying for his company. Get a grip, girl, she thought. This is *not* a first date!

She'd drunk too much; she knew it. As they dug into the tiramisu with a spoon each (thankfully), she started telling Greg all about James and what he had done, despite promising herself earlier that she wouldn't. How he'd cheated, how unreliable he was being. Greg was sympathetic, angry on her behalf and seemed to champion her in her strength to go it alone. He even expressed amazement at the age of her son, when she looked so young. She didn't bother telling him about Frankie and Imogen and the whole single for a year vow, since she was breaking it so spectacularly.

He was so nice. So understanding. She didn't know whether all this *niceness* was the act of a fledgling escort, but she hoped not. She hoped he was just a genuinely nice man. Grace began to imagine again this was a real date, but at the same time revelled in her bravery that it wasn't. She was out for dinner with a male escort. It thrilled her that no one, not a soul, knew about this. It thrilled her that James would be so *surprised* if he knew about it. Even more thrilling was the thought of turning up with this man, at James's family do, and giving James the shock of his life.

'Some men are just programmed to be bastards,' Greg was saying. Her vision and hearing were slightly blurred now. 'But not all. You may feel like that at the moment, but you won't always. There'll be someone for you, at some point in the future. When you're ready for him.'

'No,' said Grace, putting down her spoon. But she said 'no' quite happily, easily almost. 'There won't be a *someone*. No more men for me, unless I'm paying for one! Ha ha!'

She was a little more than drunk, now. She looked at his lovely face. Well, she hadn't stopped looking at it. She wished he would stand up again so she could get a better look at all of him. She wanted to see his legs, his stomach, his bum. Perhaps she should spend a little bit more of Gran's money. Perhaps she should sleep with him. Be his *first*.

'So what's the drill now?' she asked, slurring slightly, and fiddling with the salt and pepper. 'Do I have to tell you what additional services I require? Have you got a menu?' She picked up the wine list and started thumbing through it as though scrutinising his price list. 'Ooh, is it like *Pretty Woman*? Do you charge, like, £2000 or something, to stay overnight with someone? Can I chain you to a bed for a week, for a million pounds?'

'No one's chaining me to a bed,' said Greg, shaking his head with a smile. 'As for an over-nighter – I'm not sure if that's a technical term, by the way – I don't know yet. I'll cross that bridge when I come to it.'

'Cross my palm with silver,' said Grace. 'Everything has its price. I'm deciding whether to sleep with you or not,' she added, brazenly. To get my own back on James, she thought.

'To get your own back on James?' said Greg. 'I don't think that's the right reason for doing it.'

'You don't want my money?' said Grace. 'Or you find me repulsive? You can't bear to sleep with me?' He wasn't going to be a very good escort if he kept this up, was he? – if she excused herself another pun. Turning down offers.

'Of course I'd be happy to sleep with you,' said Greg. 'You're a very attractive girl. But my role as an escort – what I hope my role is going to be – is to make women feel good about themselves.' How generous, thought Grace, somewhat scathingly. He rubbed two fingers over his chin and continued, 'I think if you slept with me, tonight, so soon after James cheating on you, you'd feel very bad indeed. In fact, I can pretty much predict you'd wake up in the morning feeling terrible.'

'Cross my palm with silver,' said Grace, again. 'So now you're a fortune teller.' But she knew he was right. She *would* feel terrible. She wasn't ready to have sex with anyone: it would only remind her of James doing it…with that slut.

'Shall we get the bill?' said Greg. Subject well and truly changed, and she was glad of it, really. He was totally right. She didn't want to have sex with him tonight.

Grace paid the bill. Credit card. She had already paid for *Greg* by bank transfer, before she left home.

They called for two taxis. Gazelle, at the wooden podium, looked surprised. They clearly looked like a couple that should be going home together. Greg had his arm around Grace and she was leaning into his shoulder. She was drunk, but they looked good together. Everyone could see that.

They stood outside in the breezy air. Greg insisted she got into the first taxi.

'Call me if you want to see me again,' he said, and granted her a light hug and a fleeting kiss. His lips grazed her cheek and he said, 'I think you're a really gorgeous girl.'

He thought she was gorgeous! A lovely warmth spread through her body.

'Of course I do,' she said. 'What are you doing on the 1st of April?'

CHAPTER TEN:
IMOGEN

They were still in Chinatown and on dessert. Imogen always had dessert. Why come out for a meal if you weren't going to have *everything*? She was having banana fritters and ice cream, Richard was having lychees in syrup.

He liked his food. He'd wolfed down everything they'd been brought: dim sum in those cute wicker lidded baskets, steam escaping from the woven gaps; noodles and rice on willow-patterned dishes; aromatic pork and peppers on sizzling skillets; chilli beef and cashew chicken. He'd seemed to really enjoy the whole experience – the over-lit canteen-type atmosphere, the clattering of trolleys, the way the waiters and waitresses stamped a card with pretty Chinese characters when you ordered your dim sum. Imogen liked Richard's delight in everything and his boyish enthusiasm. It made her want to take him outside and rip his clothes off.

The muscles she could see bulging under his shirtsleeves weren't helping matters. She imagined, not for the first time, what he would look like with his shirt off. Oh, she'd imagined it several times. When they'd had a drink at the tiny bar before they'd sat down, during the starter, during the main course and every time he'd raised his chopsticks to his mouth. Oh sod it. It had been pretty much constantly.

Richard was very polite to the waiters. This was a deal-breaker for her. How a man talked to waiting staff told you everything you needed to know about him. They had a guy who was slightly nervous. He told them it was his first week. He stumbled over his words a bit, apologised that his English was not that great and spilt some white wine over the rim of Imogen's glass and onto the table. He was over-apologetic but Richard was great. He was really kind, told him not to worry about it, and even said, 'We've all been in our first week, once.'

They talked about loads of things: his job, her job, his parents, her parents, New York, London, chat shows in both countries. She was careful how much wine she drank. Not too little – she didn't want to seem boring. She wanted to look as though she enjoyed food, good wine and conversation, which of course she did; she was a seasoned old pro in going out for dinner, after all. But she was also mindful of not getting too sloshed. It was suddenly very important that she looked poised, in control. An English Rose. She didn't think many English Roses got off their heads on white wine and found themselves face down in their fritters. So she slowly sipped one glass of wine. Savouring it. Holding the glass as she'd imagined she would when she was a little girl dreaming of going out for nice meals in smart restaurants with handsome men.

The conversation was relaxed and they laughed a lot. They had an excellent exchange about silly English words, when Imogen called herself a numpty for knocking one of the dim sum lids off the table.

'Numpty?' said Richard, in delight. 'That's a new one. He got out his BlackBerry and pretended to write it somewhere. 'I've learned quite a few quaint British insults since I've been here. Wally, berk, duffer – duff*er*, is that right?' Imogen laughed and nodded. 'Git, minger, *munter*, plonker, wombat,' he continued. 'Though I thought that could be Australian?'

'Yep, Australian,' said Imogen. 'I sometimes use that one though.'

'And an Irish guy, in jest, I hope, called me a boll*ix*? I always thought it was bollocks, but I could be mistaken.'

Imogen laughed. 'Bollocks in English, bollix in Irish,' she said. 'It's an education.'

'It certainly is,' said Richard.

They really did laugh a lot. They had the *power* to make each other laugh and it was a heady power that thrilled her. It was exhilarating to have your pithy one-liners and dry, witty observations bouncing across the table like exuberant ping-pongs and making an alpha male American roar with laughter.

'You're funny,' he said, at more than one point. She took it as a compliment. He had a sense of humour she adored, too. Mocking, slightly sarcastic, so un-American – he was as far from have-a-nice-day, straight-down-the-line blandness as you could get. They laughed all the way through jasmine tea and those minty chocolates that come out on a saucer.

'You're my kind of girl, Imogen,' said Richard, as they sat and waited for their bill to be brought to them. He looked all serious, suddenly, and she felt a thrill of heat surge all the way down to her toes.

'Am I?' she answered flippantly but doubted she concealed her delight.

'Yep. You're smart; you're kinda sassy. You have a lot of chutzpah.'

'Thanks!' She grinned. 'You're not so bad yourself.'

She glanced away and smiled at a passing waitress. She felt incredibly *naughty*, sitting here with this man. She was supposed to be single. She was supposed to be *ignoring* men. But she was finding him irresistible. Was he her kind of man? He was exactly what she'd been after all these years. A rich, successful businessman, somebody with perfect manners who would treat her right. It was all she had dated for a long time. There was supposed to be a safety in these type of men – as disappointing as they'd all turned out to be – an unspoken assurance that she wouldn't fall in love with them. She suddenly felt afraid she couldn't guarantee her own safety, not with this man…but she pushed that fear aside. Why couldn't she just enjoy him?

Their bill arrived and Richard paid it, despite Imogen insisting it be split.

'My treat,' he said. 'I invited you.'

'Thank you,' she said.

She didn't want to get up. She wanted to sit at this table, with this man, all night. Talk about everything, talk about nothing. Just be with him. She was shocked at the intensity of this feeling, that she wanted to be with this man. She'd only just met him! Up until the moment she'd met him she'd been really enjoying being single. What was happening to her?

As they left, their waiter was walking briskly towards the kitchen, a look of intense worry on his face. Richard stopped him and put a hand on his shoulder. 'Hey, good luck. In a couple weeks you'll be flying. Heck, you'll be running the show.' It was really lovely of him; she hoped to God it wasn't an act.

'So where can I drop you?'

They were outside the restaurant, on the pavement. Ah. This was new. A *really* perfect gentleman, although she wasn't sure she wanted him to be. She was slightly aggrieved he was not asking her back to his place, or to a hotel. They always did!

She tried to arrange her face so she didn't look disappointed in the slightest.

'Don't worry, I can walk to the Tube from here,' she said. It was fine and dry now. And it was only ten o'clock. It was early! The night was still young. She didn't want to go home. She didn't want to walk away from him just yet. They'd had such a great time.

'Okay,' he said. 'If you're sure.'

'I'm sure.' She had never been an actress, but she'd been around them long enough to pick up a few tips. She made her face bright and nonchalant and gave him a dazzling smile. 'Thank you ever so much,' she said in the Queen's best English. 'I've had a wonderful evening.' Okay, so she wouldn't be picking up an Oscar any time soon. She probably wouldn't even pass an audition for am-dram Noël Coward at the local village hall. She sounded like an idiot. An idiot who'd swallowed a plum.

'My pleasure,' said Richard, ignoring her Celia Johnson from *Brief Encounter* impression, and he stepped forward and kissed her lightly on the cheek. It was thrilling, having his face so close to hers, his warm but cool lips on her flushed skin. He smelled wonderful, like honeysuckle and testosterone.

'Bye, then,' she said, and she walked away from him and towards Oxford Circus Tube. She felt sad and sorry to be leaving him but at the same time excited and buzzing. She'd felt like this once before… Oh God. The fear was back. She suddenly felt like she was at the top of a very tall building and perilously close to the edge. She had nothing to grab on to and she was terrified. She was in very near and proximate danger of falling for this man.

And he didn't have her number and she'd refused his card.

'Wait!' called Richard. 'I don't have your number! Do you have a card?'

Oh thank God, thank God.

'Yes!' Knowing she didn't look at all cool, she literally ran back to him, pulled a card from the little inside pocket of her swish bag and thrust it into his hands. And then, because she couldn't trust herself not to fling her body onto his and beg him to take her to bed, she turned on her heel and fled.

Imogen frowned to herself as she put her ticket through the barrier in the Tube station. She was in big trouble. Really big trouble.

She was in grave danger of being a giant, absolute fraud.

CHAPTER ELEVEN:
FRANKIE

Frankie walked to Tesco's. She wouldn't run; she didn't want to look all dishevelled and out of breath before she even got there. She wanted to look cool, composed and wedgie-less. She'd got new gear, including a pair of leggings that actually fitted her and a T-shirt in a normal colour that didn't say anything.

She'd decided to go to the Couch to 5k meet-up. Just to see what it was like. Train with like-minded people. Beat her personal best. See that handsome guy again… Why not? It was another Sunday without the kids and, to be honest, she was bored stiff and desperate to avoid another drop-in visit from her parents.

She'd run, on and off, since that first time two weeks ago. She was getting better at it. She could now go twenty minutes without a stitch and was beginning to enjoy that feeling of satisfaction when she got home and knew she'd done what she set out to. She liked it. She was a *runner* again.

He hadn't been quite right about the car park. It was empty of people – there were only cars – but there was a group of sporty-looking people in Lycra and fleece limbering up in the parkland behind it. As she walked over, the man she'd met by the river was lolling against a tree, wearing black shorts and a turquoise T-shirt, and easing on sweatbands. She made a beeline for him. The other people looked scary: a couple doing mirror-image star jumps, a guy in a red tracksuit and matching towelling headband doing hamstring stretches, a woman thrusting a black and pink bum in the air as she tied her laces.

'Hey! You came!' He was as gorgeous as she'd remembered. His hair slightly longer and even more George Wickham. His eyes just as heavenly. He had a slight designer stubble thing going on this morning as well, which made him look incredibly sexy.

'I did.'

'And you've got new trainers.'

Frankie looked down at her new Adidas running shoes with the natty netted sides.

'Yep. Cool aren't they?'

He had a neat pile of stuff at his feet: sports bag, water bottle, perfectly folded sweatshirt. They were all lined up in a row. He even had what looked like three individually wrapped protein bars aligned like soldiers in a manly blue Tupperware box.

'Well, you look great,' he said, as she looked up. She noticed for the first time his voice had a slight northern quality to it. With his full and floppity hair, his impressive but tidy sideburns and his mesmerising full-lashed eyes, she half expected a neighing, saddled horse or a discarded pair of breeches to materialise behind him.

'Thank you.'

'My name's Hugh, by the way.'

'I'm Frankie.'

'Well I'm ever so pleased to meet you, Frankie,' he said, mock-formally. And he held out a hand, which she took. As their skin made contact he smiled and his gorgeous eyes crinkled at the corners. Wow. He was gorgeous. She felt all funny. 'Right,' he said, letting go of her hand despite her trying to hang on to it for a bit longer. 'We'll be off in a minute. Are you ready?'

'Ready as I'll ever be.'

'Let's go for it then.'

He ran next to her for the entire twenty-five minutes. It was hard to chat when your knickers were up your bum (damn! New leggings, same problem), your boobs were one big wobbling block and you were out of breath. But she did her best. Hugh was very encouraging.

'All right?'

'Yes, thanks.'

'Do you need to slow the pace?'

'No, I'm okay.'

'Think you'll make it to the end?'

'I hope so.' She looked at his muscly legs pumping in impressive rhythmic fashion. 'You're very fit,' she noted.

'I'm a PE teacher.'

Of course he was.

At least she didn't get a stitch this time, and when they got to the end of the run she mercifully didn't feel like she wanted to die. She just had to sit down for ten minutes with her head on her knees saying, 'I'm fine, I'm fine.'

Afterwards, he walked her to the edge of the car park.

'Can I ask you something, Frankie?' His beautiful eyes were boring into her. She was transfixed by them. 'Are you married?' Of course, he must have noticed her wedding ring. She still wore it. Actually, she didn't dare attempt to try and get it off – she feared it wouldn't pass her knuckle.

'I'm separated.'

'Oh. Good. That's great.' He looked really pleased. 'Would you like to go out sometime? Could I take your number?'

Her heart gave a little leap. Would she like to go out sometime? She'd split with Rob to give her some time on her own. She was supposed to be single, and single for a year. She'd taken that pledge, with the girls, and she thought she'd keep it, easily. But he was so handsome, she was bored, she could do with some fun in her life and she needn't tell anyone…

'Yes. Okay. I'll give you my number.' He pulled his phone from his sports bag and tapped it in. Then slid the phone back into the front pocket of the bag. All the while he had a really intense look on his face. He was really looking at her. In her eyes. At her lips. Now she felt really funny. She felt all *wibbly*. She looked into *his* eyes. She looked at *his* lips.

'Great,' he said again. He stepped towards her. Then another step. When she thought he couldn't get any closer, he got closer still. Her heart started pounding – what was happening? – and, before she knew it, they were kissing. Kissing! He had his hand on her left sweaty bum cheek. She had her fingers in his lovely hair. They were really going for it. They kissed for ages. Ages. She clutched on to him like a drowning woman to a lovely big, life-saving rock. He finally leant away from her, his lips flushed and a big grin on his gorgeous face.

'I'll text you,' he said and bounded off into the car park.

'What have you been up to? Your face is bright pink.'

Imogen had texted her as she walked – or rather swooned – home from Tesco's, asking if she was free to meet for a quick coffee. Imogen was with Grace in town (James wasn't having Daniel this weekend – he'd gone to the New Forest, with *that bitch*) and as Frankie was too wired to go home, she'd detoured to meet them. What the bloody hell had just happened? She'd kissed a man she barely knew, a man she'd met twice. They'd just kind of leapt on each other. It was unprecedented. It was so out of the blue… It was absolutely bloody fantastic.

'I went for a run. The clue is in the outfit.' She looked down at herself. It was a dry day and the trainers were still pretty pristine.

'You?' said Imogen, getting her purse out of her bag to pay for coffee.

'I used to run, remember? I've decided to take it up again. I've joined a running group.'

'Yeah, I remember. Good for you. Any hot men?'

'If there were, I didn't notice.'

'So there were some?'

'No.'

'Well, great,' said Imogen. 'I'm pleased you're running again. You used to love it.'

'Does running make your chin all red?' asked Grace. She was peering into the counter and deciding between a blueberry muffin and a millionaire shortbread.

'Apparently,' said Frankie vaguely. 'So what have you two been up to?'

Imogen shrugged. 'Not much. Just working.' She started studying the Starbucks menu, above the counter, though they all knew exactly what was on it.

'Just working,' echoed Grace. 'And staying in a lot. You know how it is.'

'You've got that big do coming up haven't you? James's grandmother's thing?' said Frankie. 'You still going?' She wished she hadn't met up with them now; she was feeling far too flustered, but she thought as long as she kept the conversation off her, she could get through it. When she got home would be the time to jump up and down and screech her head off.

'Yes,' replied Grace. 'I've decided just to go on my own.'

'Really?' said Imogen. 'I could come with you?'

'It's not your thing,' said Grace. 'And thanks again for *your* offer, Frankie, before you say anything. Honestly, I'm fine going by myself.'

They were now at the front of the queue and gave their order. Frankie knew it wasn't really post-workout fare but she ordered a hot chocolate with whipped cream – she needed the sugar. As they sat down at a table she said, 'Well, I'm impressed, Grace. Going on your own. I think that's fabulous.' Grace never went anywhere on her own. Frankie *was* really impressed.

'Thanks, Frankie,' said Grace. 'I appreciate it.'

'Good being single, isn't it?' said Imogen.

'Hmm,' said Frankie and Grace, and the three of them sat with their heads lowered and stirred their drinks.

CHAPTER TWELVE:
GRACE

Anyone coming out of the Tube, as Grace was, in the five o'clock April sunshine, would have thought 'Blimey, that's an attractive man.' A *really* attractive man. He was leaning against a glass-fronted poster and wearing a perfect dinner suit and a handsome, amiable face that said he would make a great friend, boyfriend or husband. What a catch. He was gorgeous. He simply looked *lovely*.

Grace was surprised someone hadn't got there before her and dragged Greg away. She wouldn't have blamed them. He was a technicolour dreamboat. He certainly made all those terrible online dates she'd been on fade away, which was quite a feat, as most of them were still messaging her. She had to block Tasting Menu guy; he kept sending her photos of his pudding. Even on the way here she'd had a message from Tim, the man who'd bailed out on her, asking if she still wanted to go on a date. He did seem fairly normal and had provided a photo at last, of him halfway up a mountain (a real rock climber this time!) looking smiley and genial, but of *course* she didn't. She had Greg.

He was outside Her Majesty's Theatre in London's West End. Nana McKensie's one hundredth birthday treat was to take one hundred members of her family and friends to see

The Phantom of the Opera – her favourite musical; she'd seen it over thirty times, apparently – followed by a private party in one of the theatre's bars. Grace had been thrilled with the plan when she'd first been told of it, almost a year ago. She'd lost count of the number of times she'd asked James to take her to see a musical. He'd said West End shows were for girls or for gays, which was typical James. She always said, well, *she* was a girl, but that had never held any sway. James was not known for his political correctness. 'How's the gay?' he always used to ask, about Gideon.

The girls had never wanted to come to the theatre with her, either. She understood their reasons: Frankie said it was all too poncey for her and she never understood what on earth was going on, and Imogen didn't do musical theatre as she saw enough *normal* theatre. It was okay. To Grace, it was a romantic thing to do, going to a West End show. Some things she didn't want to do with the girls. Some things she wanted to do with a man. Thank God she'd found her *plus one*.

'Hello, again,' said Greg.

'Hello,' said Grace.

'You look lovely,' said Greg.

She was in a long velvet evening skirt, corset top and choker, and some sparkly black pumps. She'd tried on and discarded several outfits, before going for this one. She really wanted to look special tonight.

'Thank you, so do you.' Some men didn't suit a dinner jacket and bow tie. Greg did. He looked like he'd had another haircut since she last saw him. In the sunlight she could see some grey at his temples; it was very attractive.

'Shall we?'

Greg took her hand and they walked up the small flight of steps and into the lobby. Sun was streaming through the windows and Grace had to narrow her eyes to make anyone out. Ah, yes, there they all were, most of James's family, dressed up to the nines – earrings and necklaces and shiny shoes and well-polished bald patches all catching the light. Maggie, in a long tie-dye skirt and ruffly blouse, rushed up to give Grace a huge hug.

'The guy from the sandwich shop?' she whispered in Grace's ear. 'He's *gorgeous*!'

'Yes,' said Grace, pulling back. 'This is Greg. Greg, this is Maggie.'

'Hi, Greg.' Maggie beamed as Greg shook her hand. 'And don't worry,' she said, giving Grace's arm a congratulatory squeeze, 'my far from punctual brother's not here yet. Hopefully you won't bump into him at all. Mum's over there.'

Gloria, James's mum, gave Grace a small wave and then came over, rustling in black taffeta. 'Grace,' she said, enveloping her in a light embrace. 'Nana told us you were coming. I'm so glad you have. And you've brought a date!'

'Er…yes,' said Grace nervously. 'This is Greg.'

'Well, hello. Lovely to meet you. And what does Greg do?'

'Service industry,' said Grace.

'Marketing,' said Greg, at exactly the same time.

He laughed. 'I'm currently in the service industry but hoping to start my own business. Marketing.'

'Fabulous,' said Gloria. 'And where did you two meet?'

Grace looked at Greg. They should have worked all this stuff out. Never mind meeting him in advance to check he looked like his photo, they should have compiled a cheat sheet for tonight.

'We met while out walking,' he said. 'I have a very friendly Labrador.'

'How lovely,' Gloria smiled as Grace gave an internal sigh of relief. 'Well, I hope you have a good night. Nana's holding court somewhere. Oh, yes, there she is.'

She pointed out Nana McKensie over by the ticket office, resplendent in faux fur and pearls and surrounded by a circle of people all laughing their heads off. Grace smiled. She adored the lady.

'Well, I'll see you later.' Gloria stepped forward for another brief hug with Grace. 'I'm sorry about everything, dear. But, he's my son, what can I do?'

Grace nodded. 'It's okay.'

A bell sounded and a baritone voice came on the Tannoy to announce four minutes until the start of the performance. Greg put a protective arm around Grace as they slowly climbed the plum-carpeted Victorian staircase with smartly dressed family chattering excitedly around them. There was an air of glamour and anticipation, of this being a wonderful treat and celebration. He steered her gently and expertly towards her seat – Nana McKensie had booked the entire balcony – and smiled benignly at the elderly theatregoers seated near them as they took theirs. He was the perfect gentleman. Grace sat down, taking a quick look around her. There was still no sign of James.

'Okay, Grace?' Greg asked.

'Fabulous,' she replied. And the lights went down and the curtain went up.

Grace loved it, right from the start. The music, the set, the atmosphere – she soaked it up, every drop. She caught Greg looking at her a few times, and knew her face would be rapt and full of delight. She glanced at him, too, his profile fixed in concentration, his eyes taking it all in, and smiled to herself. She was delighted to be sitting next to such a gorgeous man.

The Phantom made his first appearance. Greg suddenly reached for Grace's hand, in the dark. She almost gasped. He'd taken her hand as they'd walked into the theatre, but there was something about this, in the dark, and the way it took her by surprise, that caused a heavenly tingle to travel up her arm and along and around her whole body. She revelled in this feeling; it was gorgeous, thrilling. She hadn't experienced such a feeling for a long time. That tingle didn't go away until the house lights went up for the interval and she reluctantly let him release her hand.

'So, you're really into musicals,' he said, as they made their way to the bar. Grace had pre-ordered interval drinks, a beer for him, a red wine for her. He looked so handsome in the glow of the red velvet and dark wood bar. She was happy just to stand and look at him. Everyone was in high spirits, women in sparkly cardigans and hairspray, men in smart casual and hair gel, all talking ten to the dozen and laughing and drinking. There was a lovely whiff of olden-day luxury and good times. Maggie waved from across the bar and gave a thumbs up.

'I used to be,' said Grace. 'I saw quite a few, growing up. *South Pacific*, *Joseph*, *Les Mis*. You?'

'I've never been to one before,' he admitted. 'But I'm really enjoying it. It's great. Thank you for inviting me.'

Booking you, Grace thought. She'd be transferring the money to him when she got home tonight. She tried not to think about it. 'My pleasure,' she said. She smiled. He smiled back. They slipped into a companionable silence and sipped their drinks.

'Tell me about your relationship history, before James,' he said, after a few moments.

'Why?' She was taken aback.

'I'm interested. I want to know.'

'Okay.' What did it matter if she told him? She took a gulp of red wine and rattled off a potted history, as quickly as she could, considering hers was a long roll call of boyfriends. She started at school and ended with James.

'So, no gaps?'

'No, not really.'

'Is that why you've hired me? So there isn't a gap?'

She thought about it. He was absolutely spot on. *No gaps!* That summed up her whole romantic life. 'I think it is. Gaps frighten me.'

'They shouldn't. It's nice sometimes to have an empty space. A blank space. Time to clear your head, think about what you want in life.'

'Yes, I suppose so.' Grace hugged her glass of red wine to her; there was nowhere to put it. She wasn't sure if she agreed with Greg. *Did* she want to think about what she wanted from life? *Did* she want to work out what she was going to do next? She wasn't sure she was ready. She wasn't sure she wasn't absolutely terrified.

'Grace.'

A different, but horrifyingly familiar, male voice was speaking. Cutting across the air between them like a scythe. Grace turned her head.

It was James. His hair was all gelled, like he did it for nights out. He was in his best, going-out clothes. If she didn't hate him so much she would have said he looked good.

'James,' she said flatly.

'I'll just go and get some water,' said Greg and he stepped away into the crowd. *No! Come back!* she pleaded silently, at his retreating back. *I know you think you're doing the gentlemanly thing, but please don't! Don't leave me with him!*

She turned back to James. Her bastard ex-husband had a stupid look on his face she couldn't read.

'You always said this was a good show,' he said. 'Who's the guy?'

'*You* said it was for girls and gays!'

They were standing very close to each other. They had to. The bar was packed. It was hot in there. People were laughing loudly, men were braying, women were cackling. There were lots of bare arms jangling with jewellery jostling against each other, bottoms being squeezed past, wobbling liquids in small glasses being carried. One of James's cousins, who she'd met once at a party, slapped another on the back and they both roared with laughter. It suddenly seemed incredibly claustrophobic. She wondered if she punched James low in the gut, if anyone would notice. She wished she actually *had* taken up Taekwondo.

'Yes. I suppose I did.'

'Is Joanne here?'

'Yes. She's at the bar. Who's the guy?' said James again.

'His name's Greg.'

'Where'd you meet him?'

'None of your business.'

'He doesn't look your normal type.'

'What, cheaters and bastards?'

James was finally beginning to squirm a little. 'No, he looks dapper. Very smart.'

'He is. He's a gentleman. He wouldn't hurt a fly. Unlike some.'

'Oh.' James looked around the bar, pretending he were just casually taking in the scene. 'Well, this is awkward.' He tried to smile conspiratorially. Grace ignored him and finished the rest of her wine.

'For you, yes.'

Greg approached with a glass of water. The ice was clinking; someone had just knocked his arm slightly. 'Okay, beautiful?' he asked, smiling widely at Grace.

'Yes, thanks.'

Greg stroked her arm and her ego, just when she needed both attended to, and looked into her eyes. Yes, that would do. Perfect. 'This is my ex, James. The one who cheated on me.'

'I see,' said Greg, in a friendly tone laced with steel. 'You're *James*. Well, you're an idiot, mate. An absolute buffoon.' He put a warm arm round her and gave her a little squeeze. 'Grace is one of the loveliest women I've ever met.'

Grace blushed and felt absolutely wonderful. This was the way to be treated.

'Right,' said James. He had a stricken look on his face, suddenly. He started looking desperately towards the bar. A girl there caught his eye and smiled. Ah. Joanne. She had a pint in one hand, a glass of white wine in the other. Classy, thought Grace, and so typical of James – sending his woman to the bar for him.

Joanne started walking towards them, looking quizzically at James. He halted her with a sharp glare and a shake of the head. She was frozen to the spot, excitable people bustling around her drinks. Beer sloshed over the rim of the pint glass and down onto the ancient carpet, but she didn't seem to notice. No one did. It would just blend in with the thousand other spills that carpet had absorbed over the last hundred and fifty years. It had probably seen it all.

Grace studied her. She was really attractive. Dark brown hair. Brown eyes. A little bit of the Zeta Jones about her. Silky blouse. Black skirt. Grace could just make out the outline of the infamous breast – breasts – underneath. She was sleek, pretty, almost understated. A rictus smile was anchored to Joanne's face like it had been face-painted on.

'Right, well, see you around,' said James and he bowled off in Joanne's direction, with that confident walk of his.

Grace shook her head. *See you around?* She was actually seeing him on Monday. He said he had a day off and could pick Daniel up when his coach got back from Paris and take him out for tea. But that wouldn't sound half as dismissive, would it? Or arrogant. That's if he even turned up. You never knew, with him.

'Thanks, Greg,' she said gratefully, turning to face him.

'I aim to please. Would you like another wine?'

'I'd love one.' She handed him a ten-pound note.

The bell rang for the second half of the performance as they were finishing their drinks. Grace felt a little tiddly. Warm. Excited.

'Forget about him,' said Greg, his arm back around her. 'I promise you'll soon realise just how easy that is.'

I could forget about anything with you by my side, thought Grace.

As they re-took their seats, she realised James was a few rows behind them. He was leaning into Joanne and smiling towards her ear. Gloria was sitting next to him. It was typical that most of James's family had accepted his new relationship so quickly. The man could literally commit murder and they'd still think he was the best thing since sliced bread. In Grace's opinion, he and Joanne shouldn't be out in public. They should be hiding out in some dingy room somewhere. They shouldn't be *out* and showing off.

She *should* try and forget about him. Greg was so much better-looking. Women had been looking at him since they came into the theatre. In the foyer, as they went up the stairs, in the bar. With appreciation. She wasn't blind to it. She loved it. She knew she and Greg looked like a dream couple. They looked like they belonged together. She wished it was real.

After the curtain call, Grace and Greg returned to the bar for Nana's after-show party. Nana beckoned for Grace to come over. She was high on a barstool, sipping a dirty martini. She put down her drink and grasped Grace by both hands.

'Gracie, my darling. There you are! Thank you so much for coming. You've brought a young man, I see. Let's have a look at him.'

'Not that young,' laughed Greg, but he did an amusing little turn for her.

'Very nice,' said Nana, looking at Grace intently with her piercing blue eyes. 'You don't let the grass grow, do you, Gracie? When I said plus one I thought you'd bring a friend. Did you not need a little time to take stock?'

'James didn't.'

'No. Quite.' Nana nodded sagely. 'But you could try being an independent woman for a while, you know. You might like it. You could Google a few of them… Amelia Earhart, she was one. Someone who flew solo.'

'Amelia Earhart flew solo then disappeared somewhere over the Pacific,' said Grace.

'Oh, details, details,' said Nana, in her raspy, cut-glass voice. 'Don't think about the end but the journey. She was brave. She was a pioneer. I had ten years on my own, once, you know.'

'Did you?'

'Of course I did – 1935 to 1945, the best years of my life. I gave quite a few men the runaround, I can tell you.

I had an absolute ball. I sang to my own hymn sheet, danced to my own drum…'

'If you had men, though, Nana, you weren't really on your own.'

'Let's just say I dipped in and out. I wasn't *saddled* to anyone. Right, get yourself some drinks,' she said, flapping them away. 'Enjoy the evening. And if you want to abscond with this handsome devil away from all the old farts and my recalcitrant grandson, I don't mind… I would!'

Grace took her advice. After another hour of small talk with people she didn't know, or slightly cringey talk with people she did, who gave her the 'sad face' about James then proceeded to quiz her relentlessly on Greg, they decided to make a move. She had made her point: if James had someone else then so did she. Sort of.

As they walked back down the staircase – she a little unsteadily – she studied Greg's face. He really was gorgeous. She hoped the show hadn't bored him, even if he was obliged to say he'd enjoyed himself. He'd had a sleepy look on his face in Act 2, a sexy one. Had he nodded off a little? If he had, she didn't mind. And he'd behaved impeccably in the bar. He was attentive. He was gracious to anyone who came to chat to them. He said all the right things. Oh God, she liked him, she thought. She really mustn't. He wasn't hers. He *wouldn't* be hers. He was just the hired help.

They stepped out onto the warm London street, teeming with post-theatregoers, diners, drinkers and lovers, and headed towards the Tube station. She had her hands in her jacket pockets. Greg gently removed the one from her left pocket and took it in his. He also let her walk on the pavement while he walked on the road. She knew if it was the olden days (not exactly sure when;

history was never her strong point) and it was raining, he would have laid down his cloak in a muddy puddle for her.

When they got to Liverpool Street, she saw *them* further down the platform, getting on the train. They must have left early, too. Joanne had a white jacket on now. James had his arm round her. James and Joanne. He's in a new couple, she thought. A brand new couple. While she was paying someone to be the temporary other half of hers. It suddenly made her feel unbearably sad.

Greg said goodbye to Grace at Chelmsford station. She now knew she'd definitely drunk a little too much. She knew she was clinging on to him too tightly as he kissed her on the cheek. She knew she looked a little smitten when he bent his head down and gave her a brief kiss on the lips. She knew her eyes were like saucers. Her breath hot and expectant. She wanted to grab hold of the back of his neck and never let go.

She'd spent the train journey with her head on his shoulder. Her hand on his knee. She really liked him. Oh no! She really, really liked him.

A black cab pulled up, Greg said, 'This is yours, Grace,' but she just stood there, wrestling with her emotions. Should she dip into Gran's money and ask him to come home with her for the night? What would it matter? No one need ever know.

She was so, so tempted. She was also unbearably tempted to ask him if he wanted to come home with her anyway, without it being a transaction. She wondered what his skin felt like. How it would feel to run her hands up his back and smooth them down his arms. She had had a sudden urge for him to really like her. To find her attractive, irresistible, to want to sleep with her.

The cab driver beeped his horn and reluctantly, she got in and let herself be driven away from him. She looked back to Greg, who was giving her a half wave.

He did like her, didn't he?

Damn, she didn't really know.

Under the circumstances, it was impossible to tell.

CHAPTER THIRTEEN:
IMOGEN

Imogen walked across the marble-tiled lobby in her click-clacky heels and got into the lift. She admired her reflection as she smoothly ascended to the twenty-eighth floor. She knew she looked good. Buttery soft leather pencil skirt. Off the shoulder, close-fitting black top. Hair blow-dried and just so. Perfect no make-up make-up.

At the top of the Gherkin, Richard was waiting.

Richard. She loved his name. It was sexy. It made her think of Tom Selleck's character in *Friends*. She'd always thought Monica should have chosen Richard, not Chandler. Chandler was a child. Richard was a full-grown, fully mature man: large, tall, sexy. And that voice! Her Richard had that voice.

It had been a month since their dinner date and Richard had texted her every day since. He'd spent most of that month in Singapore on some important business, having been called there a few days after their encounter, and a text from him would usually arrive about 7p.m., when she was on her way to a dinner or a play, and he was back in his hotel room after a long night entertaining clients. He would ask her how her day had been and she'd text something amusing that had happened, and he'd laugh (as you can laugh, by text) and come back with a funny comment about his own day. There was usually some banter about insurance or re-insurance, and the pompous world of actors, daaahling, and England and America and which country made better use of the word 'fanny'. They'd decided it was much more fun to tease each other about their nationalities, after all.

She knew she shouldn't be doing it. She knew when his first text arrived, the day after they met, saying how much he'd enjoyed meeting her and he hoped they could do it again, she should have ignored it. Deleted his number. Put the barriers up and shut up shop. But she couldn't. She couldn't resist him. Making contact with him. Thinking about him nearly every minute of every damn day. When he told her he had to go to Singapore, she'd thought 'good', but it hadn't stopped them, they'd carried on texting and she'd carried on thinking about him *all* the time. The distance just made it all the more tantalising.

He made her laugh. His texts made her day. Although her days were pretty fabulous anyway, it had to be said. The new job was going great. She'd already signed up eight actors she'd been desperate to get her mitts on and had found two of them work already, one in a brilliant sitcom about life in a mobile phone shop, the other in a hot ITV drama about adultery.

It was great fun working with Marcia; she knew it would be. Marcia was loud and funny and enthusiastic and they laughed pretty much all day long. The upbeat mood of the office meant loads got done. Imogen couldn't be further from Carolyn Boot and her fascist rule of terror and she loved it.

She also loved the location of her West End office. She could pop into Soho every lunchtime for a lovely ciabatta panini, or a duck wrap, or a Greek salad with loads of feta and mint, or whatever she fancied. Not that she was eating a whole lot. She often didn't finish her feta salad. She was excited, jittery. About Richard. Every time she thought of his eyes, his nose and his smile, his head, shoulders, knees and toes (okay, she hadn't seen those, but she could imagine they were pretty special), she had a fluttery feeling in her tummy. He was just really sexy. Charming, funny, American. That *voice*. She couldn't wait to hear it again.

Yesterday's text, which he'd sent at 7.30p.m. on his way to a dinner meeting at the top of the BT Tower (he was back from Singapore, at last) had said, *Are you free for a picnic lunch tomorrow?*

Depends where it is, she'd texted back, on her way to a production of *Disastrous Assignations* at the Barbican. Apparently, the lead, Aggie Monthammery-Smythe was someone to keep her eye on. *And what time.*

My office, he'd written. *12.30?*

As you know, I'm a highly important, super busy person, she tapped in, gleefully. *But if I jiggle my diary I may be able to fit you in.*

Jiggle your diary?

It's a technical term.

Then he sent a screenshot of his business card, *Because you wouldn't take it the first time.*

Thank you, she'd texted back, adding, *Serial killer* and a smiley face.

The lift pinged expensively and the door glided open with a luxurious swish. Sweeping before her was a huge chrome and glass reception desk. Yup, just how she had imagined Richard's office. She approached. The girl on reception was, of course, young and beautiful.

'I'm here to see Richard Stoughton,' said Imogen, her heels sinking satisfyingly into the soft, pale green carpet.

'Oh, yes,' said the beautiful girl, 'he's expecting you.' She rose from behind the desk and beckoned for Imogen to follow her through a large, open-plan office. Workers at desks looked up at them as they strutted past. The girl had hair you could see your face in and a tiny, pert bottom, which wiggled cutely under her tight, navy power dress, but Imogen was not jealous in the slightest. Why would she be? *She* was having lunch with the most gorgeous American in London.

They reached a heavy wood and steel door, the girl pushed it open and Imogen stepped inside. Richard's office was massive. About twenty feet from her was a huge desk, a large leather chair and a dazzling backdrop of the London skyline framed in the Gherkin's iconic windows – floor to ceiling but triangular in shape and latticed like a magnificent pie. The room was jaw-droppingly stunning. Bright and light. Corporate and streamlined. Cushioned underfoot with expensive, pale grey carpet. It smelled of efficiency and a subtle Jo Malone-y fragrance. She wrinkled her nose. Sandalwood and pomegranate?

Between Imogen and the desk was a small square table laid with an artfully draped white tablecloth, which was origamied beautifully at the corners. Imogen stepped towards it. The table was adorned with gorgeous dishes of amazing-looking food, all on dinky white plates and bowls: salmon and tuna sashimi, tiny goats' cheese and tomato bruschetta, shiny black and red grapes, prosciutto and slivers of Brie, cute custard tarts and miniature doughnuts. Plus two tall champagne flutes and champagne on ice in a silver bucket to the side, all lit up in the sun, which was streaming in from those amazing windows. Everything was perfect. Richard had really gone to town.

Actually, where was he? He wasn't here.

'Would you like to take a seat?' gestured the girl, to the table. 'Mr Stoughton won't be a moment.'

'Thank you,' said Imogen, 'I'll stay standing. I can have a little nose around.'

'Mr Stoughton's work is highly important,' the girl said haughtily, drawing her perfect breasts up. 'I don't think he'd appreciate it being *nosed* at.'

'I'm joking,' said Imogen. 'I'm not a corporate spy or anything. I work in the entertainment industry. I'm an agent.'

'Oh!' said the girl, now looking like a bad smell had been thrust under her nose. She turned her back and walked smartly out of the room.

Imogen didn't want to be sitting when Richard came in. She feared her skirt would crease and her stomach would muffin-top unattractively over her waistband, not that it was massive – it had shrunk to nothing over the past few weeks. Still. She wanted to be upright, smoothed down, composed.

She wandered over to the window and looked out at the view. Then she approached Richard's desk. It was so tidy! Some of the high-flyers she'd been out with had been messy so-and-sos. She picked up an exquisite-looking pen, flicked it on and off a couple of times, then put it down again. She tapped a key on Richard's PC, hoping to see his screen-saver. All that popped up was a screen full of figures. Boo, boring, she thought, but all the same she felt slightly relieved. She'd had a sudden dread of seeing photos of a wife and children, even though he'd definitely told her at their dim sum dinner he wasn't married.

A door to the right of the desk opened, making Imogen jump, and Richard entered the room. Bloody hell. Immediately, that room was *filled*. He was tall, broad. White shirt, grey suit and plain navy silk tie. Sexy eyes and mouth. Shiny shoes, salt and pepper hair. He was utterly sublime. She'd had that thing all month, where she couldn't remember exactly what he looked like. That thing you get with people you fancy that never happens with normal people. She could remember bits and bobs, but not the whole. And now the whole of Richard was in front of her she was almost *floored*.

He was monstrously good-looking. The whole package, and just the kind of package she liked: out-of-this-world looks, great personality, with a dash of corporate power. You've been here before, she thought to herself. Well, she had, literally; she'd once dated someone ten floors down. She'd certainly been with this kind of *man* before: charming, good-looking, rich and powerful. Oh, she'd dated dozens of them. She'd even *had* one or two on similar-looking desks (yes, the old secretary/boss role-play routine. She once had to flick her hair down from a bun and everything.) And they'd all, with monotonous predictability, turned out to be either dull, disastrous or dishonest. Or all three. *Big* disappointments. Why she was putting herself back in that well-worn, slightly grubby saddle again, she didn't know. Especially as she had the feeling this man may not turn out to be a disappointment at all, which petrified her.

Then Richard smiled, and she knew.

'Hello, Imogen,' he said.

Oh good God, that accent. She couldn't bear it. It was like molasses dripping down a stack of pancakes, a punctured egg over easy oozing over a muffin – all American, sexy-sounding clichés. He made it impossible to avoid them. As she smiled back she did one of those embarrassing nervous involuntary swallows, which she prayed he hadn't noticed. Highly uncool. 'How are you?'

'Good, thanks. You?' God, her voice was all weak-sounding; she had to clear her throat slightly.

'Just great,' said Richard and he stepped forward to kiss her on the cheek. She took him all in at this mouthwateringly close range: face, suit, shoes (oh shoes! Immaculate!), citrusy cologne, the warmth and wonderful smell of his face. Bloody, bloody hell.

'You look nice,' she managed, her voice barely above a whisper. Ugh! She really had to snap back to sassy. Her texts had been great, all month. She'd been on fire. Now this man was actually in front of her again, she'd fallen apart. She was close to becoming a wreck and needed to pull herself together, sharpish.

'You too.' He smiled and looked her up and down, his eyes resting on hers when they came back to her face. Intent, suspense and bare, delicious lust hung in the fragrant, air-conditioned air.

Quick! Think of something else to say. 'Champagne at lunch?' she enquired in what she hoped was a cheeky manner. There. That was better.

'Who doesn't like champagne?' said Richard. His mouth was doing that sexy, curling up at the corners thing again. She wanted to step forward and lick it.

'I thought you Americans were super conservative,' she said. 'Not like us Brits. If we can help it we'll take a four-hour lunch and come back to the office at 5 p.m. absolutely rat-arsed.' Her words were fun and flippant – much, *much* better – but her voice now had that slight waver to it that signalled a raging, inner sexual fire. Luckily, it didn't seem to register with him. He laughed.

'Rat-arsed? You are an education, Imogen.' God, that bloody, bloody voice. Keep talking, mister, she thought, and I'll be gone. Your staff will have to slap me round the face and drag me out by my ankles. 'Shall we?'

He pulled back a chair that had been swathed in white fabric, like one at a wedding. It just stopped short of having a giant bow at the back. Had this whole ensemble been hired in? She wouldn't be surprised. Richard seemed the sort of man who would click his fingers and have things happen. She sat down and could immediately smell the freshness of the linen.

'Help yourself to whatever you fancy.'

You, she thought. She wondered, if she casually suggested it, whether he would care to take her there and then, on his desk. She had a hair band in her bag; she could do a bun.

He shook out his napkin and put it on his lap. 'Oh,' he said teasingly, 'do we need to say grace or something first?'

'*Grace*,' said Imogen, with a smirk. 'She's one of my best friends, actually.' Grace! For God's sake don't think of Grace! She'd have a fit if she knew what you were doing, letting the side down spectacularly. 'No, no need. I'm not of a religious persuasion. I've hardly been a nun, in my life!' She laughed shrilly. God, she was nervous. Calm down, she told herself. Why are you talking about nuns? Don't let him think you're a slut! Say something cultural, intelligent. 'And we're very much a secular nation these days. God-fearing went out with the Tupperware party and the landline phone.'

The look on his face said he obviously had no idea what she was talking about and neither did she. She ploughed on. 'I like to bow to my own conscience. Not that of a higher power.' What gibberish! And her conscience seemed to have disappeared, right at this very moment. Well, since the moment she'd met him, actually. She was supposed to be a man-hating, ball-breaking kick-ass woman who had spurned all men. Not a woman who wanted to bonk this one then cuddle up to him afterwards like a purring kitten. Pfft! That would hardly happen if she continued being so nervous, random and unfunny. Where had the feisty, highly amusing woman from the dim sum restaurant gone? She'd clearly done a bunk, along with all of Imogen's resistance.

She really, really liked this man.

She tried to concentrate on the food. 'This is quite a spread.' Spread. No, not a word she wanted to be thinking of. Good God. 'It looks lovely.'

'I hope you're hungry,' he said.

She wasn't. She'd scoffed loads in Chinatown without a care in the world. Now she didn't think she could eat anything. Thank God it was what Frankie's mum famously called 'picky bits'. She toyed with a goat's cheese tart then dropped it back on her plate. Champagne. She needed champagne. She threw the bottle a longing glance. Hopefully it would loosen her up. Richard took her hint and poured her a glass. Taking a large guzzle, she felt herself relax a little. She'd have to be careful though; she had a meeting with a casting director later that afternoon.

'So,' he said, 'the new job's still working out?'

She picked up a black grape and tried to chew it. Damn it, she couldn't eat and talk to this gorgeous man at the same time. Just look at him! His face was lightly tanned above his crisp white shirt. His eyes were mesmerising. His mouth was tantalising. Everything had an 'ing' at the end of it. He just gave off *heat*, from the other side of the tablecloth. He was the best-looking man in the world. Come on, she thought. Pull out the stops. Wow him with your dazzling conversation and witty repartee, you know you can. Pull it out of the goddamn bag!

'Oh a blast,' she said, and after another fortifying gulp of champagne, she began to regale him with tales of agenting and the ML agency and Marcia and her Dictaphone. She quickly got into her stride. Soon she was telling him about the actor who'd come into the office for a meeting with a tree-shaped air freshener in his jacket pocket. He'd forgotten to put deodorant on and had nicked it from a taxi – it had taken them two days to rid the office of the smell of pine. Richard was laughing his gorgeous head off. She loved making him laugh – she could rapidly see it becoming her new favourite thing.

There was a knock at the door. It was the reception beauty.

'So sorry to disturb you, Mr Stoughton, but Jim Lamb, the new underwriter, would really like to speak to you. It's kind of urgent. Would it be okay if he came in?'

'Sure,' said Richard. 'He can come in. Thank you, Veronica.' He laid down his cutlery and rose from the table, leaving Imogen to follow his bum with her eyes and prepare her next funny story.

In shuffled a timid-looking red-faced man. He was young and skinny, the back of his neck was all red and his shoes were too try-hard shiny. He started apologising profusely, his head bowed. Richard put his arm round his shoulder in a fatherly manner – his hand like a big gentle bear paw – and led him to the corner of the room. There was a lot of muffled discussion. The young man actually sniffed at one point, and took a screwed-up, damp-looking hanky out of his pocket to dab at his nose with. Then Richard was seeing him to the door. Imogen could now catch what was being said.

'Hey, it's fine, don't be nervous,' Richard was saying, in that amazing voice. 'I'm happy to mentor you personally. Come see me at 9a.m. every morning, for fifteen minutes, and we'll run through any problems and issues. Get things all straightened out at the top of the day. It'll all be fine, Jimmy, trust me.'

Jim nodded, looking much brighter, and scuttled out of the room. He reminded Imogen of a young, modern-day Bob Cratchit.

Wow, she thought, Richard was a really nice boss. Caring, understanding, powerful. She nearly swooned, but brought herself up. It could all just have been for her benefit. Perhaps after she'd gone he would call in and bawl out this same employee, reducing him to tears. Demand he get him a coffee then tell him off for making it wrong, before sending him back to his little desk and his flickering candle and his grey, scratchy fingerless gloves…

Richard returned to the table and sat down. He pushed up his cuffs slightly as he prepared to dive into the sashimi. She was pleased to see he didn't have a stupid watch on. One of those flashy million-pound ones that some men liked to wear – as if all their stupid wealth and power could be displayed in a huge, silly clock face embedded with millions of ridiculous Swarovski crystals. Richard had a nice plain, manly looking watch with a brown leather strap. And sexy hairy wrists.

His phone rang. It had a sensible, normal ring tone. No *Rocky* theme tunes or Crazy Frogs, thank goodness. She'd heard them all.

'Sorry,' he said, 'I really have to get this. It won't take long.'

He picked up his mobile from the table and took it over to his desk, where he sat down on the huge leather chair.

'Hello, Patrick,' he said, then laughed lightly. 'Yes, absolutely.' And he launched into some indecipherable stuff with lots of numbers. Imogen switched off. She was looking round Richard's office again. There really wasn't much in it. She supposed all the dull stuff, like photocopying and filing and faxing (did they still fax any more? Telex? Was that still a thing?) happened elsewhere. Only the top stuff happened here.

Richard had a couple of tall, imposing stainless steel cabinets. She wondered if he kept a stack of clean shirts in a top drawer, like in the movies, Gordon Gecko-style. She had a sudden – and not unprecedented – wonder of what he looked like bare-chested. If only he would change his shirt now. She'd love to see it. Should she throw a glass of champagne over him and force his hand, arm, pecs, whatever?

He put down the phone. She decided to wander over and sit down on the brown leather swivelly chair opposite him. She was a tiny bit tiddly now, so she started spinning on it.

'Since you're taking a ride on that thing,' he said, 'do you want to scoot round here so we're on the same side?'

Her stomach did an energetic somersault. He waited while she trundled her chair round, feeling slightly silly. Once she'd rounded the corner, he grabbed the edge of the chair and pulled it towards his until they were facing each other, knees touching. She looked down at their knees – his under expensive grey fabric; hers with tan leather stretched over them. It was a new kind of intimacy, and actually more erotic than the bumping of other body parts she had known. Or maybe it was just the man.

She had to fight the urge to stroke one of his knees with her hand. Knees, eh, she'd never found them sexy before – now she was irrationally desperate to see at least one of Richard's.

He was looking at her quizzically, once she'd dragged her gaze upwards, and said, in an amused voice, 'Is it *okay* if we touch knees, or is it too much for you?'

'I'll let you know,' she said. His face was dangerously close. If she wanted to, she could lean in and kiss him. And she did want to. Usually, by now, she would have done it. She would have played out some seduction routine much earlier in the lunch: crossed her legs enticingly; fed him a grape or two, hitched something up or down, whatever she thought would work best. She may have even done one of her specials – leaning directly across a dinner table and brazenly sticking her tongue straight into someone's mouth. She'd done it before, sending cutlery and crockery crashing. It had been a very hot night with an ultimately cold fish of a man – another of her disasters.

She was too close to him. She'd drunk too much champagne. She liked him too much. This was all getting too dangerous. What was she thinking? She had to go on the counter-attack and quickly. She had to regain some composure here, some ground. Collect herself. She thought, with shame, of her two friends, their vow to have a year of being single, her supposed new code of conduct. This man could be no good for her. She wasn't supposed to be falling for anyone.

She shunted her chair a foot away from him. He looked surprised. He looked even more surprised when her voice took on what she hoped was a haughty froideur.

'You seem to have me all wrong, Richard,' she said.

He looked totally taken aback. Those blue eyes widened.

'You think I'm an English ice maiden, don't you?' she said. 'And that with a bit of warm American maple syrup and a dusting of cinnamon, I'll melt in your arms. So you can *have your way*. But it's not a dead cert, you know. I might *not* melt.' Champagne favours the brave. Her voice ratcheted up to *def con* hauteur. 'I may be sworn off men, for all you know.' There, she'd told him. 'I might not want to go near your American hot dog with an English barge pole.'

He roared with laughter, throwing his head back. His throat was sexy. Firm, tanned, with a lovely sprouting of hair at the base of it. It looked like it needed nuzzling.

'I'm not quite sure what a *barge pole* is, my English Princess,' he said, his eyes mocking and gorgeous. 'And *sworn*? What, you took an oath or something?' Christ, that American accent was bloody sexy, she thought, as the champagne continued to take hold. No more booze around this man, she thought. It's not a safe area.

'No. I didn't swear on the Bible or anything like that. I told you, I'm not religious,' she said, continuing to inch her chair away from him. 'I just decided. Well, there are three of us. All off men. We're supposed to be single for a year. We've come up with a charter.' She was saying too much. She'd had too much booze. Next she'd be telling him all about the losers she'd dated. Or about Dave Holgate's belly. It was tempting. Richard would laugh that delicious laugh. It was suddenly more important than anything else in the world, that he find her hilarious. It wouldn't hurt, would it, to tell him she'd been enormously unlucky in dating?

'A *charter*, hey? And there's three of you?'

'Three of us. Friends. Me, Grace and Frankie. We live in the same street. We've had enough of men. It's not that unusual.'

'Someone hurt you?' he asked gently.

'No, not at all,' she snapped. 'Just a long, long series of disappointments.'

'The wrong kind of men?'

'Men like you, actually. But I keep coming back for more, it seems.'

'Ah, a pattern. I see.' He looked amused, where she thought he might have looked angry. 'So, I'm your next disappointment?'

'I'm not sure,' she muttered. Damn it. She'd said too much. The point was he was *not* disappointing, far from it. But she wouldn't tell him that.

'Hmm. Interesting. All these men…all these disasters… and you. Do you think there could be a common denominator here?' He was teasing, but she was unnerved and terrified.

'I haven't *made* these men disappointments! They've done it all on their own, believe me.'

She was more than a bit annoyed. Good. Annoyed was good. It was better than being scared witless. Annoyed meant she could *go*. And she really should go. Make an exit. Get out while the going wasn't good. What a shame she hadn't eaten anything. Her appetite was back now, booze-fuelled. Those egg custard tarts had looked so delicious. She wanted to stay for pudding. She wanted to stay for Richard. God, he was bloody gorgeous.

'I've got to go,' she whimpered. 'I don't trust myself.'

She could have *punched* herself. No, don't say that! It immediately shifted the balance of power. It told him she fancied him. That she really liked him. That she was under his spell, his control. Why, why, *why* did she say that? Ironically, she'd said it before as a casual line in seduction. When she trusted herself all *too* well, when she knew exactly what she was doing. It usually preceded leaping on someone with wanton abandon. Now she said it as bare fact, a fact that she was vulnerable and petrified.

'I need to go,' she repeated. 'I've got somewhere I have to be... I...'

He grabbed the base of her chair and pulled it back towards him in one deft move. This time they were thigh to thigh. His turned his upper body to face her. His face, mouth, lips were close to hers, so close. She could smell his skin. She could see straight into his eyes. He leant forward, placed his left hand softly under the side of her face...and kissed her.

Oh. My. God. His lips were warm, almost hot. There was a heat coming off his face in citrusy wafts. He was kissing her. He was kissing her. He was kissing her. She never wanted it to stop. She'd never been kissed like this before. She was spiralling down a delicious tunnel to total oblivion. It was tender, it was teasing, it was tantamount to heaven. *Richard...*

Finally, his lips were gone from hers. She felt bereft. She could have kissed him all day. She opened her eyes to see him sat there, smiling at her. She smiled back, then, suddenly, she was horrified. This was wrong! So, so wrong. She was supposed to be off men. For a year! She was supposed to be a single woman, enjoying her freedom. She *couldn't* fall in love with him. He would only end up breaking her heart. The type of man she'd always thought she was *safe* with was going to break her heart. She had to get out of here *now*, or she would never get out alive.

'I've got to go,' she said again, weakly.

'Why?' He looked…satisfied. Sexy as hell. 'We haven't even had dessert, or pudding, as you call it. Would you like to have some *pudding* before you go?' He gestured over to the table. She glanced at it. The egg custards were glistening in the sun. How did he know she loved them? He was mocking her a little, she knew, but in a way she was frightened she really liked.

She was undone, all over the place. Oh my God, that kiss. So warm, so American, so amazing, so…hazardous. 'I'll take a custard tart for the road,' she said, standing up and trying to get her voice to sound somewhere near normal.

'Sure.' He was smiling. Relaxed. He had just kissed her. As he walked over to the table, she examined his back view again. It was nice. Too nice. He wrapped a custard tart in a sky blue napkin for her. Nimble fingers. Lovely fingers. She wanted those fingers dipping in her custard. Stop, stop, stop! She had to get out of here, NOW!

She nearly ran to the door. She fled, without looking back.

The heavy office door shut softly behind her, like an anti-climax.

As she made her way back through the open-plan office, veering slightly but determined to look sober, her head was held unnaturally high. She was channelling all her favourite female television characters. Carrie Bradshaw walking through *Vogue*, Ally McBeal strutting through the law firm, Scully walking purposefully wherever it was she used to walk.

Several pairs of eyes looked up as she passed.

'I love your shoes,' said a woman's voice from inside a grey cubicle.

'Thanks,' said Imogen. She felt obliged to stop. They *were* kick-ass shoes. They were the type of shoes you put on as soon as they arrived in the post, and then you sat on the sofa with them, holding one leg aloft in turn so you could admire them. The kind of shoes you kept by the side of your bed so you could see them as soon as you opened your eyes in the morning. They had been carefully chosen for her lunch with Richard. She had stuck them out one end of the white tablecloth to make sure he noticed them. He had.

She peered inside the cubicle. The woman looked friendly. Nice cardigan. Teal. She had photos of beaming children stuck all over her work station. A large box of tissues in a floral case. Imogen was transfixed. This was the feminine side of re-insurance. She was aware she was staring. Nosing. What would snooty reception girl say?

'Lucky you,' the woman whispered with a smile, over the top of her computer, and at first Imogen thought she was still talking about her shoes. 'He's lovely.'

'Thank you,' said Imogen, again. She didn't know what else to say. She smiled at the woman in a way that she hoped said 'poised, sober and lucky', not 'pissed, just been kissed and all over the place', and walked a very straight, measured line through the office, past the impressive reception desk and to the lifts.

Once inside, with the doors closed, she looked at her face. She looked deranged, changed. She leant her cheek against the cool metal flank of the lift, and saw the London street loom larger and larger below her until she was level with it.

She'd fallen for him, hadn't she? He'd kissed her and she'd fallen for him. There was no going back.

The door opened and she stepped out. As she click-clacked back over the marble floor and out of the revolving door into the breezy city street, she believed herself to be the weakest person she knew.

CHAPTER FOURTEEN:
FRANKIE

A couples' triathlon?

I'm washing my hair that night.

Ha ha. What about driving down to Southend and taking a jog along the seafront?

Maybe. But only if we get fish 'n' chips!

There had been two more Couch to 5k meet-ups since Frankie and Hugh had snogged by the car park (she could only make alternate Sundays – she was going again tomorrow) and they had kissed goodbye – very energetically – both times. It was becoming a lovely habit. She'd got over her complete astonishment at it happening, that first time, and now expected it and looked forward to it. It was fun.

In between snogging meet-ups, they texted a lot. Hugh was pressing her to go on a date with him, but so far, Frankie had resisted. Despite her eagerness to give him her number, once she'd really given it some thought, she'd decided she was reluctant. She'd only recently got rid of Rob and wasn't sure if she wanted a boyfriend or any kind of new man. She was happy to kiss Hugh – really happy – and enjoy their textual flirting, but she wasn't sure if she was ready for more. She relished the periods of time to fantasise about him; if she went on a date with him those fantasies might disappear in a puff of smoke. She really didn't want another Rob.

Hugh was keen and persistent. This morning he was trying to pin her down to a day and time. They'd been volleying texts between them like tennis balls since eight a.m. and it was now quarter past ten. His text speak was appalling and he used lots of horrible things like 'gr8' and 'TTFN' and far too many 'lol's, but he was fairly amusing and he wanted to go out with her, and that made her feel good. Thinking about their delectably infrequent, frantic kissing at the edge of the car park made her feel *really* good.

She grinned as another text came through. Oh. It was from Rob.

Harry forgot his homework.

Oh no! Can't he do it when he gets home tomorrow?

He said it'll be too late. It's maths. I can help him with it. You're useless.

Thanks! Can't you print it off the internet?

No. He needs his textbook.

Ah, okay.

Can you bring it over? You can see where I live.

Frankie stared at the text. She wasn't sure she wanted to see where he lived. Rob's flat, house, home, place, pad whatever. It would be a bit weird. How long had he lived there now? Three months? Where he lived was now a world apart, his place had nothing to do with her.

A text from Hugh arrived:

We can do fish 'n' chips. Then a 2k run to burn it off ;)

She sent a quick reply.

I'll think about it. Got to go out now. Speak to you later x

She put a kiss because she felt bad, but she had to think about whether or not she would go to Rob's flat. She had often wondered what it was like. It was strange and often horrible not to know where her children were sleeping every other weekend. She couldn't picture them there, asleep at night, and it was weird. Their bedrooms, their pillows, their duvets. They were unknowns and she didn't like it.

She'd cried last night, actually, out of nowhere and into her pillow, panicked that she couldn't picture Alice's face because she was unable to visualise her sleeping. She'd had to get out of bed and fetch the photo she had of all four of her children, from her dressing table. She'd examined them all. Traced over their faces with her finger. Perhaps she *should* go and see their bedrooms at Rob's. Witness where they spent all that time. And, if she really admitted it to herself, she did have the tiniest, tiniest desire to go and have a nose at his flat.

Okay. Text me the address. The lady will help me find it.

Rob would know what she meant. The 'lady' was the satnav lady. Frankie liked to talk back to her, thank her for her instructions and call her a 'dozy bint' if she sent them the wrong way. She'd once forgotten her satnav (it was one of those stick-on ones) when driving Josh to a camp at Mersea, and Rob, at work, had looked up the route on Google Maps and spoken to her on loudspeaker as she drove, in satnav lady's lilting Irish accent. It had been really funny.

As she pulled up outside a new-build row of terraces, featuring four storeys of windows with little balconies, she could see why Rob had chosen to live here. It was walking distance from an Asda and right up his street: quiet, clean and with no work needing doing to anything. Rob had been pushing for a new build when they'd moved to their house in New Primrose Road. He thought one would be less 'grief', as he'd put it. He'd been over-ruled; Frankie had wanted a rambling doer-upper and she'd got it. On the other hand, he'd made her move *not far enough away* from her parents, so it was a kind of payback.

Rob's own parents had lived in an ancient, ramshackle farmhouse, up until his dad died and his mum moved into sheltered housing. It had constantly needed work doing to it, work that Rob was often roped into helping with, even as a kid. He was painting bannister spindles by the age of ten and regrouting by thirteen. When he grew up, he dreamed of owning a brand spanking new place that needed zero work: uPVC windows that never needed painting; walls that didn't crack in the same places every year no matter how carefully they were filled in; rooms that were *warm*, but Frankie had come across the 1930s house in central Chelmsford, Rob's required area, and thought it perfect. She liked a period feature, a tiled fireplace and a dado rail or two; she was partial to large rooms, good ceiling heights and a garden that was larger than a handkerchief. She persuaded Rob that it had the space and potential they needed and he spent the next two years with a power tool or a paintbrush in his hand.

He hadn't always been a lazy git, thought Frankie ruefully, as she got out of the car. At one time, he'd made a real effort. He'd worked really hard on their house. So, where had it all gone wrong? she wondered. At what point exactly had he turned into an idle, good-for-nothing slob?

Rob loved Chelmsford. He loved living there. He always declared that he was a Chelmsford Man. Strictly speaking, though, he wasn't. The ramshackle farmhouse he grew up in was in Danbury, a village five miles away. He and Frankie had met in the village, at The Ram pub and restaurant. She'd been on a girls' night out, with work; he was out for a family dinner with his mum and sister.

They'd seen each other at the bar, when he'd let her get served first, and later, she'd literally bumped into him in the narrow beamed corridor as they were both coming out of the toilets. Romantic!

'We must stop meeting like this,' he'd said.

'Yes.' She'd laughed. He looked nice. Jeans, a short-sleeved shirt. Short, fair, curlyish hair. Not fat, not skinny. Cute.

As they'd passed each other, he'd turned and called back to her. 'We're going on into town tonight,' he'd said. 'Well, me and my sister Beth are – I don't think my mum can be persuaded.' He laughed, showing all his teeth. 'I know this is a bit cheeky, but I'll be in The Schooner if you fancy it.'

'Oh, right,' she said. 'Thanks.'

She didn't know if the girls would be going into town after the meal or not, but by the time they'd polished off dessert and the last of the seven bottles of red, Frankie definitely was. She'd been glancing at Schooner man, over at the other side of the restaurant. He'd been laughing a lot. His mum and sister were laughing a lot, too. He left the restaurant at half ten. By eleven o'clock Frankie was drunk enough to call a taxi for herself and head into Chelmsford.

Rob was alone at the bar of The Schooner and the rest, as they say, was history. A whole lot of history.

His modern, low-maintenance flat was on the top floor. Frankie supposed Rob would have to buzz her in, but a girl in a denim jacket was heading in through the heavy glazed door in the centre of the block so she skipped in behind her, into a stark white communal hall. There was a pushbike there – wasn't there always, in these places?

It wasn't Rob's. His was still in the garage at home, flanked up against the wall next to the kit car.

She went up the grey, concrete stairs. Four flights. She counted along the blank white doors to Number 54 and rang the bell. There was a shout of 'Mum's here!' and Harry came to the door.

'Mum,' he said. He didn't look ecstatic to see her. He looked wary. Almost suspicious. It must have been as strange for him to see her here as it was for Frankie to be at the door of her husband's unknown home. 'Dad!' he yelled, as though calling for backup, in the way that fathers who answer phones to their children always call for their wives. Then he took the textbook Frankie was proffering and hopped back into the flat.

Rob appeared. He had an apron on. An actual apron. It wasn't even a comedy one with boobs on. It was a proper, serious apron. With blue and white butcher's stripes and a wholesome smear of flour across the front. Alice was balanced on his hip, her chubby legs wrapped around him. She reached out for Frankie with a huge toothy grin and Frankie grabbed her with near relief and took her in her arms.

'Hello,' she whispered, into Alice's perfect, pink ear. 'So this is where you are.'

'Come in!' Rob said, all jolly, like Abigail at *Abigail's Party*, welcoming her guests. 'Excuse the pinny. Tilly and I were just making some fairy cakes. Or cupcakes, or whatever they call them these days. Come on in,' he said again. Frankie followed him down a short hall and into an open-plan living room that had a kitchen shoehorned at one end, behind squeezed-back concertinaed doors. A lovely vanilla-y smell was wafting from a very clean-looking built-in oven.

'Hi, Mum,' said Tilly distractedly. She had an apron on, too, and was sitting on the sofa next to Harry. They were watching cartoons.

'Hi, darling,' said Frankie, going over to kiss them both. 'You both okay?' Her eyes were filling with tears and she felt ridiculous, but it was just so *weird* seeing them here.

'Yeah,' they said, in unison, without taking their eyes off the television.

'Where's Josh?'

'Playing outside,' said Tilly.

'Oh.'

'He's out on the communal lawn,' said Rob, 'with some of the neighbours' kids. He's made loads of friends.'

'Especially Jonathan,' said Tilly in a sing-song voice. 'And *Daddy* is friends with Jonathan's mum.'

'It's just one of the neighbours,' said Rob, shrugging and looking slightly sheepish. 'Jenny. No biggie. We've been to Kaper Kids together.'

'You don't have to explain,' said Frankie, but she was quite taken aback. Rob had a new friend? A Jenny? How was she supposed to feel about that? She didn't know, but she supposed she didn't have a right to feel anything about it. *She* sort of had a Hugh.

'I'll show you round,' said Rob. 'It won't take long.' He grinned. He looks happy here, thought Frankie. Really content. Perhaps he *was* happier. Now he was away from her. With his new flat and his freedom and his *Jenny*.

She followed him to the window where he pointed through the glass to the tiny balcony. He had a couple of pot plants on it. They didn't look like they were on the brink of dying. They looked like he actually watered them.

'Balcony,' he said, unnecessarily.

She nodded. 'Very nice. Those plants look like the kind Mum's always bringing round for us. Er, for me,' she added.

'They are,' he said. 'She popped round.'

'Oh! How did she know where you were?' asked Frankie, incredulous.

'She phoned me at work.' Rob shrugged. 'I got a lot of *poor Rob*'s.'

'I bet you did,' said Frankie.

'There's Josh,' he said, pointing, and she could see him, kicking a ball around with a couple of other boys. Laughing his head off, a jumper tied round his waist.

'Yes, I see him,' she said. For some reason she felt incredibly sad.

Rob turned back to the room. 'Living/dining/kitchen, as you can see.' He swept his arm round the space. His sofa was a rather nice dark brown leather one, all antique-looking. She wondered where he'd got it from. Had he hired it? Or did it come with the flat?

'Three bedrooms,' he said, almost proudly. 'Follow me.'

She followed, still holding Alice – although she was getting a heavy old lump, she didn't want to put her down. He led her to a small bedroom that housed a double bed and a single. 'Mine and Alice's room,' he said. The double bed had a pale blue cotton duvet and was neatly made. The single bed had a duvet and pillowcase set that was pink and had roses on it. It was very pretty.

'A big girl's bed,' lisped Alice.

'Yes, darling,' said Frankie. 'It *is* a big girl's bed.'

At home, Alice still had a cot bed so it was a lot smaller. Alice's big girl's bed had her favourite rabbit on the pillow. There was a white bedside table next to it, with a little pink lamp and a drawer with a heart-shaped cut-out. Everything was so neat and tidy! Was Rob sure he lived here? Did he actually live in a fleapit next door and had broken into this pristine show home especially for her visit?

There was nothing else in the room, just one of those clothes rails you get in Argos, with a few of Rob's things neatly hung on it. *Neatly*! It was unheard of! Perhaps the flat was so small he simply couldn't be untidy here. Perhaps he'd been abducted by aliens and replaced with someone who gave a toss.

She would reserve her judgement. He was a messy so-and-so and always had been, she bet all the bedrooms weren't as nice as this. If they were, she'd be quite angry, actually. How dare he be all tidy and conscientious here, when he never was at home?

Rob led her into the room next door.

'The boys' room.' The next bedroom had two single beds. You couldn't swing or *squeeze* a cat between them and surely the boys had to crawl up from the bottom of their beds to get in, but, again, it was *tidy*. She was flabbergasted.

'And Tilly's room.' It was the other side of the narrow hallway.

Rob let her go in by herself. There probably wouldn't have been room for both of them anyway; it was tiny. A single bed, chest of drawers and wardrobe. Flat-pack. She wondered if he'd put them up himself, without swearing. The last time he'd attempted any kind of flat-pack assembly at home, he'd ended up saying the F word fifteen times and they'd had to get a man in to finish the job. She was rather proud of herself, as last week she'd put a wooden shoe rack together all on her own. No fuss, no drama, no F words. Just the help of a forum on Google and a quick call to Grace. Who needed a *man* to cock it up?

A cuddly toy Frankie didn't recognise was on top of Tilly's bed. Everything was neat and tidy, tidy and neat.

That was a line from the *Mr Men* book Rob used to read Tilly at bedtime, if he got home from work early enough. *Mr Messy*. Tilly loved it. As Rob put on a sing-song voice and described Mr Tidy and Mr Neat, who sorted out Mr Messy and made him a better person, Frankie used to stand in the doorway and laugh, thinking, 'Nothing like Rob, then.' That was before things got too bad. Before Rob became a Mr Messy who couldn't be helped.

On the bookshelf in Tilly's new room were a stack of about thirty *Mr Men* books. Square white books, all stacked together. He'd re-bought them. All of them. Her anger at his new tidiness momentarily disappeared and her eyes welled with tears. Stop it, she thought and shook them down. You wanted this. He lives somewhere else. He's bought a few books – so what?

She went back into the living room. Rob was picking up a toy car from the floor.

'It's very tidy,' said Frankie. 'Have you got a cleaner?'

'Nope.'

'Has your mum been round to tidy up?'

'No.'

'Has *my* mum been round to tidy up?'

Laughing. 'No!'

'Then how come it's so tidy?'

'I tidied it.'

'And you made the beds? I didn't know you knew how.'

'I've had to learn. I looked it up on YouTube.'

She didn't know if he was joking or not. He leant over the back of the sofa and retrieved a basket of folded washing from behind it. Everything – T-shirts, children's vests, socks – looked clean, smooth, folded. Where had this apparition of good housekeeping appeared from? Rob had always managed to crease a shirt transporting it from a hanger to his own body. How on earth was he able to materialise a whole basket full of nicely laundered clothing? As far as he was concerned, clean and pressed laundry just appeared from nowhere, done by the laundry fairy.

Rob's washing smelt nice. Different from hers. A lavender smell. *Rob's washing*. It was almost hilarious.

'And you know how to use a washing machine as well.' She realised she was sneering.

'Of course. I learnt that too. I've learnt a lot of new things,' he added, after a pause. And smiled. He held her gaze. She looked away, furious. There was a time he couldn't even tell the washing machine from the tumble dryer, let alone how to operate either of them. Why couldn't he have done any of this at home?

She glanced down to the basket and, finally depositing a now unbearably heavy Alice on the floor, picked up the corner of a clean white T-shirt.

'Did you *iron* all this?'

'Yes. Well, some of it. I've learnt a good technique. Hang straight from the machine to minimise ironing. It's a good tip.'

'I'll remember it, thanks,' she said sarcastically.

Bloody hell. He was giving her housekeeping tips. She couldn't believe it.

Alice held up a podgy little hand and said, 'Mama' and Frankie gave it a gentle squeeze, then bent down and kissed her daughter on the cheek, breathing her in. She exhaled deeply. She supposed she should be pleased Rob was coping so well, for the children's sake at least. She thought she'd be walking into a chaos of filthy-faced urchins and takeaway boxes. A social services job. But she'd got it all wrong. It was calm there. Organised. The children seemed happy. It was confusing. So, separately, they could each run a calm, ordered household, but together they were a disaster?

'Rabby,' said Alice.

'It's on your bed,' said Rob.

'I'll get it,' said Frankie.

As she walked to Rob and Alice's room, she passed a door set into the wall of the hall. A cupboard. She opened it and a football magazine immediately fell on the floor. She was surprised more didn't tumble out. The cupboard was jam-packed full of *stuff*. Toys, clothes, books, an empty cereal packet. A badminton racquet. Shoved in, rammed in. Stuffed to the absolute hilt.

He had a Monica Cupboard, like in *Friends*! A cupboard crammed full of junk to enable the immaculate apartment around it.

Weirdly, it made her smile. She felt better: he hadn't turned into a completely saintly housekeeping robot, after all. Maybe the tidiness she had witnessed was proof of some kind of *effort*, rather than some warped male Stepford transformation purely to spite her?

She went back to the living room/kitchen and gave Alice her rabbit.

'Do you want a cup of tea?' Rob said. 'I've got Hobnobs.'

She hadn't planned on stopping very long, but she felt more relaxed, somehow, now she'd seen the secret cupboard. And Hobnobs were her favourite. 'Okay.'

'And chocolate digestives. And Clubs…'

'Clubs?'

'Oh yeah, we know how to live, over here. If you like a lot of chocolate on your biscuit…' he sang.

'…join our club.'

She couldn't help but grin. God, they were both really old. They knew the same silly advert jingles. The same lines. It had always been that way. They shared the same jokes, finished each other's sentences. They had a

few stock phrases they would complete for each other,
including:

'You'll always find me…'

'…in the kitchen at parties.'

'You're terrible…'

'…Muriel.' Then, '*Mariel*,' they would both drawl in
unison, in over-exaggerated Australian accents, referring to
Muriel's more glamorous alias.

'We were on…'

'*A break.*'

How they'd laughed at that episode of *Friends*, many
moons ago. They loved *Friends*. They'd watched it every
Friday night, with a Domino's pizza, Ben and Jerry's
Funky Monkey and a bottle of Sol each with a lime
segment stuffed into the neck of the bottle. Joey's Man
Bag, Monica's Secret Closet and Ross and Rachel On
a Break. How they'd laughed. And now they were on a
break too. Frankie didn't know how Rob felt about it. She
thought, again, that he seemed pretty content. She hadn't
seen this far ahead, how he would be without her… She'd
just wanted to get away from him.

She looked at the back of his head as he turned to put the
kettle on. He'd had his hair cut. It looked neat around the
ears. He hadn't bothered getting it cut in the months before
they'd split. It had started curling round the bottom of his
ears and growing down his neck. It looked nice now, with
its not unattractive sprinkling of grey.

They'd talked about that sort of thing loads of times.
About getting old, going grey. They'd both assumed it
was something they'd do together. She'd said she would
always, *always* dye her hair, although maybe when she
was a hundred she'd let it go a soft silver. He said he was
dreading losing his hair and it going grey, and that this part
of ageing was the one women had over men – they could

dye their still-apparent hair and not look ridiculous, whilst men risked an odd, copper-coloured comb-over. She'd told him not to worry, that she liked grey hair, and if he started receding, he could just shave it all off and do a Grant Mitchell, as she found it sexy.

Rob's hair hadn't receded, but it *was* going grey. Frankie had an urge to reassure him, to say, 'Your hair looks quite sexy, all grey like that,' but she couldn't, could she? She'd dumped him.

The one thing he'd done for her, at home, was to make her the occasional cup of tea. As the kettle boiled and he rummaged in a cupboard for teabags and sugar, it was almost just like old times. She felt conflicted. She'd dumped him because he was hopeless. He was probably *still* hopeless. But, at this moment, she missed him.

He turned and smiled at her, held her gaze. The smile hung between them like the Clifton suspension bridge. They'd been there once, the day after going to a friend's wedding in Bristol. It had been a dreadful day, weather-wise, characterised by that soft summer drizzle – warm and very annoying. They had cagoules on with the hoods up. But buoyed by the romance of the wedding they'd just been to, and the fact that they'd only been married a year themselves, they had kissed at one end of the bridge. It had been a fantastic day. A fantastic kiss. And now, in Rob's new flat, it seemed that either one of them could climb that smile, that bridge, to reach the other.

After a few awkward seconds, they let the smile fall. He wasn't allowed to smile at her like that any more. They were separated. Estranged. 'My estranged husband'. What an odd phrase. It made her think of a Victorian gentleman wearing a funny hat and pulling a cat's bum face.

Rob handed her a mug of tea. She realised it was his *Fimbles* mug, from home. She hadn't noticed it had gone.

Then he reached to a high cupboard to get the Hobnobs. He'd lost a bit of weight. His jeans were hanging off his backside a bit. Was he eating properly? Proper meals? Was he feeding the children well? He must be. They certainly weren't coming back home to her like starving waifs.

'Are you eating okay?'

'What do you mean?' said Rob. 'Does my mouth work? As far as I'm aware. I don't think I've got an eating problem.' She knew he was thinking of the 'drinking problem' scene in *Airplane*, the one where the drinking problem is Ted Striker missing his mouth every time. They'd seen and loved that movie a hundred times.

'Ha, no. Are you eating properly? The right stuff? What are you giving the children?' The mood immediately changed. She was nagging.

'We're all eating properly, thank you. Me and my children. How about you? Tinned spaghetti bolognaise and Cadbury's chocolate fingers?' He knew they were her favourites, when she could eat alone and have whatever she wanted. Things that required No Cooking.

'As an occasional treat,' she lied.

'I hope you're looking after yourself, the weekends I have the children,' he said. Now *he* was nagging. His voice took on a hard edge. 'Are you going out drinking? Having a lot of "me" time?'

He was being sarcastic, with the 'me' time nonsense. She knew he hated that ridiculous phrase. Still, it put her back up. She had never had any 'me time' when they were together. None. Except five minutes in the loo, from time to time. Even then, someone was usually banging on the door, demanding something. Whereas he had all the 'me' time in the world. Even his commute to work on the trains he moaned so much about was a blissful chance to just sit and do nothing, whilst she wrestled breakfast and nappies and mess and uniforms and tea and bath and homework and reading and bedtime.

He was also fishing, she knew, about what she was doing in his absence. She knew him. He wanted to know was she going out? Meeting other men. Had she met another man? Oh dear. No way was she mentioning Hugh and all the snogging…

'It's not really any of your business,' she said coolly, bristling.

'I hope you're being careful,' he said. 'You know what I mean.' If he'd been a jolly uncle figure or Sid James, he may have winked at this point, but he didn't. He looked serious and a bit hacked off. He actually *does* think I'm going out and shagging other men, thought Frankie. And he looked bothered about it. Did *he* still fancy her?

'Of course,' she said, breezily. He could make of that what he wanted.

'Anyway, right,' he said, putting the biscuits back in the cupboard. 'So…we have plans…'

Frankie baulked. 'Oh…okay…plans, with the children? Of course. Anything nice?'

'We're going to the Natural History Museum. Going up on the train.'

'Oh, great. Fab.' They'd all wanted to go. *She'd* wanted to go. They'd talked about going this year, in the summer holidays. He knew that.

'So, what are *you* up to today?' He wasn't going to invite her, then. For a family outing. It would just be the five of them.

'Oh, plans, as well, you know. Things to do…places to see…'

'Okay. Well, have fun,' said Rob. He was actually ushering her to his front door. His clean, white front door.

He'd even thought to buy a mat, too. It was all brown and unsullied. It said 'Welcome', like this was a proper home.

Before she knew it, she was outside his door and it had been shut – shut on him and his weekend with their children.

She stood for a second, like you do when you suddenly think of the perfect retort for a conversation you left ten minutes ago, then she turned and walked down the stairs.

CHAPTER FIFTEEN:
GRACE

Greg was waiting under a tree. A temporary outdoor rink, for the spring and summer, had been set up in the beautiful surroundings of Admirals Park, on the edge of Chelmsford. It was the prettiest rink Grace had ever seen. Her teenage roller-skating excursions had been to orange-lit hell holes with neon plastic everywhere. Here the rink was surrounded by trees and summer blooms. How scenic and civilised. Lovely. And it was the most perfect early May day – warm, with a gentle breeze, and not a cloud in the sky.

Greg was wearing jeans, black trainers and a black and white checked short-sleeved shirt, which showed off his great forearms. His dishwater blond hair was…perfect. His eyes flickered with merriment when he first spotted Grace and his lovely mouth broke into a grin. She'd made an effort with her appearance too. Skinny jeans. A long pale blue vest with a long white vest layered over the top. White canvas sneakers. She wanted to look cute.

She had sneaked out of the house again, this time via the overgrown back alley behind her house she'd forgotten about until she'd started lying to everyone. The path was so overgrown she had to keep high-stepping over stinging nettles and she kept her arms clamped to her sides so they didn't get wrenched by brambles. She'd managed to make it unscathed.

'What on earth have you got me doing?' said Greg, as she neared him.

'Sorry!' She laughed. 'It'll be fun, I promise.'

'Please don't tell me you're a British champion at this or something.'

'No,' she replied, drinking in his gorgeous face. He looked amazing. He wore the casual look as well as he wore a dinner suit. 'I used to love it as a teenager, though. Hopefully I can remember what to do.'

She'd booked him for roller-skating and it had taken her a while to decide to do it. After Nana McKensie's theatre evening, she'd been a little freaked by how attached she'd got to Greg. She'd cringed when she'd remembered leaning her head on his shoulder on the train and clinging to him at the train station. She hadn't contacted him for a few weeks and had been proud of her willpower. Then James had collected Daniel, last night, and had said, while Daniel was getting in the car, 'No sign of that bloke again, then? Has he dumped you?' and after they'd gone Grace had sent Greg a text and asked him when he was free.

She'd had to go out last night. On her own. It was an evening drinks do at the school, a fundraising cheese and wine night. Every year she and James had gone together. She'd been frightened about going alone. She'd had a brief moment when she'd considered booking Greg for that as well, but luckily she'd had the sense to dismiss the idea as complete and utter madness.

It had actually been okay. She had felt so daunted walking in as a single parent amongst all those couples she knew, all those lucky people who were still together, but it had been absolutely fine. She'd been most nervous about answering the question, 'Where's James?' but she'd coped with it rather well. To some people she'd just said James was 'busy'; to others, including the headmistress – a matronly jolly hockey-sticks type with a Louise Brooks, silent movie bob – she'd said, 'We're separated.' The headmistress hadn't batted an eyelid.

'Well, splendid,' she'd said. 'Good for you,' which had left Grace quite taken aback. Still, she was amazed at herself. She'd happily spent the evening in a circle of mum friends whose husbands had formed a rumbling pack at the bar, and had had a pretty good time.

Greg stepped towards her and kissed her on the cheek. They stood grinning at each other. They made a lovely couple. Anyone looking at them would have said so. Look at them! They were a hot couple out enjoying themselves: she was as far from a heartbroken, slightly desperate single mother paying a male escort to do things with her that her husband had never wanted to, as you could imagine. She must play it cooler with him today, she thought. No more clinging.

'Oh God,' groaned Greg sardonically as they handed over their shoes at the outdoor counter and were given heavy, multi-coloured skates with unfathomable laces.

'Think of it as a kind of initiation.' Grace giggled. 'I'm preparing you for all the weird and wonderful things you'll have to do as an escort.'

'But I'm really looking forward to Ascot!' joked Greg.

As well as booking Greg for roller-skating, Grace had booked him for a day's racing at Royal Ascot in June. Every year she sent dozens of lucky women off to the races in beautiful hats. This year *she* was going. She'd bought the tickets – Saturday the 20th of June – and had booked their train fares. She couldn't wait.

'Come on then,' Greg said, grabbing her hand. 'If you want roller-skating, I'll give you roller-staking. I can't guarantee I won't fall flat on my bum, though.'

'Now that I'd like to see,' she laughed.

He was actually good, really, really good. She found it hard to keep up with him.

'You've done this before,' she shouted after him. 'Cheat!'

'I didn't *actually* say I hadn't done it before,' he called over his right shoulder as he sped in front of her looking annoyingly graceful and accomplished. All he needed were knee and elbow pads and a pair of giant headphones and it could be 1982.

There was a boy in a lime green T-shirt, who kept staggering right across the middle of the rink. Everyone was avoiding him. On his next foray to the centre, chopping along like a stilted flamingo, Grace had the misfortune to be coming out of the bend. She saw he was in her path, tried to swerve to avoid him, but he lurched the same way and they collided. His splaying, Bambi legs went under hers, upending her, and she landed with a painful thwack on her bottom. She didn't have the best padding there. James always said she had a scrawny backside. Her eyes sprang with tears, which she rapidly blinked away. Greg, swooping by, came to a professional-looking gliding stop by them.

'I'm all right,' spluttered the kid, and he grappled to his feet and lolloped over to the side of the rink. Greg grabbed both Grace's hands and pulled her up, while she had an urge to pull him down on the rink and just lie there with him for a while, in the sun. Greg looked over to where the annoying kid was hanging off the side rail.

'You sure you're okay?' he called out.

'Yes, I'm okay,' shouted the boy, fiercely brushing away tears with his fist.

'Where's your mum?' called Greg.

He pointed to a woman at the other side of the rink. She'd seen the kerfuffle and was standing up from a camping chair and gesturing for the boy to come to her. Then, to Grace's horror, she looked towards Greg and Grace and her face froze with recognition. Not at seeing Grace, but at seeing *Greg*. She smiled, shyly, then looked away, back to the boy, who was making his way over to her.

'Do you know her?' asked Grace, her heart chilled and afraid.

Yes,' said Greg, in a way that decisively said, 'Don't ask any more,' and Grace immediately knew she was a client. *Another* client of his. It made her feel ill. He'd been busy in the last few weeks, then.

'Okay,' she said, lightly. But as she took to the rink again for another circuit, she purposely skated past the woman, her heart pounding, and slyly studied her. She was plain. With brown hair, and wearing a navy T-shirt and some sort of beige trousers. She looked…ordinary. Mousey. She didn't look like a woman who hired male escorts.

Grace had a million questions for him. Where had he taken her? What did they do? What was she like? Was she nice? Was she married? What did they *do*? She knew she shouldn't be asking any of them; it was none of her business. So she asked just one, the one she really wanted to know the answer to. She caught him up and pulled at his arm.

'Have you had sex with her?' She felt sick as she said the words.

'Gosh!' he said. 'You can't ask questions like that! Here, of all places. Think of the children! And,' he dropped his voice to a smiling whisper, 'I don't know who you're talking about.'

'You know exactly who I'm talking about. That woman. So have you?' She *had* to know.

'That would be telling. If I told you, I'd have to kill you.'

'Very funny. Can't you just tell me without killing me afterwards? *The Apprentice* is on tonight.' She was attempting to smile but it hurt her.

Greg sighed. 'If you must know, no I haven't. I haven't slept with a client yet.'

She was stupidly pleased. Relieved. She took off away from him. Started to glide. She felt satisfyingly warm, but at the same time there was a nice breeze going through her hair. A song she loved was on – 'Breakfast at Tiffany's' by Deep Blue Something. She'd loved that song when she was young, when her life still stretched out before her, unwritten. She felt strangely free, at this moment. Free of James, free of stress and misery.

After her third lap, she realised she didn't know where Greg was. Oh, there he was. Over at one of the side railings, sandwiched between a gangly teenager and a little girl with neon safety pads on.

'You were enjoying yourself,' he said.

'I was.'

'Shall we get a drink?'

'Okay.'

There were some wooden trestle tables round the edge of the rink. They sat at one, in dappled sunlight, and as leaves rustled gently in the trees above them, they drank from Coke bottles with straws. She'd paid for them, of course.

'So how is it all going, with your ex?' They were sitting across from each other. Grace hoped the dappled sunlight was flattering, like candlelight. She remembered he had called her gorgeous, after their first date, and wanted him to think it again.

'He's being pretty awful still,' she said, 'but it's okay. *I'll* be okay.'

'You deserve more,' said Greg. His hands were wrapped round his Coke bottle. He was tapping one of his index fingers on it. 'I know we don't know each other very well, but I'm certain you do. I think you're a lovely person.'

'I bet you say that to all the girls, women, whoever.' She laughed.

'No, actually. I'm saying it to you.'

She lowered her eyes, suddenly bashful. And, yet again, she wished she was on a real date with him. That he'd asked her out. That he'd *chosen* her, not that she picked him up online for a fee. But then James had chosen her, James had asked her out – that winter's day when he'd wandered into John Lewis and she'd helped him pick out a hat for his mum – and look how *that* had worked out. It was better this way.

'Thank you, Greg. Where do I send the cheque?'

He laughed. They both knew it was bank transfer.

'Anyway,' she said, 'how do you know I'm lovely? I might be awful. It might all just be an act.'

'I'm a good judge of character,' he replied. 'I just know. Right,' he said, draining the last of his Coke. 'One final spin on the ring of death?'

As they skated a final circuit, he slipped his hand into hers. His hand was warm, firm, comforting. She felt secure. Holding hands at the roller-skating rink! They were like a teenage couple. Or a grown-up couple enjoying a silly afternoon of childhood nostalgia. Except they weren't any kind of couple, were they? One of them was soon going to be having sex with women for money and the other was a sad woman in her thirties who had only this – dates with a male escort – to cling to.

Don't forget, she told herself, it's all false.

But it was better that way.

CHAPTER SIXTEEN:
IMOGEN

Imogen closed her desk drawer and sighed for about the two hundredth time that week. She was alone in the office – Marcia was out for a 'blue sky meeting' with Tarquin, whatever that was. It probably involved a big old nosh-up and several bottles of plonk. Tarquin was on the brink of a second audition with *EastEnders* and Marcia had gone off with a book on cockney rhyming slang and a leather jacket catalogue.

Imogen's sighs were deep and huffy, often accompanied by an unhappy shrug of the shoulders. Thoughts of her aborted lunch with Richard – even after six weeks – were driving her crazy.

She felt so ashamed about running out on him like that. She was mortified she'd fled after he'd kissed her. But she'd had to. The man, the kiss… She had to run, and run for her life. She'd wrestled with it for weeks, but the truth was – and the truth really, *really* hurt – she was in love with Richard.

Damn, damn, damn – this was *not* supposed to happen. She had been in love once before and it had been catastrophic.

When she told people she didn't date actors it wasn't strictly true. When she was nineteen, and working at her first agency, she careered from her sensible path of finding a 'great man' and embarked on a passionate, whirlwind two-month love affair with an actor called Sebastian. Yes, 'The Blip'. He was twenty-five. He was long-haired and ambitious. Wildly romantic. Impoverished and poetic. All the clichés. She'd fallen hard, she thought he had too, and she didn't doubt he loved her ('You're the one for me, Immy,' he always said, while brushing his hair from his eyes), but there was a problem. She wasn't the *only* one. Sebastian was enjoying a rather large 'overlap' with a ballerina who was away training in St Petersburg. A woman he called 'incredibly special' and didn't want to give up, no matter how hard Imogen begged. He'd had to choose, eventually, and he hadn't chosen Imogen. She'd been devastated. Absolutely devastated. She'd cried for five months, she'd sworn she'd never fall in love again. She wouldn't let herself. And she never told anyone about Sebastian.

Sebastian was the reason Imogen had done a one hundred and eighty degree turn and gone for a completely different type of man. Businessmen, city types, the Good on Paper men who could love her and make perfect husbands, but not hurt her. They couldn't be further from the starving artiste in the garret, the *act-or* who pretended she was the only one. They were the safe choice who would ultimately disappoint her. Until Richard.

Richard was right, wasn't he? She *was* the common denominator, but not in the way he'd meant. It wasn't that she'd turned all her ex-men into disappointments; they were disappointments right from the start because she knew she was never going to fall in love with them. That's why she picked them. None of them were *ever* going to be amazing.

Now Richard had come along and turned everything on its head. Her plan of safe smooth sailing with a man she couldn't love had been chucked over the side of the boat.

With Richard, she was on uncharted waters, but all the same she knew how it would go. She would love him and he would leave her. The fact that he lived in New York made it even more probable.

She couldn't put herself into someone's hands like that again. When she was dropped she knew it would be unbearable. With Sebastian it took her for ever to get over the hurt. She'd only been nineteen then, think how much harder she'd fall, how much harder she'd hurt now. Better to not see Richard again. Better to put him out of her mind. Keep well away. She could do this. She could resist. There. No Men. No Richard. Done. It was easy.

That's what she'd decided and she was determined to stick to it, however much she huffed, and however much it went round and round in her head like knickers in a washing machine. She'd ignored Richard's texts and calls until they petered to nothing and she felt empty and sad. She valiantly tried to erase him from her mind. On several occasions, especially after a few drinks, she had to sit on her hands to stop herself from calling him.

Imogen sighed again and stared blankly at her computer screen.

There was a clatter and a shuffle. Marcia was back, Tarquin ambling into the office behind her. They were both clearly three sheets to the wind. Marcia was doing that over-exaggerated shushing thing, a stubby finger to her lips. Their neighbouring office was an acupuncture treatment room – Marcia had been told off by them before, for loud screeching when someone was having their chakras or something done.

Once the pair of them were in, and the door was closed, the finger went down and the volume went up.

'Tarqy, darling,' she boomed, 'be careful now. Keep a safe distance from Imogen – she's put a hex on all men.'

Imogen, ignoring her, walked over to the tiny sink they had, and started pouring two large glasses of water. They looked in dire need of them.

'You're both drunk,' she accused, taking on that old classic role of Superior Sober Person. 'Did you get all the *EastEnders* stuff done?'

'We're Mitchells; you don't mess wiv no Mitchells,' growled Tarquin, showing his perfect, upper-class teeth and advancing towards Imogen in what he probably thought was a menacing manner. She shoved a glass of water into his hand.

'Good, *great*.' She nodded. 'Well, it's in the bag, certainly.'

Marcia threw her giant handbag on her desk and plomped down on her chair. The force of it made several papers on her desk waft onto the floor. She left them there. Then she grabbed her Dictaphone and went over to the window where she started whispering manically into it. It was a stream of near unconsciousness but Imogen could make out the odd thing: 'doof doof', 'Prince Albert' and 'faaamily'.

Tarquin tried to plonk his bottom on Marcia's vacated chair but missed and landed on the floor. Instead of trying to get up, he threw both legs in the air and pushed his bum up with his hands like he was attempting a move from BAGA 4.

'What on earth have you been drinking?' said Imogen.

'Two bottles of vino blanco and a round of flaming Sambucas,' said Marcia, returning to her desk.

'At lunchtime?'

'Oh, don't be such an old killjoy,' said Marcia, leaning on her desk for balance. 'You and me used to get hammered all the time, in the good old bad old days. Just because you're *over forty* –' she sneered, doing quotation marks with her fingers '– there's no reason to be so *boring*.'

Marcia was fifty-eight. Age was definitely just a number to her and the more the number increased the less attention she paid to what society expected of it. If society wanted a demure middle-class lady, they weren't going to get it.

'Imogen's become dull, dull, dull,' continued Marcia, suddenly sitting on the trunk where they filed contracts. She swung one black opaque leg over so she was astride it, like a child on a Trunki. 'She's practically a *nun*! She's not *having* any men.'

Imogen froze at the word 'nun'. She remembered her silly conversation with Richard, at the lunch. Before it had all gone wrong. Damn it, she should never have gone.

She wished she'd stayed.

'Not having any men,' muttered Tarquin, to no one in particular, then added, 'we had the cheese board. A nice bit of Stilton.'

'She *hates* men,' said Marcia.

Imogen regretted, not for the first time, telling Marcia about Grace and Frankie and the year of being single. Back in February, she and Marcia had spent a very entertaining evening at the Savoy Grill, despite Marcia's claim she was now highly boring, when she'd enjoyed a glass of wine too many and told Marcia how they'd all sworn off men. Marcia had thumped her own leg in hooting laughter all night long, thinking it the funniest thing she'd ever heard. Her co-agent had got loads of mileage out of it since. If it was the equivalent of an ever-rechargeable electric car, Marcia was constantly zooming up the M6 on it, with Britney Spears in the CD player. Every time anyone vaguely male came into the office Marcia made a cross with her fingers and held them up in front of her mock-disgusted face, each time Imogen went out to meet a male actor, Marcia would hand her an old key she had in her desk 'to lock her chastity belt with'.

'I don't *hate* men,' protested Imogen, and not for the first time. 'I just think I could do without one.' I *know* I can do without one, she said to herself. She was right to walk away from Richard, very right. She was safer going it alone.

'Did you know Tarquin dries his entire body hair with a hairdryer every morning?' said Marcia, apropos of nothing. She was now doing a silent 'oops upside your head' on the trunk.

'No,' said Imogen. 'How interesting.' What a nice vision, she thought. Tarquin stark naked in his bedroom directing a Remington at his furry bits. Yuk! But, hey, this was good: revolting images of men – good, good. More reason to be off them, she thought. More reason to be off Richard.

Then, against her will, a vision came to her of Richard naked with a hairdryer. Uh-oh – he looked great. Better than great. He looked *magnificent*. Strong, hairy, resplendent, his gorgeous chest hair oscillating under the hot, hot air of the dryer as he prepared himself for another gorgeous Richard day, a day where he'd be simultaneously rescuing kittens, ending national debt and re-insuring the globe. Damn him! Perhaps she shouldn't have fled from his office, perhaps she should have let him kiss her for the rest of the day.

Tarquin did an almighty burp, which brought Imogen back to earth with a bump. A boozy, slightly blue cheese, slightly aniseed smell was issuing from his direction. She knew if she lit a match in front of his mouth the whole of Soho would go up in flames. The pair of them were incorrigible. Marcia – now slumped over her desk and snoring – would be useless for the rest of the afternoon and Tarquin was just plain useless full stop. After fifteen minutes and a not inconsiderable effort getting them out of the office and down the stairs – during which a diminutive acupuncturist popped her head out of a door and told them to shut up – Imogen packed them off in a taxi.

She returned to her desk, ready to enjoy another good sigh and shrug, when a text message flashed up on her phone. She picked it up quickly. Richard. Oh my God. Her heart leapt up to her chin. She started shaking.

Hey Imogen, you're driving me nuts here. I can't give up on you. I want to see you. Don't be a berk, come to Ascot with me?

Despite herself, she burst out laughing. He was so funny. He was so great. She had that image of him naked again, saving the world. She didn't want to be dull and boring and fearful.

Before she could stop herself, Imogen took a deep breath and tapped words into her phone.

Hi, you duffer. I'd love to.

CHAPTER SEVENTEEN:
FRANKIE

'I love you, too! Now *get on with your homework*!'

Kids, muttered Frankie to herself with a shake of the head and a smile – how she loved them, how they drove her round the bend. She returned from shouting at the bottom of the stairs and bunged a handful of cutlery and a roll of kitchen towel on the dining room table. Grace and Imogen were coming over for pizza tonight. Takeaway pizza. They would never expect her to cook for them. She would hate to have to provide napkins and side plates and decorum. They were such *great* friends. She was ever so sorry she was secretly lying to them about keeping away from men for a year.

The doorbell rang. It was Grace, with Daniel, and a green salad with feta and mango. Daniel took off his trainers and charged up the stairs to cries of 'Daniel! My maaan!' from Josh, in an over-the-top American accent.

'Oh, you're a classy cow,' said Frankie, pleased, as Grace came in. Her more domestic friend could be relied on to spruce up proceedings to a respectable standard and often supplemented Frankie's credit card suppers with a little non-plastic yumminess. Frankie took the salad from her and put it in the fridge. 'You know how lazy I am,' she said. 'You'll be lucky if I get plates out.'

'No problem,' said Grace. 'Daniel helped me make it.'

'Did he?' said Frankie. 'Wow.' *Her* children had helped her this evening by scattering football cards all over the sitting room floor, doing multiple wees in the toilets without flushing a single one away and trampling mud from the back garden all up the hall.

The four of them had been banished upstairs. Alice and Tilly to bed and Josh and Harry to their rooms, to do their homework until Daniel arrived. Frankie didn't think much homework – if any – had gone on. For the last half an hour all she'd heard was distant squealing and the thwack of cardboard on cardboard. Now there was just the noise of what she called 'thundering around'.

'New shoes?' said Frankie, to Imogen as she arrived. She'd brought Prosecco and a *huge* smile and was wearing a stunning pair of black and white court shoes, the ones with the black tips on the toes and the nice stitching. 'Uh-oh! Got something to tell us? You always buy new shoes when you've got a new man! You're not doing the dirty on us, are you?'

'No!' said Imogen, stepping into Frankie's hall and nearly tripping over a skateboard that had been left on the floor. 'How dare you! No, I'm going to Ascot in a few weeks. I'm wearing them in.'

'Ascot?' said Grace, casually, appearing in the doorway to the kitchen with a glass of white wine in her hand. 'You're going to Ascot? Which day?'

'The 20th, the Saturday,' sighed Imogen, with an over-exaggerated grimace. 'Corporate thing, *again*, with a load of luvvies. It'll probably be *deathly* dull.'

'Will you be in a box?' asked Grace, with a slight cough. She was fiddling with her hair and sipping her wine. She tipped the glass too quickly and some dribbled down her chin. 'Oops,' she said, pulling a folded tissue from the back pocket of her jeans.

'Yeah, stuck in a stuffy, boring box with a load of screeching morons,' replied Imogen. 'What fun! Still the food will probably be good. Speaking of which, double pepperoni tonight, Franks?'

'Of course,' said Frankie. 'Let's see these shoes, then.' She couldn't wear heels – they crippled her after five minutes – but enjoyed cooing over Imogen's. Imogen sat on a kitchen chair and held one leg aloft. Frankie ran a finger over the stitching.

'Wow! Bloody hell, Imogen! They're amazing.'

'Gorgeous,' agreed Grace.

'Thanks,' said Imogen, flicking her foot from left to right as she admired them. 'If I'm going to be bored out of my brain I may as well look fab doing it.' She grinned.

'Hey, Grace, didn't you say you were going somewhere on the 20th of June?' said Frankie.

'Er, yes,' said Grace.

'Where you off to?' asked Imogen, looking up.

'Magical mystery tour,' said Grace quietly, 'with Taekwondo.'

'There's a combination of words you don't hear every day!' Imogen laughed. 'How wonderfully old-fashioned! So you've really no idea where you're going?'

'None whatsoever,' said Grace. She looked quite miserable at the prospect, thought Frankie. Why on earth was she going then?

'I bet it's Stratford-on-Avon,' Frankie said, opening Imogen's Prosecco. 'My nan's Magical Mysteries were always Stratford.'

'Yes, it probably is,' said Grace. 'Yes, I bet it's Stratford.' She smiled, but her smile looked slightly forced, Frankie noted. Still miserable over James, poor girl, she surmised. She hoped this trip would cheer her up. 'I've always wanted to see where Shakespeare was born.'

'*Have* you?' said Imogen.

'I know I'm not always at the Globe watching some up-and-coming playing a randy, naked Coriolanus,' said Grace, 'but I *have* read some Shakespeare, you know.'

'I'm sure you have, honey,' said Imogen, touching her lightly on the arm. 'We've all read the bloody stuff. And *anus* is the right word.' She giggled. 'I've seen far too many naked arses with a sword in their hands. Right, Franks, what time's our dinner turning up?'

'So what have you been doing recently?' asked Frankie, to Imogen, as she dropped plates into the dishwasher. 'You've been really quiet. I haven't been receiving my usual stream of hysterical texts.'

'That's because I'm not dating, darling,' said Imogen, sitting at the table and examining her nails. They looked newly done – a soft peach, immaculate. 'It's just been work, work, work. I've been throwing myself into it feet first.'

'Difficult, in the shoes you wear, I should imagine.' Frankie smiled. 'Is it all still going well?'

'Oh tremendously well.' Imogen beamed. 'Marcia's a scream and I've got *loads* of clients now.'

'No new hunky actors you've been tempted by?'

'No. Ugh, God no! Absolutely no one I'm remotely tempted by. *Remotely*.' Frankie and Grace raised their eyebrows at each other. Was the lady protesting too much?

'Does that mean there is?' teased Frankie.

'No!' said Imogen, slightly huffily. Frankie let it lie. She knew that Imogen *never* dated actors. Why would she start now, when she was on a Man Ban?

'How's it all going with you, Grace?' said Frankie. 'With James? Is he still being unreliable or have things calmed down now?'

'No, he's still being unreliable,' said Grace. She took Frankie's plates out of the dishwasher, rinsed them, then put them back in again. Frankie let her get on with it. She knew such stuff was a comfort to her.

'He's such a loser,' said Imogen. 'You're feeling better about him now though, right?' she asked. 'It's been, what, four months?'

'Much, much better, thank you,' said Grace.

'Is the Taekwondo helping?' enquired Frankie. 'You know, beating six bells out of people. Or chopping them with your hands, or whatever it is you do.'

'Yes,' said Grace, smiling. 'Chopping people with my hands is really helping.'

'How was the tournament?' Frankie said.

'The tournament?'

'Wasn't there a tournament a few Saturdays ago? You were out all afternoon.'

'You been twitching curtains again?'

'Twitching my nets? You know I'm always twitching my nets!'

'Yes, the tournament was great, thank you.'

'Let's see some moves, then.'

'What?'

'Show us some moves!'

'No! Don't be silly! I'm not showing you any moves!'

'Come on,' said Frankie, standing up and grabbing Grace by the hands. 'Hi-ya!' she shouted, like Miss Piggy and started doing kung-fu fighting arm waving.

'No!' insisted Grace, quite firmly. She shook Frankie's hands off hers. 'I'm going to the loo.'

'I still can't see Grace doing martial arts, can you?' queried Frankie, once she'd left the room.

'It's self-defence, isn't it?' said Imogen, shrugging. 'It's exactly what she needs.'

'Mmm,' said Frankie. 'I guess so. So, have you *really* not met anyone, or not even got your eye on anyone?'

'Frankie, I have no plans to let the sisterhood down!' said Imogen. 'I'm a new woman these days. A new woman with no man. And I've never felt better.' Imogen tossed her hair like a marauding pony and gulped down a mouthful of wine.

Such *strong* women, Frankie thought. Grace with her Taekwondo, Imogen with her fabulous new job and new lease of life. Strong, single women. And there was her with her guilty little secret. Wouldn't they be shocked if she told them about Hugh! The man with more than a passing resemblance to Willoughby from *Sense and Sensibility* (she was working her way through all the Austen hotties, in her mind) who she snogged with abandon every other Sunday. Notice how no one asked *her* if she'd met a new man. She was tempted to put it out there, just for the shock value.

'How are kids coping with everything?' asked Imogen. 'Are they happy with the whole alternate weekends thing?'

'They seem to be,' replied Frankie. She hadn't noticed any problems since she and Rob had split. Alice and Tilly were as happy and as loving as ever and there'd been a parents' evening at Harry and Josh's school on Monday night, and they were both doing really well. Extremely well, in fact. It had all run late as it always did – she and Rob had to stand by the stage underneath a mural of The Great War and chat for twenty minutes while they waited for Miss Capron to stop talking to Alfie Donaldson's mum. They'd grinned at each other a couple of times while the teachers talked to them about their boys' achievements. Rob had winked at her when Mr Butler said, for the fifth time, that Josh was 'spirited'. Once upon a time they would have held hands at these evenings, although those days were a long, long time ago. 'No problems at home, no problems at school.' Frankie was proud how well her children had adjusted to it, actually. Although they could still drive her mad.

'Well that's fab.'

Grace came back from the loo. 'I'm doing one of those wedding fairs this weekend,' she announced.

'The ones James wouldn't let you do?' said Imogen. 'How come?'

Grace had often mentioned how James insisted on weekends being for 'family time' and he didn't want her working, and how Gideon had always been sniffy about it but secretly thoroughly enjoyed being a martyr by doing the wedding fairs on his own. 'Gideon's got to go to a civil ceremony in Cornwall. He's reluctantly handing over the reins to me.'

'How exciting!'

'Not really. I'm really nervous. I won't have a clue what I'm doing!'

'Oh, you'll be fine!' said Frankie. 'Do you want me to pop in? For moral support? I'm on my own this weekend. I can start raving about the hats and pretending to buy them all or something? Come with me, Imogen, it'll be a scream!'

'I can't, I'm afraid,' said Imogen. 'I promised I'd take Mum into town.'

'Ah, shame. Well I can drop in, can't I, Grace?'

'I'd love it if you did,' said Grace, although Frankie thought Grace looked less than enthusiastic. 'I'm feeling so jittery about it.'

'Perfect. I can pretend to be a bossy older bride and create a bit of a buzz. Right, I reckon the pizza's gone down by now. Shall we break out the chocolates?'

CHAPTER EIGHTEEN: GRACE

James would have hated this, Grace thought, as she climbed the steps to The Finch Rooms with several huge bags of hat boxes and cellophane-wrapped bridal headpieces and fascinators. When they'd got married, he'd half-heartedly gone along with the whole wedding planning thing – florists and caterers and photography studios and cake-makers – but had hardly thrown himself into it. Far 'too girly', he would have said, about wedding fairs. 'Full of giddy women with no taste and too much money to spend.'

She was glad it was being held here and not at some giant aircraft hangar of a conference centre. The Finch Rooms was a large Georgian house, set in picturesque grounds, with dozens of small, fabulously decorated rooms for people to wander in and out of. It was a perfect venue for small weddings, although a marquee could be attached at the back of the house for larger receptions. She remembered she'd looked round it when she and James had got married, before they'd plumped for Huntingdon Manor.

Directed to a small drawing room at the rear of the house – a carpeted square with a large sash window and duck egg wallpaper – she began setting up. She'd brought a dozen or so hatstands, but also utilised the gorgeous shelving units either side of the huge marble fireplace. Gideon had never trusted her with the displays in the shop. She always had to stand by as he executed his artistic flair, and coo enough times to satisfy him as he arranged and rotated hats and headpieces and faffed with ribbons and bits of lace. Now it was her turn, and she didn't think she'd done a bad job. She stepped back and admired her handiwork. Actually, she'd done a *great* job. She could create a beautiful display of hats.

Grace's silent moment of satisfaction was short-lived. A girl wearing a short sixties-style dress and black opaque tights, despite the balmy June weather, bashed noisily into the room with a folded-up table under one arm and a massive long, flat cardboard box under the other. She had dyed crimson hair scraped into a top-knot and appeared to be wearing slippers.

'Hi, I'm Nancy,' she said breathlessly. She expertly opened up the table with her knee, dropped the box to the floor and began to pull from it large pieces of lace and sheaths of gorgeous cream and white embossed wedding stationery. She fanned out the stationery on the lace then studded the arrangement with artfully placed fountain pens. It was a very romantic-looking display.

'Your stationery is beautiful,' said Grace, walking over and taking a closer look.

'Thanks. People seem to like it.'

'It must sell itself!'

'Well, I have to do a bit of sales patter. Spin the whole *marriage is wonderful* line.'

She pulled a face. Grace almost wanted to shush her. You couldn't speak like that at a wedding fair! 'Oh. You don't think it is?'

Nancy smiled wryly. 'No! Not since my fiancé left me at the altar. But, hey, it's fine. I went off on our honeymoon by myself and ended up spending two years backpacking around South East Asia.'

'Oh, okay.' Grace didn't know what else to say.

'But people keep doing it, don't they? Marriage. The daft beggars. I can't stop them, so I may as well earn a crust helping them. It's not my fault I design incredible wedding stationery!' She laughed. 'Hey, I like your hats and stuff.'

'Thank you. I'm a bit nervous. I've not done one of these before.'

'Oh, you'll be fine. Just take a deep breath and tell yourself you can do it.' She smiled and adjusted one of her fans of envelopes, then glanced at Grace's left hand, and her wedding ring. 'You're married?' Grace realised she'd been unselfconsciously twiddling with it while they'd been talking.

'Separated.' There, she'd said it again. She'd said it at the school do and no one had dropped to the floor in a dead faint or clamped their hand to their mouth in horror. The headmistress hadn't exploded in shock. Nancy looked delighted.

'Great! It's so much fun being single, isn't it?'

'I hate it, actually,' said Grace. 'I like being with someone.'

'Have you got kids?' Gosh, this woman was blunt. She had a slight accent; Grace wondered if she was Australian.

'A son.'

'Well, you'll never be on your own, then.'

What a strange woman she was. 'Actually I like having a man in my life.'

'Oh.' Nancy frowned. 'Are you seeing someone?' As though it were a huge betrayal to womankind.

'Yes.' Not that it was any of her business.

'You jumped out of the frying pan into the fire?'

Grace was about to respond about it being a very nice fire and in any case it *really* was none of her business, when a young couple, hand in hand, came into the room and went straight to 'ooh' and 'aah' over Nancy's beautiful stationery. Nancy started talking to them in a new, high voice about romance and how the more expensive the card, the more sincere the wedding vows…

A couple of hours went past. The room was a hive of activity. Nancy had a constant stream of couples; Grace had plenty of brides and mothers-of-the-bride, plus six texts from Gideon demanding to know how she was getting on.

Fabulously, she replied, to each and every one of them.

At lunchtime, she had the shock of her life.

'Hello, Grace.'

Oh God, it was Greg. He was standing in the doorway in jeans and a white polo shirt, smiling and looking absolutely gorgeous. His hair had seen a bit of gel and it looked like he had new shoes on. What the hell was he doing here? She'd mentioned she was doing this today, when they'd chatted by text last night, but why on earth had he turned up?

She blushed crimson down to her toes.

'What are you doing here, Greg?'

'Sorry, I didn't mean to disturb you. I was in the area. I've been to see a mate. I thought I'd call in and see how you were doing.' She blushed even more. It was so clearly a lie, he *so* wasn't just in the area! He'd just wanted to see her, hadn't he? She beamed at him, feeling monumentally excited. He really liked her. He just wanted to *see* her! Nancy glanced over from showing an eager couple some save-the-date cards and raised a pierced eyebrow.

'Well, I'm doing very well, thank you,' said Grace.

'Great, great. Glad to hear it.' Greg went over to one of the shelves. He picked up a peach cloche and, grinning at her, plonked it on the top of his head. He put it down again and reached for a fascinator dripping with pearls and jet black beads. 'So, Grace –'

'Ah, *here* are those fabulous hats I've been hearing all about!'

Oh my God. It was Frankie, dressed up like a character from an Oscar Wilde play. She had about four scarves draped round her neck, was dangling the handbag she usually thrust over her shoulder on the end of an extended wrist and had half her face obscured by huge, fashion magazine editor sunglasses. She took off the glasses, winked theatrically at Grace, then flew over to a hatstand to examine a white trilby with silver ribbon. 'Beautiful hats!' she exclaimed, in an over-loud voice. Grace, horrified, tried frantically to shoot a warning glance at Greg, but he had the fascinator on and was checking out his reflection in one of the dozen mirrors Grace had propped up. He didn't notice her exaggerated head flicks and darting, warning eyes. Nancy did. She was obviously trying hard to conceal a laugh.

'I think this is really me, Grace,' said Greg, turning round.

Frankie's head also shot round, at lightning speed. One of her scarves – butterfly-printed chiffon – whacked her in the face. She stared at Greg. Greg froze. Grace froze. Even the couple at Nancy's table froze. Nancy had a very mischievous look on her face.

'Is there anything in particular you're looking for, *Frankie*?' stammered Grace.

'Aw, you're not supposed to know my name!' said Frankie, her high, silly voice abandoned. 'How can I be your mystery shopper and big you up if you say you know me! Don't blow my cover! Who's this?' She was still looking directly at Greg.

'This is Michael, one of our suppliers,' said Grace quickly.

'Yes, hello, I'm Michael,' said Greg. 'I supply…er… pearls. From the Indian Ocean.'

'That's right,' said Grace. 'Michael was just popping in to see how his fascinators are selling.'

'Yes,' said Greg, 'my fascinating fascinators. They're… marvellous.'

'Pearls from the Indian Ocean, eh?' said Frankie. 'Very flash.'

'We try our best,' said Greg.

'Right, Michael, so you said you had your next appointment to get to…?' said Grace.

'Yes, absolutely, better get going. People to see, pearls to…erm…sell.'

And Greg removed the fascinator, gave a short bow and left the room.

'Blimey,' said Frankie, her eyes flashing. 'He's gorgeous!'

'Michael? Yes, he's not bad.'

'Not bad! He's an absolute dreamboat. Is he single? Why don't you ask him out? Can *I* ask him out?'

'I'm *single*, remember. For a whole year. Just like *you*.' Frankie looked momentarily sheepish. 'We're not supposed to be asking anyone out. And he's probably gay.'

'He doesn't *look* gay.'

'How would you know? Your gaydar's absolutely rubbish.'

'True.' Frankie nodded. 'But, wow. You should definitely find out if he is or not, next time he comes calling, with his *pearls*.'

'I'm single for a year,' said Grace. 'Don't deter me from my path.'

Frankie stayed for the next couple of hours and had great fun flitting in and out, and squealing at hats when there were customers around, and generally being quite annoying. Grace sent her packing fifteen minutes before the end of the day and she and Nancy started packing up their stalls.

'See,' said Nancy, putting paper and envelopes into her lidded box. 'You did it. You did it on your own.'

'Yes, I did,' replied Grace, carefully placing hats back into boxes, using fresh tissue paper. She was very happy with the way the day had gone.

'That was quite a performance, by the way,' said Nancy. 'Before. That your bloke?'

'Yes,' said Grace. She didn't bother to try and hide the pride in her voice.

'Your friend's right,' said Nancy. 'He's really good-looking. Why are you keeping him a secret? Is he married?'

'No,' said Grace. 'It's complicated. But as you may have heard, I'm supposed to be single.'

'Clear as mud,' said Nancy, shrugging. 'Well, none of my business.'

There's a first, thought Grace.

'I must say, though, he looks almost too good to be true.'

'Well, he's not,' said Grace firmly. 'He *is* true.' Thank goodness it was the end of the day. She'd had quite enough of this awful Nancy and her unsolicited comments. Still, nothing, not this annoying woman, or even the near miss with Frankie, could dent her fabulous mood. Greg had turned up out of the blue on the flimsiest of excuses. She hadn't paid him; there was no business transaction. He'd simply wanted to see her. Grace sighed happily and felt a tingle up and down her body. He must like her. *Really* like her! And this could work – if she could just persuade him to give up the escorting. It couldn't be that difficult, could it? He'd already taken the first step.

After Nancy had left the room, saying she hoped to see Grace again, which Grace pretended to agree with, she went to the sash window. A young couple, their arms round each other, giggled in the car park and got into their car, and Grace twisted her wedding ring then slowly eased it off her finger. Yes, she could make it on her own. She'd proved that today. But she was so glad she didn't have to.

She smiled as she wrapped her ring in a square of pale pink tissue paper and put it in her bag. It was time to take things to the next level with Greg. And Ascot was where she would make it happen.

CHAPTER NINETEEN:
IMOGEN

It was windy and not quite warm enough. Dresses were blowing up. Fascinators were hurled off heads and into puddles. Pashminas were turned into billowing kites. There were goose-bumped arms and legs. Bright, dry lips smacked together. False eyelashes flapping in the gale. Red soles, real and fake. Tottering. Tittering. Skittering.

A lot of women looked under-dressed and over-done, but some looked *amazing*, elegant in beautiful dresses and show-stopping heels, and with the most sensational hats Imogen had ever seen. She must take a few surreptitious photos later, so she could show Grace.

Imogen hoped she matched up to the best of the bunch. She felt pretty amazing herself, as she walked through the coach car park at Ascot, with Richard. The new shoes, a buffed bod, an exquisite tight-fitting cream silky dress. She'd barely eaten all week. She knew it was wrong, and today she'd eat like one of Ascot's champion thoroughbreds, but she wanted to look sensational.

Huge coaches were rolling in from Brighton, from Essex, from Surrey, from Kent. Screeching women in glamorous dresses were clambering out of them. The sharp edge of an enormous hat nearly caught Imogen's eye and Richard took her hand. She could tell women were looking at him. He didn't look stupid in the top hat and tails. He didn't resemble the fat controller in any shape or form. He looked like he was born to wear such a get-up. He was majestic. A woman in peach headgear shaped like a Babybel was gawping, her mouth open like a guppy's. If Richard had uttered anything at that moment, in that rumbling American accent of his, she probably would have dissolved into a peach polyester heap.

Mitts off, thought Imogen. He's mine.

Her resolve had crumbled as soon as she'd got his text. It felt like a minor miracle and you don't ignore minor miracles. He wasn't giving up on her. He didn't care that she'd ignored him and hadn't taken his calls. He wanted to see her and *she* didn't want to be a woman who was frightened. It was time to put fear to one side and take a very deep breath. He wouldn't hurt her if she didn't let him, would he? It was a just a day. One day out. He was gorgeous, *she* was single and fabulous; she was going to Ascot and she was bloody well going to enjoy herself.

She grinned unashamedly as they walked through the entry gate and into the main concourse of the Grandstand. They were greeted by umbrella-canopied bars, hordes of wandering people dressed to the nines, chatting and laughing, and understated officials in smart suits strategically placed to direct people where they needed to go. One approached Richard, and chatting politely, led them to some very posh silver grey lifts. Imogen called out, 'Thank you!' with unconcealed delight, as the lift door closed on them. She was effusive, full of it, brimming with fun and possibility. Fear had been put in its place.

'Excited?' said Richard, in his lovely voice, as they glided to the fourth floor.

'Thrilled!' replied Imogen.

He'd picked her up from outside her office. It was a bit of a pain pretending she had to go into London for an early Saturday morning meeting, and going up on the train and getting changed and ready there, but there was no way Richard could collect her from home, for obvious reasons. He'd pulled up, with Nigel at the wheel of a long black limo, complete with champagne. She'd almost jumped up and down with excitement. And when Richard had swung open the door for her like he had before, she'd almost swooned. In his Ascot suit he was divine. She was pretty much powerless.

She'd grabbed the champagne greedily; it would give her something to do with her hands – she wanted to jump on Richard and put them all over his body. They'd kept doing that thing, where two people who fancy the pants off each other keep grinning. It made the journey fly. Every time he grinned, it made her knickers leap. Glorious.

He'd started telling her who else was in his box at Ascot. Imogen was the only 'friend' he'd invited – she'd been asked to save his sanity, apparently – the rest were 'corporate folks'. He reeled off a list of very boring-sounding people, casually giving the names at the bottom of the list as Phil and Carolyn Boot.

Oh. My. God.

'Carolyn Boot! You know *her*?' she asked Richard, startled.

'Yes, I do business with her husband. Do *you*? By the horror on your face I'd say you do!'

'I used to work with her. *For* her.' She grimaced. 'I gave her a piece of my mind when I left the company,' said Imogen. 'I don't think she'll relish spending any time in mine.'

'Oh, really? Will you be okay?'

'I'll brazen it out and rise above,' said Imogen. 'I'll be fine.' She was bricking it, slightly, but yes, she *could* brazen it out. Nothing, not even Carolyn Boot, was going to spoil this day.

The lift opened. Richard took Imogen's hand and together they walked along the plush corridor and into Box 356.

It was wonderful. Hugely smart and very, very corporate. There was a large table with white linen, on which coffee and tea pots and interesting-looking biscuits were displayed. A bar. A huge television up on the wall. And a corner balcony outside with full vista of the track and all the hordes of well-dressed people below. When she'd been to Ascot before it had all been quite posh but not like this. The acting and directing circle she moved in didn't run to *boxes*.

'Amazing…' she said, looking round her.

The word died on her lips but she kept her smile going – Carolyn Boot was walking into the box. She was trailed by a tall thin man – her husband, Imogen presumed – who looked like a much uglier Richard E. Grant. He'd always been a bit of a crush of Imogen's. What was it with these *Richards*? She wouldn't have said no to a bit of Branson, either, once upon a time… Even a Madeley was not an unattractive proposition. God, was she on heat?

Carolyn turned a laser-like stare on Imogen and raised her eyebrows. She had obviously not been forewarned, like Imogen had.

'Abigail, is it?' said Carolyn, alarmingly coming over.

'Imogen,' said Imogen. Richard had temporarily deserted her. A man with a goatee had commandeered him and he was over by the floor to ceiling windows. She knows damn well what my name is, Imogen thought.

'Right.' Carolyn held out a claw for her to shake. 'And your connection is?'

'To?' Imogen knew she sounded insolent, but she didn't care.

'Richard Stoughton.'

'Oh, we're dating.'

'Really?' said Carolyn, looking incredulous. 'Are you sure?'

'Of course I'm sure. I think he may be in love with me,' said Imogen. There. That told the old bag.

'I find that very doubtful,' said Carolyn, with a sneer. She looked about to say more, then her face closed down to a blank glare. 'Excuse me, I need to get some champagne…' She started looking round her and clicking fingers at the substandard E. Grant. He made to take her pashmina.

'No, no, not that, darling,' she said, brusquely. 'Champagne. Get me champagne.'

The poor man practically ran to the bar to grab a glass of champagne off a waiting tray.

Imogen stepped away. So Carolyn was going to be imperious and icily friendly, she thought. She could handle that. At least there'd been no mention of her terrible departure from Yes! Productions. Perhaps it would come later. Carolyn's revenge. She couldn't imagine Carolyn was the type of woman not to execute it.

Fortification. That would help. Imogen went to the bar and got two glasses of champagne, one for herself, one for Richard.

'Cheers,' she said, walking over and handing it to him.

'Bottoms up, me old mucker.' He grinned.

'Uh-oh, Bert's back,' said Imogen. Richard laughed.

They bumped glasses and each took a sip. That fizzing sip of champagne held all the promise of the day. Fun, frivolity, slight inebriation, excitement. She could take Richard on. One day at a time.

Several more people entered the box. A horsey couple – she couldn't decide whether the man or the woman looked more like a thoroughbred showjumper – a big American lady in a straw hat and an embroidered tent, and two or three indistinguishable city types who already looked well-oiled and were braying like donkeys about the FTSE 100. They were the type she used to go for, until she knew better.

A smiley, very posh bloke came in to talk about the horses and to give tips on the bets. It was almost like a stand-up comedian's routine, all his asides and in-jokes seemed well rehearsed. Imogen listened as intently as everyone else and laughed in all the right places. She didn't have a clue. She wasn't a horsey person and had never bet on anything in her life. Carolyn was earnestly marking things down on a piece of paper and circling things in her programme. *She* knew what she was doing – of course she did.

Out on the balcony it was blowing a gale. They all had to troop out there for the first race. It was real *hold on to your hats* weather, and like a welcome vacuum when you swooshed back inside. Imogen was happier in the warmth of the box, hovering around the buffet table or chatting randomly to the characters in there. She only braved the balcony again when the Queen rumbled down the track in her carriage. Imogen, buoyed by champagne, gave her a wave, clutching her pashmina to her with her free arm. The Queen didn't wave back.

When she was suctioned back into the room, a spread was laid out on the table replacing the tea, coffee and biscuits. There were salads, flans and quiches, cheeses and breads, smoked salmon – all delicious-looking. Imogen knew she was going to eat loads; champagne always gave her the munchies.

'Everything okay?' said Richard, coming to stand by her side as she finished her plateful. She hadn't wanted to shadow him; he had people to schmooze. She'd pretty much done her own thing since she'd been in that box. She'd chatted to people, been friendly to the women (the Boot excepted) and acceptably flirty with the men, had eaten and drank...and had watched Richard from the corner of her eye as he worked the room.

He was so good at it. He was charming, disarming, friendly, all-inclusive and all-encompassing. He had the large American lady laughing like a drain. Even Carolyn, in his current circle, appeared to be tittering, slightly. Simpering. She almost looked girlish. She had one foot hooked behind the other, the toe of her sandal rubbing the back of her calf as though she were playing footsie with herself. It amused Imogen no end. The ice lady melteth in the hands of the right man, clearly. Did her husband know?

Imogen wondered, not for the first time, what it would be like to put herself in Richard's hands. Naked, preferably. Perhaps tonight she would find out. She hoped so.

'Everything's great, thanks.'

He whispered in her ear. 'There's something about you.'

'That's a Level 42 song.'

'Level who?'

God, he was sexy. His eyes glinted, like the bubbles in her champagne. His lips looked warm and inviting. 'Do you want to take a stroll down to the Royal Enclosure with me?'

'I'd love to, sir,' she said, placing her champagne flute on the table. 'Let's do it.'

By the time they got to the paddock, the wind had dropped and the sun had miraculously come out. Imogen was feeling quite warm now. She slipped her pashmina off her shoulders and enjoyed the heat of the sun on them. They stared at a few horses, admired a few coats, saddles, whatever. It was not really her scene. But it was fabulous. She was with Richard. They always found things to laugh at.

After half an hour, after they'd looked and laughed and seen everything there was to see, they made their way back across the busy concourse, to the lifts.

Imogen suddenly stopped.

'What's up?'

'It's my friend, Grace! I thought she was in Stratford!'

There was Grace, standing next to a man with dark blond hair and queuing at one of the Pimm's stands. She was rummaging in a pink clutch bag and smiling at something the man was saying.

'Grace!' called out Imogen, releasing Richard's hand and sidestepping a few feet from him. She'd remembered, just in time.

Grace dropped whatever it was she was getting out of her bag. A pair of sunglasses. The man she was standing with bent to pick them up but she more or less shoved him out of the way, to her left, and grabbed them herself. She then rapidly stepped forward, aligning herself with a group of women in mega-tight dresses who were shrieking and laughing in the queue.

'Imogen!'

They stepped towards each other in unison, like the couple coming out of the cuckoo clock. Grace was smiling, but looked terrified.

'I thought you were traipsing round Shakespeare country?' said Imogen.

Grace laughed. A very high, unnatural-sounding laugh. Was she drunk? She didn't usually laugh like that when she was drunk.

'The Stratford rumour was wrong,' said Grace quickly and stumbling slightly over her words. Maybe she *was* drunk. 'It turned out to be Ascot. One of the gang must have heard it wrong.' Imogen was a bit confused. Grace didn't look dressed for what she'd thought would be sightseeing round Stratford. She was in a pale pink sheath dress and nude heels. Unless she'd thought it was going to be a theatre thing. Grace liked the theatre. Or perhaps the mystery coach had a stash of fascinators to hand out, for any eventuality. Or perhaps Grace had brought some from work, for everyone on the trip… It was all a bit…strange. She looked…shifty. Would Grace *lie* about coming to Ascot? And if so, why?

Grace waved her hand vaguely in the direction of the gaggle of hefty women next to her. 'The gang,' she said, airily. They looked…up for it. There was a surplus of ugly platform shoes on pasty legs. One girl was straining for release from a sausage-tight lime bodycon dress, her bottom like two puppies fighting in a Lycra sack. She was snorting with laughter and truffling into a bag of popcorn. Wow, Grace was a rose amongst thorns in that little lot. They didn't look very fit for Taekwondo people.

'Oh, right. Actually, I thought you were with that bloke, for a minute!' laughed Imogen.

'Which bloke?'

'Him,' said Imogen, pointing at the dark blond guy, who was now at the front of the queue and relieving a huge jug of Pimm's from a girl serving.

'No,' said Grace, quickly. 'Who are *you* down here with?' Mercifully, Richard had been grabbed by a passing toff and was having his ear bent about something clearly terribly interesting, his back to them.

'Some awful media finance man,' Imogen said, pointing faintly his way. 'You know the sort. Thinks he knows it all.

I've got a right day of it. I'm having to drink an awful lot of champagne just to get through it!'

'Is he good-looking?' asked Grace. 'He looks just your type, from the back.'

'God, no! And I'm *off* my type, as you know. My type are utter no-hopers, remember? Don't forget the charter, miss!'

'Ha, yeah.'

'So where are you then?'

'Silver Circle, with the riff-raff. How's the box?'

'Fabulous, darling.'

'Of course it is.'

The gaggle of girls were on the move. They had turned and were walking left, towards the Silver Circle.

'Right, well,' said Grace. 'I'll get back to the hoi polloi, madam. Enjoy!' And she took off in the direction of the girls, weakly warbling, 'Wait for me!' and tottering along in her heels. The guy with the jug of Pimm's was hovering, a blank expression on his face, as Grace ran past him. *He* was a good-looking guy, thought Imogen.

She walked over to Richard who was still in deep conversation with the toff, but looked like he was trying to edge away.

'Well, great to see you,' Richard was saying, 'but I have a beautiful woman I must attend to, so if you'll excuse me…' He sidled away, leaving the man still talking.

'I don't need *attending* to,' said Imogen, grinning at him.

'Of course you don't. It's just a bullshit thing men say to get away from each other. How was your friend?'

'Good. A little odd, actually. I've got a feeling she's here with a man.'

'So? So are you, lady!'

'We're not supposed to be though, are we? I told you about the charter, didn't I?'

'Oh the *charter*,' he said, with amused sarcasm. 'Well, charters are meant to be broken.' And he stared at her for so long she thought she might spontaneously combust, and then, when she couldn't bear it any longer, leant down and made Grace, Ascot and the world disappear by placing his soft lips gently on hers. It was a kiss that was by description only, chaste. They were surrounded by people, after all. This was not the boardroom. But how it felt... Good God. It was a delicious reminder of the amazing first kiss they'd had, and a promise of everything she hoped was in store for her with this amazing man.

She feared she kept her eyes closed far longer than the kiss and when she finally dragged them open, Richard was grinning at her. She had a very funny feeling at the bottom of her stomach. He was heavenly. Heaven sent. Heaven scent. His cologne mixed ethereally with the blooms of arranged flowers all around them. Ascot was in bloom. And so was she. Sod the bloody charter. She was mentally tearing it up and chucking it out the open window of a speeding car, travelling along Route 66. She'd have to come clean to the girls tomorrow. She had not sworn off men. She could swear Richard was the best man to ever come her way.

They made their way back up to the box. Imogen felt thrilled, happy, excited. So much of the day and night was left to come. All of it with Richard. She was walking steadily on her heels, but inside she was dancing the tango. And fancy bumping into Grace like that! She thought her friend would have been more pleased to see her, had more to say. It was, after all, quite a coincidence.

'I'm just going to pop to the loo,' said Imogen, as they came out of the lifts on the third floor. 'You go on ahead.'

'Pop to the loo?' mimicked Richard.

'Use the bathroom, visit the powder room, whatever. You Americans and your euphemisms. You're so damned *polite*! See you in a min,' she said, and dashed into the toilets.

She got waylaid in the loos, the way slightly drunk, giddily happy women do. She got chatting to a group of women who were at the mirrors doing their make-up, as she tried to squeeze between them to get to the sink to wash her hands. There was a lot of 'Sorry, love'-ing and giggling and 'I like your shoes,' and 'Ooh your hair looks nice,' and 'Ooh, are you in a box too, what number?' and 'That's a lovely dress; you've got an amazing figure' etc. She was in there for a while. It was nice to have a drunken girly chat in the women's toilets now and again.

On her way back to the box, along the tiered landing, she passed a girl walking in the opposite direction. She was young, late twenties-ish and crying. Really sobbing. Imogen gave her a sympathetic smile. The girl gave a sob and dashed past her to the lifts. Poor love, Imogen thought. Too much booze, probably, and perhaps a row with an equally drunk boyfriend. It happened, even at posh Ascot.

She pushed open the heavy door of the box, and went back in.

CHAPTER TWENTY: FRANKIE

Frankie and Hugh finally decided to go to Paper Mill Lock, in Little Baddow. She'd finally given in. Embarrassed the cat and mouse shenanigans had gone on so long, she'd ended up confessing to him she wasn't looking for a boyfriend and Hugh had said that was fine, no pressure, but if she changed her mind it was okay with him. In the meantime they'd just have an afternoon out. Imogen and Grace were both out for the day, she reasoned, so why not? And she wouldn't be seeing Hugh for a 5k meet-up snog-fest tomorrow; it had been cancelled as he had a family christening.

She'd been to Paper Mill Lock with Rob and the kids before. It was lovely. Grassy banks and gorgeous walks along the river, loads of boats to have a nose at and a gorgeous tea room. On a summer's day there was nowhere nicer and today was a perfect English June day. Blue sky, what weather presenters now called wall-to-wall sunshine, a nice breeze that fanned you but didn't have you reaching for a cardigan, and one of those rare days that you knew would stay like that *all day*. There was no chance of it all going to pot by four o'clock when everyone would run shrieking to their cars, their bags over their heads and their toes sodden in their sandals.

Frankie pulled into the car park just as Hugh was expertly reversing a black Volvo into one of the two remaining spaces. She gave him a cheery wave and parked her car next to his.

'Hey,' he said, slamming his car door and bounding up to her to give her a kiss on the cheek. 'How are you doing?'

'Good, thanks. You?' She felt all shy. The last time she'd seen this man they'd been snogging enthusiastically behind one of the town's main supermarkets. It was weird, frankly, seeing him somewhere else. She felt herself going all hot under the collar of her pretty white top.

'I'm absolutely great. Right! Let's get going then. What a lovely day.'

They walked to the riverside. It was hot. Frankie was glad she'd worn shorts and sandals. Hugh took her hand and she grinned. This was going to be a perfect afternoon. She wondered how soon they could be kissing again. As they started to stroll past the water, a flotilla of primary-coloured canoes glided past.

'All right, Hugh?' called out an uber-sporty looking character with yellow Lycra zipped up to his neck.

Hugh let go of her hand to wave. 'Hey! Yeah, how you doing, pal?'

'Good, mate, good. We're heading down to Maldon.'

'Good stuff, pal!'

'See you at the next Canoe Baloe!' called uber-sports over his shoulder as the flotilla slid out of sight.

'I'll be there, pal!' hollered Hugh, taking Frankie's hand again.

Hugh was attracting a lot of attention. Mothers with buggies were gawping; men were glancing sideways at him. They could all see it too – he was *very* good-looking. He was wearing those mountain boot things, some chino shorts, and a white shirt, with the sleeves rolled up. His forearms and his calf muscles were equally impressive. Ultra-firm and beautifully hairy. He looked – as they say in Bristol – lush. Frankie felt girlishly pleased to be walking next to him. She could pull a hot guy! She could attract a damn fine-looking man! She'd traded up from Rob and she felt fabulous.

They walked about half a mile down river. Frankie loved peering into all the boats. Houseboats with curtains, hanging baskets and the remains of lunch on tiny tables spied through equally tiny windows; small speed boats with white leather steering wheels; boats that looked rusty and knackered but still exciting; boats called *Marion* and *Sylvia's Hope* and *Gone Fishing*. Frankie saw a boy who looked like Josh atop a boat and teasing a gambolling dog with a piece of string. It gave her heart a horrible pang. She quickly looked in the small, round window below. A woman was crocheting, a glass of wine at her feet.

A green barge painted with roses was at the lock they were approaching. One man was on the lock and winding some ancient-looking cog mechanism with a gigantic key thing. Another was astride the deck and attempting to throw a lasso of rope over a bollard at the water's edge. Hugh immediately leapt over and started to help secure the rope. His calves tensed and relaxed in a very enticing way. He tied a very decisive knot.

'Thanks, mate,' said the man on the boat.

'No worries, pal.'

Hugh looked all pleased with himself. He was brushing his hands together in the manner of a job well done. He shrugged faux-modestly and said proudly, 'You'll always find me…'

'In the kitchen at parties?' offered Frankie.

He looked at her strangely. 'No, tinkering about on water. I might bring my canoe down for a go next weekend. Do you want to come and watch me?'

'Oh, maybe.' She'd have the children. Did she really want them meeting this man yet? She hadn't even told him about them. Their texts had hardly been in-depth.

'I could borrow one for you.'

'I don't think I'd be able to get my bottom in one.'

'No, maybe not.' She looked at him but he didn't appear to be joking. They fell into step again and carried on walking. 'So, tell me more about yourself, Frankie.'

Okay. Now was as good a time as any.

'Well, I've got four kids.'

'Four!' He spluttered and a polo mint fell out of his mouth and onto the grass next to the narrow path. He left it there. 'Blimey. But you're separated… You have alternate weekends off, right?'

'Well, yes.'

'No worries then,' he said, looking all happy, like he'd solved something.

'Do *you* have kids?'

'Me? God, no. Never been married, never had kids. Hey, let's have something to eat. They do a champion cream tea.'

They sat at a wooden trestle table, by one of the locks. Frankie watched as Hugh went into the café to order for both of them. She hadn't even told him what she wanted. And he didn't seem thrilled about her having children. Oh dear. She wasn't sure where this was going. He was a great kisser though, really fantastic. Perhaps she could just continue to hook up with him for kissing and he'd never have to meet her kids? It was workable. And at least if it was just casual kissing she'd have nothing much to lie about, to her friends. She felt another clang of guilt on breaking their pact and wondered how they were both getting on today.

She hoped Imogen wasn't too bored stiff at Ascot, schmoozing with all those people. She hoped Grace was having fun on her day out too, on her magical mystery tour. Frankie wondered about that Michael. He was a bit of all right, wasn't he? Was Grace hiding something?

Hugh came back with the cream tea. 'Hugh Trafford always gets his man,' he said, randomly, as he carefully placed the heavy tray on the table. He sat down, with a smile. 'Okay, gorgeous,' he continued, 'seeing as we're getting to know each other, let me tell you about the time I ran the Brighton Mile…'

CHAPTER TWENTY-ONE:
GRACE

Damn! Grace had been convinced she wouldn't bump into Imogen! That Imogen would be up in her high-falutin' box somewhere and wouldn't deign to come down amongst the masses. What bad luck she had run into her.

Thank God she'd made up that stuff about the mystery tour round at Frankie's and hadn't told an outright lie about where she was going. She knew the whole thing had sounded ridiculous, but she also knew it would give her an excuse if – horror of all horrors – she was unlucky enough to see Imogen at Ascot. She could say that stupid thing she'd said, about Stratford-Upon-Avon being just a rumour. Ugh. She wished she'd practised saying it in the mirror – she'd hardly sounded convincing, had she? Had Imogen believed a word of it?

She hoped so. Thank goodness that group of women had been there, for her to pretend to be with, although they'd looked none too pleased she'd started following them. One of them had actually sneered and said 'Who's the weirdo?' before Grace was able to turn back, once the coast was clear. She'd so nearly been rumbled. She *so* didn't want to be found out. To have to explain Greg and how she'd met him. Not only a man – but a male escort! She was supposed to be anti-men, not paying one for company.

The sisterhood would never ever recover. She'd be thrown out of the coven.

Yet, he was worth it. She and Greg had travelled up by train. They'd laughed about their encounter at the wedding fair. They'd walked into Ascot holding hands and looking like they'd been together for years. When she'd returned to him after pretending to run after those women, he'd laughed.

'Ashamed to be seen with me?' he'd said. 'I got the hint, although I thought I was supposed to have the opposite effect!'

'Ha. Well, I'm *supposed* to be single. There was no way I could let Imogen see me with you. But you *are* gorgeous though, of course you are.' She stroked his arm reassuringly. 'Any woman would be proud to be with you.' She wanted to make him feel better. She felt awful she'd denied his existence.

'And you are, too,' he said, pulling her in close to him and thankfully not asking for any further explanation. 'Any man would be proud to be seen with *you*. You're lovely, Grace, and you look stunning today.'

'Thanks,' she said, frowning a little. 'Listen...' She pulled her face back from his, but not wanting to release her body from his embrace. She liked it too much. '...You don't have to keep saying things like that. You've said quite a few nice things to me now. It's been great for my ego, and all that. But you need to stop.'

'Why?'

'Because I like you too much. Because I want it to be real. Not fake.' This was it. She was putting herself out there without a safety net. Next level. The miraculous close shave with Imogen and the champagne she'd already drunk were making her brave.

'It isn't fake when I tell you you're gorgeous and how much I like you. It's true,' he whispered in her ear.

'Is that why you came to see me at the wedding fair?'

'Yes,' he said. 'I really do like you.'

'But you're an escort.'

'I am.'

'Are you going to stop being an escort?' She pulled away from him. Crunch time. She held her breath.

'I can't. I need the money.'

'There's always McDonald's.'

'Very funny.'

'Have you slept with anyone yet?'

'No.'

'Not that woman from the roller-skating?'

'No.'

'Have you seen her again?'

'Yes, another date. Lunch.'

'What about other women? Please. I want to know.'

'I've been out with a few other women. Dinner. Business functions. Family dos when they want to score a point with an ex.' He winked at her. 'No sex.'

She ignored the wink. Greg took both of her hands. 'Do you want to carry on doing this? Seeing me?'

'Paying you, you mean? Yes, I do. No, I don't. I don't know!' Damn. The power was all his. Again. Someone else's. Not hers. He had the power to hurt her, after all. By not liking her enough. For not liking her enough to drop the transaction and do this for real. *She* was the one supposed to be in control.

'Look,' he said. 'Let's just enjoy today. Forget you're paying me, we'll act as though we're actually dating, and we'll see how things go. How about it?'

Her heart leapt. What did that mean? Did that mean he *did* want to do this for real? Was he giving her hope? It sounded like it! Oh, she was ecstatic, if he really meant it. This was wonderful.

'I *really* do like you, Grace.'

He pulled her close to him again, and she believed him.

'Yes. Okay,' she said. 'Let's just enjoy the day.' She could do that. See how things went. Then think about how they felt tomorrow.

Even though she already knew.

CHAPTER TWENTY-TWO:
IMOGEN

Imogen went back into the box and Richard was holding court, laughing his loud American laugh and waving his large American hand in the air as though stopping traffic. He was obviously telling some anecdote or other. He was ebullient. Confident. Genial.

She tried to look at him objectively. *Tried*. But whichever way she looked at him, the truth stared her in the face. He was perfect. If her other men had been pavement lowlifes, then Richard was the top of the Empire State Building. Her New York kind of guy. He had charm. He wasn't self-obsessed. He was funny. He liked *Goodfellas*. He knew 90s Britpop bands. And he seemed to really, really like her. A week ago she'd been really frightened by this, now it delighted her.

Oh Lord, what on earth would she tell Frankie and Grace? They'd kill her! How could she be a member of the Year of Being Single club, when she was secretly romancing a not-so-quiet American? How could she be sworn off men if she was secretly swearing an allegiance to Richard? Thank God Grace hadn't rumbled her. What an amazing coincidence she was there. Actually, thinking about it, she supposed, it wasn't *that* unlikely. There were a lot of coach trips to Ascot, and not all roads led to Stratford-on-Avon. Imogen picked up a glass of champagne and savoured the cool bubbles tickling her throat.

Carolyn was in Richard's circle again. She looked enraptured. Her hatchet face had softened. She was actually laughing, *really* laughing, her head thrown back. She looked girlish, carefree. She's as charmed as I am, Imogen thought. Richard really could charm the birds out of the trees.

Was Carolyn a threat to her? No, not in that way. She didn't think Richard was in any danger of fancying Carolyn – she was only attractive if you liked small axes with short handles. No, in terms of some sort of revenge against her. It still worried her. Imogen doubted Carolyn would just let it go, what she did to her in the office that day. She could imagine a desire for retribution simmering for ages, before Carolyn struck, like a shoeless praying mantis…

Stop it, thought Imogen, you're being silly. If Carolyn wanted revenge she would have taken it by now, and so what if her old Boot of an ex-boss liked Richard? Who wouldn't? The man was a god.

Imogen approached the group. Also enjoying Richard's story were the horsey couple and a pair of the posh, boozed-up city boys all braying and neighing so loudly they surely belonged down in the paddock. Richard smiled broadly at her as she stepped towards them.

'Imogen,' he said. 'I was just telling these lovely people about my first ride on the Tube.' He said it as 'toob'. She loved that. 'And how I sat for thirty minutes at St Paul's because there was a handbag on the line at Bank.' She laughed. He pulled her towards him. She slid her arm around his back, under his jacket. It was warm – she could trace his skin under his shirt with her hand. Carolyn gave her a look that was hard to interpret. Imogen decided it was a mixture of contempt and envy, all bound up in a supercilious smile Cruella De Vil would have been proud of. *Sorry, love*, thought Imogen. *I win.*

The balcony was not such a hideous wind tunnel now the weather had brightened, so they all ventured outside to watch the next race. Richard had put a bet on for her, a horse called Avoid The Traffic. She had an urge to shout out, 'Move your bloomin arse!' like Audrey Hepburn in *My Fair Lady*. It was quite exciting.

After the race finished, and her horse had come a respectable third, Imogen and Richard stood for a while, feeling the sun on their faces. It was glorious now.

She leaned into him. Richard gave her a pair of binoculars and she looked down to the crowds of people below. The Silver Circle. She wondered if she could see Grace and her group of friends. She scanned the hordes. People were laughing, drinking, having a great time. Faces were red from the sun, and booze, and roaring at horses.

There she was! Grace. Laughing and holding a champagne flute in her hand. Tossing the curls that framed her face. Hang on, there was that guy again, the one at the Pimm's stand. They were standing very close to each other. *Very* close. There was no gaggle of women nearby. No 'gang'. Grace and the man looked very much à deux, and it didn't look much à deux about nothing. He now had his arm round her. He was kissing her cheek. She was still laughing. Well, well, well. Grace, you *dark horse*, thought Imogen. She was with someone, and very handsome he was, too. Quite an improvement on that bastard, James. Good for her.

Richard stepped closer and put his hand lightly on Imogen's waist. She smiled up at him. So she and Grace were both at it. She wouldn't say anything. She couldn't, could she? She didn't have a leg to stand on. She almost willed Grace to turn round and catch her in the act, too.

The Single for a Year club looked like it was rapidly disbanding. They hadn't even managed six months.

After the final race, Imogen presumed they would make their way out of Ascot and home. She thought Richard would call Nigel and tell him where to wait for them. She could get used to this driver business. How nice it was, having someone to just drive you around. She was a rubbish driver, a terrible parker and a perennial 'scraper' – of bollards, road signs, whatever. Her car was a scratched mess and she avoided driving it unless she absolutely had to. How wonderful to just glide in and out of a car that was always just waiting where you wanted it.

Richard didn't call Nigel. 'There's a party,' he said, holding her hand as he led her out of the box. She never wanted to let it go. Her hand felt safe in his.

'A party? Where?'

'In one of the car parks. An Owners' and Trainers' party. Would you like to go?'

'I'd *love* to go!'

Owners, Trainers and Rich Americans, clearly. Exciting. Although to be honest, Imogen was torn between not wanting the day to end, and getting to Richard's hotel, or wherever he was staying, as soon as possible so she could rip his clothes off. Just the touch of his hand was making her desperate to sleep with him. But, no, it was fine, she could wait, she could party on. Those fabulous shoes may have to come off, though. They were killing her.

They walked through Ascot's tarmacked open areas in the fading June sun. The Grandstand was scattered with the aftermath of a typically boozy day. There were wandering, puce-faced men carrying battered top hats; shrieking women hobbling along the tarmac hanging on to each other, fascinators missing or woefully lopsided; staff members sweeping up litter and collecting empty plastic glasses. Heading through the now virtually empty Silver Circle, they came across a crescent of top-to-toe drunk women snoozing face down in the grass. Discarded empty champagne bottles were littered amongst upended stilettos shoes displaying scratched dirty soles, and hitched dresses revealed cellulite and scarlet knickers. She was pretty sure one of the women was the monstrous girl at the Pimm's stand, conspicuous in a lime green wiggle dress that was concertinaed up her thighs and showcasing a bum sliced by a black thong. Grace was definitely not with them. Was she already on the coach? Or had she never been with these girls at all? Was she copping off somewhere in the bushes with Handsome Man, then following him home?

Imogen decided to check her phone. Just in case Grace had got separated from this gang of fools and needed to find her.

There was no text from Grace, but one from Frankie. The text said, *Ha, well we know what that means ;-) And I'd like to see you try!!* Hmm. That was odd. It sounded a bit flirty. Who on earth was that supposed to be for? Was Frankie texting a *man*?

I don't think that was meant for me!!!! texted Imogen. She and Richard were almost at the gate. He was being really attentive and she loved it. He was subtly steering away drunk posh city bloke number two who was trying to link arms with her, country dancing style, and breathing into her face. City bloke's breath stank of beer and burgers and he had a repulsive, boozed-up red nose. Richard extricated his arm and placed it down by his side.

'There you go, fella,' he said. 'We don't want you falling over and dragging the lady down with you.'

'Sorry, old chap,' muttered the bloke. She could see why these idiots were still hanging around. Richard had been fabulous company and had kept them in as much champagne as they wanted, all day long. At least they had ditched Carolyn Boot. Dancing in car parks was hardly her scene. She had said a polite goodbye not long after the last race. Had seemed quite friendly with Imogen. Had shaken her hand and said it had been nice seeing her. But her smile had looked false and painted on and there was a steely glint in her eye Imogen didn't much like the look of. Oh well, Carolyn could sod off – hopefully she would never have anything to do with her again.

Another text arrived from Frankie.

Ha, no. Soz. To another friend. How's your day going with your mind-numbing clients?

Mind-numbingly awful, thanks. What u doing?

Not a lot. Just chilling out. ☺

Enjoy.

You too. Spk soon.

Imogen put her phone back in her bag. She and Richard walked through a large metal gate and out into a wide open area that was a mixture of sandy grass and concrete. Flash sports cars and Range Rovers were parked to one side, and in the field beyond, a huge white marquee awaited them. It had reams of twinkling fairy lights strung all round it and as they approached she could see a huge, under-canvas bar where staff dressed in black were shaking stainless steel cocktail shakers. Wow. Top hats and tails and dresses and heels were all converging, heading towards the marquee like it was that mountain in *Close Encounters*. Thumping music was coming from somewhere. The Black Eyed Peas. This looked fun!

She weaved away from Richard and headed to the bar to get them both a drink. Her treat. Mojitos. But everything was free. She carried them over to Richard, who was leaning against a tree, his jacket slung over one shoulder.

She had never been more in lust, more excited, more exhilarated, than on this perfect night.

Before long, shoes were off and she was dancing barefoot in the prickly grass, the evening breeze in her hair, fascinators and pashminas flung to the centre of the circle of people they'd randomly found themselves dancing with. It was a very posh update on dancing round handbags and brilliant fun. Richard was across the circle from her, making some quite impressive shapes.

'Not bad for a Yankee Doodle!' she shouted over Pharrell.

'Thanks, English Rose,' he called back. 'Not so bad yourself!'

She was quite a good dancer, she knew. Yes, she was not the youngest there, by any stretch of the imagination, but she was totally fabulous. She *felt* young. She felt glowing and vibrant and full of life. She felt like life may well last for ever. It would, wouldn't it? Why wouldn't it?

The evening was lovely and warm. Heavenly. As the music switched to a Bruno Mars number, with a slower tempo, and the sun went down over a low bank of trees in the distance, Richard took her in his arms and held her in close, by the bottom. She pressed herself further into him. It felt saucy, lovely. She was reminded of the Jilly Cooper book cover for *Riders*. Recently, the PC brigade had demanded the hand on the jodhpurs be moved upwards, to look a bit less sexual. She wanted the original *Riders*' hand on her bottom.

'Hey, you,' he said.

'Hey, *you*.'

God, she fancied him. His eyes were boring into her brain, relinquishing her of her knickers, stripping her of inhibition, moral protest, underwear, the charter. Oh God, the charter. It was not quite dramatic enough to simply chuck it out of a car window – it was currently on a long scroll, in twirly writing, being held aloft by someone in doublet and hose, whilst a serf lit one corner with a flaming torch... Oh dear. She was a traitor. Her bravado briefly went up in smoke, too. How on earth was she going to break this to the others?

CHAPTER TWENTY-THREE: FRANKIE

After they'd eaten – and it *had* been a champion cream tea – Hugh gathered and piled up all their dishes and put them at the corner of the table, laid their cutlery parallel and straight, mopped up spillages and lined up the condiments.

'There,' he said.

'You're very tidy.'

'Hugh Trafford likes a tidy table.'

Ugh, why had he started talking about himself in the third person? That was a bit weird. And he said he didn't drink – ever – which was even weirder. Adding that to the fact he hated children and didn't get her jokes – she'd tried to make a crack about a character on *Coronation Street* and he'd just looked bemused – a cloud of disappointment and despondency began to gather above her head, like in a cartoon. She feared it would unleash a comic bucket of heavy grey raindrops at any moment, all over her head. What had gone wrong?

She was getting to know him better, that's what. Exactly what she'd been worried about. And she didn't know if she could be with someone who called everyone 'pal'. For the first time since they'd split, she missed Rob. He got *all* her jokes – they were the same as his.

Nevertheless, she let Hugh kiss her again. In the car park when they said goodbye. She may as well make the most of it; she knew she wouldn't be doing it again.

'Another date soon?' he said, as they finally pulled apart.

'I'll call you,' she said.

She got home to a cold, empty house and it wasn't pleasant. She wished her children were here – shrieking, laughing, messing about. Fighting over the remote control. She wondered what Rob had done with them today. Another fabulous trip to London, maybe?

She missed them. She wasn't sure how much longer she could go on like this, especially as her major distraction had just come to an end. She went into the kitchen and poured herself a glass of white wine. Her phone was on the table and she picked it up. She might just send Rob a little text, see how the children were doing…

Frankie finally stopped texting Rob at half midnight. What the hell had happened? They had had such a laugh. Their humour sparking off each other. It had been almost *flirting*. Like the old days. Although, of course, in the old days, when they'd met, there had been no mobile phones. Their courtship did not involve texting. It involved drinking, dancing, kebab shops and landline telephone calls. But tonight's texting reminded her of their old-days' banter, when it was just them. When they were a new, fresh shiny item, not an old, used, slightly grubby *thing* that was dragging an inordinate amount of baggage down the street with it.

Her first text had just been asking about the children and making a joke about Josh's refusal to get his hair cut. He'd replied with something funny about nits, and it had just gone on from there. They'd slipped back into in-jokes, puns, plays on words and film and music references. Teasing each other. Having a laugh. They must have sent about fifty texts each. She scanned over the day's messages. Actually, it was more like a hundred each. Minus the one she'd sent to Imogen by mistake. Oops.

She had a grin on her face and her cheeks were all flushed. How could they be laughing and bantering so easily? He'd been a lazy slob; she'd hurt him badly. How had they got from that to this easy familiar flirting?

Careful, she thought. At this rate she'd be tempted to get back with him and she wasn't sure that could ever happen. She enjoyed her nice clean home every other weekend. Her space. Her freedom. The house was less chaotic generally, too, in Rob's absence, with one less person sabotaging her domestic efforts. Her bed was always smooth and un-rucked when she got in. She had less stuff to pick up, less mess to clear up in the kitchen. The bin was no longer a toppling mess of things not pushed down properly. It had worked, hadn't it? She shouldn't let the small matter of missing Rob a bit tonight ruin everything she had achieved.

She sighed.

She couldn't go back to the crush of husband and mess and chaos every single day, could she?

CHAPTER TWENTY-FOUR: GRACE

Greg.

Grace sat on the edge of her bed and stared at the floor.

Greg.

Her head was full of him.

It had all gone wrong. They'd said goodbye at Chelmsford train station again. It was becoming a very unsatisfactory habit. Saying goodbye and going their separate ways. Why? They'd been so relaxed in each other's company on the way up to Ascot. Things had been great the whole day, especially after that conversation they'd had. How had things gone so wrong on the way home?

It all seemed to change the moment they'd got on the train. They'd been fine on the Tube across London, the same as they'd been all day – happy, chatty, affectionate and easy in each other's company. They'd sat holding hands and giggling at silly things. But as the Chelmsford train pulled out of Liverpool Street, after a brief spell of reading out her horoscope to her from his phone (Luck and Love were coming. Brilliant), Greg went silent. Attempts from her to continue the wonderful time they'd had were met by him staring out of the window, until she'd stared too…at fields and houses where people with normal relationships were living normal lives. Watching telly, making cups of tea. Going to bed with each other. She knew exactly what was on her mind; she had absolutely no idea what was on his. She'd kept looking at him, wondering what he was thinking. She wished she'd spent some of Gran's money on a nice luxury taxi all the way home from Ascot. It would have been easy then. She would have just asked the driver to take them back to her house…

'What's wrong?' she'd asked him, several times.

'Nothing,' he'd said. 'I'm just tired. It's been a long day.'

And at the taxi rank he'd said, 'Goodbye.'

'Where are you going?' asked Grace, panicked.

'I'm going home.'

'Oh.' She wanted to scream. *Come on, Greg – ask me to come home with you! Beg to come back to mine! Say you find me irresistible. Say you're falling in love with me, that you can't live without me. Say something!*

'So, see you again soon, Grace.'

She could barely respond. All her bravery, from earlier in the day, left her. 'I hope so,' she whispered, miserably. And then, as she felt the crush of disappointment descend on her and pictured a depressed night tossing and turning in her bed, for all the wrong reasons, Greg kissed her. It was sudden. His lips weren't on her, then, suddenly, they were. They were pressed on *her*. Warm, insistent. The kiss took her breath away. It was amazing. Oh, God, she loved it. This kiss was everything. And when his tongue tangled against hers and probed tantalisingly, she clung on to him for dear life. He was gorgeous. And she realised he was clinging on to *her*. He liked her! He had to. A man didn't kiss a woman like this if he didn't.

But, once it was over, he still didn't say he wanted to take her home.

He released her and said nothing. He just looked a weird mixture of confused, regretful and resigned. A black cab pitched up and he walked over and got into it. She saw him take his phone out of his pocket and look at it as the taxi pulled away.

And now Grace was sitting on her bed bloody frustrated and bloody angry with herself. She'd fallen for an unattainable man. Fallen for a male escort! It was stupid, ridiculous, self-inflicted and unnecessary. It was devastating. But why had he kissed her like that? That kiss was not fake! She knew it wasn't. He had bloody well meant that kiss, and so had she.

She was so confused by his behaviour. They *could* have a relationship. He hadn't slept with anyone yet. He'd only been on a few dates. He'd only been an escort for five minutes. He could give it up. Surely there was another way for him to raise the money he wanted? Surely there was a middle ground between male escort and McDonald's?

Perhaps she hadn't been clear enough. Perhaps she hadn't made herself *fully clear.* She'd been pathetic. She had to take more control. Be far more proactive. Force his hand. She knew where he lived; he'd told her. She'd go there in the morning and *demand* he give up the escorting.

And then they would be together.

CHAPTER TWENTY-FIVE: IMOGEN

Imogen crashed through the door at 2a.m. Giggling, with Richard. He'd insisted on coming back to hers. She'd been disappointed. He probably had a lovely, sexy hotel room in London with a huge double bed and fifty-five fluffy pillows to romp on. But Richard had said, very convincingly and with a twinkle in his eye she couldn't possibly say no to, that he wanted to see where she lived, that he wanted to see the whole of her, that he wanted to see her in her natural habitat.

'Like a chimpanzee?' she'd enquired.

'Exactly like a chimpanzee. No,' he'd said, in that delicious voice of his, as they'd sat in the back of the car, pressed tightly together. (She had to resist the urge to clamber up on his lap.) 'I just want to get to know you better. I want to see your house, your style. I want it confirmed.'

'You want what confirmed?'

He leaned towards her and whispered in her ear.

'That you're the woman I'm going to fall in love with.'

Her stomach had flipped like a small child on a trampoline and her heart leapt higher than an Olympic high-diver.

'Okay, Nigel,' she'd called to the front, unnecessarily – he was probably already heading that way. 'The only way is Essex. Turn the car around!'

And here they were. Richard the American was in her boxy, suburban hall. She wished, not for the first time, she was in her trendy little flat in Putney. The tiny hall there had uneven bottle green walls and an antique church pew. This hall was smooth and blank and soulless. She hoped he'd managed to clock her stylish prints in their black frames, before she'd quickly switched off the light.

'Well,' he said. Her shoes were off again. She felt diddy, standing next to him towering above her. She loved the way that felt.

'Well, what now?' she enquired, looking up at him. His face was half in shadow, illuminated only by the dim light from her porch.

'Do you want to get naked?' he asked, his voice low and incredibly husky.

'Yes. Please.'

And he stepped forward, gently grabbed the bottom of her dress with both hands, warm hands grazing her thighs, and slowly, slowly started peeling it up her body. He did it slowly enough that she knew she could stop him at any time. Slowly enough that she thought she couldn't bear it.

Oh, but she could. As he really, really slowly, centimetre by centimetre, pulled up her dress, it was delicious, languid. She was being peeled like a sexy prawn. It also meant there was lots of grinning, and a bit of giggling, and some oohing and a bit of *ooh-er*-ing, and a couple of ooh missuses – she loved that he knew that very British brand of sexy talk – until she was there, standing before him in her underwear, and grateful for her fab forethought of highly expensive matching rose-pink silk, with black ribbon. She'd always done good underwear.

'Don't leave me this way, American boy,' she said. 'Now you.' And she took off his jacket. Unbuttoned his shirt. Very slowly. Undid his high-quality formalwear trousers.

They weren't from Moss Bros, that was for sure. Imogen wanted him. She had to have him. And the time was now. She held out her hand and led him to her well-made bed. She may not have the fifty-five pillows of a hotel bed, but she had a very springy mattress.

CHAPTER TWENTY-SIX: FRANKIE

Across the street, in her bed, her window wide open as it was a hot night, Frankie heard Imogen crash in at God knows what time of the morning. She heard a car pulling away, then the sound of keys thwacking with a metallic jangle against Imogen's front door. There was giggling and a low rumble. A man's voice? Really?

Frankie had been awake on and off all night. Her brain was whirring after the date with Hugh and all the texting with Rob, and the slightest noise had disturbed her: the bark of an urban fox, a car going down the street, her friend bringing a man home for a shag... Imogen was back to her old tricks! She must be. Funny, realised Frankie, Imogen had never brought a man back to Chelmsford before. Her stomping grounds were historically hotels, apartments, London town houses and after-hours offices. That definitely sounded like a man's voice, though. There was *definitely* something going on.

Frankie turned over in bed and put a pillow over her head.

What the hell was Imogen up to?

It was ten the following morning. Frankie was in her dressing gown and on her way to put something in the outside bin. As she crossed her drive with the bulging black sack, Grace was just coming down her front path. She looked startled when she saw Frankie.

'How was the magical mystery tour?' Frankie called across. 'Did you have a good day?'

'Yes, brilliant, thanks.'

It didn't look that brilliant, thought Frankie. She noticed her friend had smudged dark circles under her eyes and a smile that looked contrived, despite her lovely outfit. She looked nice for a Sunday morning.

'Where are you off to?'

'Tesco's.'

'Oh right. You look nice for it. I hope you're not going to be flirting with the man on the cheese counter.'

'Of course not,' said Grace. 'See you later.'

'Yes, see you later,' said Frankie, feeling dismissed.

Grace got into the car and drove off. Frankie went back to her house and shut the door. There was a smudge on one of the long, narrow panes of glass either side of the door. *Kids.* She pulled her sleeve over her hand and rubbed it off. Then spotted another one, on the other side. She was half-heartedly considering going to get the Mr Muscle and a duster when she heard the sound of a car again and peered through the glass. Grace was driving back up the road and there was a man striding down Imogen's drive. She opened her door again almost as a reflex.

'Morning!' called out the man, breezily. It sounded like an American accent. Frankie and Grace, who had parked back outside her house and stepped out onto the pavement just as the man passed her – his hood up – raised eyebrows at each other. The man looked odd. A very smart suit with a grey hooded fleece over the top was a very bizarre fashion statement. Didn't Imogen have a fleece like that? And he had a white carrier bag with something bulging in it.

Frankie could see a circle of grey. Imogen's door suddenly opened.

'Gasman!' she shouted and then slammed the door.

Grace and Frankie raised their eyebrows even higher.

'I forgot my phone,' Grace said, with a shrug, and dashed back into her house, leaving the front door wide open.

Frankie was left alone, in her doorway. The man was now swiftly disappearing up the road, his carrier bag banging against his right leg. Where was his van? All she could see was a car that looked a bit like a limo, at the end of the street. Imogen was cheating, wasn't she? She had to be. Frankie would have to get to the bottom of it.

As she closed the door, she remembered she'd forgotten something, too. She hadn't packed Alice's sun-hat in her overnight bag this weekend. Damn. She'd need it. It was a boiling hot day and Rob had told her last night he was taking the children for a picnic at Hylands Park.

They used to go there all the time. Hylands House itself was beautiful – a majestic white stucco neo-classical mansion – and its parkland boasted acres of greenery, a lake and an excellent wooden play area for kids. They used to spend a couple of hours at the play area then walk up to the house, to explore the stable centre, the second-hand bookshop and the artists' studios. It was one of their favourite places. It meant a lot to them.

Frankie would take Alice's hat to them.

She parked her car and walked up the gently sloping hill. All around her were families, running dogs, laughter, kites, picnic bags, blankets and sandwiches in tin foil. Frankie scanned the hill for Rob. Ah, there he was, right at the top. She could just make him out, kneeling on a picnic blanket. Alice was a plump bundle next to him. Harry and Josh were playing some kind of fun-looking, two-handed rounders. She couldn't see Tilly at first, then realised Rob was leaning over her. He was probably on nose-wipe duty.

Frankie had quite a way to walk. She did a kind of slalom, between all the people and blankets. A marauding sausage dog meant she had to round a massive oak tree at the top of the hill and approach Rob and the children from the right. They hadn't yet seen her.

Rob's hair looked nice. He'd flicked it up slightly at the front into a less deep Tintin quiff. There was gel in it – that was unusual – and he was wearing a really nice shirt. Blue and white checks. Short-sleeved. She bet he didn't have any sun cream on. He'd burn. Burn, then go brown, that was his usual style. He was wearing those jeans that Frankie liked, the ones she'd bought him from TK Maxx. He was all scrubbed up, and she was reminded of how he looked on their first date – clean and gelled – and how excited she had been at the sight of him, how she sneaked sideways glances at him when she thought he wasn't looking. And how much she fancied him, and how she knew she would love him, one day soon.

A lovely scene, so far: pastoral, picturesque. But something was off. There was a picnic blanket joined to Rob's – its red and white stripes perpendicular to his blue and green ones. On the other blanket was a woman in a stripy Breton top and a pair of cut-off jeans, crouching by a wicker picnic basket. A small boy was lifting up one corner of the blanket with his big toe whilst he stood chattering away.

'Hi, Mum!' said Tilly, as Frankie got nearer.

'Mummy!' said Alice, reaching up her delectably tubby arms. Frankie stepped towards them and tried to envelope both her daughters in a hug. Alice wrapped her arms round one of Frankie's legs. Tilly gave her a brief squeeze round the middle then skipped away.

'Oh hi, Frankie,' said Rob, shoving a screwed-up tissue in his back pocket. 'Thanks for bringing the hat. I've been trying to keep her in the shade. Couldn't face the shops in all this heat.'

She'd texted him to say she was coming. He hadn't told her he wouldn't be alone. All the fun and near-flirting of last night's texts disappeared into the ether.

'That's okay,' she said, handing him Alice's gingham sunhat. 'Looks like you're having a nice day.'

'Yeah. Yeah. Gorgeous weather, eh? We're all enjoying ourselves.'

'Hello, boys!' called out Frankie to her sons.

'Hiii, Muuum,' they chorused, not even looking over.

'Oh, this is Jenny,' said Rob, and the woman smiled. 'My neighbour. The one I mentioned? She's a lone parent, like me. You don't mind me saying that, do you, Jen?'

Jen.

'No, of course not. I try not to be *alone* though, too much.' And *Jen* gave a shrill laugh and popped a miniature Scotch egg in her mouth.

I bet you don't, thought Frankie, releasing a now struggling Alice, who wandered off to peer into Rob's carrier bags. You're certainly not alone at the moment. And *lone parent*? That sounded really final. Rob sounded quite proud of it. Pleased.

'This is Frankie.' My wife. No, he didn't say that. She was though, wasn't she? She was still his wife.

He leant across the blanket's dividing line and handed Jen's kid a chocolate Mini Roll. Sharing. Nice.

'This is Jonathan,' Rob said.

'Hello,' said Frankie. Jonathan gave a shy smile.

'Do you want to sit down for a bit?' asked Rob. 'We've got plenty of food. Or is there something you've got to do?'

'Er, no, I'm okay, thanks, Rob. There *is* something I've got to do. I'm on my way there…now.' There was nothing. There was nowhere. No one. She was going home to an empty house and nothing to do for the rest of the day. But no *way* was she sitting on a blanket with Rob and Jen, even though her heart had a pang in it the size of a rock at the sight of her children, looking so clean and beautiful and happy and well fed, enjoying the hazy sunshine and a perfect summer's day in the park. It made her want to cry.

She bet Rob and Jen would mosey on up to the house later, like *they* always used to: go to the stable centre, get an ice cream. Peer in through the windows of the house at the gorgeous stately rooms inside. Peer into the room that was so special to Frankie and Rob…the room where they'd held their wedding reception, a decade ago. It had been packed full of people. She had looked the best and slimmest she'd ever looked. Rob had looked unbelievably smart. They'd both been so joyous and happy, with so much to look forward to. Perhaps Rob would say nothing about it; there would be no flicker of recognition or nostalgia across his face as he took Jen's hand and they walked back across the grass down to the lake…

Frankie had a feeling she'd never associated with him before: jealousy. Why was his best, scrubbed-up self coming to the park with this woman?

'I'll be off then,' she said, feeling utterly dejected. The girls were giggling over daisy chains. The boys were now doing a disjointed, laughing *haka*. She started to walk away.

'See you,' said Rob. 'I'll bring them back at six tomorrow, shall I?' There was a non-pupil day this Monday. He was taking the day off and they were staying an extra night. He was rummaging in another Tesco carrier bag. Why didn't he bring the cool box? Frankie thought. Then she remembered; it was at her house.

'Bye.'

There was no begging for her to stay. No wailing at the thought of her going. They were used to it, she thought. Used to not seeing her on these weekends with Rob. They didn't need her. None of them did. Least of all her husband.

As she got to her car she looked back up the hill. She put on her driving glasses, to see them better. The three boys were haring around. Rob and Jen and Tilly were sitting on Rob's blanket, Alice on Jen's lap. Jen was passing Rob something. He was leaning towards her and it looked like he was laughing.

Anyone near them walking a dog, or flying a kite, or screwing up the last piece of tin foil from their last cheese and pickle sandwich, would think they were a family.

CHAPTER TWENTY-SEVEN: GRACE

Grace was excited, jittery. So jittery she'd forgotten her phone and had to go back for it. She needed it for Google Maps. There had been a strange man on their street, leaving Imogen's drive. She hadn't seen his face, but according to Imogen men from the gas company now sported suits and ill-fitting grey hoodies. *Very* strange. Still, she couldn't concern herself with that now. She was on a mission. She was on the brink of starting a wonderful new relationship. Farewell James and his cheating bastard heart for good! She'd found someone better. Someone better-looking, nicer…someone who would be faithful to her and treat her right. She couldn't wait to get to Greg. She would put away her purse, he would put away his escort plans and they'd start the rest of their lives.

He lived on Chelsea Road, in Chelmsford. He hadn't told her the number but he'd told her the street when she'd asked him. Escorts didn't usually give out their addresses, she was sure, but he'd told *her*. He was different. *She* was different.

She'd go to his street and look for his car.

To get to Chelsea Road, Grace had to drive through the centre of town. She made steady progress – traffic wasn't too bad on a Sunday. Turning right at the roundabout by the university, she passed the Pacific Hotel. Greg's car was quite distinctive: an electric blue Beetle. He'd dropped her to the end of her road in it, after the roller-skating. It was there, in the hotel car park. She was sure it was. She had no choice but to swiftly put on her indicator and turn at lightning speed into the car park. A car beeped behind her angrily; she'd braked quite suddenly.

She parked two rows behind Greg's car and instinctively – feeling like a ridiculous rookie cop on a stake-out – ducked and peered up through the windscreen. She could see the doors to the hotel lobby.

An older couple with matching rucksacks came through them. Then a giggly group of young women wheeling those hand luggage cases. Hen night – one of them was still wearing pink fluffy deely bobbers. Then, in a flurry of *huge* leopard print scarf and laughter, a blonde fifty-something in a black maxi dress emerged. She had an expensive-looking red patent bag over her shoulder, leopard print shoes to match the scarf, and her hair was flicky blonde and mid-length.

Greg appeared behind her, in the trousers and shirt he'd worn to Ascot. The woman, mid-laugh, stepped forward and planted a kiss on his lips. It was a long peck, almost a smooch. Then she reached behind and, although Grace wasn't sure, seemed to squeeze his bottom. They laughed. Oh God. A client! Grace felt sick.

The woman turned and skipped down the lobby steps to a red sports car parked close to the lobby. With a swish of a fancy key fob thing, she got in, fouffed her hair in the mirror, put on some shades and sped away.

Greg started walking down the steps to his car. Without daring to look over at him again, Grace took off the handbrake, slammed her car into reverse, and got the hell out of there. As she drove away, hot, stupid tears ran

down her cheeks. She'd been a bloody fool, all over again.
A bloody idiot. Why had she thought for a minute that
dating Greg was her being *controlled* and *in charge*? What
a joke! She hadn't been protecting her heart. Her heart had
come way off the rails and was careering down a one-way
track on one of those pushy-pulley things. She was way,
way out of control.

Gutted wasn't the word. How *could* he? Somehow,
between saying goodbye to her at the station last night, and
now, he had managed to sleep with his first client. Well,
congratulations, Greg! How much did he get for it? £200?
£500? She angrily googled his agency website again,
when she got in. It didn't say, but everything he did had a
price. Everything was fake. Everything he'd done, all those
nice things he'd said. Fake, fake, fake. How could he kiss
her like that and then go and make some cold hard cash
shagging Mrs Fifty-something Leopard Print?

It was a done deal. Greg was a proper escort now. He
was initiated.

And it was all over for him and Grace. She was
absolutely gutted.

CHAPTER TWENTY-EIGHT:
IMOGEN

A very happy woman sighed contentedly and languidly stretched her arms above her head. A happy woman who had gone back to bed after seeing Richard off up the drive. She didn't care that he'd been spotted, not really. It was bad luck that both Grace and Frankie had seen him, but Imogen would explain to them properly later…that she was sorry, but she'd fallen in love. Maybe she'd pop over to see them tonight. For now, she was going to spend the rest of the morning in bed, chilling out and reliving the amazing sex she'd had with Richard.

And wow, it had been amazing. Amazing! He had been considerate, tender. Loving, exciting. He knew exactly what to do and when to do it. They had some music going: something 90s, Brand New Heavies, 'Midnight at the Oasis'. The lighting had been just perfect. Half moonlight, through her open window. There was a gorgeous eye-locking moment about 80 per cent in.

Everything had been perfect. He'd not attempted to talk dirty once. Talking dirty was an absolute bugbear of hers. If she heard the mere sniff of a 'Do you like it when I do that, baby?' her libido took off in a jumbo jet to Timbuktu, never to return. Thankfully, there was none of that. He was lovely and silent, except when it was appropriate to be otherwise.

And afterwards, he'd been fabulous. He'd stroked her cheek and told her she was beautiful and then early this morning – they were both too wired to sleep in – he'd made her a bacon sandwich, and she'd put on his shirt, like they do in the movies, *and* she'd looked dead sexy in it, just as she was supposed to.

When he'd left, she'd lent him her huge grey fleece, to put over his suit – not a brilliant disguise for a lover, clearly, despite her making him pull up the hood (Gasman! Was that the best she could do?) – and he'd kissed her and told her he'd see her very, very soon. She told him she couldn't wait.

'Happy?' he'd asked her, just inside her front door, looking faintly ridiculous.

'Deliriously so.'

'Me too. You're the one for me, Imogen. I knew it as soon as I first saw your stroppy face.'

'And you're incredibly corny, Mr Stoughton. As well as being slightly rude. Now off you go.'

She lay in bed until eleven o'clock before she got bored. She wasn't really a lying-in-bed person, even when she tried to be. She sat up and reached under it for her small laptop. She'd check her emails, have a mooch around the fashion blogs she liked to follow. She plumped up several pillows behind her and, sighing contentedly, opened up Outlook.

She had eleven new emails. A lot of it was junk: handbag sales, new beauty products on the market, newsletters she'd subscribed to but really should get around to unsubscribing from. There was an email from Marcia about Melissa May Scott, an actor she was thinking of signing up. Marcia wanted her to check out the notices for a play she'd done. Yep, yep, she'd do that later.

She was just about to close down Outlook and scoot over to Google when another email popped up. The subject said 'Information' and the sender was Carolyn Boot. The email sent the customary nervous chill down her spine, coupled with internal eye-rolling. That doomsday sense of oh flip, what does the old dragon want now? Carolyn had always had Imogen's home email. When she'd worked for her, Imogen had to be on call for the old bat 24/7. What on earth was this about?

She opened up the mail.

Dear Imogen,

I thought it would be in your best interests to know that Richard Stoughton is in a relationship with another (much younger) woman. She was at Ascot yesterday. I'm not sure whether you saw her – she's very slim and blonde and much younger than you. I suspect the relationship is a tumultuous one (aren't the best always!) as they had words and she seemed quite upset. Furthermore, my husband and I were in New York last November and after meeting Richard for lunch, we saw him with the same woman and a child in Central Park. I believe Richard to be the boy's father. Forearmed is forewarned, I believe, Imogen. I'm sure you will thank me for passing this very pertinant information onto you.

Regards,

Carolyn Boot

Strangely, Imogen's first sensation was glee at the fact that Carolyn had made a spelling mistake – 'pertinant' not *pertinent*. Her second was a mixture of fear, despair, horror and nausea. What? Oh my God! It all came flooding into her brain in a horrible, awful rush – the young girl walking up the landing and crying, Carolyn's cool smile when she said goodbye, Richard's effusive display when Imogen returned to the box, which she now saw was a show of automatic recovery. No wonder he was laughing so loudly, showing off so heartily, it was a loud American smoke screen to cover whatever scene had just taken place.

Another woman? In a relationship? A child! Oh God, a child! Richard was father to that young woman's son. She felt sick. She hadn't had a hangover but one swept over her now like a brutal tidal wave. She needed water, she needed carbs, she needed Nurofen. She needed to have not just read this bloody email. In a horrible click of her laptop mouse, Richard was no longer her Richard from *Friends*, he was no longer *her* Richard at all.

Carolyn's delayed revenge. That's what this was. She *knew* I'd sleep with him, thought Imogen, in a cold sweat. She knew I would, and she'd tell me afterwards. Strike while all irons were still hot. Bitch. Bloody bitch. But Imogen was also culpable. She should have known Richard was too good to be true. Too charming, too nice, too funny, too good-looking: too bloody perfect.

She wailed. He had been. He'd been perfect, for her. Oh God, oh God. This couldn't be happening. 'You're the one for me,' he'd said. Sebastian had said the same. How could she have been so stupid?

Unless…Carolyn had got it wrong. It was his sister, right? It was *always* his sister, in the movies. The girl the hero is talking to, mopping up tears from, having a brief kiss or cuddle with by a car or outside a shop or something. It always turns out, to huge relief all round, to be his bloody sister, and the heroine always goes, 'Of course, how silly of me!' and slaps her own forehead for being so dumb and not having seen the *clearly obvious* family resemblance. The woman was his sister and the boy was his nephew. Not his *son*. Carolyn had got it all wrong.

But. Why would his *sister* turn up to Ascot? And have sexy tumultuous *words* with him, in the box. It didn't make sense. His sister would be in America, surely?

It wasn't his sister, was it? It was a girl he was in a relationship with. A younger, slimmer, blonder girl. A girl who'd had his baby. A girl who was on one of those boozy Ascot coach trips, who'd had a lot to drink, who knew exactly where to find Richard. Or was she supposed to be a guest in his box all along? Had she rocked up and discovered he was there with another woman? Had he *double-booked*? She didn't know. All she knew was, this girl had shattered all her illusions. That's what they'd been. Illusions. He was a liar, a man who made women cry, a man who had babies with women and then met other women and didn't tell them, a man who could not be trusted. Imogen felt like banging her head against the wall. She was right to have been afraid. She was right to be terrified of falling in love. But she'd gone and done it anyway. And now she must pay the price, just like she had all those years ago.

She'd been an utter fool.

The rest of the day was spent lying on a sofa in a pair of jersey pyjamas and angrily reliving all the ways in which Richard had been an absolute tragedy of a disappointment. And sobbing into a whole roll of toilet paper. And eating Twiglets. The only constructive thing she did was block his number from her phone. She should have done it the moment he kissed her.

On Monday morning, she left for work early. She didn't take the Tube to Leicester Square as usual, but came out at Liverpool Street and walked to the underground car park under Richard's office. She knew he got into the office at six a.m. and that between six and seven Nigel parked the car underneath the office and went to the local greasy spoon for a cup of tea and a bacon butty. She found Richard's car, that gorgeous car with the leather interior, and put a Post-it note on his windscreen that said, *'It's over. I know about the woman at Ascot and your child. Imogen'*, and then she walked back to Liverpool Street Station, got on the Tube and went to work.

CHAPTER TWENTY-NINE: FRANKIE

At around nine o'clock, long after Frankie had got back from Hylands and a while after she'd spent all afternoon not watching Wimbledon, she did something she'd made herself not do, ever since she and Rob had split: she looked at their wedding album.

On the first page was a large picture of Rob outside the church. He looked nervous, cheeky, expectant. There was one of him and his sister, Beth, his arm round her shoulders. They were both grinning from ear to ear. He looked excited. Beth had told her that Rob had been ready super early that day. *Really* early for him. He hadn't drunk a drop the night before either, she'd been told, or eaten a kebab, like the others had. He'd wanted to be *fresh* for the day, he'd kept saying. Beth said all his mates had teased him for it, trying to get him to have a beer, but he'd refused. 'No, not tonight,' he'd said, apparently.

Frankie was excited too – she'd arrived ten minutes too early, and had to go round the block twice as she could see some of their friends, animated and laughing, still making their way into the church. Even when she'd finally told the car to stop, one minute after 2p.m., there were still a couple of stragglers making their way in. Everyone had been so on form, so happy. There were photos of some of their friends, outside the church before she'd turned up, taken with Rob. There was a funny one of someone doing bunny ears, behind Rob's head. Then there were photos of her, in her dress, with her dad. She'd worn a huge meringue, in the palest of pale pinks, her hair pinned up into waves. She'd looked gorgeous; everyone had said so.

She turned the next page and smiled. She and Rob were coming down the aisle, after signing the register. With tears springing to her eyes, she remembered how Rob had practically marched her down there, laughing, as though he couldn't wait to get her outside, into the sunshine and the pealing bells and the confetti, so they could begin their married life.

She looked at the photos again, slowly, from beginning to end, and she cried and cried and cried. For the people they'd been. For the people they were now. And for the huge gulf and four beautiful children that sat between the two.

After two hours of crying, her nose was red raw from being blown into less than soft kitchen roll and her eyes felt like onions. She lay on the sofa, slippers on, despite the heat. Every time she stopped and thought, *enough now*, she started bawling again. But she still didn't know what she wanted. She thought she wanted him back. But she was terrified that having him come home would set them on the same road again – just slightly further back. Before they knew it, they would reach the exact same point again – the point where she'd had enough of it all and kicked him out.

She reckoned she could easily spend the entire night this way. Thinking and crying. Crying and thinking. She was just entering another ready bout of sobbing when her mobile phone rang. It was Rob. She sniffed a giant sniff and tested out her voice, ridiculously saying, 'Hello, hello,' into the silent living room, to make sure her voice wasn't too wavery or croaky. Then, she pressed the green phone symbol and said it to him.

'Hello?'

'Frankie. Hi. It's Rob. Tilly's not well. I don't know if it's an A and E job or not but if it is I can't go because the others are all asleep.'

'A and E!' Frankie sat up and one of her slippers fell off. 'What on earth's the matter?'

'Sorry, I didn't mean to scare you. But she's all feverish. Burning hot, all shivery. I'm pretty worried.'

'Have you given her the pink paracetamol stuff?'

'Yes, but it's not doing anything yet. It was half an hour ago. Can you please come over, Frankie. I'm sure it's *not* anything serious, but I'm beginning to panic a bit.'

'Oh God,' said Frankie. 'Yes. I'm coming over. I'll be there in fifteen minutes.' She grabbed a jacket and her keys, changed her slippers for flip-flops and flew out of the front door.

When she got to Rob's flat, he was pale and couldn't muster a smile.

'How's she doing? She any better?'

'I think so. I'm not sure. Come and have a look.'

Tilly was lying on Rob's brown leather sofa, on a cotton sheet that he must have laid there for her. She was in her One Direction pyjamas and was fast asleep. Frankie placed a hand to her forehead. She felt hot and her face was all flushed.

'Have you called the NHS number, whatever it is these days?'

'No, I hadn't thought of that. That was always your – '

'Department?' She smiled ruefully. 'What's her temperature?'

'Thirty-seven.'

'That's fine then. Normal.' She had a sudden thought. 'Have you checked her for spots?'

'Spots?'

'Chicken pox.'

Tilly was the only one who'd never had it; the others all had. Frankie had even taken her to a chicken pox party when she was two – they were all the rage at the time – and Tilly still didn't get it.

Frankie gently pulled up the bottom of her daughter's pyjama top. There, on her tummy, was a smattering of the tell-tale, irregular-shaped spots, just emerging.

'I'm sure that's chicken pox,' she said, with a sigh of relief. 'I know it well.' She did. She'd been the one to nurse the other three children through it: running tepid baths, applying cold flannels, giving them lectures on not scratching and scars. Rob hadn't been involved. 'I'm sure the paracetamol will kick in soon. Keep a note of the time you gave it to her. It's every four hours. You can wake her, even through the night, to keep her dosed up. Or,' she said. 'I can take her home with me.' She wanted to. She wanted to take Tilly home with her.

'I don't think we should disturb her,' said Rob. 'She's out for the count. Can you stay, Frankie? Stay with me, to look after her?'

There was only one answer. 'Okay,' Frankie said. 'I'll stay.'

He put the kettle on, then they sat on the floor in front of the sofa, and the telly, which had some old comedy show on, turned down low. They talked in low voices. They talked and talked. About Tilly. About all the children, in turn, how they were doing at school, the wonderful and funny things they said, how they were growing up so fast. Then they started talking about TV programmes they used to watch together but had watched separately over the last few months, until Rob looked at Frankie and said, 'I don't blame you for chucking me out. I was awful, Frankie, I'm sorry.'

'You were,' she said.

'I know.' He nodded. 'I was a lazy, self-centred, unappreciative git.'

'Yes, that pretty much sums it up.'

'Okay, enough about me…' he joked. 'I'm trying here. I want to try and make things right. I think I can change, if we got back together…'

Rob straightened his back and his eyes, which had been blinking sleepily, focused on hers. She hadn't looked into his eyes for a long time. She'd forgotten what nice eyes they were. 'I really want us to get back together, Franks. If you want to, that is. Would you consider it?'

Frankie sat up too. She realised she was shaking. It took her by surprise. 'If we do, you *have* to change. In a lot of ways.'

'I will, Frankie, I promise.'

She took a deep breath. 'I really need you to know, that as awful as it was, it wasn't a mistake – me kicking you out like that. It was the opposite of a mistake.' Rob lowered his head and stared at the floor. 'I know it's really hurt you,' she continued, 'but I needed this to happen. I needed to be on my own.'

'You needed to get rid of me.'

'I did.'

'As bad as it's been,' said Rob, looking up, 'and it was *really* bad, in the beginning. I was so angry with you – my own fault, I know, I know,' he said, holding his hands up, 'it's been good for us. I hated you at first, really hated you. Then I came to realise, it was me I hated. What I'd become. The lazy so-and-so I'd become.' He leant back and sighed. 'You know, I felt like I'd never been a proper father to them, until I had them on my own. That first weekend I had them, bloody hell, it was hard, but I realised that's what it's like for you, all the time. That first weekend I became their father.'

Frankie nodded.

'Then I wanted to show you that I could do it – that I could scrub up, shape up, look after them properly and without complaining. That I could keep somewhere clean and tidy, do the washing and the ironing and all that stuff.'

'I'm glad you got to experience how mind-numbing all that stuff is. I saw your Monica cupboard, by the way.'

'Did you? Oh God! I wanted to create a good impression. I'm afraid it did involve shoving a load of junk in there ten minutes before you turned up!'

'Don't beat yourself up. I do the same, in a multitude of cupboards, before Mum and Dad come over. You just never noticed. You didn't have to.'

'I'll change,' he repeated. 'And I want to help the kids to change, too. To be *better* – we don't want them growing up to be like me.'

'No, we don't,' said Frankie. 'Or to be too soft, like me. I've been thinking about this a lot. How they got so bad. You've been lazy and I think my own parents were so strict with me that I've completely gone the other way with the children. Over-compensated. Tried to be their friend, the best, most brilliant mum in the world. It's back-fired, hasn't it?'

'It may have done. I think if we put in more rules and boundaries then we'll all have a better time. Kids love boundaries; I heard it on the news the other day.'

'Who knew?' She laughed, but she felt hopeful. It sounded like Rob was finally ready to be a help not a hindrance. They could work on things *together.*

'And I'll get rid of the kit car.'

'Really? You love Kit!'

'Where can we go in it, unless we get a sidecar? It was a selfish pursuit, with a selfish end – me going off on my own. I don't want to be on my own. I want to be with you.' He locked eyes with her. She remembered the green fleck he had in his left eye. She hadn't noticed it for a very long time. 'Remember that day you came over here? I really wanted to ask you to come with us, to the museum. But I couldn't, I wanted to make you see I could do it on my own.' He ran a hand through his hair. He looked knackered. 'You did look lovely that day, though.'

'Did I?'

'You always look lovely, Frankie. I should really have told you more often.'

'You never told me at all, Rob.'

'I know. I'm sorry.' He looked her right in the eye. 'I promise I'll bring some romance back into our lives. You deserve it. You're still lovely, Frankie.'

Frankie gulped. She knew she looked terrible after all that crying earlier, but it obviously wasn't bothering Rob. Blimey, this *was* bordering on romantic. There'd been no romantic moments with Rob for about fifteen years. She'd love romantic moments in her life again.

'I love you,' said Rob.

She got a funny feeling in her stomach. A feeling Rob hadn't generated for aeons. She could see in his face that lad she'd met in The Ram, all those years before. He looked handsome, tender, earnest, and utterly delighted with her. Could they get it back, what they'd had before life got in the way?

'Are you sure?'

'Yes, I'm bloody sure. I want to be with you.' His face took on a hurt puppy look. 'Frankie? Help me out here, for God's sake!'

She'd enjoyed her time on her own, going it alone. She'd proved she could do it. She'd rediscovered her sense of fun and adventure. She'd even kissed another man.

It was now time to be part of a team again. On better terms.

'And I want to be with you, Rob.'

His face relaxed; his eyes lit up. 'You do? Really? Do you mean it?'

'Yes, I mean it.'

'So we can get back together? Can I come home?'

She'd loved being single. She was sorry she hadn't managed it for a whole year. But she'd made her decision.

'As long as you bring your new laundry skills with you, yes, you can come home.'

'Thank God for that!' said Rob and he sat, with his head down, and exhaled for what seemed like for ever. When he looked up he had tears in his eyes. 'Come here.' And he bundled her into a massive bear hug and held her so tightly stuffed into his neck she could hardly breathe. When he released her, he put his face close to hers and kissed her, in a way he'd done once upon a time. Way back when. It felt lovely. It felt like coming home. Then he put his arm round her and she nuzzled into his warm, familiar shoulder.

'Were you on a date with that woman, that Jen?' she suddenly said, pulling away from him slightly.

'No, we're just friends. But I like that you think I was.' He grinned.

'I don't actually,' she lied, sticking her tongue out. 'Why would you be? She's nowhere near as attractive as me.'

'No, she's not.'

'And you've always hated Breton tops.'

He laughed. That way he laughed by throwing his head back and showing all his teeth. She'd missed that. 'You're terrible…'

'*Mariel*,' she added.

And he pulled her close to him again and they sat like that, in each other's arms, for ages, and watched *The Love Boat*, which somebody had decided was just right for putting on telly at one in the morning.

They were back together, and everything was perfect.

CHAPTER THIRTY: GRACE

*I need to see you. This morning. Will NOT be paying you.
11 a.m. at Luigi's*
  That's me told, lol! OK. See you there.
  Inappropriately flippant, but what did he know?

On Monday morning, after she'd taken Daniel to school,
Grace walked into Luigi's. She'd taken the morning off
work. Pretended she was unwell. Gideon had not been
happy, but when was he ever? And she *did* feel unwell.
After she'd witnessed Greg and his client at the hotel, she'd
spent the rest of Sunday staring at the television, seeing
nothing. She knew she had to talk to Greg. She knew she
wouldn't rest until she had.

Greg was sitting at the same table, although he was
dressed a lot more casually this time. T-shirt and jeans
instead of shirt and trousers. He still looked completely
gorgeous. He was a very attractive man. But he was a
man who last night had been paid for sex. And he would
continue to be paid for sex. He would not give up his job
for her so. He was not the *man* for her.

He smiled that slow, sexy smile as she walked over
to the table. Damn! She had a fleeting hope – and she

knew it was just a hope – that he hadn't done anything last night. That Leopard Print Lady had just wanted some company. She'd wanted to talk, to hold his hand and pour out all her troubles as she drank cheap house white from the mini-bar…

'Hi,' Greg said, cheerfully, 'to what do I owe the pleasure, on a Monday morning?'

'Less of the charm speak,' she snapped. 'We can dispense with all that now. I'm taking you off the payroll.'

Greg looked shocked but slightly amused. 'Taking me off the payroll? What do you mean? You don't want to see me any more?'

She sat down, with a bit of a bump. Banged her bag down on the table. It made quite a loud noise. No one else was in there. It didn't matter. Nothing really mattered.

'The pleasure was all someone else's, last night, wasn't it?'

He looked uncomfortable. 'Meaning?'

'Meaning, I saw you and Mrs Leopard Print come out of The Pacific Hotel yesterday morning. Looking quite happy. Quite *satisfied*, in fact. I was on my way to try and find you. I wanted to talk to you.'

'Ah.'

'Ah, indeed. And lots of other noises, no doubt.'

'You saw me with Gill.'

'Gill.' *Thanks for that. I'm not sure I wanted to know her name*. She felt so flat. Gill. Just a name. Just a woman. It could have been anyone. Anyone with some cash in her bag and a little free time she wanted filling. *He* certainly didn't care. It was money. 'What happened?' she said, sadly, although she was trying to add a cutting edge to her voice. She doubted it was working. She expected she just sounded pathetic. 'After we left each other on Saturday night? How did your night end with a paid booty call from *Gill*?'

'She texted me when I was on the train.'

'Oh.' When was that, then? When he was reading her horoscope? Was *that* why he went so quiet afterwards?

'She wanted to meet me for a nightcap. I went to the hotel.'

A *nightcap*. That old, rotten chestnut.

'How nice. Why did you kiss me, Greg?' Grace's voice was rising. She felt sick. 'You shouldn't have kissed me like that, then slept with that woman. It's disgusting!'

She hated this. This loss of control and power. She'd gone back exactly to how she felt when James had cheated. James had all the power, now Greg had it. She hated them both. She pushed back her chair with a harsh, metallic scrape and rose from the table.

'Please don't go, Grace,' pleaded Greg. 'Let me explain. I liked you. I really, really liked you. I meant all those things I said to you. Every word.' She sat down again, deflated, but kept her chair where it was, away from the table. 'I couldn't resist kissing you. You're gorgeous, you're a lovely person. I think you're amazing. You deserve someone amazing. But I *can't* give up the escorting. I need the money. I'd never be able to make it another way…'

She cut him off. 'No, Greg, this is the way you *want* to make money. You've chosen this. You *want* to do everything you've done, including sleeping with that woman.' She knew she was sneering when she said *that woman*, but she couldn't help herself. 'You lied to me. You said to forget I was paying you and to see how things went. Those were your actual words, Greg.'

'I'm sorry.'

Grace's anger was escalating, but she knew she was most angry with herself – she'd gone into this with her eyes wide open. How could she have been so stupid, so naive?

'You're a prostitute now, Greg. That's what you are. You've crossed that line and there's no going back. Welcome to your new career; I hope it's a great success.'

Greg shifted a little, in his seat.

'Oh my God,' whimpered Grace, feeling like she was going to faint. 'I wasn't your first client, was I?'

Greg had the audacity to actually blush a little.

'You lied to me,' she groaned. 'Oh God, you say that to everyone don't you, to make them feel special? *I bet you say that to all the girls*,' she mocked. 'How long have you *really* been an escort?'

'Three years.'

'Three years!' Her stupidity and naivety knew no bounds. She'd been a blind, trusting idiot!

'Grace, Grace, look, it's all academic. I'm sorry. I'm sorry I can't be the man for you. But I never was. Perhaps in another life…' He tried to smile.

'I hate it when people say that,' she barked. 'We're not in another life, we're in *this* one.' Her voice lowered to a whimper. 'You've lied to me on every level.'

'Why were you coming to find me, anyway?' Oh, change the subject, why don't you? He's so bloody calm, she thought, while she was falling apart.

'It doesn't matter now.'

'I'm sorry,' he repeated. 'Look, before you go and I never see you again, can I say something? I think you need to grieve for your marriage. I don't think you've given yourself time to get over it.'

'Well, thank you, Dr Phil!' she said. And then she really couldn't stand it any more. She pushed back her chair further, with another terrible screech, and stood up. 'I've got to go. This whole thing has been a mistake.'

'Take the good things from it, not the bad,' said Greg. He stood up, too. He tried to hold out his hand to her. His eyes seemed to be pleading with her.

'Goodbye, Greg. Enjoy the money.'

She walked out of Luigi's. She headed down the street. And she began to cry. Finally, the tears she'd refused to cry for James, for her marriage, came flooding out. It wasn't the best place for it – in the middle of town in broad daylight – and she must have looked ridiculous, walking down the high street sobbing and with tears running down her cheeks, but for once she was beyond caring what she looked like. It all came out: the hurt, the betrayal, the lies, the grief. James and that woman. The loss of her marriage. She sobbed and sobbed and sobbed, at one point having to duck into a shop doorway for a particularly loud bawl.

Once she'd finished, and blown her nose on a whole pack of floral-printed tissues, she started thinking. She had to find a way forward. A way to live now. *Were* there any good things to be taken from Greg? She really wanted there to be something, so this whole episode was not a complete waste of time. All the wasted years with James, now a wasted few months with Greg. The bastard and the escort. It would make a good book title.

What on earth was she going to do now?

Her phone chimed with a text. She extracted it from the neat little pocket inside her bag. Who on earth was this? Oh, it wasn't a text, it was a 'Hook' from Hook, Line and Sinker. A message. It was that Tim again. The one who climbed mountains.

Hey, Grace, me again. Hope you are well. Are you by any chance free for that date we never had? I've had some absolute shockers, I can tell you – you may be my only hope!

There was a new photo in a circle next to the message. She enlarged it. It was Tim in a dinner suit, laughing, and clearly cropped from a group picture. There was a hand on each of his shoulders. Tim. He looked nice. He *seemed* nice. He liked her. He wanted to go out with her. She could message him back, arrange to meet, start all over again.

She could do that, couldn't she?

CHAPTER THIRTY-ONE:
IMOGEN

It was the night of Imogen's forty-first birthday party and she was as miserable as hell. So much for her distant dream that she'd be married by thirty! She hadn't been married by thirty, or forty, or forty-one. She wouldn't ever be getting married.

On her fortieth birthday – a cruise up the Thames and a night dancing in Mahiki – she still had hope. Now, that was gone, along with any desire to date, hook up with, sleep with or have anything to do with *any man ever again*. Being single wasn't the worst thing. Single she could live with, happily. Being utterly *heartbroken* was the worst thing. Richard had shone a brief and heavenly beam of light on her life and now it had been taken away. She was left in the dark, alone and devastated.

It was Saturday night, almost a week to the day since she'd discovered the truth about Richard. June the 27th. Happy bloody birthday. As she sat on the train opposite Frankie and Grace, all of them dressed up with somewhere special to go, she tried to muster up some – any – enthusiasm for tonight's get-together. She couldn't be doing with it. She couldn't face going to The Summer Garden at London's swanky, five star Residence Hotel with her two best friends, and Marcia, for a gorgeous dinner and some cocktails. She wanted to stay at home and sob under her duvet in despair because she'd lost the best man she'd ever known.

She hadn't planned anything for her birthday. She'd been so caught up in Richard, she'd almost forgotten it was coming. And after it had all gone so tragically wrong with him, she'd rather it didn't. Her friends hadn't mentioned it either. For women who'd decided to simplify things by ditching men from their lives, they all seemed to be losing the plot.

Imogen gazed out of the train window and sighed. She was *so* not up for tonight. It was completely wasted on her that Marcia had booked the best table at The Summer Garden. That strings had been pulled. Marcia knew the maître d' there, some old flame of hers she'd had a passionate fling with twenty years ago. She'd never forgotten him. Imogen suspected Marcia had had a string of passionate flings with unforgettable men. And there was no danger *any* of them had forgotten *her*.

Marcia had strong-armed Nicholas Longbottom (Imogen couldn't wait to have this physical attribute confirmed or denied) into giving them the best and most fabulous table in 'The Alcove', a cosy, candlelit nook of the restaurant usually reserved for celebrities and Ronnie Wood. And Imogen had drummed into her how lucky they were to get a table there.

'Darling, it's fabulous,' Marcia had said on Tuesday, as she sat at her desk flicking through headshots. Imogen was at hers, under the eaves, catching up dejectedly on some paperwork. That morning Marcia had noticed Imogen's birthday on the calendar, was horrified nothing had been arranged and got straight on 'the blower' to The Residence. 'It gets booked up way in advance. You're lucky I could wangle it, at this late notice. Tell your friends to dress up.

I know you anti-men lot like to wear sackcloth and ashes, but you must go full *glamorama*.'

'I don't think I'd suit sackcloth and ashes,' Imogen had said, sighing and looking down at her crisp navy suit with the nipped-in waist. 'And it's not as though we're going to flog ourselves with birch twigs at the sight of any men. A nice dress and some heels – will that do you? What are *you* going to be wearing?'

'Oh, I'll be hoisting the mainsail to full mast, sweetie, don't you worry about that.'

Whatever that meant, thought Imogen, though no doubt Marcia's enormous bottom would be clad in some kind of huge, chiffony skirt and she'd have a whole treasure chest full of costume jewellery on.

'You look like you need feeding up a bit,' said Marcia, ploughing on; Imogen had a sudden image of her roaring round a field in a blinged-up combine harvester. 'You can't be all frugal-*stroke*-hessian-*stroke*-lesbian at The Summer Garden, you and your man-hating friends. We've got to stuff our faces and drink buckets of alcohol. You won't be able to get wheatgrass shots there, you know.'

'When have I ever drunk wheatgrass shots?' spluttered Imogen. 'And we're not *lesbians*. We're just normal women who don't need men in our lives.' Less than ever, she thought miserably.

Marcia looked at her pointedly and then burst out laughing. 'Okay, whatever you say.' She suddenly seemed to remember something, grabbed her Dictaphone from her desk and coughed, 'Deluded' into it, followed by the louder, '*Deluded*. New play At the South Bank. Stephen Mathers or Nigel Pendleton-Smith? Pink sky it tomorrow,' then threw it back down. 'We'll have cocktails in the bar and then dine,' she exclaimed. 'It's your birthday, Imogen! Celebrate!' And she actually swivelled right over to Imogen on her chair, grabbed Imogen's right cheek and gave it a little squeeze.

'Bog off, Marcia!' said Imogen, swatting her away. 'Squeeze your own cheeks!'

She couldn't bear to tell Marcia she didn't feel like celebrating, or what had happened with Richard. She'd never mentioned him to Marcia – there was no way she could, after confiding in her about all that single for a year guff. And thank goodness she hadn't, now Richard was gone.

The train lurched and Imogen's bag slipped from her lap. She grabbed it just in time, before her favourite lip gloss clattered to the filthy floor. She'd worn it on the lunch date with Richard, she recalled despondently, as she stuffed it back in her bag. That bastard. She couldn't think about that, or him, now.

The three friends were glammed up, just as Marcia had hoped. Imogen – black leather jeggings, high ankle boots and a charcoal grey silk loose-fitting blouse with a pussy bow. Frankie – capri pants, black T-shirt and tuxedo jacket – she looked great. And Grace – soft gold shift dress – amazing as ever.

They all looked slightly away with the fairies, though, Imogen thought. Grace looked miserable and had her mouth set into a firm line as she stared vacantly out of the window at passing fields. Frankie looked like she was permanently trying to suppress a massive grin and had a silly look on her face, like Worzel Gummidge when he was thinking up a plan.

They all looked like they had things they should be telling each other, but there was no way Imogen was *ever* telling them about Richard. They'd both quizzed her about the man they'd seen outside her house, especially Frankie, who was very sceptical about it being the gasman. She said she could have sworn she'd heard a man's voice the night before, but Imogen told her it was the taxi driver, helping her into the house as she was drunk, and that the gasman just had a very strange uniform. She didn't care if they believed her or not. It didn't matter. Nothing mattered any more.

She just wanted to forget the whole sorry episode – another tragic blip she should never have succumbed to. If she told her friends what had happened, she couldn't guarantee she wouldn't burst into mascara-ruining tears, for falling for Richard so badly and so heavily, for sleeping with him, for entertaining the entirely ridiculous notion that he could love her back. She couldn't do it. She would not and *could* not succumb to being a pathetic woman wailing over a man.

The train trundled on. Fields gave way to the backs of terraced houses with huge satellite dishes, which gave way to the O2 ex-Millennium Dome and the Olympic Park, and finally, Liverpool Street Station. As the train came to a stop, they all looked at each other and smiled. Grace's was tight-lipped, Imogen's was fake and Frankie's was wide and beaming.

What on earth had happened to them all?

CHAPTER THIRTY-TWO: FRANKIE

She and Rob were back together. It was just like starting over. Frankie had to tell Imogen and Grace at some point, but she didn't dare just yet. She couldn't collapse the sisterhood, break the charter, let the side down, whatever, especially not today.

For the sake of birthday harmony – not that Imogen seemed too bothered about it, and Frankie was slightly ashamed she'd forgotten all about it too, until Imogen had rung to say Marcia had booked a swanky restaurant for tonight – she would have to pretend that Rob was still persona non grata, man-us horribilis, ex under fire. She could do this. Pretend she wasn't filled with enormous relief, renewed love and massive hope for the future. Pretend she didn't have a man again, a *new* man. He *was* a new man: Rob really did seem to have changed, and she had to take a chance on him. She'd enjoyed being single but she wanted her family reunited more.

She would toast to independence, female solidarity and telling men to sod right off, but keep her delicious secret to herself. And at the end of their no doubt fabulous evening, she would go home to Rob and her children. Tomorrow they'd have the sort of Sunday she'd really missed – chaos and mess and mayhem (but not *too* bad; they were having new rules, remember?) and snuggling up on the sofa to watch something fun like *Ghostbusters*. She couldn't wait.

Rob had moved back in last night, after days of constant texts between them saying, 'Are you sure?' 'No, are you sure?' He'd arrived on the doorstep with the same bags he'd left with, but there seemed to be less in them and they were packed better. When she'd opened the back door, he'd flung them to the ground, smiled his lovely, familiar smile and said, 'Hi, honey, I'm home.' She had virtually jumped on him, *Dirty Dancing* style and had dragged him into the house. She'd laughed at the burrs like beads of Velcro stuck to his shoulders – his car was parked in the next street and Frankie was making him use the back alley until she had a chance to tell Imogen and Grace he was back.

The kids were thrilled, mostly. Frankie told them they weren't going to Daddy's flat any more, and that Daddy was coming home. Harry had looked a bit disgruntled; Dad had an Xbox. 'Dad can bring it home with him,' she pointed out. And Josh had pulled a bit of a face about leaving Jonathan behind, but Frankie had promised he could come for tea. Without *Jen*.

'Will our house be Daddy's house again?' asked Tilly. She was feeling better, though she looked awful. She had bright red, blistering spots all over her face and body. A finger wandered up to her cheek to a particularly angry-looking one.

'Don't scratch your spots!' pleaded Frankie. 'Yes, darling, it will. We're all getting back together.'

Was he sad to let his flat go? she'd asked him, last night.

'Of course not,' he'd said. 'I'd rather be here, with you, than anywhere else in the world.' They were snuggled up in bed. She didn't mind the rucking up of the covers, or the way he'd created a chilly space when he'd rolled to the side to turn off his phone when they'd first got in.

She still believed in the Single for a Year Club, in theory.
She liked its ethos. She would use it to help her devise a
new framework for life with Rob. She wouldn't be taking
any more nonsense. She wouldn't be treated like a servant
or a doormat. She wouldn't put up with mess, laziness and
selfishness. The worm had turned. By the same token, she
would no longer be a martyred screaming fishwife. If she
had a grievance she would air it, in a calm and measured
manner. She would stand up for herself with *reasoned*
arguments. She and Rob would operate in compromise,
collaboration, co-operation. There was going to be discipline
and sticker charts and boundaries and guidelines and love.
They were both going to try really hard, and so were the
children (whether they liked it or not). They were both
determined to put the romance back where it belonged…
And they were going to go running together again.

'Looking good, Franks,' Imogen said as the three of
them met at the station.

'Thanks.' Frankie grinned. Her face looked all-aglow
tonight, she knew, and her eyes were shining. She felt
happier than she had in months – years! – yet, she tried not
to grin too broadly or have her eyes look too sparkly. She
didn't want to give the game away just yet. She knew she
looked great, though. She felt it from the top of her newly
washed head to the bottom of her strappy sandals.

It was lovely having a night out in London together,
actually. What Frankie's mother would call a 'bit of a
jaunt'. Frankie smiled to herself, imagining her mother's
reaction when she told her she and Rob were back together.
Her mother would be *ever so pleased*. She'd think things
were back to their rightful place, the status quo reactivated,
the world restored to its natural order. The posting of
snippets could be resumed. That service had stopped in
the last few weeks, a (welcome) silent protest, Frankie

knew. Now she and Rob were back on track, the 'helpful' hysterical missives about the perils of modern technology would start up again.

They got on the train. Imogen started a caustic, dryly hilarious monologue about Marcia, warning them all she was like a rolling thunderball. Frankie was dying to meet Imogen's work partner-in-crime; she'd heard all the stories. It was going to be enormous fun, tonight. Just girls, food, wine and chat. Perfect. And she would have her New Rob to go home to at the end of it.

Imogen was different tonight, Frankie noted. Usually she laughed and waved her hands around while she told her tales of Marcia. Tonight she was sort of muttering and, funny though she was, she looked a bit miserable and scowly. Imogen had insisted there'd been no man at her house the night she'd come home from Ascot, but Frankie didn't believe her. Grace looked miserable, too. After Imogen's speech about Marcia, they all quickly fell silent. Neither Imogen nor Grace seemed to be sharing Frankie's enthusiasm for the night ahead. She tried to start several conversations about what had been on telly that week, but each time they trailed to nothing. She hoped her friends would perk up when they got there. Especially the birthday girl! Good Lord, you're only forty-one once!

They took a taxi from Liverpool Street to The Residence, which was opposite Green Park. As they neared the huge, elegant hotel, flanked by bay trees in enormous pots, a woman who Frankie presumed was Marcia, from all Imogen's descriptions over the years, was standing outside the main entrance. Her head was lowered, sunglasses were perched on top of her head and she was having a good old rummage in an enormous mustard-coloured bag. She pulled out a gold compact, shouted, 'There's the bugger' and turned to the man loping next to her in a bright turquoise suit and white shirt with ruffles on it, who looked like an over-coiffed Italian gangster. As he leant his waxen face towards her, she patted him enthusiastically on the nose with a powder puff.

'Oh God, she's brought Tarquin Soprano with her,' hissed Imogen in a sotto voice, as they crossed the road to the hotel. 'What the hell has she done that for?'

'Tarquin Soprano? You are kidding, right?' said Frankie, suppressing a gigantic giggle.

'Gosh, look at him,' asked Grace, a little too loudly, as they arrived on the pavement outside The Residence. Tarquin had topped off the turquoise suit with a pair of really shiny spats and was carrying a kind of clutch bag. His hair was styled to within an inch of its life.

Marcia was equally overstated. She was wearing a *huge* teal green shawl flung dramatically over one shoulder and fastened with an enormous elephant brooch. Underneath Frankie could see navy taffeta. She also noticed that Marcia had the tiniest, tiniest feet, squeezed into weeny red suede peep-toe court shoes. A slightly twisted red toe peeped accusingly from each hole, like tortoises' heads from their shells.

'Darlings!' Marcia exclaimed and she embraced them all in a theatrical group hug. Frankie got a faceful of over-perfumed cashmere and too-orange BB cream.

'Hello, Tarquin,' said Imogen a little tersely, once she'd got Marcia off her. 'I didn't know you were coming.'

'Oh, I had to bring him!' gushed Marcia. 'He was at a terribly loose end, weren't you, poppet? You don't mind, darling?' she said to Imogen, laying a burgundy-taloned hand on her arm. 'He'll be the life and soul, I absolutely promise.'

Tarquin was puffing up his ruffled chest like a dodo and trying to catch Frankie's eye. She was expecting him to say

'How you doin?' like an ageing Joey Tribbiani but when he spoke his voice was very English, very posh and very high. 'How do you do, ladies?'

'Fine thanks,' said Frankie, trying not to laugh.

'Nice to meet you,' said Grace, politely, although it looked like she was trying to back away.

'Okay, he can join us, but this was *supposed* to be a girlie night,' Imogen hissed at Marcia, 'I'm really not in the mood for men.'

'Well, we know that, darling,' said Marcia. 'But Tarqy's hardly a threat. And perhaps after a few cocktails, you'll see things differently. You never know, there might be some highly eligible men in there tonight.'

'I doubt it,' said Imogen, tersely. 'And I don't need *cocktails* to realise that all men are dicks.'

'Sometimes a dick is *exactly* what we need,' said Marcia, and she raised one caped arm and swept into a passing section of the lobby's revolving doors like Zorro, leaving them to haphazardly jump in the one behind her. As they scuttled out the other side – Frankie had missed the exit, somehow, and had to go round again – a weasly-looking man in a grey pinstriped suit was waiting like a sentry to meet them.

'Nicholas, darling!' cooed Marcia, pinching poor Nicholas lightly on one loose, grey buttock.

'Marcia,' said Nicholas, in a thin little voice, and gave her a weedy kiss on each cheek. Marcia was beaming like a camping torch. Nicholas looked moderately terrified. He and Tarquin looked each other up and down and didn't look particularly impressed with what they saw.

'Shall we?' he said, and escorted them through the white marble lobby, down a soft-carpeted corridor and into a magnificent bar. It was fabulous: twinkling optics above a shiny stainless steel bar, white leather sofas and squashy armchairs, low lighting and high glamour. Frankie had never seen anything like it.

'It's gorgeous,' she said.

'Thank you,' said Nicholas proudly, as though he took sole credit for it. He held out his arm and saw them to their seats, then clicked for a cocktail waiter to come over.

'I'll be back to escort you to The Summer Garden,' he said, bowing slightly and turning to go.

'Thanks, ducks,' said Marcia, with a wink and two clicks that people make to horses. 'And I hear the beds are really bouncy here, if you fancy a bit of a fiddle later.'

'I'm not really in the market for a *fiddle*,' said Nicholas, 'if you don't mind. Thanks all the same.' He gave a small bow. 'See you in a while.'

'Parting is such sweet sorrow,' cooed Marcia. 'I bet you're still a horny bugger underneath all that grey. What a shame I won't get to find out.' And she slapped him merrily on the bottom in full view of the young, handsome waiter who had just arrived at their table. The waiter tried hard to suppress an almighty smirk; Nicholas looked absolutely mortified and fled, his violated bottom a flopping rhapsody in grey pinstripe as he ran to the exit.

'Cocktails, ladies?' said the handsome man.

'Ooh, yes please,' said Frankie, settling back in her gorgeously comfy chair.

It was going to be a very good night.

CHAPTER THIRTY-THREE: GRACE

Grace ordered a pina colada and looked around her. This bar was incredible. Really swanky. And so *clean*. She was going to have to 'buck up', as they said in books, and do her best to enjoy tonight. Good friends, good conversation and good food. That was a good thing, right? She needed it. She'd been in a horrible, emotional limbo since the denouement with Greg. Confused, sad, resigned and with a kind of flatness as though a large iron had been plonked on her. She'd cried a lot more over the past few days. Sometimes over James. Sometimes over Greg. Sometimes over what had become of her life.

She sighed and reached down to her bag. Her phone was chiming from inside it. (Was it Maggie? – she was babysitting.) Grace allowed herself a small smile as she glanced at the screen. It was a text from Gideon, wishing her a fabulous evening.

Amongst all the flatness, something miraculous had happened with her boss, and it happened when she got to work on Monday after her showdown with Greg. Gideon had been in a right mood. He hadn't appeared to be talking to her, which suited her fine. God knows what had rattled his cage this time; his cage was extremely flimsy and could be rattled at the slightest provocation.

At three o' clock, he'd disappeared for over half an hour and she was astonished to discover him in the stock room, sitting on a step stool and sobbing into an enormous hanky.

'Sorry!' said Grace, taken aback. 'I didn't mean to disturb you.'

'It's okay.' Gideon gave a huge sniff. His voice was a wobbly squeak.

'What's wrong?'

'Nothing, nothing. I'm fine.'

'You don't *look* fine.'

'I'm *fine*, Grace.'

She'd pulled over another stool and sat down next to him. The horrible meeting with Greg and all the tears she'd shed made her feel brave, or was it reckless?

'Can I ask you something, Gideon?'

'If you must.' He looked up at her and his eyes were red raw.

'Why are you so miserable? Why are you *always* so miserable?'

He fixed his bloodshot eyes on her.

'Do you really want to know?'

'Yes.'

'It's my ten-year anniversary.'

'Oh, well, congratulations,' said Grace, hesitantly. 'Isn't that supposed to be a happy thing?'

'Not when someone died ten years ago, it isn't.'

'Oh Gideon, I'm so sorry. Who was it, your mother?' Gideon had never, ever mentioned his family. He'd never really mentioned anything.

'No. I'm afraid to say the old gay-bashing bag is still alive and living in Basingstoke,' snorted Gideon. 'No, my partner, Dominic.' He did a gigantic sniff and balled the hanky in his fist. 'The love of my life. My partner. For thirteen years. He died.'

'Oh God, Gideon, how horrible for you. How did he die?'

'Electric shock. At work.'

'Oh, Gideon, that's awful. I'm really sorry.'

She was. She realised she was actually really sorry about a *lot* of things, mostly that she had never tried to get to know him, as difficult as he had made it.

'I really *am* sorry,' she repeated. She tried to take his hand.

At first, he resisted, flinched and moved his hand away, onto his lap. Then he let her take it. They sat there for a while, in silence. She rubbed the back of his hand. It was soft, and surprisingly warm.

'Do you want to go to the pub?' she said, suddenly.

'What?'

'The pub. We could go for a drink. A chat. Get to know each other.'

'What about the shop?'

'We'll close the shop. It'll still be here tomorrow. Let's just bunk off.'

She had been taking a massive chance here. She had half expected Gideon to fly into a sweary rage.

'Okay,' said Gideon. 'I'd really like that.' And he'd looked at Grace properly for what seemed like the first time ever.

She thought about it now. They'd had a good chat. A really good chat. He'd told her his entire life history – and there was a lot of it! – she told him about James, about Greg, about the whole sorry state her life had descended to. They'd got drunk on Baileys and it had been fabulous. A fabulous relief amongst all her angst and despair. She and Gideon were now friends.

A second text came through. Gideon again.

By the way, I've had some amazing feedback on you re. the wedding fair. You were a hit, girl! I'm happy to step aside and let you do them all on your own in the future.

She'd forgotten all about the wedding fair, with everything that had gone on since.

And don't forget what I said to you. Don't jump out of the frying pan into the fucking fire!

He *had* said that. She remembered now. It was after their seventh or eighth Baileys and he'd clutched her hands imploringly as he'd said it. She replied something about fires being warm and better than being out in the cold, but she considered his words now. It's what Nancy, the girl from the wedding fair, had said too. Grace took a large sip of her pina colada, which had now arrived, through a bright pink straw. People had been saying a lot of things to her recently she'd been totally ignoring. Gideon, Nancy, Frankie, Imogen, even Greg. That she was amazing just as she was. That she could make it on her own. What had Nana McKensie said? Be a *pioneer*.

Why hadn't she been *listening* to anybody? She'd been focusing on all the things she hadn't got and none of the things she had. She had been *blind*, but not in the way she'd thought. She'd been wanting to plug the gaps of her life when a gap was exactly what she needed. She looked around the bar again, at her friends – so proud and single – and thought about her life. Friends, Daniel, a job with – finally! – a nice boss. She didn't need anything else. She'd been to the school fundraiser on her own and survived. She'd done the wedding fair and been a 'hit'. She'd given Greg what for, confronted Gideon at last and had shown James she could live a perfectly decent life without him, thank you very much. She could be a pioneer in her own life, couldn't she?

She could make it on her own. With her friends, and Daniel – the very best thing in her life – she could make it on her own.

She was about to put her phone back in her bag when she remembered something else. Tim's message. She had never replied to it. Now was the perfect time.

Hello, Tim. I'm sorry, but I'm not dating at the moment – I've had some shockers too and am taking a break! If you haven't been snapped up, I may be free next January. Give me a try then?

There. Single for at least a year. Sorted. She smiled to herself and took another big sip of her cocktail.

Two pina coladas later, Nicholas re-emerged to take them all into The Summer Garden. Marcia was even more on heat, but Nicholas was wise to her. He attached himself to Grace and talked politely to her as they made their way through the hotel. At one point she helped physically steer him away from Marcia's clutches. He was almost sprinting to keep a safe distance from her. Nicholas would be pleased to clock off tonight, Grace thought.

As they walked into The Summer Garden, Grace gasped. It was amazing. They were in a huge atrium, flanked on all sides by eight magnificent storeys of hotel. Each level was festooned with cute, shuttered windows, Juliet balconies and cascading foliage, and the atrium was topped with a stunning glass roof through which you could see the stars. It had elegant, marble pillars, wrapped in reams of twinkling lights. Huge palm trees, their glossy leaves gleaming in candlelight. White tables with silver candelabras. Blooms of the most gorgeous flowers in pale summer pinks and creams were everywhere. Peonies, sweet peas and roses spilled from huge, ornate vases and tumbled from rococo plinths.

In one corner was an enormous white piano where a tiny bald man was tinkling the ivories. They walked in to 'Strangers in the Night'.

Nicholas showed them to their table with a flourish, pulling out their chairs for them, and he flamboyantly shook a huge linen napkin onto each of their laps. Imogen and Marcia were on one side, Grace and Frankie the opposite, and Tarquin looked proud to be head of the table.

Grace was almost transfixed by Marcia. First, she held Nicholas' hand down on her leg as he laid down the napkin and he yanked it away, as though burnt. Then, after he'd escaped – with Marcia laughing and calling out, 'Tonight's the night, Nicholas!' – she started an inordinate amount of faffing and rummaging in her bag. She finally unearthed her reading glasses and her Dictaphone and set them on the table next to her wine glass. Meanwhile, Tarquin was rearranging the ruffles on his shirt and pulling faces in the back of his knife.

Frankie was beaming, glowing. A little smile kept creeping up on her face. Single life was really suiting her, thought Grace. It was going to suit her, too, now she was properly ready for it. By contrast, the birthday girl looked miserable. She smiled when someone addressed her directly, but otherwise she just looked morose. On the train up, several times Grace had caught her staring blankly out of the window looking like her dog had just died, not that Imogen had ever had one. She was not a dog person, not with those floors.

'I'm going to the loo,' said Frankie, getting up and leaving the table. Marcia and Tarquin started bickering about wine.

'White wine has me pie-eyed within ten minutes, Marcie,' Tarquin was insisting. 'I'll be all over the place.'

'You are anyway,' said Marcia. 'Well, I can't drink red. It exacerbates my irritable bum.'

'You have an irritable bum?'

'Oh, grumpy like you wouldn't *believe*, Tarqs! There's things going on down there they'd be too squeamish to put in *The Lancet*!'

Grace stood up. 'I'm going to the loo as well,' she said. 'All those cocktails.'

'I'll come with you,' said Imogen. 'Order some champagne, Marcia. It'll make things simple.'

'The bubbles will make me burp like a navvy,' warned Marcia, holding her stomach as though she were shoring up a balloon, 'but okay, that sounds like an excellent plan. We *have* got a birthday to celebrate!'

'Another year wiser,' said Imogen, ruefully, as she got up from the table. There was definitely something up with her, thought Grace. All Imogen's previous birthdays as long as she'd known her had been riotous affairs, with Imogen on top form. Her fortieth had been an absolute scream. Oh dear, she feared the *returns* tonight would not be happy ones. 'Good God, those two are unbearable,' hissed the birthday girl, as they moved away.

'Aren't they!' said Grace. 'Marcia's even worse than you described her! Fascinating to watch, though.'

'Oh, never a dull moment with our Marcia!' said Imogen. 'Great fun to work with, but by God, sometimes you just want to strangle her with a pair of tights!'

'Ha, I bet. Are you all right, Imogen?'

She was now a few steps behind Imogen as they weaved through tables of laughing and drinking diners. It was probably not the right moment to ask. Imogen turned her head and called back over her shoulder, 'I'm fabulous, honey' but Grace wasn't convinced. She would have to try and talk to her later, maybe she'd be able to get it out of her on the drunken train journey home.

Frankie was standing outside the ornate cream door to the women's toilets. From the back, it looked like she was smoking. Grace knew that she and Imogen both did, as rebellious teens, until the legendary night they'd almost set their tent on fire with a packet of Camels Imogen had brought back from Spain. Grace knew all the stories.

As they neared, they realised Frankie was on her phone.

'Give them all a kiss from me,' she said, and her voice softened. 'I love you too.'

'Who are you talking to?' asked Grace.

Frankie turned, blushed and stuffed her phone into her shoulder bag. 'Er…no one,' she said. 'Well, Rob, actually…' she added, sheepishly, lowering her shoulders and putting her hands in her jacket pockets.

'You're back with Rob?' said Grace, incredulous.

'Er…yep.'

'Traitor!' exclaimed Imogen, shaking her head.

'Well, what about you and the *gasman*?' Frankie countered. 'And come on, tell us the truth! I couldn't see much of his face, but I've never seen a gasman who looks like that. The one we normally get looks like Blakey from *On the Buses*.'

Imogen laughed hollowly. Then she tried and failed to look indignant. Then she just looked sad. 'Okay, you've rumbled me. It wasn't the gasman. It was a mistake.' And her face fell further. She looked down at her fabulous shoes as though she wanted to disappear into the ground.

'Do you want to tell us about it?' said Grace.

'No! I can't. Not today. Maybe in about five years. When I'm over it.' Imogen looked awful, Grace had never seen her look quite like that before. Imogen sighed, then raised her head. 'We're not doing very well, are we? Grace, you're the only one who's kept to the charter.'

That stupid charter. It wasn't worth the paper it wasn't written on. So much for her two best friends staying single. Then again, she'd hardly kept to it. Grace swallowed. Was it time to come clean?

'Not exactly,' she said.

'What do you mean, not exactly?' demanded Imogen.

'Not exactly.'

'What on earth's going on in here, ladies?' It was Marcia, looming behind them like a battleship. 'I can't sit and help Tarquin count his age spots all night! What are you doing? It's like a scene from *Macbeth*. Are you plotting the downfall of the male species?'

'Yes, we're just sharpening up the birch twigs, Marcia,' said Imogen. 'And please don't call us "ladies", Marcia. I've told you that before.' She shuddered. 'It makes me think of misogyny and feminine wipes.'

Marcia hooted with laughter. 'But you *are* ladies! Come on, back to the table! Chop chop! We can't leave Tarquin there all by himself – before we know it he'll be up at the piano doing a Liberace, Lord knows he's got the temperament.'

They all went to the loo and headed back to the table, in a slightly inebriated troop. The truth will out, thought Grace. It always did. Frankie was back with Rob and she and Imogen had both been up to no good with men. So much for a year of being single. They should be ashamed of themselves.

CHAPTER THIRTY-FOUR:
IMOGEN

The man on the piano finished playing 'Moonlight Sonata' and Imogen looked around her. The restaurant was crowded and buzzing. There were a lot of men with dates – their wives, their girlfriends, their mistresses? Mostly wives, she suspected. Marriage didn't seem to be a dying art, no matter what anyone said. It was funny, she thought, how when men made a speech at a wedding reception they were always bursting with pride when they said 'my wife' for the first time – it always got an 'aah' and a round of applause – yet years later the same phrase become a mock-terrible thing that came with a tut and a grimace. My wife. *The* wife.

She wouldn't ever be anybody's wife, to be proud of in the first flush of marriage or affectionately scorned in the distant future. She didn't even want to be anybody's girlfriend now Richard had gone. She couldn't see herself with a man again. She'd fallen in love, and she'd had her heart broken. She wasn't planning on repeating either experience. Ever.

She'd have to tell Frankie and Grace everything. She couldn't believe Frankie was back with Rob, and Grace had been seeing someone as well! They were all a disgrace. And *she* was a heartbroken disgrace.

Marcia had ordered three bottles of Veuve Clicquot and Imogen sipped slowly from her champagne flute as she surveyed the scene. She couldn't bear to get drunk; she didn't want to get maudlin and end up sobbing on anyone's shoulder. Instead she'd taken solace in the amazing food. She'd had seared scallops with bacon and pea puree, followed by beef Wellington with dauphinoise potatoes and spring vegetables. She was halfway through a sublime chocolate almond fondant. This could be the way forward. The only way forward. She'd be fat and miserable. Happy bloody birthday.

The piano was still silent. There was a man with his back to the restaurant, half obscured by a palm and leaning down to the pianist. The pianist nodded. Imogen rolled her eyes. Some champagne-soaked idiot saying *Play it Again, Sam*, no doubt, or requesting something by Michael Bublé. Git. She put down her glass and returned to her fondant.

As she demolished the last mouthful, she looked up in surprise. She could hear the opening strains of a song she knew well. Blur, 'The Universal'. That was strange. And quite a departure from Frank Sinatra and the hits of The Carpenters.

She looked over to the piano again and dropped her spoon. It glanced off her plate and clattered to the floor. A passing waiter picked it up and whisked it away into the front of his apron.

'Sack the juggler!' giggled Marcia.

'Oops!' said Frankie. 'Butter fingers. Hey, are you okay, Imogen?'

'I really don't think I am,' said Imogen, staring straight ahead.

'Drink some water,' suggested Grace. 'If you're feeling a bit sloshed it'll dilute the alcohol.'

'I don't think water can help me,' said Imogen.

Walking towards their table, in blue jeans and a white, open-necked shirt – his eyes glinting, his hair just right – was Richard.

She froze. Her heart was going like the clappers. She'd only ever seen him in a suit, or his birthday suit. In jeans he looked sublime. He was like a mirage before her – Colin Firth coming out of the lake in *Pride and Prejudice*, Brad Pitt sitting by the side of the road in *Thelma and Louise*, Tom Selleck being anywhere and doing anything at all…

'Blimey, *he's* good-looking,' said Frankie, a quizzical look on her face as though she was trying to remember something.

'Isn't he?' said Imogen in a near whisper. Damn, damn, *damn* him for being so gorgeous. What the *hell* was he doing here?

Marcia and Tarquin both flicked their heads round.

'Christ on a bike!' said Marcia. 'Sexy man alert!'

'What about *me*?' said Tarquin, eyeing Richard up and down.

'Yes, yes,' said Marcia. 'Same meat, different gravy.' The woman was practically salivating.

'Is he coming over to *us*? Do you know him, Imogen?' said Grace.

'Yes,' whispered Imogen. And there, suddenly, he was, in front of her. Her perfect man. Her imperfect man. If only he'd been what she wanted him to be. He was the best-looking man she'd ever seen.

'Hello,' said Richard.

'*Hi*,' said Marcia. She was both doe-eyed and fluttering her eyelashes like a camel.

Frankie was nudging Imogen, and hissing, 'Who *is* he?' Imogen ignored her.

'Hello,' said Richard, again.

'Hello,' said Imogen hesitantly. Then, accusingly, 'How did you know I was here?'

'Well, you wouldn't answer my calls,' he said, his rumbling American accent cutting through the clatter and chatter of the restaurant. She could hear nothing else. 'So Nigel and I drove to your house.'

'Oh,' said Imogen.

'Oh!' said Frankie, agog. She was clutching onto Grace as though in the presence of a deity. 'Hang on, are you the gasman?'

'I guess I am,' said Richard. 'Are you *Frankie*?'

'I am,' said Frankie, looking pleased as punch.

'I'm Grace,' volunteered Grace. She started fluffing up her hair then seemed to think better of it and lowered her hand.

'Hi, Grace,' said Richard. 'I've heard all about you.' Grace smiled. Frankie grinned. Marcia was ramping up her cleavage with both hands and attempting a duck pout.

He turned back to Imogen. 'So, you weren't home – obviously – and I was about to leave when a couple pulled up in a car. The lady seemed pretty keen to find out who I was. She asked me a ton of questions.'

'Fiat Panda?' said Frankie.

'I'm sorry?' said Richard.

'Were they in a Fiat Panda? A black one?'

'It *was* a black car,' said Richard. 'And the lady had some sort of a plant on her lap, if that helps.'

'Mum and Dad!' exclaimed Frankie. 'I knew it! Then what happened?' she said, pulling her chair nearer to the table.

'They said you weren't home,' said Richard, turning back to Imogen. 'They said you were out in "That London", for dinner at a swanky hotel. She couldn't remember the name, but said it was somewhere five star. Nigel and I rang round them all on the way up here, until I found you.'

'I booked us in the company name,' said Marcia, loudly. She now had her chest displayed proudly on the table. 'Always claim it on expenses, duckie,' she said to Tarquin.

Tarquin nodded, as though making a mental note. He hadn't taken his eyes off Richard.

'That's what I tried,' continued Richard, 'when I got nowhere with Henderson. I thought it might be a business dinner.'

'No,' said Imogen. 'I'm with my friends. People who *care about me.*'

A very barbed remark, but Richard was refusing to cut his fingers on it. He looked round the table genially. 'The famous Single for a Year Club?' He smiled.

'Three of us,' said Imogen, brusquely. 'Not these two.'

'God, no!' said Marcia and Tarquin in unison.

'Although we've disbanded,' added Imogen. She stuck her tongue in her cheek and looked pointedly at Frankie and Grace. Frankie raised her eyebrows in return, as if to say, 'You can talk!'

'It's Imogen's birthday,' said Grace.

'*Is* it?' said Richard, looking surprised. 'I'm sorry, I had no idea. Happy birthday.'

'Thanks,' said Imogen sourly.

'Look, can I sit down? I feel a bit of a *plank* standing here.'

Richard *was* drawing a lot of attention to himself. A lot of people were gawping at him. A lot of women and quite a few men. And he's learnt another new English phrase, thought Imogen. He sounded cute when he said it.

'I don't know, to be honest,' she said.

'Oh, go on,' said Marcia, leaping up to pull out the vacant chair at the opposite head of the table. She jutted her huge bottom in Richard's face as she did so, in what she probably thought was a seductive manner.

Richard ignored Marcia's bottom and just stood looking at Imogen. Good God, he was virtually irresistible.

'Imogen?'

'Okay.'

He sat, and his solid right thigh brushed against Imogen's leather-clad one. She made a point of shifting hers out of the way.

'I'm pleased to meet you all,' he said. And he leant and shook everyone's hands around the table. He had a rapt audience. Frankie's mouth had not stopped hanging open since he arrived. Grace was absent-mindedly twirling a long curl around her finger. Tarquin was doing some competitive preening by smoothing his ruffles with one hand, his coiffed hair with the other. And Marcia just looked like a glam version of Kathy Bates in *Misery*, the grinning Number One Fan, before things got crazy.

Richard faced Imogen. She was shaking slightly. She was trying not to look at him. She was desperately trying not to be caught up in his gorgeous web of lies again.

'Imogen,' he said, again.

'Yup,' she snapped.

'I don't have a child with that woman or anyone. I'm not with *that* woman.'

'Okay,' she said dully.

'I was seeing her, back in New York, for a couple months. Just casually. She has a five-year-old son. She brought him along to the park once. As I say, it was all very casual. I think she was dating a few guys while she was in the city.'

'Slut!' interjected Marcia.

'Let him finish!' snapped Imogen. A tiny spark of something was igniting in her heart.

Richard stared down at his hands. 'Look, maybe we could go outside someplace, you and me, and talk privately?'

'No. Whatever you have to say, you can say in front of my friends.' Imogen was rooted to the spot. She didn't trust herself to go outside with him.

'Okay, it was over between me and – Sarah – quite some time ago. Her contract finished and she went home to England. Until Ascot I hadn't seen her since December.'

Sarah. The name made her feel ill.

'Are you *sure*?' asked Imogen. 'Are you sure there was no overlap?' It was the most important question she'd ever asked.

'Oh, I love an overlap!' snorted Marcia.

'Shut *up*, Marcia,' said Imogen. She was leaning forward in her chair now, her fingers clasping the edge of the table.

'There was no overlap,' said Richard. 'It was finished once she left New York. I wouldn't do that. Even if I'd been seeing her when I met you – which I wasn't – it would've been over that minute. Don't you see? Once I saw you, I couldn't think of anyone else.'

Imogen felt faint. 'Go on,' she said weakly.

'Okay,' he said. 'For months now Sarah's been emailing, calling, asking me to hook up with her again. Pleading for another chance. Saying that she loves me.' He grimaced. 'She hardly knows me. I didn't tell her I was coming to England, but she called the New York office and they told her. Then, God knows what she said to her, but Veronica told her I was going to be at Ascot.'

'Who's Veronica?' asked Frankie.

'Hot PA,' muttered Imogen.

'Do you think so?' said Richard, looking surprised. 'Not enough spark for me.' He stared at Imogen. She stared right back at him.

'*Please* go on,' she said. She was beginning to feel the stirrings of real hope.

'So, Sarah came to Ascot with her girlfriends. She got drunk. She found me and asked me to reconsider.' He gave an apologetic smile. 'I said no. I was very sorry, I didn't want to hurt her, but *no*.' He said the 'no' very firmly. 'I hope that face-to-face she finally believed me.'

'I think she did,' Imogen said quietly, 'I saw her crying as she came out of the box. Then Carolyn Boot emailed me to say you were in a relationship and had a child together.'

'Right,' said Richard coldly. '*Carolyn Boot*. So that's who stirred all this up. God knows how she even knew Sarah had a child!' He looked furious.

'She said she saw the three of you in Central Park.' Imogen was fiddling with the bow on her silk blouse. Did she dare believe him, dare expose her heart again?

'Ah,' Richard said, with a slow nod. 'Now I get it. The Boot got the wrong end of the stick, as you Brits say.' He sighed. 'I hope Sarah's okay. I tried to let her down gently… I swear to God, Imogen, what I've told you is the truth.' He took her hand. She felt helpless with desire. 'I'm single and I have been for a while.'

The pianist was now playing 'Wonderwall'. Had Richard told him to do a whole 90s Britpop repertoire? Imogen looked over and spotted Nigel at a far table, tucking into a plate of food, his napkin stuffed into his collar.

Richard reached across and took her other hand.

'Although I don't want to be single.' His beautiful eyes were locked onto hers. His eyebrows were perfect. His face was – heaven. 'Oh God, I'm nervous as hell,' he said, and he actually swallowed. Out of the corner of her eye, Imogen could see Grace's 'Aw' face coming on and she halted it with a glare. 'I want to be with you,' he said.

Now she could speak.

'I don't know,' stammered Imogen. 'I don't know if I can trust you. I don't think I can believe in any man. I'm not sure I can do it.'

'I can't give you up.'

'I don't know, Richard.'

'When have you ever been so uncertain, Imogen?' His eyebrows knotted together and he actually looked tormented. His voice was strangled. 'Never, I bet! Dammit, Imogen, will you just let me date you? You're the most beautiful woman I've ever met.'

'She does look good tonight,' interjected Frankie.

'Shut up, Frankie!' said Imogen. A smile was spreading across her face.

'She really does,' said Richard, catching her smile. 'She's the most crazy, infuriating, brilliant, perfect woman I've ever met.' He was grinning and it was infectious. They were all grinning round the table. Marcia looked like the Cheshire cat. Tarquin's tombstone teeth were studded with sesame seeds. His chair was tipping back at an alarming angle. Richard caught it and set it level.

'Hang on,' he then said. 'I can do better than this.'

He levered one muscly arm on the table and lowered himself to the floor. 'I've a funny feeling one day I'll be doing this again,' he muttered. He steadied himself on one knee and looked up at Imogen's startled face. 'Imogen, will you do me the honour of being my girlfriend? My one and *only* girlfriend. Exclusive, we call it where I'm from. Going steady?' he said, with a wink.

'Yes, yes, *going steady*. We do that here.' It was Marcia. Richard didn't take his gaze from Imogen.

'You make me not want to return to my New York apartment. You make me not fussed about seeing The Mets play ever again.' His whole face was lit up and his eyes were fixed on hers. 'You make me want to live in a garret in Belsize Park and listen to Blur.'

Imogen smiled, her eyes filling with happy tears.

'*Imogen.*'

'*Yes.*'

'I'm not going back to the States. I've been offered a permanent post here. I want to ask you for your hand in dating. No more secrets, no more lies. Proper dating, out in the open. What do you say?' Imogen looked into that gorgeous face. He looked so serious. So earnest. So delicious. 'Imogen Henderson, I love you, will you date me?'

Her heart soared. Her stomach somersaulted, did a couple of backflips and finished off with a do-si-do. Then she grinned. 'I don't know,' she said. 'Frankie?'

Frankie considered for a moment, her head on one side, then slurred, 'Is he a loser, or do you think at any moment in time in the future, he could become a loser?'

'He's not a loser,' said Imogen. 'I'm pretty much sure he's not a loser. As for being a loser in the future, I really don't know. There's no guarantee, is there?'

'No,' said Frankie. 'I've a further confession. Rob moved back in last night.'

'I'm happy for you,' said Imogen.

'Thanks.' Frankie grinned. 'So, take a chance.'

'Grace? Be my voice of reason. This would be a mistake, right?'

'I'm happy for you too, Frankie,' said Grace. 'And, by the law of probability, Imogen, they can't *all* be bad,' she added. 'If you think this man is amazing, then go for it. I've been seeing a male escort by the way.'

'What!' shouted Imogen and Frankie in unison.

'That's your mystery man?' said Frankie.

'The guy at Ascot!' said Imogen.

'Oh God, is he *Michael*?' said Frankie.

'Who the hell's Michael?' said Imogen.

'It's a long story, but yes,' said Grace. 'He was all of those people. But he's gone now. I'm single and I'm determined to be single for a long time. No more frying pans, no more fires... I'll tell you later.'

'I think you should go for it,' trilled Marcia.

'Me too,' squeaked Tarquin.

There was a slight cough. 'Do you have an answer for me?' asked Richard. Imogen turned her gaze back to him. He was still on the floor. He looked worried and slightly pained.

'Oh, sod it,' said Imogen. She could *do* single with style. She was brilliant at it. But she chose this man. She chose not to be afraid. She took a really deep breath and looked into Richard's eyes. 'Yes, I do, Richard. I want to date you. I would *love* to date you… But you better make them bloody good dates.'

'Yes, ma'am,' said Richard, with a wink. 'I can do good dates.'

'I love you,' said Imogen. It was as simple as that. She loved him. She'd loved being single but she loved Richard more. 'Now get up off that knee, you silly bugger, before you do yourself a permanent injury.'

They all stood in the lobby. Imogen and Richard were wrapped round each other. Frankie and Grace were giggling together and lolling against a pillar. And Marcia and Tarquin were attempting some kind of waltz around the lobby. Tarquin was wearing Marcia's cape and prancing like a flamboyant Batman.

Imogen pulled her face out of Richard's warm neck. 'Can you give me a minute?'

She squeezed his hand, moved away from him with a smile and walked over to Frankie and Grace.

'Group hug?' she asked.

They circled their arms round each other and squeezed each other tight until they were laughing and hopping round in a mad circle.

'I'm sorry I couldn't manage a year of being single,' Imogen said, as they came to a stop. 'But now you've seen what I was up against.'

'He's amazing,' said Frankie. 'Nor me. I couldn't manage it either. But I know I'm doing the right thing.'

'That just leaves me,' said Grace. 'And I reckon I can do it.'

'Good for you, Gracie,' said Imogen. 'You carry that single flag with pride. And it *is* something to be really proud of.'

'We're going to be okay,' said Frankie.

'We are,' said Grace.

'We really are,' said Imogen. And they circled their arms round each other again and grinned happily in each other's faces.

ACKNOWLEDGEMENTS

Thanks go to my brilliant editor, Charlotte.

To Elizabeth Davies, for reading my first ever manuscript and helping me in so many ways.

To Mary Torjussen – I couldn't have done it without you. See you at *The Ivy*!

And to Phil and Emma Cunningham for inviting me to Ascot and being wonderful hosts.